Relic of Haven

Other works by Alex Kingsley

The Bastion Cycle:
Empress of Dust
Relic of Haven

Short Stories:
The Strange Garden and Other Weird Tales
The Things I Made
The Small God of West 54th St
Shroomscape
Three-Inch Grave
Would You Still Love Me if I Was a Wyrm

Plays:
The Suit
A Question of Legitimacy
Unplanned Obsolescence
The Dreamless Patron
The Bearer of Bad News

Relic of Haven

BOOK 2 OF THE BASTION CYCLE

Alex Kingsley

Space Wizard Science Fantasy
Raleigh, NC
www.spacewizardsciencefantasy.com

Cover art by MoorBooks
Editing by Courtney Brooks
Illustrations by Ines Maria Eckermann
Book Layout © 2015 BookDesignTemplates.com

Empress of Dust/Alex Kingsley.—1st ed.
ISBN 978-1-960247-46-9

Author's website: Alexkingsley.org

To Noa. You are worth so many shrimp to me.

CONTENTS

Part One: Home

Prologue

Excerpt from A Brief History of Bastion

There is a pre-Quake folktale about swine squabbling over the fundamentals of infrastructure. It's not widely circulated any more, as few pre-Quake stories are, but some historians have noted its parallels to the founding of Bastion.

The original tale involves three pigs and a wolf, an extinct predatory canid. Of course, an aggressive dog would never be taken seriously as an antagonist in modern day Bastion, not when compared to a desertwalker. Who could be afraid of a harmless little wolf?

In the story of Bastion, the antagonist is the Earth itself.

The legend says that the Earth grew tired of lending its water, its nutrients, and just about everything it could offer to mankind. Mankind wasn't giving it anything in return. So the Earth started to shake from hunger and devour everything it could.

To flee the Earth's wrath, mankind hid themselves in cities scattered across the globe. The City of Glass, the City of Air, the City of Ashes, and on and on.

The only survivor, Bastion, was the City of Concrete and Steel. Each summer, Bastioners celebrate the purported day that they became the last humans on Earth.

Is it not strange that we don't mourn the lives lost to the Quakes?

Is it not sad that we're all alone?

Evidently, Bastioners don't believe so. Is it not our own intelligence that allowed us to survive, and the folly of others that doomed them?

Surely our shared survival is an indication that we are the chosen people—chosen not by a deity, or by fate, or by the Earth itself. Chosen by logic and reason. A pre-Quake philosopher once called this "natural selection."

The citizens like to imagine that the invisible hand of this "natural selection" selected us. In actuality, their survival was just dumb luck. Don't try to tell that to a Bastioner, though. They will assure you they live in a city of ideals. City of innovation, city of survivors, city of synthetics.

The final city.

CHAPTER ONE

A Deal

Chavi dreamt, as they often did, about being buried alive. In this particular iteration of the same nightmare, they were enclosed in a metal box, not wood, with no chance of clawing their way out. There was a grate in front of them, and something was pouring through it, though the exact nature of the substance kept changing. First dust, then water, then some kind of thick black sludge that stained their skin. They moved to paw at the grate but found their hands manacled, chained down by some invisible force. All they could do was watch as each little metal hole poured out a substance that gathered at their feet, like hundreds of weeping eyes.

"Let me out!" they screamed. "Please!" But no answer came. "Why are you doing this to me?" they asked, but already the dust that turned to water that turned to sickly sweet tar made its way into their mouth and filled their lungs.

Chavi awoke gasping for air, sitting straight up in bed. They closed their eyes and focused on their beating heart, willing it to slow. They glanced down to Harvard who, mercifully, was still asleep next to them. Good. Their nightmare hadn't disturbed his sleep. It would happen eventually, of course, given the frequency with which they'd woken up gulping down air ever since they were a child. But for now, he could rest blissfully unaware of their abnormality.

With a jolt, Chavi remembered they had an appointment.

They reached for the clock on the bedside table—three thirty-seven. So they hadn't missed it. They planted a kiss on Harvard's forehead and carefully slid out of bed, dressing themself in the grey hoodie they'd recovered from their mother's apartment. She'd given it to them for their fifteenth birthday. They expected the door to protest on its hinges, but luckily this door had just been replaced. Thanks, August. It opened silently, and Chavi disappeared into the dark hallway, glancing one last time at the rise and fall of Harvard's chest as he slumbered undisturbed.

The latch clicked into place almost imperceptibly, and with extreme precision, Chavi made their way down the stairs, tapping into their old sneaking-out expertise from their Academy days. They made it to the kitchen without detection, unlocked the front door, and stepped out into the cool night air. The townhouse they were unofficially "borrowing" from the Taheris conveniently opened directly onto the central thoroughfare of Lower Bastion, which meant the meeting location was just a few blocks south on a backstreet only frequented by garbage collectors and the occasional smoker. Chavi looked up and down the street when they arrived, but no one seemed to be waiting for them, so they leaned against and waited.

"Hey," a familiar voice hailed them from the shadows, and Chavi turned to see Mellie approaching, her features shadowy as she came into the sparse streetlight. The two of them hadn't known each other very well back at the Academy, so it was awkward to be meeting with her years later, in the middle of the night.

But if she offered any kind of relief, Chavi would take it. The two of them had reconnected at a party shortly after the Ivies arrived back in the city, and Chavi realized she was their best link back to their old dazzle crew. They could bear a little bit of awkwardness, but they couldn't bear...well, whatever was happening to them. It had started when they woke knowing full well that they should have been dead. When they'd been shot at the Galvin Conference, they knew with grim certainty that the wound would kill them. Having survived it felt deeply *wrong*.

"What's up?" Mellie nodded, her pink pigtails swaying. Chavi shrugged. There was no simple way to answer that question. *Still recovering from getting shot and trying to figure out why every day feels like hot sand grating against the inside of my skin* was probably too much to pour out to a relative stranger. When Mellie leaned against the wall next to them and pulled out a dazzle joint and a lighter, they figured she wasn't in any rush, so they relaxed.

She lit up the joint and took a long drag, then gave Chavi that crooked smile of hers as she gestured for them to take it. They smiled and accepted. It wasn't that being high actually dulled the pain at all, but when they could get their mind to the point of just barely functioning, it was easier to forget, even if only for a few seconds.

"Ariel says you were a scavenger," Mellie said, her eyes flicking over them. "That true?"

Ariel was another tangential acquaintance, one they'd only had a brief and admittedly confusing interaction with since returning to Bastion. Chavi nodded, and Mellie's smile widened.

"No shit?" she said. "Never actually known any scavengers. None who made it back, anyhow. They say it changes you. Do you feel changed?"

Yes, obviously. Chavi couldn't possibly begin to describe all the ways they'd been changed. But the dazzle had put them at ease, and they didn't want to ruin that pleasant buzz, so they just shrugged and said, "I don't know."

Mellie looked disappointed. "Damn, thought maybe you'd done some cool stuff."

"Being a scavenger is not that cool."

"You ever kill anyone?" she asked, eyes sparkling with morbid curiosity.

Chavi scoffed, hoping to hide the grimace underneath.

"You hardly even run into people in the desert," they evaded.

"Yeah, but I heard when you do, things get weird," Mellie pressed. "That the desert makes people crazy."

Chavi had certainly seen their fair share of the desert...affecting people when they were at the mercy of the sandheads, but they were not about to admit that the only time they had actually come close to killing anyone was back in the Academy when they were sixteen years old. Not including Minty, of course. But they hadn't killed Minty, not really. Even still, they'd been responsible for his death, and had been punished accordingly—

"You sure you're good?" Mellie asked, mercifully derailing their thoughts.

No, they very much weren't, but if they wouldn't even admit it to their own boyfriend that anything was wrong, they definitely weren't going to start spilling their guts to a virtual stranger. It would be easier, though, to pile it all on someone who didn't matter.

They could feel the dazzle in their body, a sort of warmth in their muscles, a tingling on their skin. For the first time in a long while, they felt they truly could relax a bit. They held out their hand for another hit on the dazzle joint. They breathed out twin streams of smoke.

"I'm not." They surprised even themself by saying it aloud. "I think I'm dying."

* * *

Harvard awoke abruptly as he was jerked to his feet. Only when he tried to scream did he realize there was a hand clamped over his mouth. He instinctively wriggled to get free, but an arm wrapped around his body pinned his arms to his sides. Someone was behind him, restraining him. Someone in his room.

He cried out, even though it was only a muffled wail.

"It's okay," a gruff voice assured him, despite the fact that it was decidedly *not* okay. His mind was still in a sleepy haze, but the sight of the empty bed snapped him into reality.

Chavi. Where was Chavi?

"Don't worry," the voice said. "You're just gonna go right back to sleep, alright?"

No, no that was *not* alright. Harvard squirmed against his captor, but the hand over his mouth shifted its position and pinched his nose.

His eyes widened with terror. His heart raced. He clawed desperately at the hand cutting off his air supply, but whoever was holding him, they were much stronger than he was. All he could do was scream soundlessly while he suffocated.

* * *

Mellie laughed, which was not the response Chavi was expecting.

"You're not special," she said with a congenial pat on the shoulder. "Lots of people die. Everyone, in fact." She left her hand there, studying them as though she were trying to sort something out. "All we can do is have a good time before it's over, right?"

Chavi shrugged. "I guess so," they said, though they weren't having a particularly good time, just a slightly-better-than-baseline time due to their altered state. Apparently this was enough of an opening for Mellie, because she snaked an arm around their waist and pulled them close. Chavi sighed and extricated themself from her grip.

"Mellie, I have a boyfriend."

Mellie scrunched up her face. "Yeah, yeah. I heard."

"You did?"

"I guess I just didn't really believe it," she shrugged. "You used to be *fun*. That's what people said, anyway. I wanted to find out for myself. Guess they were wrong."

"Or, I changed." That was true, wasn't it? They say the dusts change people. Well, out there, Chavi had been a leader. They had been Yale, captain of the Ivies. That meant something.

A shadow passed over Mellie's face. "People don't really change."

Chavi felt a flare of indignation in their chest. Their head snapped toward her. "Do you know how old I was when I built that reputation for myself, Mellie?"

"How old?"

"Sixteen. I'm going to be twenty-one soon."

"Happy birthday."

"Maybe people don't change," they conceded. "But they grow up."

"If you grew up," Mellie needled, "why are you having a secret meeting with a girl in a back alley to buy drugs?"

"Because I like drugs."

"Bullshit."

"It's true. I do."

Mellie's eyes flashed as they flicked over Chavi. A lopsided smile pulled at her lips.

"Is that all?" she asked.

"What do you mean?"

"You really *are* dying, aren't you?" She didn't say it with the kind of pity or empathy that usually goes along with such a statement. More like grim fascination. "Shit, I thought you were joking. You dustsick or something?"

No. Worse. "Maybe."

Her smile widened. "How would you like to join our circle?"

Chavi wondered if they were supposed to know what that meant. "Your what?"

Mellie pulled a card from her pocket and proffered it. It bore the address of an apartment in western Midtown and Ariel's name. They hadn't known each other well at the academy. Something about them had always made Chavi feel ill at ease. It didn't matter, though, since Ariel had never taken much interest in Chavi—they never seemed to take much interest in anyone. They had always been alluringly aloof.

"It's a community," Mellie explained. "And we all share in Harmony together."

"So, a drug, then?" Chavi guessed.

"It's not a drug, exactly," Mellie said, eyes gleaming. "There *is* a drug, but...that's only part of it. It's hard to explain unless you've experienced it yourself."

Sounded tempting. Also sounded expensive. Time consuming, too. A brief late-night rendezvous for a hit of dazzle was one thing, but joining an organization sounded like a whole *commitment*, and commitment was something Chavi was only selectively capable of. At this point, though, it seemed unwise to discount any solutions.

"So, Harmony...what does it do?"

"*Everything.*" Mellie took their hand and closed their fingers around the card, then turned to leave. She waggled her fingers, then started down the alley, her pink pigtails swishing. Chavi didn't stay to watch her go. They wanted to get back to bed before Harvard realized they were gone. As they sped back toward the townhouse, Chavi wondered if it was really true what they'd said—that they'd grown up. Years ago, when they'd first joined the Commission, Jasmine had said she hoped they would, and at the time, it stung. Had they managed it? Or was Jasmine still disappointed?

Chavi slowly turned their key in the lock at the front door. They treaded carefully, afraid of waking the other Ivies. Their bedroom door creaked almost imperceptibly as they slipped in, moving to the dresser to put away their hoodie. They placed the card Mellie had given them on the surface. Probably they'd throw it out, but right now they just wanted to—

They caught a glimpse of something in the dresser mirror—a figure, silhouetted in the streetlights streaming in through the window. A figure that was not Harvard.

Instinct took over as they reached for the knife and spun around, already swinging and ready to strike, but the intruder was prepared, and they were quicker. The figure parried the blow easily, using Chavi's momentum to throw them off balance. Chavi felt a foot hook around their ankle and pull. They stumbled but managed to stay upright. In one neat movement, the assailant grabbed their wrist and jerked it behind their back, eliciting a cry of pain as they dropped the knife. They heard it clatter to the floor and skid across the ground as it was kicked to the side.

One hand on their wrist and the other planted on their shoulder, the attacker shoved them, sending them sprawling. Chavi's head cracked against the bedside table as they fell heavily to the ground, stranger standing above them.

And then the figure walked away. Chavi struggled to their feet as the intruder walked to the door and flipped the light switch.

"I told you, Chaverim, that I would be needing a scavenger friend," said a familiar man with a crisp suit, gold glasses, and sharp features. "I can't imagine you're really all that surprised."

"You," Chavi hissed, one hand gripping their throbbing head, the other clinging to the wall for balance. The brief but painful fight had left them dazed.

"Yes, me!" the man said, clapping his hands as though he was delighted by his own existence. Devrin. That's what he'd called himself back at the Conference. "But let's not forget you. You're looking very well. If I remember correctly, you were shot in the stomach. That's not something most people recover from. But you"—he gave Chavi a quick look up and down—"you seem to be doing just fine."

Only once Chavi managed to fully right themself did they register the conspicuously empty bed and a spike of panic shot through them.

"Where is Harvard?" they demanded.

Devrin shrugged. "He's fine," he assured them.

"That's not what I asked."

"He's with some of my trusted associates on the other side of town. You don't need to worry about him. Yet."

"What do you mean, yet?"

"I'd like to talk to you, Chaverim."

"So. Talk," they said through gritted teeth.

He chuckled. "You misunderstand. Not here. Elsewhere. I have a job for you. I need to know that you'll do it."

"And if I don't?"

Devrin looked taken aback, as though he were shocked Chavi would even suggest such a thing, "Well, then I'll kill your boyfriend. Sorry, I thought that was obvious."

They felt a sudden weight drop into their stomach. "You'll *what*?"

Devrin gestured to the empty bed.

"Did you think we just took him for fun? No, clearly this is a *threat*. I didn't think I had to spell it out for you. Pay attention, Chaverim!" he snapped his fingers. "If you don't cooperate, we'll have no choice but to kill him. I really did think this was quite clear from the beginning. We'll be waiting for you in the building at the corner of Locke and Curie. Arrive by sunrise," he said, then as an afterthought added, "I don't think I really need to say 'or else' as it's implied, but just in case it wasn't *perfectly* clear: or else."

"By sunrise?" Chavi repeated. Locke Street was a few miles west of them.

"Yes."

Their heart hammered. "I don't know if I can make it in time."

"Well, you had better hope for Harvard's sake that you do," he said as he headed for the open window. As he slung one leg over the windowsill, he added, "Oh! And one more thing. Dress for a fight."

With that, he gave an impish little wave and disappeared out of the open window.

Chavi knew they should think but they did not have time to think. What was happening? *Why* was it happening? It felt surreal, dreamlike— no, *nightmare* like. What time was it now? How long did they have? How far away was the address? What did they need for a fight? What kind of fight?

They pulled up the drawer where they'd kept their old equipment from the Commission—things they had thought they'd never have to touch again. They snapped their old hunting knife sheath into the belt loop of their jeans. Was that enough? On instinct, they pulled out their sledgehammer holster and snapped it on underneath their hoodie.

Chavi glanced over their shoulder—was that sunlight already? They threw open the door and ran downstairs, their feet hammering on the wood. They would just barely make it—but they *would* make it. They'd make sure of it.

CHAPTER TWO

The Challenge

Harvard wasn't entirely sure when he woke up, as the hazy room came into focus. He found himself staring at a metal cabinet up against a cinderblock wall. Only once he reached up to rub his eyes did he realize that his hands were bound in front of him. Once he had enough presence of mind to be afraid, he sat upright, remembering.

"Oh, you're awake," said a gruff voice from the foot of the bed. Harvard turned to see a strangely familiar burly man with a thick blond beard, putting aside an incongruously small book and standing up to approach him. Immediately Harvard's eyes fell on the knife that hung sheathed from the man's hip and his instincts took over. *Run*. He had to run. But where? The man now blocked what looked like the only door. There was no place for him to go. He scurried backward on the cot, which squeaked underneath him as he pressed himself into the corner.

"Don't be scared." The man put up a hand as he pulled his chair to the foot of the bed. "I'm not gonna hurt you."

Harvard found the questions flowing out of him before he could stop himself. "What's happening? Where am I? Where are my friends? Are they okay?"

"Your friends are all fine," the man assured him. "We only came for you."

Harvard felt himself relax—a little. At least he didn't have to worry about Chavi or Jasmine or Princeton—*August*. Harvard was still getting into the habit of calling him by his real name. But if the rest of the Ivies weren't involved, that made everything worse. What was so special about *him*? With a sinking sensation, he worried he already knew.

"If this is about my family," he said, "they won't pay for me. They don't care about me."

It didn't even sting to admit anymore. It was just a fact of life that he had long since accepted. The man beside the bed, however, looked genuinely confused.

His thick brow scrunched like two kissing caterpillars. "What? No."

Now it made even less sense. If someone had discovered he was the lost Bell twin, then perhaps this was some kind of ransom situation. But the look on the man's face told him that he'd had no idea his family was even important. Harvard sniffled. He hadn't even realized he'd started crying.

"My crew doesn't have any money," he explained.

"We don't want money."

"Then what's happening?"

The man sighed deeply and gestured for Harvard to come forward. Cautiously, he moved toward the edge of the bed. If the man was going to kill him, there was nothing to stop him.

"Harvard—your name is Harvard, right?"

He nodded meekly.

He extended a hand. "We haven't properly been introduced. I'm Pierce."

Harvard numbly took the man's hand in both of his.

"Harvard, I'm very sorry that you're involved in all this. You have accidentally become a player in a very dangerous game. My suggestion to you is to play your role without question, then you can go home. Understand?" His voice was like a warm rumble, a pleasant earthquake.

Harvard nodded again.

"Think of this as a bad dream. It will all be over soon."

"I just—I don't understand—" he stammered.

"And you won't understand," Pierce interrupted him. "And that's okay. Now I need you to believe me: I'm not going to hurt you, alright?"

"Alright." And strangely, he did believe it.

"But if you don't do exactly as you're told"—the man's intense blue eyes locked with Harvard's—"you *will* be hurt. Understand?"

"Yes," he whispered.

"Good."

He stood and walked toward the head of the bed, where Harvard could hear him opening some drawers of the metal cabinet.

"We'll have to be there soon."

"Be whe—"

Suddenly there was a piece of cloth in his mouth, being tied so tight it hurt his cheeks. He yelled in surprise.

"Sorry about this. It's all about putting up appearances."

Again, Harvard didn't understand. Appearances for whom? And how was *this* putting up appearances? He didn't just *look* like he'd been kidnapped. He really *had* been kidnapped.

Pierce guided him out of the room into what looked like a loading dock, toward a rickety wrought iron elevator. As they ascended, Pierce squeezed his shoulder. Harvard wasn't sure if this was meant to be comforting, or to remind that there would be no use in trying to flee. They entered a sort of atrium, full of tall, shrouded boxes that threw shadows across the concrete ground. It smelled like mildew. There were shattered display cases and torn posters lining the walls. Harvard wondered if this was some kind of old museum, and if so, he wondered what the covered boxes were for.

Waiting at the center of the peculiarly shrouded cubes was the suited man from the Galvin Conference. The Head Enforcer of the Delian Group. Devrin. Harvard's panic increased tenfold. His skin suddenly felt cold.

"Oh there he is!" Devrin said, like an aunt at a dinner party who's excited to see the little nephew all dressed up. "You look wonderful. Keep that facial expression. Yes, exactly like that!" He inspected Harvard like a stage director examining an actor in costume. "You look perfectly pathetic!" This may have been true, but Harvard still took umbrage at the remark.

"Don't you worry," Devrin assured Harvard with a paternal pat on the head. "You're about to be bravely rescued. It will be terribly romantic. I know how much young people love it when things are terribly romantic."

Actually, I was having a really romantic night before you kidnapped me, Harvard thought but could not say for obvious reasons.

Devrin's eyes lit up.

"What's *that?*"

He froze, his eyes fixed on Harvard—no, not on Harvard, on something else. The key he wore around his neck, the one Chavi had procured for him when they returned to Bastion so he could access a rehearsal piano. With one fluid swipe, Devrin grabbed the key, easily snapping the cord that held in place. Harvard gave a muffled cry in protest. That was his gift. His first gift. It had been given to him.

"A key?"

Devrin held the key by the cord slightly above his head, watching it glint in the scant aquarium light as it dangled. His keen eyes locked in it like one of the crows Harvard had grown up with, fighting over coins. In fact, Harvard was suddenly struck by how corvid the man appeared, eyeing the glimmering treasure—his pointed nose like a beak, his suit and shirt like a magpie with its black and white plumage.

The Enforcer abruptly broke his gaze, pocketing the key, which again elicited a cry of discontent from Harvard.

"Oh, you'll get it back," Devrin assured him. "I just want to take a look at it. I have a thing for keys, you see. Now!" He clapped his hands. "Get into position, you two. It's almost curtains."

* * *

"Is this a joke?" Chavi muttered to themself.

They'd followed Devrin's instructions. This was definitely the place.

It was the disused Bastion Aquarium.

The Rubira Association often took it upon itself to open museums in Lower Bastion in the name of charity. Most, like this one, had fallen into disrepair. A torn poster boasted the display: Deep, Dark, and Dangerous! Chavi groaned inwardly. They'd had enough deep, dark, and dangerous out in the dusts. Did Devrin know about that? About the sandheads, and the ritual? Did he pick this place on purpose, to make Chavi feel like they were drowning? Surely he hadn't put that much thought into it. Or *did* he?

Why? Chavi wondered. What was the point? Just to torment them? Just for fun? It didn't add up.

Chavi steeled themself, then pushed open the boarded-up double doors, which creaked in protest on their rusty hinges. They entered a room that had once been a lobby. Shattered glass covered the floor, and insects had made homes in what was left of the tanks. Fungus grew in the cracks, and Chavi trudged under a discolored sign that encouraged onlookers to "Venture Deeper!"

"Harvard!" Chavi cupped their hands around their mouth. Their voice echoed in the vacant hallways. It reminded them of the crab den they'd slept in back in the dusts, with all its abandoned tunnels.

"Mmmph-mm!" came a distant reply.

"Harvard?" they asked.

"Mm-hmm!"

"I'm coming! Stay right there!"

Not that he had a choice. Chavi followed the sound of his voice to a corridor labeled "Ocean Predators." These tanks were larger than the ones in the foyer, about twice Chavi's height, and most were either covered up or empty. The largest tank, at the center of the room, was draped with black fabric, and it reminded Chavi a bit of the curtain in front of the screen at the Bastion Cinema. Chavi heard a metallic clang, and they looked up to see a catwalk surrounding the edge of the tank, probably used to feed the creatures inside back when this place was actually a suitable home for creatures.

Devrin leaned against the railing.

"Chaverim! So glad you're here. I know how disappointed little Harvard would have been if you didn't make an appearance."

He gestured to the side of the catwalk, and for the first time Chavi saw Harvard, partially hidden in shadow, gagged with his hands bound in front of him. Even from a distance they could see him trembling, his eyes wide with panic. The assistant—Pierce?—had an arm wrapped around his front. In the other hand he held a knife—not directly threatening Harvard, but the point was clear enough. Chavi felt guilt roiling in their chest. This was all their fault, wasn't it? If they hadn't left to go meet Mellie—No, even before that. If they hadn't been stupid enough to wear their captain's band into the Conference, and catch Devrin's eye, he wouldn't even have known they existed. And they'd given him their name, which had no doubt allowed him to keep an eye on them. His fixation on the Ivies was entirely Chavi's doing.

It didn't matter. They were here now, and they were going to fix it.

"Did they hurt you?" Chavi asked Harvard.

He shook his head. A subtle movement, and Chavi could tell he was leaning away from Pierce's knife hand.

"I'm gonna get you out of here, okay?" Chavi reassured him, though admittedly they weren't sure if they were saying it for his benefit or their own. "You're gonna be fine, alright?"

Harvard nodded, but Chavi doubted he believed them. They turned to Devrin.

"What do you want?" Chavi asked.

"Oh, right to business!" He clapped his hands. "That's what I like about you, Chaverim. So direct. To the point."

"I think what you like about me is that you have my boyfriend hostage," they growled.

"Oh yes, that too. I do particularly like that. Now, to the task at hand, since I know you're in a bit of a rush. I have a job for you."

"So you said."

"And so long as you complete the job, no one has to die." He glanced meaningfully at Harvard. "Come join us. I'll show you."

He kicked a switch, and a metal staircase unfolded itself. Chavi climbed the stairs to join the others on the catwalk. They turned to face Harvard, wishing they could do something to reassure him. All they did was lock eyes for a moment before Chavi turned away, ashamed.

From their vantage point on the catwalk, they could see into the tank. The bottom was filled with sand, and churning through the sand was a desertwalker. It wasn't the biggest Chavi had seen—at about meter wide, would have been dwarfed by a creature like Skrack. However, it had an extra appendage extending from the back of its shell and reaching upward, like a dog with an upright tail. The crab tapped a claw against the glass, as though pleading for escape.

"Are you familiar with this creature?" Devrin asked.

"Haven't seen it before. Looks like a scuttler of some kind."

"Very astute of you. That it is. Specifically, this is a scorpioncrab."

"You want me to kill it?" Chavi guessed.

"No. I mean, killing a scuttler isn't easy, but if that were all then I could just do it myself. No, I want you to *steal* from it."

Chavi's eyes narrowed. "Steal from a crab?" they repeated.

"Do you know what's special about a scorpioncrab?"

Chavi felt themself growing impatient. "No, I don't. Why don't you tell me?"

"It has a sack of poison just below the stinger, and it's only exposed when it's about to strike." Devrin pointed down into the tank, and Chavi could see the pale pocket of fluid waggling beneath the forbidding stinger. "I want you to swipe the poison sack for me."

"Why not just kill it, then take the sack?" Chavi asked, watching the creature tap on the glass with powerful carapaced legs.

Devrin nodded, as though he was hoping for this response. "Well, evolution anticipates nasty little tricks like that, now doesn't it? When the creature dies, the sack explodes. Think of the creature as a sort of...Darwinian suicide bomber."

Chavi made a mental note to ask Jasmine later what "Darwinian" meant.

"So, you want me to steal the poison sack without killing the creature?"

"And, preferably, not die in the process." Devrin held up a finger. "That's the sticking point those before you couldn't seem to manage."

"So you have had others before me," Chavi said. The whole situation shifted in perspective. No, Devrin wasn't just tormenting them for the sheer joy of it—though he was definitely enjoying it. He'd put others up to the task and they'd no doubt met a gruesome end, likely in this very tank. So of course he'd decided to recruit a former scavenger, one of the few people in Bastion with any actual experience dealing with desertwalkers. And—Chavi had the moment seared into their memory—Devrin didn't think of scavengers as people.

"I just know *you'll* be able to do it. Because you have some extra motivation!" Devrin gestured across the tank at Harvard—no, at the clock mounted on the wall of the tank. "You see, I'm on a bit of a time crunch with this venom, so time is of the essence. I need you to be quick about it."

"I think not dying will be plenty of motivation to be quick about it," Chavi retorted.

"Oh, I'm sure. But I've added a bonus challenge, because I just know you'll be up for it. Every minute that passes and you haven't delivered the venom to me, I'll break one of your boyfriend's fingers."

"*What?*"

Harvard made a horrified "Mph?" as Pierce sheathed his knife and grabbed one of Harvard's hands.

Before Chavi could say something along the lines of, "you're insane," Devrin gave them a firm shove on the back, and they fell sprawling into the tank.

Chavi landed awkwardly on the sand, scrambling to right themself. They brushed off the sand that clung to the lenses of their glasses, then took stock of the beast in the corner of the tank, watching them with beady black eyes, stinger held aloft and ready to strike. They guessed they were out of range, but their instinct sent them backing away until they bumped against the glass.

They unsheathed their hunting knife, feeling naked. Without vapor, what chance did they stand against this thing? They hazarded a glance at the clock. Ten seconds had already passed. They caught Harvard's eyes, wide with terror. This was a deathtrap, and they knew that. But they'd do it for him.

Chavi carefully inched toward the beast, knife in one hand, the other held up as a shield. The stinger darted for them, and they managed to dodge before it could strike them. The tip planted itself in the sand. Chavi couldn't help but laugh. A few weeks back home hadn't dulled their hard-won scavenging instincts.

The stinger whipped to the side, catching Chavi not with the tip but with the tail. It threw them in the air, and they slammed into the glass. They heard it crack. From above, they could hear Harvard scream.

Chavi checked the clock. Just past thirty seconds, and all they'd managed to do was get themself thrown across the tank. The scorpioncrab moved for them, and they managed to crawl out of the way just before the stinger came down again.

Maybe they could get behind it? No, it was too fast for that. What if they allowed the stinger to strike them, to get the venom sack in reach? That seemed stupid. Like, not so stupid they wouldn't try it, but that plan went solidly at the bottom of the list.

They managed to get back on their feet and out of the scorpioncrab's reach. It hissed.

Chavi glanced at the clock again. The second hand was nearing the minute mark, but Chavi couldn't even imagine a way to get out of this tank alive, let alone complete the task that was asked of them. They looked pleadingly toward Pierce.

"No. Please," Chavi begged. Pierce looked down at them with pity, and for a brief second Chavi thought this would be the moment he stood up against his boss. That he would say, *"That's it. That's too far. I can't do it."* How could he, the way he looked down at Chavi with such sympathy in his eyes?

Then he snapped Harvard's right index finger like a twig.

Harvard gave a muffled shriek.

"Oh, calm down," Devrin said from across the tank. "It's just one finger. You've got more."

Chavi gritted their teeth and turned back to the creature. With renewed commitment, Chavi paced the tank, the beast turning nimbly to keep them in its sights. They thought back to the way Harvard had managed to get the desertwalkers on his side. How did he do it? Was there just something special about him? Chavi yearned for Harvard's competency when it came to forming bonds. If diplomacy were an option, this would be much easier.

Please, they begged internally, *make this easy for me.*

The creature froze.

How did you do that? Chavi heard a voice in their head. A voice that was *not* supposed to be there.

Um.

They remembered Harvard's claims about talking to crabs, how he heard their voices in his head. But he hadn't been able to *think* to them. He could just *hear* them.

I asked, how did you do that? Do not make me ask again.

I don't know, Chavi thought, wondering if it was possible to get so high on adrenaline that they'd started having hallucinations. No, this was real. They weren't sure how they knew, but they felt a certainty deep in their gut that they were not imagining this.

Okay so I'm communicating telepathically with a desertwalker, they thought, this time to themself. *That's a cool and normal thing to do.* But they didn't know how to answer its question. *How* were they doing this? Crab...magic? There was only one explanation, and admittedly Chavi didn't fully understand it. They weren't exactly lucid to witness it.

I was injured, once, and a desertwalker saved me. I think it maybe...made me part of it. That sounded weak and they knew it, so they added hopefully, *We gained the trust of Empress Kryaka.*

Ha! Your allegiance to the Southwest Plains means little to me. I hail from the Northwest.

Okay. I mean, I can still talk to crabs though. That's got to mean something to you, right?

The beast shuffled in the sand. *I admit it is...unusual.*

Unusual enough that you'll help me?

I cannot claim to understand the whims of Kryaka, but she has no sway over me.

But if you don't, I'll have to kill you. Chavi brandished their hunting knife as though it were actually threatening, which they knew very well it wasn't. It was like waving a sandstaff at a duststorm in hopes of convincing it to turn the other way.

Bold assumption I will not kill you first.

But I'm the first human you've ever met who can speak to you! That means I'm special, right? Too special to kill.

The creature's stinger tensed. *It means you are an abomination that must be destroyed.*

Okay that's definitely not, like, the direction I was hoping—

Their thought cut off when the beast rushed them. It lifted a thick leg and knocked them to the ground, planting it on their stomach to pin them in place. Chavi heard Harvard scream from above, and they weren't sure if the scream was for them, or if another minute had passed and he'd lost another finger.

The scorpioncrab poised the stinger to strike.

"Wait!" Chavi held up a hand, before remembering to think at the creature instead. *Wait! Wait! Before you kill me. I'll tell you the truth.*

The stinger lowered slightly. *The truth?*

Chavi glanced at the clock. Two minutes had passed. They were rapidly approaching the third.

Don't you want to know? How I became this unholy abomination?

It was not a gift from Kryaka?

No. It wasn't a gift. And if you get off me, I'll tell you.

The creature stayed put, seeming to consider this offer. Chavi took short, shallow breaths, lungs constricted by the weight pressing into them. Finally, the creature obeyed, lifting its leg off their chest and retreating backward to give them space. Chavi took a grateful breath, shakily regaining their footing on the sand. They glanced at the clock. Almost three minutes. Not enough time. They had to end this. Somehow.

I stole it.

The scorpion bristled, as much as a scorpion could bristle. *How?* Even with its voice projected directly into their mind, Chavi could hear the beast's rage. No, it was something stronger than rage. Bloodlust.

You must promise not to kill me, they bargained.

I promise to wait until I've learned of your treachery. Then I will kill you.

Okay. Fair enough.

They crept closer. Harvard gave a muffled shriek above them, and they knew the third minute had passed. They looked up to see him limply leaning against Pierce, and they wondered if, mercifully, he'd passed out.

You see that boy up there?

Yes. What does he have to do with this?

I'll tell you. The truth is...that I would do anything to protect him.

With that, Chavi jerked their shoulder back, and their sledgehammer fell into their hand. Before the creature had a moment to respond, Chavi slammed the head into its shell. It made a sickly cracking sound, followed by squelching. The creature wailed in agony, blinded by pain, its tail stabbing wildly in hopes of catching Chavi. They dodged it easily and gripped it, ripping the exposed venom sack free. The stinger surged forward, catching Chavi in the shoulder. Without the poison, however, it could do little other than stab them and shove them backward. They dug their feet into the sand so as not to be forced to the ground again.

You...are vermin, the creature hissed, its voice now weak and distant, as though retreating deeper and deeper down a tunnel.

I know. And I'm sorry.

The beast's strength faltered, giving Chavi the opportunity to rip the stinger from their shoulder with a pained grunt. Chavi lifted the hammer and brought it down one more time. The tail went limp, and the voice in Chavi's head fell silent.

They stared at the mangled corpse, feeling...disgusted. But were they disgusted with the monster, or with themself?

The sound of clapping pulled them from their trance.

"Well done, Chaverim!" Devrin kicked a switch and another metal staircase unfolded itself into the tank. "You may come out now."

Chavi shook themself off, brushing away sand. Their injured shoulder screamed in agony, leaking blood all over their hoodie. The thing was probably ruined, anyway. They shucked it off and threw it on the sand so they could get a better look at the wound. It wasn't a wide gash, but it was deep. They probably wouldn't be able to use this arm for a while. Before ascending, they checked the venom sac, still gripped in one hand, miraculously unpunctured. They really hoped that just touching it wasn't enough to kill them, but if that were the case it was already too late.

By the time Chavi reached the catwalk, Devrin was already on the ground outside of the tank. They descended the stairs at the front of the tank to meet him.

"Alright here's your venom or whatever," Chavi shoved the sac at Devrin, happy to be rid of it. Devrin turned it over in his hands, appraising it. When he was satisfied, he gestured for someone in the shadows to come forward. An attendant in a white lab coat bustled in and started examining the wound on Chavi's shoulder.

"Where's Harvard?" they demanded.

"Pierce took him back to his room," Devrin said, handing off the venom to another attendant.

"You said if I got this shit for you, you would let him go!" The person bandaging the shoulder jumped. They hurriedly finished wrapping Chavi up and looked to Devrin for confirmation. He dismissed them with a nod.

"No, I said if you got 'this shit' for me then I wouldn't kill him, not that I'd let him go. He's going to stay here with me a bit longer, actually. Pay attention, Chaverim." Again, he snapped his fingers in their ear.

They didn't mean to lash out. They didn't want to. But their fury took over their whole body, puppeting them. They grabbed him by the lapels and shoved him against the tank so hard they heard the glass crack behind him. He didn't look scared. He didn't even look surprised. Chavi wanted to change both of those things.

"If you don't let him go right now, I will kill you," they hissed.

Devrin raised an eyebrow. "You do realize if this becomes too inconvenient for me, I'll simply have his throat cut and be done with it?"

Chavi studied him, and their group loosened. They allowed themself to be pushed away, Devrin's hand resting on their shoulder.

"Good," he said. "That was the smart move. Maybe you're not as stupid as everyone thinks. Oh, don't make that face. I have access to all your records, remember? That includes your education history. I know you didn't get a high school education past the age of sixteen. And judging by your grades, one could hardly call what you did receive an 'education' at all."

Chavi deflated. "What do you want from me?"

"I want you to go out there"—Devrin gestured vaguely to the outside world—"get your little crew together, and bring them back here."

"Why?"

"I have a job offer for them."

"You want to offer us a job?" Chavi repeated. They wondered if he realized they would have been a lot *more* likely to accept a job from him if he hadn't gone the whole kidnapping-route. "I thought this *was* the job."

"No no no! This was just a test to see if you could *do* the job," Devrin gestured to the tank holding the now desiccated desertwalker corpse. "And you passed! So now it's time to bring in the whole gang. And I want you all to make your decision about whether or not to take it right here."

Chavi wondered if he realized that there was a zero percent chance the Ivies would ever work for him. Still, if they wanted to get Harvard out of this alive, they had to at least pretend to be interested, right?

"What do we get?" they asked.

Devrin looked at them like he thought they were stupid, which, actually, he'd just said that he did. "Money. Or are you unfamiliar with how the hiring process works? I suppose it is true that no one has hired you to do anything, well, ever."

Chavi's fists clenched. It took all the restraint they had—which was not very much—not to launch themself at him again. "You threatened to kill my boyfriend. We don't want your money."

Devrin smirked. "Really, Chaverim? You know what's more likely to kill your boyfriend? Starvation. You're squatting in a property that isn't yours. What are you going to do when the owners find out? Go crawling back to your mother, ask if all of you can stay in her tiny little basement? No, you're too proud for that. And you know it would break her heart to see her only child grow so pathetic. No, I think you'd live on the streets first. The streets, however, are a dangerous place. So, yes, I did threaten to end your boyfriend's life. But if you think I am the biggest threat to his life, then you would be mistaken. Now go. Get out of here and come back with your friends."

Chavi slumped in defeat. He was right, and that made them hate him even more. "Can I at least see him?" they asked.

He rolled his eyes exaggeratedly. "You're so needy," he groaned. "Fine. Come with me."

* * *

Harvard awoke gasping as all the pain rushed back to him. He'd never broken a bone before, even in the two or three years he spent scavenging. Now he felt like thousands of needles were pressing into his fingers. When he saw them bent at unnatural angles, he let out an agonized groan. He thought he might faint again, or maybe just vomit. Then he remembered the sight of Chavi dodging blows from that desertwalker, and he almost forgot his pain in the wave of panic that washed over him. He became aware of Pierce in front of him, holding pieces of wood, gauze and medical tape.

"Where's Chavi?" Harvard demanded, "Are they okay? Are they hurt?"

"Chavi is fine. Now I'm going to splint your fingers," he explained levelly, "and it's going to hurt. I'm sorry. Just talk to me, okay?"

He took Harvard's massacred hand in his own, careful to avoid the fingers. Harvard was too shaky, too stunned to pull away, though his instincts told him he needed to put as much distance between himself and this man as possible.

"You—you said you wouldn't hurt me," he panted.

Pierce pressed Harvard's index finger against one of the wooden sticks. He cried out, and Pierce winced.

"I know, and I'm sorry I lied to you. But I don't regret it." He pulled some medical tape with his teeth, and began wrapping it around the finger. "I told you what you had to hear."

"You broke my fingers!" Harvard said through gritted teeth, and his pain melting into anger. He'd been tricked into trusting this man, and he betrayed him.

Pierce paused his work on the splint to look into Harvard's eyes.

"Would it have been better if I told you? If I'd said Harvard, I'm going to hurt you very badly and there's nothing you can do about it?"

Harvard said nothing, just swallowed hard. He clenched his jaw to keep from wailing in anguish.

Pierce wrapped a second piece of tape around the first finger.

"Alright I'm moving on to the second one. Keep talking to me, okay? Your name is Harvard. But that's a brand name. That's not your real name, right?"

"No, it's—AUGH!"

Pierce aligned another finger with the wooden splint.

"What's your real name?"

"R-Ronan," he breathed, his uninjured curling into a fist around the bed sheets.

"That's a good name."

"Thank you," he responded instinctively.

"But you prefer to go by Harvard?" Pierce ripped off another strip of tape.

"Yes."

"Why?"

"That—that's what Chavi calls me."

"Okay great. Let's talk about Chavi. You love Chavi?"

"Ye—AH!"

"That was the last one. It's easier from here. When did you meet?

"About…about two years ago."

"And what do you like about them?"

Maybe it was just the fact that his mind was clouded with pain, but Harvard found himself struggling with the question.

"They're just…they're just so good," he finally answered.

"Yes. They seem like a good person. I can tell. I'm glad you have a good person who cares about you."

"Th—thank you," he again responded without thinking. Why was he thanking the man who'd just mutilated him? Yet he couldn't help starting to trust Pierce again. He had a gentleness about him that put Harvard at ease.

"Oh, before I forget…" Pierce put the key on its cord back around Harvard's neck. "He wasn't lying about giving it back. Hope that makes you feel better."

He went back to wrapping the last finger, and let out a relieved sigh as he finished.

"Done," he announced. "Obviously you should avoid using these fingers—though believe me, the temptation will be there. They won't take long to heal, but until then, favor the other hand."

Harvard nodded as the door burst open and Chavi appeared in the room, eyes frantic.

"Harvard!" they cried, barreling toward him.

"Chavi!"

And then he was wrapped up in their arms, feeling that familiar sensation of warmth and, despite everything, safety. They buried their face in the side of his neck.

"I am so, so sorry," Harvard found himself saying, and he realized he was crying.

"You're sorry?" Chavi pulled back. "No, I'm sorry."

"Are we going home now?" he asked. He didn't like how childish he sounded, but right now, he felt like a child. He needed home. Sleep. Comfort.

They ran a hand through his ginger curls, now moist with sweat.

"I can't take you home," Chavi said, and their voice was strained, like it pained them to say, "but I'll be back for you, I promise." They whirled abruptly on Pierce. "You," they seethed, "I swear if you touch him again, if you even think about it, I'll kill you."

Pierce accepted the threat impassively, silent, hands folded together, as though this was more or less the reaction he had been expecting.

"Chavi," Harvard called them back weakly, worried that they would lose what little time they had together.

They were kneeling by his side again in an instant.

"Everything's going to be okay," they assured him, grabbing his good hand. Harvard nodded, even though he didn't believe that for a second. Everything was already very much not okay. His fingers, though better, still throbbed, and he had no idea when he would be back home or what else these people might do to him. Or *why*, which was what terrified him the most. And Chavi—for the first time he really got a good look at them since the fight with the scorpioncrab.

"Your shoulder!" he cried, seeing the blood-soaked bandage for the first time. "What happened? Are you—"

"I'm fine," they assured him, squeezing his good hand.

Devrin appeared in the doorway and Harvard felt his stomach lurch.

"Time's up, I'm afraid," he said with a pout, as though he truly felt guilty about separating the two. It was all a lie, of course, and Harvard knew that. Two Delian group guards appeared behind him as though to reinforce his mandate.

Chavi ignored him. They wrapped their arms around him one more and kissed him hard, and when they broke away Harvard saw the two guards gripping their arms, dragging them back to the door.

"Get off!" Chavi shouted, jerking wildly to get out of their grasp.

"Wait!" Harvard found himself shouting. He moved to follow them, but a hand descended on his shoulder, keeping him seated on the bed. He looked up to see Pierce, restraining him, shaking his head.

"I told you not to touch him!" Chavi cried as the two guards struggled to get them through the doorway. Devrin had since disappeared.

"I love you!" Harvard called after them, and he felt his throat tighten around the words, as his eyes welled with tears.

"I—" Chavi began, but the door slammed shut before they could finish.

* * *

Once the door safely separated the two of them, the guards' duty was done. Chavi shook them off, and they departed hastily, like scuttlers disappearing into the desert haze. Devrin, of course, was waiting for them.

"I'm terribly sorry about your hoodie, by the way," he said amiably. "I'm assuming you won't be wanting it back?"

Chavi stalked toward him, and it took all their meager willpower not to deck him.

"I'm gonna come back here," they promised, "and when I do, I better find him alive and unharmed, or I will *quaking kill you*."

Devrin snickered pityingly.

"That's adorable," he said, "but that entirely depends on him. If he can behave himself for the rest of the day, then we won't have any trouble."

"It's not that hard to just not hurt someone!"

"I think"—Devrin looked down his nose condescendingly—"you'll find it's much more complicated than that. Come. You've got a crew to gather."

Devrin waved a hand to indicate Chavi should follow, and he guided them toward the creaky wrought iron elevator that had brought them down to the lower level.

"You really don't have to coddle him like that," Devrin advised them sagely. "He's an adult, after all."

"He's nineteen!" Chavi shot back, and then realized they didn't actually know if that was true. If they were almost twenty-one, Harvard must be at least twenty. When was Harvard's birthday? They didn't know. So not only were they a condescending partner, they were also an ignorant one. And Devrin was the one to point it out, which of course made it even more infuriating.

"See you soon, Chaverim," Devrin said as he ushered them to the door. "I can't *wait* to meet your friends! Meet them *properly*, this time. We're going to have fun!"

Chavi doubted that.

They stepped out of the aquarium and were hit with the overwhelming urge to scream. Everything was horribly wrong. Instead, they bent over, placing their hands on their thighs, and breathed. This was undeniably a bad situation. A super fucked up situation, actually. But they were still in control. To some degree. At the very least, in that moment, they could choose what to do next.

They collapsed against the wall of the aquarium and started to sob.

CHAPTER THREE

Fallout

Less than an hour later, Chavi was seated with Jasmine and August in the townhouse living room. Someone had draped a blanket over Chavi's shoulders—they weren't sure who. Jasmine had put a mug of tea in front of them. They hadn't touched it.

"So," August said, lying back on the couch, "let me make sure I understand." He looked so jarringly different than he had as Princton, having traded in his dusts gear for a surprisingly vibrant wardrobe. His shirt was so colorful it made Chavi's eyes hurt. Or maybe it was just exhaustion. They couldn't tell.

"The guy from the Conference—the dude with glasses—you're saying he broke into our house and stole Harvard in the middle of the night?"

"Yes."

August sat up abruptly. "Wait, why weren't you there?"

"I was...in the bathroom," Chavi lied.

Jasmine and August both stared at Chavi for a moment.

"Um, how long did you take in the bathroom?" August asked.

"I don't—how long does it take you to piss, August?" Chavi deflected.

"Don't answer that, August," Jasmine said. "Chavi—"

"Fifteen to twenty seconds."

"You share a wall with us!" Chavi pointed out, hoping to avoid any suspicion that this might sort-of-kind-of be their fault like they knew it definitely was. "Didn't you hear anything?"

August flushed. "I...I mean, no."

"You could have stopped them from taking Harvard!" Now it wasn't an evasion. Now they actually were angry at August. Why hadn't *he* come to Harvard's aid? He had been in the room next door!

"I didn't hear anything!" August said, reddening.

"I got thrown against a wall! How did you not—"

"There were a lot of noises coming from your room last night, Chavi! I was sort of trying to block them out!"

He immediately looked embarrassed for saying it, blushing deeper, gripping his elbows and curling up on himself in a distinctly un-August position.

"It's fine," Chavi said, relaxing. "It wouldn't have mattered anyway."

"Chavi, I know you're upset right now," Jasmine said, leaning against the kitchen counter, "but you need to work with us."

"I am working with you!" Chavi protested. "I'm telling you what happened. I got back, Harvard was gone. Devrin—"

"Glasses man," August clarified, mostly to himself.

"—was in our room. He said if I didn't show up to the aquarium by sunrise, he'd kill Harvard."

"Holy shit," August murmured.

So Chavi recounted the whole ordeal in as much detail as they could without crying again. When they reached the end, they leaned forward, elbows resting on their knees. They took a deep breath. Dusts, their heart was still racing. "He said he had...a job for us. Wanted us all to be there to hear him out. He wants us all back there tonight."

Chavi expected some kind of reaction from the other two—ideally something along the lines *"fuck that, let's rescue Harvard and be done with this whole thing"*—but their faces were impassive.

"What kind of job?" Jasmine asked, and Chavi felt irrationally irritated at her for even asking.

"He didn't say. He didn't wanna tell me anything before we were all there."

"So...this job." August leaned in. "How much we talking here?"

"August!" Jasmine chastised.

"I'm just asking!"

"He kidnapped my *fucking boyfriend!*" Chavi shouted.

"I don't think there's any point in discussing this," Jasmine held up a hand. "If we need to go back tonight, then we'll go back. And assuming Chavi has told us everything"—she eyed them and they shrunk into the couch cushions—"maybe we should give them some time to rest."

August nodded before retreating upstairs, mumbling about having work to do anyway.

Jasmine leaned in.

"Will you be alright?" she asked.

Of course not.

"Sure," they said with a shrug, avoiding her gaze.

She nodded. "I'm going to go get Avi. She should have a look at that injury on your shoulder before we go."

Admittedly, Chavi had forgotten they'd been hurt at all. Jasmine left, and they were alone, turning the events of that night over in their head.

Chavi couldn't stop seeing him, trembling, eyes wide with terror though he was trying so hard to be brave, chin upturned as he strained to get away from the knife that pressed into the skin under his jaw.

This is my fault, they thought. *And it's my job to fix it.*

Interlude One: Kathy

Katherine Bell's brother was dead, and it was her fault. She hadn't meant for it to happen of course—he'd just made it so *easy*. There was a kind of satisfaction in it, to needle him until he cried. She'd been doing it ever since she could remember. And at the time, it never seemed wrong to her. In fact, it felt natural. It cemented her place as the superior sibling. Isn't that what Mother wanted? For her to prove herself as the strong, capable heiress that she knew herself to be?

Putting down Ronan was something she did without even questioning—until, of course, he disappeared. She easily could have sloughed off the blame on her parents, but she knew the truth: she was the one he spent his days with. She was the one who nudged him closer to breaking every day. She was the one who'd tempted him into trying to steal from their mother, which had been the tipping point. And somehow, the whole time she'd seen it as her duty to the family, like she was slowly hacking away at a vestigial limb. So when she woke up one morning to find that the bedroom that shared a wall with hers was vacant, and heard the servants whispering to each other in worried tones, she was under no illusions about who was to blame.

Her mother assured her that they'd scoured the city. The Bell family had a *personal* connection to the Delian Group, after all. Every Delian Guard in the city had been on the lookout for him. And when they turned up nothing, Saoirse Bell reported that she could only draw two conclusions: either he'd died in the streets, or he'd fled the city and died in the dusts. Kathy drew her own conclusion: she was the one who had killed him.

This was a truth that she kept wrapped up in the depths of her soul, one that she never spoke aloud, and that she masked with the cordial smile of the heiress she was supposed to be. But she knew beneath it all that she was a monster, and swore never to let anyone else see it.

But then she *saw* him.

She wasn't sure what had drawn her gaze to him, but in the back room of the Galvin Conference, she locked eyes with her own reflection. For one stunned moment, she felt as though she were looking in a trick mirror—one that showed her a version of herself in another world. But that expression was one she knew well, one she'd seen him wear every time he knew he was going to be chastised, and there was no doubt in her mind that it was him.

"Ronan?" she'd whispered.

He darted away like a frightened animal, and instinct propelled her to charge after him, shoving aside researchers and investors in her wake.

"Ronan!" she cried. "Wait! Ronan!"

She followed him out the door in the hallway, which was starting to fill with workers bringing presentations to the stage. She weaved through the growing crowd, keeping her eyes locked on Ronan's ginger hair just a few paces ahead of her. She reached out to grab him, but her fingers only managed to brush the back of his suit jacket.

"Ronan!" she called one last time as he burst through the door into the main exhibition hall. By the time she made it to the door, he was already lost in the crowd.

"Are you...feeling well, Mistress Bell?" said a voice behind her, and she remembered that before the chase, she'd been conversing with a representative of the Zuri Institution about a potential internship. He was puffing with the effort of keeping up with her.

"No," she said numbly, staring into the crowd. "I am not feeling well. I think I should go home."

* * *

Weeks later, Kathy Bell still couldn't stop herself from replaying the memory again and again in her mind. She sat at the foot of her bed, staring at the wall. She was almost angry.

Years she'd spent putting him out of her mind, shoving his memory deep down where no one could find it, alongside her own culpability. And in one moment, he'd shattered all of it.

But had it even been him? How was that even possible?

He was dead. She knew that.

But also he'd been there.

But maybe it was just someone who'd looked like him.

But it had been her own face. She was sure of it. And besides, if it was a stranger, why would he run away?

It was definitely him.

But he was dead.

She found herself standing and walking out of the room. She drifted to the bedroom door next to hers, the one that hadn't been touched for six years. The handle creaked as she turned it, pushing the door in and gliding inside.

She'd never been in Ronan's room before. She'd had no reason to. She imagined, though, that it was exactly as he had left it. Her parents had left the room untouched—she liked to imagine that it was to respect his memory, but she knew they just didn't want to deal with getting rid of his things. She opened the door to the wardrobe and examined the shirts that hung there—she remembered him wearing some of them. *So small,* she thought. Had he really been that young when he disappeared? She'd always imagined him as the same age as her, growing up with her even in death. Now she remembered him as he was before he left. Still a child. And here she was, a woman, having denied that child the opportunity to grow up.

Or maybe not. Maybe he lived.

She closed the wardrobe gingerly and glided over to the desk, still littered with papers.

What did he even have to work on? She wondered, but as she sifted through the papers, she saw it wasn't work at all, but drawings. Sketches upon sketches of birds, plants, the ocean—even some of the Bell Manor servants. None of the Bell family themselves.

She gasped quietly. Among the abandoned sketches was a single self-portrait. He'd drawn himself sitting at the piano, and below it he'd scribed a staff with some music notes.

How did he do that? She wondered. *Don't you have to draw a self-portrait looking in a mirror? Was his memory really that good?*

Kathy began to gather the sketches in her arms—she wasn't sure what she planned on doing with them, but she couldn't help the feeling that it had been wrong to let them sit here as long as they had, unseen.

"Katherine?"

She yelped in surprise, dropping the armful of sketches, gripping the portrait in her hands so tightly that she crumpled it.

Saoirse Bell stood in the doorway, watching her daughter with an expression that bordered on disapproval.

"What are you doing in here?" she asked, with the unspoken understanding that her opinion hinged on Kathy's answer.

"I was just...thinking about Ronan," she answered, instinctively hiding the crumpled sketch behind her back.

"Hm," Saoirse laughed, "I would advise against that. Any reason for your sudden bout of...sentimentality?"

He's alive, she wanted to say. *He's alive and he's out there and we have to find him.* For some reason, though, she bit it down. It somehow seemed unwise.

"No," she looked down at her feet. "No reason."

"Sentimentality is not something we strive for, Katherine. Avoid it."

"I just..." she wrestled with herself, feeling as though there were some kind of danger in pursuing the line of conversation, yet unable to stop herself. "I was just wondering...is it possible that Ronan is still alive? Living in the city?"

Her mother laughed again, a sharp sound coming from Saoirse Bell.

"No," she said, "it isn't possible. We searched every corner of the city. And you know he wasn't exactly a smart boy, so I wouldn't put it past him to try his luck out in the dusts. Do you really think he could have survived outside the city walls?"

"Well...scavengers do it," Kathy reasoned.

"And do you think Ronan would have lasted two seconds as a scavenger?"

"No," Kathy admitted.

"Well, there you have it," her mother smiled tightly. "I really should have had this place cleaned out long ago. I'll have Camilla deal with those ghastly drawings. Come here, Katherine. And shut the door behind you."

Kathy did as she was told, still gripping the sketch in her concealed hand.

He's alive, she thought again, *and I'm going to find him.*

CHAPTER FOUR

Exchange

Harvard thought he was slowly losing his mind. He sat on the bed, picked at the splints on his fingers, paced the room, jiggled the door handle, and sat back down before repeating the whole cycle over again. He didn't know how long he'd been trapped here. He knew it hadn't been more than a day. It felt like years. It wasn't just the waiting that he hated—he could wait if he had to. He considered himself a relatively patient person.

No, it was the fact that he was helpless. He felt just like he had as a child trapped in his parents' home, just as he had when he was stuck in the Commission, or when he was sick in O'Neill's pod, or every time that Skrack had to scoop him out of the way of danger. He hated the feeling that he couldn't do anything on his own. For a brief, glorious moment, Harvard had been able to take care of himself. When he was alone in the dusts, he'd managed to not only persuade Skrack not to kill him, but even help him save the rest of his crew. He'd been a hero. For the first time in his life, actually felt capable of doing something worthwhile.

Why did his budding sense of agency have to be snatched away so soon?

Now he had to sit and wait for Chavi to come back and rescue him. And what if they didn't? Was he even worth rescuing? He didn't think so. Wouldn't it be much easier for the Ivies to get on with their lives without him? He was only holding them back. The little voice of reason in his head told him he was being absurd, but in this cinder block prison, reality felt distorted. How much did Chavi really care about him? They didn't love him. Not like he loved them. He was merely tolerated, not desired. They were better off without him, anyway. No one was coming for him, were they?

Harvard had to get out. He wasn't the same person he was a few months ago.

He could do this on his own, and he would do it now. He waited behind the doorway until Pierce returned with a tray of food.

"Thought you might be hu—" he paused when he surveyed the empty room. Harvard slipped out behind him and darted into the hallway. And he ran, and it felt so good to run.

"Hey!" Pierce called after him, but he was already gone.

It had been so easy! He was in control again! He was—

He paused at an intersection between two displays. He didn't know the way out.

Voices echoed in the corridor, but he couldn't tell where they were coming from. He pressed himself up against a wall, willing the voices to pass. He peered around the corner to see two Delian guards, talking quietly. He silently padded in the other direction.

He broke into a run again.

Something rammed into his face just above his left eye, and everything exploded in white light and pain. He fell backward, and his head cracked against the ground. He instinctively thrust out a hand to catch himself, forgetting his injured fingers, which screamed in protest. A boot came down on his stomach and he grunted. He blinked into the fluorescent light shining down on him, and he could see two silhouettes up above.

"What's this kid doing out here?" one of the silhouettes asked, and as his vision adjusted Harvard could see that they were holstering a gun. His hand flew up to the place where the butt of the gun had struck him. Hot blood trickled from the wound and ran down his face. He groaned.

"Dunno," said the other guard. "I thought Pierce was watching him. Pierce!" they called.

"I'm coming, I'm coming," Harvard heard Pierce's gruff voice behind him, and the sounds of heavy booted footfalls.

"Caught your charge tryna make a break for it," the first guard said. His boot lifted from Harvard's stomach. The other guard bent down to grab Harvard by the arm and pull him none-too-gently to his feet.

"Oh, calm down," Pierce said. "You know he wasn't gonna get far."

"He mighta. Kid was pretty fast," the second guard said as she shoved Harvard toward Pierce, who caught him by the elbow. Pierce used a thick hand to tilt Harvard's head and examine the wound.

"You shouldn't have done this to 'im," Pierce said, and Harvard could have sworn he heard anger in his voice.

"You shouldn't have let him get away," the first guard said. Pierce grunted and herded Harvard back toward his cell.

His brief moment of freedom now past, it occurred to Harvard to wonder what his punishment would be. He guessed that the Delian Group did not take escape attempts lightly. When they returned to the cell, he saw the tray of food spilled on the ground. Pierce must have dropped it when he turned to pursue Harvard.

"I told you to listen," Pierce said. To Harvard's surprise, he didn't sound angry. Just...disappointed. No: concerned.

"You *saw* what that thing did to Chavi!" Harvard protested. "I can't have them putting themself in danger like that again because of me!"

"They were fine!"

"It almost killed them! And every second I'm here is keeping them in danger. I can't just sit around like a hostage."

"You *are* a hostage," Pierce reminded him. He ran a hand across his beard, pensive. "Look, you have to trust me."

"Why would I trust you?" Harvard crossed his arms. "All you've done is lie to me."

"I told you what you needed to hear and you know that. And that's what I'm doing now. Do not try to fight. Just wait until this is over." Pierce put a hand on his shoulder, encouraging him to sit. Harvard shrugged it off.

"I can't."

"Yes, you can. And if you don't, your friends will be the ones who get hurt."

Harvard felt a jolt of alarm. "What?"

"I know it seems tempting, to try and get out of here on your own so your friends aren't put in any danger. But believe me when I say that if you resist, they'll be in even *more* danger. So. Will you stay put?"

Harvard held Pierce's gaze for a long moment before he finally said, "Yes."

"Good. He didn't come to rule the city without learning how to make people cooperate."

"The six corps rule the city," Harvard corrected, straightening. "He doesn't."

"No, he does. He has for a long time. The city does not work like you think it does, Harvard. How many people do you think rule the city?"

"I don't know," Harvard shrugged. "Hundreds. Thousands. However many people are in the corps."

"No," Pierce said, locking eyes with him. "Two."

"Two?" Harvard repeated.

"Just two. And pretty soon, it might just be one. But for right now, the city is completely controlled by two individuals. He is one of them."

"Who's the other?"

There came a knock on the door.

"Harvard?" Devrin asked, and his voice was sing-songy. "Can I come in, please?" Like Harvard had any choice in the matter. Devrin was the one with the key, after all. The door swung open, and with a curt nod from Devrin, Pierce was dismissed. He moved to the door, casting a worried look at Harvard before leaving. The door slammed shut behind him.

Devrin nudged the fallen tray with his foot.

"Harvard, did you not like your food? Are you vegan? I didn't know you had dietary restrictions, but I'm sure we can rustle something up for you."

"Stop it," Harvard said, forcing himself to stand tall.

"What?"

"Stop pretending to be nice to me."

Devrin's head snapped up, and he looked genuinely wounded.

"I'm not," he said. "Believe it or not, I am *actually* trying to be nice to you. You're our guest, after all. It's the least I can do to make you feel comfortable, given the circumstances."

"Then let me go."

Devrin frowned, looking genuinely remorseful. "Well, I would if I could, but I can't. Think of this"—he waved a hand to indicate...everything, maybe?—"as a performance. We're all just pretending, telling a story, creating an illusion. You've been cast, whether you like it or not, and you have to play your role until the show is over. Understand?"

He did not understand. Devrin took one step forward, and Harvard instinctively leapt back. Devrin giggled.

"Are you afraid of me? Silly boy. You know I wouldn't hurt you."

But Harvard didn't know that. He had a distinct feeling that Devrin could hurt him, and all his instincts told him to be ready for an attack. He trembled more violently than ever, more than he had when facing down monsters in the dusts. He turned away.

"Now I'm going to tell you something, Harvard, and I'm only going to say it once, so I need you to pay very good attention."

Gingerly, he took Harvard's jaw in his hand and tilted his face up to look at him.

"Your friends will be here tonight. It would be a shame if they never left."

"Please," Harvard whispered. "Don't."

"Well you don't have to beg me!" Devrin laughed. "The choice is entirely yours. If you behave yourself, we won't have an issue. If you give me trouble, though...well, I'll have to give you trouble, too. It's only fair. I'm a believer"—his grip tightened ever so slightly—"in justice. Do you understand me?"

Harvard nodded feebly.

"Out loud."

"Yes."

"Good."

He let go, and Harvard found that his trembling made his legs so weak he collapsed to the floor.

"You should really get that tremor under control," Devrin said over his shoulder as he sauntered toward the door. "It really seems like such a hassle."

* * *

For the second time that day, Chavi stood outside the Bastion Aquarium. This time, they were flanked by the two other Ivies. That should have brought them some small measure of comfort, but it didn't. Instead, they just represented two more people that Chavi could accidentally get hurt.

"Are you okay?" Jasmine asked them.

"Yeah," they said without looking at her. Their eyes were fixed on the lopsided sign that hung above the aquarium. "I'm fine."

"I mean," Jasmine clarified, "can you do this?"

"Yeah, I can do this," they said, but in truth it sounded more like they were trying to convince themself than answer her.

"Let's go," August said, pressing an encouraging hand into Chavi's back.

"Yeah. Let's go."

The double doors at the front of the building screeched as the three pushed through them. Shattered glass cracked under their feet. Foliage that had lived a brief life free of its cage now lay dead on the floor, spilling out of broken tanks.

They came to the atrium Chavi was already beginning to despise. Devrin leaned against the covered tank, looking oddly casual, staring down at his watch. He looked up at the sound of the Ivies' entrance, grinning wildly.

"There you are!" he cried. "I was getting worried you'd be late."

"Where is he?" Chavi demanded. They swept their eyes across the room, but there was no sign of Harvard.

Devrin gave the other two Ivies a conspiratorial look.

"Right to business, this one!" he laughed, gesturing at Chavi. "Are they always like this? Must be some captain!"

The Ivies were silent, even August, which Chavi was thankful for.

"Where is he?" they repeated.

"Now hold on a moment." Devrin held up a hand. "I haven't even been properly introduced to the rest of your crew. And if they're going to be working for me, I think it's important we start off on the right foot."

We already started on the wrong foot when you decided to hurt Harvard, Chavi thought, but thought better of speaking aloud.

"I'm Jasmine."

Chavi was shocked to see her step toward Devrin, extending a hand. They wanted to protest, slap her hand away. *Don't be polite to him! What are you doing?* But Jasmine never did anything without thinking it through first—she'd already evaluated her options rapid-fire, and for whatever reason, had decided it was no use to resist. So she introduced herself.

"It's a pleasure," Devrin said.

Jasmine remained silent, which took more restraint than Chavi would have had. It didn't seem to bother Devrin in the least. August took his cue and shook his hand as well.

"August."

Devrin nodded, satisfied.

"See, that wasn't so hard, now was it? Now we're all properly acquainted. That's very important for a business transaction, I hope you know."

"*Where is he?*"

Chavi felt Jasmine's hand on their arm and they took a quick breath. It was only a touch, but the message was clear—if they lost their temper now, the consequences would be dire. They had to keep it together. They nodded their understanding to her, and she retracted her hand. Luckily, Devrin didn't seem at all perturbed by Chavi's outburst. If anything, he was amused.

"Alright, alright," he chuckled, then called out, "Bring him out!"

Chavi heard August gasp quietly when Harvard appeared, Pierce guiding him in a slow, careful shuffle toward the front of the atrium. One hand was placed on the back of his neck while the other arm crossed his front, knife poised to easily slash through Harvard's throat if he so chose. Harvard himself looked even more disheveled than when Chavi had last seen him—he had a blossoming bruise above his left eye, and a cut at the center was trickling blood down the side of head. His splinted fingers were purple and swollen. His eyes were wide with panic, and the moment Chavi came into view he locked gazes with them. Chavi ached to help him, to protect him, to clean him up and tell him they would never let this happen again—but that urge was mixed with rage, especially upon seeing the fresh wound. It almost scared them, how much they hated Devrin. They'd spent their whole life trying to avoid allowing their anger to hurt someone, and now suddenly, they knew with complete certainty that given the opportunity, they would kill this man. They wouldn't even hesitate.

"What did you do to him?" they demanded.

"Oh that?" Devrin strode over and touched the bruise above Harvard's eye. Harvard winced. "He did that to himself. Clumsy boy." Devrin knocked Harvard's head playfully, and Harvard squeaked, painfully aware of the vicinity of the knife.

Chavi crossed their arms, eager to have all of this over with.

"Alright. We're here. What do you want?"

Devrin slinked back over to the Ivies, his hands in his pockets.

"I have an errand I'd like you to run. As seasoned scavengers, I think you'd be perfect for the job. Not far off the coast of Bastion, there is an island. I have reason to believe that at the center of that island, there is a piece of pre-Quake technology. All I ask is that you fetch it and bring it to me. See? Easy."

Jasmine inhaled as though she might be about to ask a question, but Chavi gave her a glance and she was silent. They had already discussed this. They were not going to take the job, and they were not going to encourage Devrin further.

"As I mentioned," he continued, "the payment would be substantial. Enough to end your financial troubles for a good long while. I was thinking something along the lines of...one hundred thousand points?"

August gasped quietly, and Chavi nudged him. What had they talked about? August made a sort of *what-it's-not-my-fault* kind of gesture. Chavi turned their gaze back to Devrin.

"Great. Cool science project you got going on. I hope you find someone stupid enough to take you up on it. But it won't be us."

Chavi had expected Devrin to look surprised, maybe even disappointed, but his face remained unchanged. If anything, his smile grew a touch.

"So to be clear, you're saying no?"

"Yes, of course we're saying no," Chavi said.

"Very well." Devrin nodded, then turned to Pierce. "Kill him."

Pierce jerked his arm to the side, drawing his knife across Harvard's neck. Harvard screeched in fear as the Ivies all lunged forward.

"No!" they all cried instinctively. Devrin held up a hand, stopping both the Ivies and Pierce. In the split second that he had begun to carry out his orders, he had only managed to slice a thin line in the side of Harvard's neck, which now dripped blood down the handle of the knife and onto Pierce's fingers. Harvard's eyes were wide with animalistic terror, and his breathing was now so rapid that Chavi could hear him gasping for air. Chavi didn't know as much about anatomy as Avi did, but they'd spent enough time with Avi to know where all the important piping in the neck was. If Pierce moved the knife just a fraction of an inch, the cut he had given Harvard would become a fatal wound. Reluctantly, they turned their attention back to Devrin, who now looked at the Ivies with mock confusion.

"Oh. I'm sorry," he said in a voice laden with false penance. "I thought you said you *weren't* going to take on the job."

"You said we got a choice!" Chavi protested.

"You do have a choice," Devrin nodded. "But if you choose no, your choice has a consequence, and that consequence is"—he cocked his head over to Harvard—"that I kill him."

Chavi gaped, at a loss. "Okay, then, yes! We'll do it! Whatever you want us to say, we'll say it. Just..." Chavi hazarded another glance at Harvard, who was still staring at them with wide, pleading eyes. "Just don't hurt him."

Devrin laughed. "Too late for *that*, I'm afraid. Anyway. Off you go. I can give you the details in my office tomorrow—"

"Aren't you gonna release him?" Chavi asked. Devrin fixed them with a look an adult might give a child who is still having trouble grasping basic mathematics.

"No," he said.

Again, Chavi fought to hold themself back from doing something they knew they'd regret. "You said you'd let him go," they seethed.

"Yes, but I lied. I'm a liar, Chaverim," Devrin said, approaching them. "Surely you've noticed this about me by now."

"We need him," Chavi said. They looked back at Harvard. He was trembling so violently he would collapse if Pierce wasn't holding him upright. "If we're gonna do this job for you, we need the whole team."

He raised his eyebrows. "But then you'll just walk away without following through. You're a liar too, Chaverim," he said with a knowing glint in his eyes. "Just like me. I'm not going to let you walk away without leaving me something of value."

"He's not a thing," Jasmine said.

"True," he said, holding up a finger. "Which means he'd be very hard to replace as your collateral. Not many things in the world as valuable as this little man. Unless, of course, one of you wants to stay behind in his place?" he suggested, sweeping his eyes over the Ivies. "Then again, who could you really afford to lose? Jasmine here is the brains of the organization, that much is clear. August is probably the muscle. And you, Chaverim, the fearless leader."

"Which is why we're not leaving anyone behind," Chavi said.

"Well you have to leave *someone*. How about this? I'm going to count to three, and you, Captain, decide who stays with me. Alright?"

Terror rocketed through their whole body. "No! I can't—"

"One."

They were trembling, just like Harvard. Sweating. "That's impossible—"

"Two."

Oh Founders, I'm going to let him down again, Chavi thought. *There's nothing I can do. I've let him down.*

"Three."

"How about me?" a voice cut in from behind them, echoing against the walls of the empty corridor. Devrin looked past the Ivies to the newcomer approaching from behind.

"Is that the famous Avi Taheri?" he asked.

"The one and only," she said as she brushed past the Ivies. She had always held herself with a proud bearing. She was a large girl, and her presence had always been imposing, but now she looked especially regal, coming to their rescue. Blood-red headscarf commanding attention, her posture demanding respect.

"It's a pleasure," he purred, shaking her hand.

"I'm sure it is," Avi replied sweetly.

Devrin laughed good-naturedly. "I like you *so much!*" he said. "We'll get on swimmingly, I think."

Chavi gave Jasmine a questioning glance. *How did she know we were here?* Jasmine shrugged, but she avoided their eyes. She was the one who'd gone to see Avi about Chavi's injury. She must have told her everything.

"So you'll take me instead?" Avi asked. Devrin tapped his chin, seeming to consider this.

"I'm not entirely sure," he said. "The benefit of using poor Harvard here is that there's no one to notice he's gone except these three. And if push comes to shove and I do unfortunately have to kill him, he'll hardly be missed. No offense, Harvard."

Harvard looked too preoccupied with the knife currently digging into his flesh to be offended by anything.

"Well, what do these three have to say about it?" Devrin gestured to the Ivies. None of them had anything to say, as it turned out. Avi looked to the three of them for approval. Chavi stared at her blankly. It was an impossible choice. They couldn't let her do this. But they also couldn't leave Harvard. They looked to Jasmine for support. She was looking to Avi, who nodded curtly.

That was good enough for Devrin.

Devrin nodded to Pierce, who swiftly slashed at Harvard's bonds and shoved him toward the Ivies. He would have fallen to his knees if Chavi hadn't leapt forward to catch him in their arms. They pulled him to his feet, wrapping their arms around him, pressing his head into their chest, half-lifting, half-dragging him as far away from Pierce and Devrin as they could. Harvard gripped Chavi's shirt with his injured hand, the fabric balled up in his trembling fists.

They wrapped an arm around him, their whole body sagging with relief. *I'll never let this happen again*, they promised silently. *I'll take better care of him. I'll* be *better. I swear.*

"We'll be back in a week," Jasmine said, and Chavi looked up to see Avi give another nod. Avi had complete faith in the Ivies, and Chavi wondered if that faith was founded. What had the Ivies really achieved in the dust except barely escaping death?

"I think a week may be a bit ambitious. I'll give you a month." Devrin nodded to Avi, who shrugged. "One of you will meet me tomorrow at Delian Tower and I'll give you your down payment."

It was a statement, not a command. It would happen, whether the Ivies liked it or not.

"Let's go," Jasmine said. August nodded, and Chavi scooped up Harvard's legs to carry him.

"Hey Ivies," Avi called as they started to depart. Chavi turned and met their friend's eyes. Despite everything, Avi wore a little smile. Chavi didn't know if this reassured them, or scared them more. "Don't fuck up."

Chavi nodded somberly, and followed the other two Ivies out the door.

It was a silent, sullen walk home. They'd saved the person they came for only to lose someone that they hadn't even known was in danger. And Harvard was still in bad shape. They trudged into the little entry hall of the townhouse wordlessly, and Chavi carried Harvard upstairs. They set him down on the bed. He still clung to their shirt with a vice-like grip.

"We're home, babe," Chavi said gently, and Harvard's grip loosened. "I'm gonna go get you some—"

Harvard pulled on Chavi's shirt with his good hand. They shared an unspoken understanding: *Don't leave. I don't want to be alone.*

Chavi sighed, seeing panic had not subsided from Harvard's eyes. Now they could at least care for him, but it didn't detract from the anger they felt boiling underneath.

"Let's get you cleaned up, okay?" they suggested, guiding Harvard to the bathroom. They sat him down atop the toilet and pulled in a chair. Avi, of course, would never have let the Ivies go without basic first aid supplies. Chavi found some gauze and alcohol stored in the cabinet, and set to work cleaning the cut above Harvard's eyes.

"This is going to hurt a bit," they warned, "but you can squeeze my hand if you need to."

Harvard started squeezing their hand even before they touched the gauze to the open cut.

"How did you get this?" Chavi asked, then immediately worried they'd began asking questions too early when they saw Harvard's eyes fill with tears. He remained silent for a long moment, and Chavi didn't press. They'd noticed that when he was particularly upset or frightened, he didn't want to—or wasn't *able* to—talk, so they let him take his time.

Eventually Harvard whispered, "I was stupid."

"What do you mean?"

"I tried to escape," he said, his eyes downcast.

Chavi felt a pang of guilt at the confession. Had he not trusted them? Dusts, he had so little faith in them. But wasn't he right? Chavi had given him precious little to have faith in. Since they returned to Bastion, all Chavi had managed to do was get shot, and then get so wrapped up in their own self-pity that they let Harvard get abducted. Why *would* he believe in them?

"I told you I was coming for you," they said, hoping he wouldn't think they were chiding him. He nodded morosely.

"I know, I know, I just—" he cut himself off, and Chavi could tell he was holding back tears, and suddenly they hated themself for making him cry.

"I just started to get afraid." He cut himself off again, his voice strained. "I started to think that maybe you—you changed your mind— or that you didn't want—"

Chavi shook their head. The weight of his words were crushing. *I haven't been able to prove to him how much I care for him. I've failed.*

Harvard covered his face in his hands, but Chavi gently pulled his hands back down.

"Hey. Look at me," they said quietly. Harvard obeyed, but he was unable to keep a small whimper from escaping his lips. Chavi squeezed his good hand.

"It doesn't matter where you are. It doesn't matter what happens to me. I will *always* come back for you. You know that, right?"

Harvard nodded, but Chavi wondered if he really believed them. Why would he? Chavi had failed to save him twice. If Avi hadn't shown up, what would they have done then? Could they have saved him? If Harvard had any doubts, he didn't show it. Satisfied for the time being, Chavi let go of his hand and brushed a stray strand of hair away from his forehead.

Chavi delicately wiped away blood from the cut on Harvard's neck and taped a pad of gauze over it.

"I'll never let anything like this happen to you again," Chavi whispered. This time Harvard didn't respond. So he *did* doubt them.

As Harvard washed and dressed, Chavi noticed something folded on the bed. A hoodie, near identical to the one they'd lost, folded neatly. A note on top bore Avi's unmistakable print. "Sorry for showing up unannounced," it said, "but hey, I got you this. Hope that makes up for it." They folded the note and placed it reverently on the bedside table before placing the hoodie on the dresser and crawling into bed with Harvard. Chavi thought about running their fingers through his curls, then stopped. The thought of fingers made them want to puke.

"I'm guessing you didn't have a chance to sleep at all?" Chavi asked. Harvard shook his head.

"I didn't either," they sighed. "But we're here now, and we're together, and we're safe. Let's sleep, okay?"

Harvard smiled, allowing his eyes to close, and Chavi could tell he was asleep almost instantly. They were exhausted, too, but they stayed up just a little longer to have the satisfaction of watching Harvard slumber peacefully, finally safe and in their arms.

* * *

Jasmine was surprised to find Chavi awake when she entered an hour later to bring up a plate of food and some tea. It wasn't much, and she didn't have the cooking talents that Chavi had inherited from their mother, but it was food, something she imagined the two of them had gone far too long without.

"Hey," she whispered as she pulled up a chair next to the bed. Chavi sat facing her, propped up on their elbow, the other arm draped over a snoozing Harvard.

"Don't bother," they said. "He's out cold."

"Good," Jasmine said as she placed the plate on the bedside table with a quiet thunk.

"Thank you," Chavi nodded to the food.

"No problem," Jasmine said absently, looking at Harvard. Only now did she have an opportunity to see his broken fingers up close. Chavi had done their best to patch up his other wounds, it seemed, but his fingers were a more permanent injury. Even splinted, they looked so jagged and wrong.

The silence was heavy between them. They both knew what they were thinking, but neither wanted to say it aloud.

"She was never meant to get involved in this," Jasmine said. She blamed herself for inviting her over to begin with—but what else could she have done?

"I know," Chavi looked away, running a hand through Harvard's hair.

Jasmine rubbed her arm. "We were never meant to get involved in it either, but...it just feels wrong."

"I know," they repeated, still refusing to meet her gaze.

"We have to do this."

"I know."

She sighed. "I'll go to Delian Tower tomorrow and—"

"I'm going," Chavi cut her off.

Jasmine's head snapped up. "What? After everything he put you through—"

"This is my fault. I'll deal with it."

She shook her head incredulously. "How is this your fault?"

Chavi pressed their lips together, and for a moment she thought they were going to cry. Strangely, it made her panic. If *Chavi* was going to cry—who had been so stoic in the face of everything out in the dusts— then things must be very, very wrong.

"He had a point," they whispered. "I'm the captain. I'm supposed to make decisions. And when he put me on the spot, and Harvard's life was on the line, I froze. And if Avi didn't show up and save my ass, who knows what would have happened. And now she's the one in trouble and she needs my help."

"That's hardly fair," Jasmine said, reaching for their arm. They flinched. "What were you supposed to do?"

"I don't know. But I know that if I'd managed to get Harvard back when I went to meet Devrin the first time, we wouldn't have even been in that situation, and Avi would be free."

"You're not the reason Devrin is targeting us." *I don't know what that reason* is, she thought, *but I'm determined to figure it out.*

They didn't say anything, just continued to stare absently forward. She gave their arm a gentle tap to get them to face her. Finally they did, and their dark eyes were wet and full of fear.

"Get some rest, Chavi, okay?" she said with what she hoped was a comforting smile.

They didn't look comforted. They simply whispered, "Okay."

* * *

Harvard kept his breathing slow and steady so as not to clue in the others that he was listening. If they thought he was asleep, he'd hear what they said about him when they thought he couldn't hear. He'd never seen Chavi so scared, and it was all his fault. If he'd been stronger or smarter or braver...or something, he could have made it out on his own. It was *humiliating*, the fact that he'd had to be rescued.

He thought he'd moved past this. He thought he'd outgrown the part of his life when he needed to be saved, to be taken care of, to be treated like some frail thing. He thought he was done with being *useless*, as his mother had called him so long ago. He was sick of it, physically sick. He was regressing, and he refused to regress. He had befriended the Empress of the Southwest Plains. He had saved her heir. He had been a hero, once.

There was no going back to being Ronan. He was Harvard, and *Harvard* knew how to take care of himself.

And yet.

Maybe they all would have been better off without him. What would have happened if the Ivies had just left him in the dusts, like August had originally wanted? He would never been a burden on anyone else. He and Chavi wouldn't be together, sure, but wouldn't that have been better for Chavi in the end? If Chavi never cared about him, then he was never in any danger of hurting them.

It was his job to fix this, he decided. He wouldn't let them down. He wouldn't let *himself* down. Not this time. Not ever again.

* * *

That night, Chavi, mercifully, did not dream of being buried alive. In fact, they did not have any nightmares at all, despite the ordeal they had just been through. Their dream felt rather like waking up. They opened their eyes to find themself in a cavern, walls smooth from years of erosion, though they seemed to undulate with movement. There was no source of light, yet somehow they could see clearly, as though the cave was bathed in sunshine. Upon further inspection, Chavi discovered the walls themselves were not moving—they were simply covered with crabs. They were desert walkers of all shapes and sizes, some species Chavi had seen and others that were completely alien to them. Some were massive and others so small Chavi couldn't pick out individual creatures from the colony.

They all walked in the same direction, down the cavern, as though called by some soundless song.

And Chavi could feel that call, too. Something pulled them forward, some kind of force they felt in their chest and in their mind and in their bones. So they took a step forward, and something felt right. They smiled. And as they walked with the crabs, down the infinite cavern, they began to feel like they were going home.

CHAPTER FIVE

Day Job

"Chaverim!" Devrin said when he caught sight of Chavi entering Delian Towers. He clapped a hand on their shoulder. They wanted to push it off, maybe also punch him in the stomach for good measure, but decided this was maybe not the time or place. "You are early! That's unexpected. I suppose you're finally getting your act together, hm? Now come!" Devrin said, as though Chavi had a choice, as he pulled them down the hall into a sort of lounge beyond the front lobby. He stopped at a counter with a coffee machine, a kettle, and a whole spread of foods.

"Won't you have something to eat? You must be hungry."

"I'm not," Chavi lied.

"Are you sure?"

"I'm fine."

"Have a bagel."

"I don't want a bagel."

"You won't take something back for Harvard?"

They rolled their eyes and grabbed a bagel.

"Happy?"

Devrin grinned. "Exceedingly. Now come. We'll talk in my office." He led Chavi to an elevator—an electric one, unlike the creaky thing in the aquarium.

"So...this is your day job?" Chavi asked, gesturing to the building at large as the elevator doors slid shut. "When you're not kidnapping people and breaking their fingers?"

"Same job. Doesn't matter what time of day I do it."

"So, kidnapping people and torturing them in an aquarium—"

"All serves the same objective as everything happening in this building as we speak. One company, one end. You know how it is," he said with a satisfied smile.

Chavi blinked. "I really don't."

"The purpose of the Delian Group is to protect humanity at all costs. I'm the Head Enforcer of the Delian Group. That means everything I do must be in service of protecting humanity at all costs."

"So, again, the whole torturing people in an aquarium thing—"

"Is just a small piece of a much larger picture that I simply couldn't expect you to understand," he finished.

Chavi frowned. "I don't get how hurting innocent people helps make anyone safer."

"That's because—and please, don't take this the wrong way, Chaverim—but that's because you are small-minded."

"Sorry, is there a right way to take that?"

He gave them a dismissive gesture. "Like I said, I simply can't expect you to understand."

The doors slid open, and they entered directly into the office. The front wall was entirely glass. Pierce stood at the window, hands behind his back, pointedly looking away from Chavi. In the back of the room was a desk, and on that desk was a teacup. Devrin moved to take his seat at the desk, and gestured for Chavi to sit across from him.

They didn't, because the only small rebellion they could afford was to not do what he wanted them to.

"How is Avi?" they asked.

"Fine. You can go see her if you want. She's just in there." He cocked his head to a doorway on his left.

"What is this, 'bring your hostage to work day?'" Chavi sneered.

Devrin laughed good-naturedly, like this was a joke between friends and not a joke between sworn enemies. At least, Chavi had sworn they were enemies. Devrin still seemed to be a little unclear about the nature of their relationship. *"Pay attention, Devrin!"* they wanted to say with a snap of their fingers. See how he liked it.

"Actually, it's where she's living," Devrin clarified. "I have guest quarters in my office. You know. I have a lot of guests."

"I'm sure you do." Chavi stood and opened the door. Sure enough, Avi was there, seated at a desk of her own. She was reading out of a thick tome and scribbling notes.

"You're doing *homework*?" they asked incredulously. Avi looked up, grinning.

"Hi, Chavi." She gestured for them to shut the door. They did.

"How have you been?" they asked, hurrying up to her to inspect her for signs of abuse. "Are you hurt at all? Are you—"

"I'm fine," Avi waved her pencil hand. "He's actually been quite generous—"

"He's not generous! He's insane!" Chavi said, punctuating the statement with a wild gesticulation indicating the man on the other side of the door.

"Chavi. Look around. Look at where we are." She fit them with a meaningful gaze, but just because they could tell it was meaningful didn't mean they actually knew what it meant.

"We're in the headquarters of the security corp," she clarified.

"Yeah, I'm aware."

"I'm being very careful about what I say. Maybe you should too."

"I think if anyone here cared what I thought about them, they'd already have me killed." In fact, they already had. It didn't take.

"That's not what I—" she cut herself off, sighing. "I'm fine, okay? Seriously, you don't have to worry about me. They're letting me continue my research while I'm here—at least, as much as I can without a lab—and there's plenty of records I have access to—"

Again, she gave them a look that was definitely supposed to mean something, but Chavi found themself at a loss.

"Okay. Well, uh, as long as you're alright," they said.

"Chaverim!" Devrin called from the other room. "I hate to interrupt a playdate, but I'm on a bit of a tight schedule today, so time is of the essence."

Avi made a shooing motion to let them know it was okay to go. They moved for the door, then threw a last glance over their shoulder.

"Avi?" they said. She had already gone back to her book. She looked up.

"Hm?"

"Thank you. For what you did. For Harvard."

She smiled a soft sort of smile that reminded Chavi of Jasmine.

"Don't mention it."

They re-entered the office, closing the door to Avi's room behind them. Devrin held up a slip of paper—an account code.

"You'll find enough in this account to equip yourselves, with a little leftover. Consider it a down payment." With a smirk he added, "Don't spend it all on drugs."

"I won't!" Chavi said reflexively.

Devrin's smile faltered. "I was joking. Founders, were you really going to spend it all on drugs?"

"No," Chavi answered too quickly. Dusts.

Devrin narrowed his eyes. "Okay," he drew out the word. "It's just, you took that very seriously. Do you do drugs?"

"No!" Maybe. A little. For medical reasons.

"Not hard ones, I hope?" he asked with what shockingly sounded like genuine, almost *parental* concern.

"Just give me the money," Chavi said, thrusting out a hand.

"Ah, desperate as always," Devrin said, shaking his head fondly.

He extended his arm and Chavi snatched away the sheet of paper.

"Your payment upon return should be enough to sustain you for a while. I know you must feel so guilty, being unable to provide for Harvard." Chavi ignored the barb, turning to leave.

"I know you're not great with taking instructions, but do try to color inside the lines this time, yes? For all of our sakes," Chavi heard Devrin say as they closed the door behind them. They hated letting him have the last word, but they knew that if they kept fighting back, they'd never manage to leave. He was just one of those people who needed to treat every conversation like an argument that he had won. Chavi could be like that too, sometimes, and it pained them a little just to roll over and let him drive the dialogue. What else was there to do? He was rich, powerful, and had Avi prisoner—even if she refused to admit that that's what she was.

They stalked off, wishing that for once *they* could feel like they'd won at something.

* * *

Harvard paced the length of the bedroom, rubbing the key with one hand and holding a mug of tea in the other. Logically, he knew Chavi would be fine. Why would Devrin do anything to hurt them now, after they'd already agreed to take the job? Still, he didn't like the idea of them going to Delian Towers on their own. Chavi wouldn't let him come, probably for the same reason.

Jasmine had made him the tea in hopes it would calm him down, but it wasn't helping. He placed the mug on the bedside table, next to the crab.

He flopped down on the bed, sighing and staring up at the ceiling, wondering—

Wait.

"AH!" he screamed, jumping up off the bed and scrambling away, bumping into the wall. Seated placidly on his bedside table was a rotund scuttler—not much larger than the Empress, who could fit in the palm of his hand. The creature watched him innocently like a carcine kitten.

Hi, an unfamiliar voice said in his mind.

"Wh—who are you?" Harvard asked, righting himself. Though he'd learned to ally with the creatures of the desert, the ingrained fear was difficult to root out. He still viewed the desertwalker as a danger, even if it wasn't currently making any move to eat his skin.

My name is Bryk, the creature said, *but I prefer the name that you gave me.*

Harvard cocked his head in confusion.

"Me?" he asked.

During our trek across the desert, Bryk explained, *you called me "Speedy."*

"Speedy..." Harvard mused. "I remember. You were one of Skrack's hatchlings."

Yes.

"You're...bigger now," Harvard observed. He supposed that made sense—it had now been a little over a month since his time out in the dusts. Still, considering how ancient Skrack claimed to be, he'd expected crabs wouldn't grow so fast.

"Did the Empress send you?"

No. The Empress has achieved Serenity.

Harvard nodded slowly, uncomprehending. Did that mean she died?

"Um...I'm sorry for your loss," he ventured.

To achieve Serenity is no loss.

"Oh. Then. Um. Tell her I say congratulations?"

We cannot reach her in the Serenity.

"Oh. Um. Well, I guess you and Skrack must be happy for her."

It is inevitable. We feel indifference.

Speedy certainly didn't sound indifferent, but then again, Harvard found it hard to read the tone of a voice being projected into his mind. He thought he sensed a hint of regret there...or maybe reverence? Or both. Harvard had never been very good at reading people, and he definitely wasn't good at reading crabs.

"Well, um," Harvard thought maybe it would be polite to change the subject, "did Skrack send you? I mean, you're a Guardian-To-Be, right? Are you...you know...guarding?"

No, Speedy admitted, *My father...does not know I am here.*

"Oh. Won't he miss you?"

There are many hatchlings. Many are lost. He knows this.

Harvard nodded, feeling like he should understand, but he was still hopelessly confused. "So what...um, what are you doing here?"

Speedy was silent for a protracted moment.

I like you, Harvard.

"Oh. Well, thank you. I like you too, Speedy." Harvard had no evidence of this—when he'd first met the creature, it wasn't yet mature enough to speak—but he felt it was the polite thing to say.

You are in danger.

"Yeah," Harvard said slowly, shifting his weight with a sudden sense of unease. "How...how did you know that?"

Our tether to you is weakened, but...we can still feel it.

"Your...tether? Do you mean like you can read my mind?" Harvard felt himself blushing, worried that the crab may judge him for any inappropriate thoughts he'd had over the past month. And ever since the start of his relationship with Chavi, he'd been having a lot of inappropriate thoughts.

No, the crab said, and Harvard breathed a sigh of relief. *But when you feel pain, great pain...we can sense it.*

Harvard nodded, remembering the conference when they'd gone to save the heir of the Empress. He'd sensed the creature's pain so acutely that he couldn't separate the creature's agony from his own. Was that how the hatchlings had felt when Pierce broke his fingers? Did Skrack feel it too? Was Skrack...worried about him? Jasmine had said Skrack declared his debt paid, so presumably after saving Chavi's life, the creature had no care for Harvard anymore. Yet...Harvard couldn't help but hope that perhaps the great beast still harbored some affection for him deep within his hard shell.

"You've come to protect me?" Harvard asked.

I cannot do much on my own, Speedy shuffled on his perch as though embarrassed, *I am not yet a full Guardian. It will be many years before I may claim that title. But I thought perhaps...were I to watch over you...you may feel contented to know that one of my kind is still with you—*

Harvard knelt on the bed, lifting the creature in his hands, careful to avoid his injured fingers.

"I am comforted," he said, and the crab made a sort of clicking sound that Harvard interpreted as appreciation.

I understand you will be traveling, Speedy continued. *I would like to accompany you.*

"That should be fine," Harvard shrugged. "I'll ask the other—"

NO! Speedy cried out abruptly. *Please—Do not tell anyone that I am here—*

"O...kay," Harvard eyed the creature in his palms skeptically. "Why?"

I cannot explain. It just...it is best that my presence remain a secret.

"I don't...I mean, I don't really like keeping secrets," Harvard admitted. He was already lying to the Ivies about his parentage. He'd told them the blood disease story and they seemed to believe it. Adding another lie to the list made him squirm. But if that was what Speedy needed...could he say no?

"Sure," Harvard decided, affectionately petting Speedy's carapace. "I would love to have you with me."

Interlude Two: Kathy

Kathy strode into the same conference hall where she'd seen the ghost of her brother. She did what she always did when she was feeling particularly anxious, which was pretend she wasn't. She held her chin up just a little higher, walked just a little bit faster, and kept her fingers laced in front of her in a manner that she personally thought looked very business-like and adult.

"What can I help you with, Ms. Bell?" asked the clerk in the records office. Kathy was easy to recognize. She knew this, and often it played to her advantage. She didn't need to ask "do you *know* who I *am*?" in order to get what she wanted because most people saw the neat ginger braids and freckles and were able to place her immediately.

"I'd like to see the attendance list for this year's Galvin Conference, please."

"Of course."

The clerk fished around in a filing cabinet before retrieving a folder and handing it to Kathy. She scanned the list, but found the only name listed under "Bell" was herself. What was she thinking? Of course he wouldn't have used his real name. It would have drawn too much attention for the missing Bell son to suddenly appear in the middle of Bastion. But if he had used a fake name, what would it be? There were hundreds of other names on the list, and she hardly recognized any of them.

"Is this everyone?" she asked.

"Yes. After the incident we've made certain to verify the identity of every person in attendance."

Kathy's head shot up.

"What incident?"

"You...were there, weren't you, Ms. Bell?"

Her stomach fluttered at the memory. "I had to leave early. I just...I wasn't feeling well." That wasn't a lie entirely. After seeing the ghost of her dead brother, she certainly wasn't feeling like herself. "What happened?"

The clerk flushed. "Well, it's a bit of an embarrassment, to be honest, which is why we've kept the whole business hushed. But given your station, of course, you're welcome to know. A group of scavengers showed up impersonating some university students. They managed to lift a specimen off the Satsuki Group. One of them was killed, and the rest were in Delian Group custody, but...the details were unclear. It seems they got away."

"What university students?" Kathy asked, sensing this was her next clue. "Who did they impersonate?"

"Both students at that science school. One used this name," the man pointed to a name on the list—Simon Foster. "And the other...well, she was impersonating Avi Taheri."

"What?" Kathy suppressed a laugh. Someone was impersonating a Taheri and no one even noticed? "How did no one catch that?"

"The Taheri girl is young, and she's involved in her studies. No one really knew what she looked like."

"Thank you," Kathy nodded, and turned to leave. She smiled to herself, and headed in the direction of the Bastion University of Sciences.

When she located the booth, she found a boy with unkempt blond hair with an array of open books and notepads splayed out in front of him. He scribbled something down hurriedly, running a hand through his hair and muttering to himself.

Kathy watched for a moment. Could this be the boy her brother had impersonated? They had roughly the same wiry build, maybe, but other than that she couldn't see a resemblance. Besides, this boy was obviously a diligent student, something Ronan couldn't have been.

"Simon Foster?" she asked.

The boy's head shot up, and behind his glasses his eyes were wide with surprise. "Yes?" He answered as though his name was only ever spoken when he had done something wrong. *Now that* is *an awful lot like Ronan*, Kathy thought. He had that same hunted look.

"Hi. I'm Katherine Bell," she said, extending a hand. "I'm pleased to meet you."

"Oh!" Simon stood up. "Um, you mean, like—Um, hi! Sorry, I didn't—" He started to clean up his books, but swiftly realized it was a lost cause. "I'm kinda. Hi. Sorry. It's, uh, nice to meet you, Ms. Bell."

He shook her hand tentatively, as though he were afraid that touching her wasn't allowed.

"I was wondering if you could speak to you?" she asked.

He reared back. "Um. Yeah! Yeah, of course. Have a seat," he gestured to the spot across from him in the booth.

While being a Bell had its benefits, it also had its drawbacks. She experienced one of those drawbacks as she lowered herself into a booth across from a boy who refused to meet her eye, nervously tearing apart a piece of scrap paper. At least, she hoped it was scrap paper, and that she hadn't made him so nervous he was subconsciously ripping at his own notes. If she sought out anyone who wasn't from Upper Bastion, they automatically assumed they must be in some kind of trouble. She was about to assure him that she meant no harm, but he spoke first.

"So. Um. Ms. Bell—"

"You can just call me Kathy," she interrupted. He nodded, but looked vaguely uncomfortable.

"Right. Kathy. What can I do for you?"

"I understand that you were one of the researchers who was impersonated at the Galvin Conference."

His hands tensed on the paper he was fiddling with. Evidently this was a difficult topic for him, and, judging by the weary look that passed over his face, one that he'd had to discuss with authorities many, many times. "Right. That."

Kathy felt a little guilty about pressing forward when it seemed she'd already upset him, but if anyone was going to lead her to her brother, then it was going to be this boy. "I was wondering if you could tell me anything about the people who stole your identity, and how it happened."

He shoved the paper aside and put his hands in his lap. "I'm sorry Ms. B—Kathy, but I don't think I'm going to be much help to you. I was supposed to present with Avi Taheri. I'm assuming you know her?"

"By name, yes. We've never met."

"Well, on the last day, Avi told me she was having second thoughts. Something about all the pressure from being from a rich family and having to perform. I wouldn't know." He said this last bit with only a hint of acid, but his eyes flicked briefly to Kathy's face and he backpedaled. "Er, you would, I guess. Anyway, she convinced me to wait until next year. I guess they figured out we were gonna be a no-show and used our spot. I don't know how, or why."

"And you don't know anything about the people who—"

"No," he cut her off. "The Delian Group wouldn't tell me anything when they interrogated me. I'm sorry. Apparently not many people even saw the thieves, and somehow they escaped custody—everyone thinks

Delian Group made some kind of mistake and they're trying to cover it up, but they can do whatever they want, so I guess we'll never know."

Kathy sighed. So this was a dead end after all. "Right. Well, thank you for your help, Simon."

He cringed, looking disappointed he hadn't been able to be more useful. "I can put you in touch with Avi, if you want," he offered.

"No!" Kathy said hurriedly. "Er, um...look, I'm not too connected with the inner workings of the family business yet, but it's my understanding that there's been a bit of a rift between my family and hers as of late."

"Really?" Simon looked genuinely shocked. "But I thought the Taheris and the Bells always had to coordinate on building projects?"

"That's what I thought too," Kathy gave a sad laugh. She didn't like the way her mother kept things from her, but she always figured that once she inherited the family business she would know everything, so all she had to do was be patient. She was excellent at being patient, and her brother's constant impatience had always made her feel very smug about it. She didn't want to make trouble for her mother, so she added, "But still, I'd rather if you not mention this conversation to her."

"Well that's fine. She...hasn't been around."

"In fact," Kathy added hurriedly, "I'd rather you not mention it to anyone. I'm...just doing some personal research, you see."

Simon seemed to perk up at this. He met her eyes for the first time during the whole conversation. "So...you're not going to tell anyone about this?" he asked.

"No," Kathy said. "And I'd like you to do the same."

He sagged with relief. "Right."

She narrowed her eyes, leaning in. Why did *he* care if people knew about their conversation? What did *he* have to hide?

"Simon?" she pressed "Is there something you're not telling me?"

"No," he said too quickly, eyes downcast.

"You know something, don't you?"

"No! I—I really don't, and I wish I did. I just..." He lifted his head, eyes fixed somewhere distant. He looked...disturbed. "Something is happening, and I don't understand it. I just can't help the feeling that it wasn't a coincidence that we were the ones the thieves used. I feel like I'm caught up in some kind of web that I can't see. If Avi knows anything about it, she won't admit it, but...something doesn't sit right with me."

Kathy leaned back, considering this. Maybe she was wasting her time. Maybe she was finally losing her mind after six years of living with the weight of Ronan's death. Maybe this was all just some elaborate fantasy she had woven for herself so that she could convince herself she wasn't to blame. But she felt the same way that Simon did, that she was caught in the middle of something bigger. She just didn't know if it was her imagination.

"I see," she said, folding her napkin delicately. "Thank you for your time, Simon. Really, you've been more help than you know. Let me know if I can do something for you. To thank you."

"You really don't have to do that," he flushed, looking almost panicked.

"You're sure there's nothing I can do for you?" she asked.

"Yeah, yeah I'm sure," he nodded. "I like to do things for myself. Er, no offense."

"None taken." Kathy slid out of the booth, smoothing out her dress as she stood. She started back down the library corridor when his voice stopped her.

"Um, Kathy?"

She turned around. "Yes?"

He was leaning out of the booth, watching her go. "Good luck with whatever you're doing," he said. Strangely, she could tell he meant it. The two of them hardly knew each other, but they were both battling the eerie sense that something in their lives was amiss. That had bonded them, somehow.

"Thanks," she said. "And whatever you feel you're caught up in, I hope you get out of it soon."

His face darkened. "Thanks. Me too."

CHAPTER SIX

Send Off

August knew this whole job thing was bad—like objectively, he knew this was a bad situation. But admittedly, he was sort of excited. Adventuring with the crew again? Just like the good ole days! Actually those days were pretty terrible, but things in the city were getting boring, so he was ready for a change of pace. Sucked about Avi, though. She was cool. August hoped she didn't die. But still! They were going to ride a real-life boat to a real-life island and find a real-life...something. That part still confused August. He didn't actually know what they were looking for on the island (technology? What even *counts* as technology?) but he trusted they would figure it out. Well, Jasmine would probably figure it out.

Pierce drove an *actual* car up to the curb in front of the Ivies' house.

"Have you ridden in a car before?" Pierce asked the Ivies as they piled equipment into the trunk.

"Yeah, I love cars. Big fan of sitting in them and riding them. Maybe driving them, on occasion," said August, who had been in a car exactly twice in his entire life. And those car rides had both been the day of the Galvin Conference, so naturally they both sucked and he hadn't gotten to enjoy them.

Pierce drove them East, toward Upper Bastion. Toward the coast. August looked out the window, watching the houses get bigger and increasingly lavish. He was looking up at the elevated mansions of Upper Bastion when everything got all dark.

"Okay I don't mean to scare anyone but like we are surrounded by darkness. Are you guys seeing this? Or, like, not seeing this?"

"We're in a tunnel, August," Jasmine said.

"A tunnel?" August's eyes widened. "In Bastion?"

"Under Upper Bastion," Pierce explained. "It's how you get to the shore. Upper Bastioners don't want Unionists commuting through their space."

August was nearly bouncing out of his seat. The shore! They were going to the shore! That meant ocean. The Infinite Ocean! Which maybe wasn't actually infinite? Unclear. But he was gonna get to see the ocean!

"Whoa," Chavi breathed when they stepped out of the car. "Guys. Guys, get out here. You have to see this."

August got out of the car next and *holy shit what the fuck?*

"That's so much water!" he exclaimed, running his hands through his hair. It was more water than he had ever seen. "Look at that!" he pointed at the ocean, which seemed to go on forever.

"I see it!" Chavi said. "I'm seeing it too!"

"This is gonna sound weird to say, but I didn't know that anything could be that big. Like, it's like the dusts, but water?" August said, then squealed. "We're seeing the ocean! That's the ocean!" He threw his arms around Chavi and started jumping up and down. For that moment, everything else was forgotten, swept up in the simple joy of seeing the ocean for the first time.

August looked over his shoulder to see how the other two were doing. Jasmine just stared, looking contemplative. Harvard shied away. August couldn't understand the look on his face. Maybe he was scared? He was holding that bag really tight.

They met Devrin at the docks, standing by a bulky person wearing a Fishers' Union uniform. August thought the uniform looked cool. He wanted one.

"This is Sax," Devrin gestured to the Unionist. "Zey are captain of the vessel *Solidarity*. Zey will be escorting you to the island."

Sax grunted by way of greeting. Zey cut an intimidating figure, with zyr muscular sailor's arms and fancy captain's hat. August also would like a captain's hat, he decided. Everyone was pretty gloomy about this whole mission situation, so it was his personal mission to be a little silly in the name of group morale. August congratulated himself for being so very brave.

* * *

Jasmine had to admit her intellectual curiosity piqued, meeting a Unionist in real life. The ocean was the only industry in Bastion not dominated by the corps. It was ruled by the sailors, and the sailors were ruled by no one. The only group of workers in Bastion that was unionized, the sailors had an organization of their own with no leader. Most of the corps thought it was foolishness destined to fail, but after hundreds of years, the sailors were just as independent as ever. Perhaps all that time on the open sea made them hunger for freedom in a way the city could not provide.

As the other three marveled at the ships, the ocean, all of it—under Sax's disapproving glare—Devrin gestured for Jasmine to step aside with him.

"Jasmine? I'd like to have a word with you, if it's alright."

It wasn't alright, but she was hardly in any position to say no. She reluctantly made her way over to him.

"What is it?" she asked.

"Listen, Ms. Reyez, I won't mince words. You're clearly"—he glanced meaningfully to the other three—"the scholar of the bunch, let's say. I have an extra task for you."

Jasmine frowned. Wasn't what they were doing already enough? He seemed to sense her apprehension and laughed.

"Now don't look like that! I actually think you might enjoy this one. As you may have guessed, the island is going to be different from Bastion—different flora and fauna, different geography." He handed her a sleek black notebook and a pen. "I want you to keep records for me. Make a map of the island, if you can, and catalog everything on it. Everything interesting you come across, I want you to write it down. And I leave the definition of 'interesting' up to your discretion. I trust you'll know it when you see it."

Jasmine opened the notebook and drew her fingers along the pages. Thick, cream-colored sheets bound in string and leather. It was the nicest notebook she had ever owned, and she itched to fill it. She hated to agree with Devrin, but he was right. She would enjoy it. To keep records of an expedition? It was the kind of scholarship she always dreamed of.

She was instantly hit with a wave of guilt. Harvard had been abducted and tortured, Avi was a hostage, Chavi was on the brink of a nervous breakdown, and here she was getting *excited*?

Jasmine looked up to thank Devrin, and when she saw his satisfied grin she swallowed her words. What was she thanking him for? She was doing him a favor after all. She nodded curtly, slipped the notebook into her pack, and headed for the docks.

* * *

Chavi set one foot on the boat. Even in calm waters, they could feel it bobbing underneath them. It wasn't right. The ground wasn't supposed to *bob*. A wave dizziness unsteadied them, and they hadn't even managed to get their second foot on yet. They grabbed one of the ropes for support.

"Have you been on a boat before?" Sax demanded.

"I've never even seen the ocean before," Chavi snapped, more ferocious than they intended. The unsteady ground made them…edgy.

"Right. That's what I thought," Sax said, lumbering over to them. "So don't *touch it*."

"The ocean?"

"The *boat*, idiot," Sax said, taking Chavi's hand and forcibly prying it from the rope. Great. Now they had nothing to hold them steady.

"How can I not touch the boat?" they asked. "I have to ride the boat, don't I?"

"I think zey mean with your hands," Jasmine clarified.

"I'm not supposed to touch *anything*?" they asked incredulously. "The whole time I'm on the boat?" Okay, maybe they were deliberately misunderstanding a bit. But hey! They'd just been called an *idiot*, and they were standing on the *quaking ocean*. It was like all their nightmares coalesced into one.

"Zey never said that to me," August gloated, "so I'm gonna touch everything."

Chavi looked back toward the dock, where Harvard still stood at the edge of the metal gangplank, gripping his satchel. They extended a hand to him. He took it gingerly.

"Maybe this will be fun," Harvard said, looking out at the open ocean.

"Yeah," Chavi said. "Maybe."

Sax untied the last rope, and the boat lurched away from the dock. Chavi looked back to the shore, at the two figures watching them go. Pierce looked grave, his arms crossed. Devrin grinned, waggling his finger to bid them a pleasant journey.

Most people live their whole lives in Bastion, Chavi thought as the shore receded. *And this is my second time choosing to leave. What's wrong with me?* It was easier, oddly, to imagine that it was through some fault of their own that they kept finding themself beyond the safety of Bastion's walls, and not that the city itself repeatedly spat them back out.

No, it was easier to think that they were embarking on a hopelessly ambitious adventure, and not to think that the city that had raised them didn't even want them around.

Part Two: Haven

CHAPTER SEVEN

Voyage

Rationally, Jasmine knew they had only been on the boat for three days. However, she had a difficult time convincing herself that it hadn't been an eternity. She thought her time scavenging with the Ivies had accustomed her to bickering. But nothing could have prepared her for the wrath of Captain Saxifrage. Whether zey were yelling at Chavi for touching something they weren't supposed to, or at August for being annoying, or at Harvard for doing a task wrong, zey were always frustrated. And given that zey were a behemoth of a sailor, zyr rage was enough to cow even Chavi.

When zey weren't berating the Ivies, zey were complaining to Jasmine about the other three.

"You were really on a scavenging crew with them?" zey asked. "For how long?"

"Two years," Jasmine said. "And two years before that with another crew."

Sax shook zyr head. "I don't know how you stand it."

"They're not so bad," she said, but her heart wasn't in it, and Sax could tell. "They're doing their best, I promise. Just...try to go easy on them, alright?"

Sax sighed, scratching zyr forehead beneath zyr hat. "I'm not sure I believe *all* of them are doing their best," zey grumbled, "but Harvard at least is."

Jasmine nodded. "He always is."

Harvard wanted desperately to make himself useful, and this tendency, it turned out, was the bane of Sax's existence.

"I, um, did my best to patch the sail like you said," he feebly held up a poorly sewn sheet of white fabric. Jasmine doubted he'd ever sewn anything before, and besides, three of his fingers were splinted, so he was bound to do a clumsy job. Sax took it in zyr hands and sighed.

"Yeah, this'll never hold up," zey said, wrapping it up in zyr arms. "I'll just do it myself. Just like I have to do *everything* myself."

Harvard's face fell. Jasmine knew Sax wasn't trying to be mean, zey just hadn't gotten accustomed to how delicate Harvard could be. Zey also hadn't yet gotten accustomed to how stubborn Chavi could be, and seemed determined to give them the worst jobs possible.

"I'm not going to sit here holding a rope for four hours," they said, crossing their arms.

"You are, actually," Sax said, forcibly unfolding Chavi's arms and wrapping one hand around the rope, "unless you want us to get stranded in the middle of the ocean."

"Can't someone else do it?" Chavi asked.

"Quite literally, no. I'll be steering. August is already doing hull maintenance. Jasmine isn't strong enough. And Harvard—" Sax sighed. "Well, I've decided not to give Harvard any tasks that are too important."

Jasmine groaned inwardly at this, knowing it was the worst possible thing zey could have said to Chavi.

"Harvard can do anything!" Chavi asserted, which was patently untrue. Two years ago, they would have realized this. Now Jasmine wondered if Chavi was so infatuated that they actually believed what they said.

Sax, thankfully, ignored them, and Jasmine found herself relieved that another shouting match wasn't about to break out.

"Sit," zey indicated a crate where Chavi was to hold the rope. "Hold it taut. Don't move. *Don't* let go."

Chavi muttered something Jasmine couldn't hear.

"What was that?" Sax asked, and suddenly Jasmine felt as though she was back in the Academy, watching Chavi get scolded for talking back to a teacher.

"Nothing," they sighed, taking a seat on the crate as instructed, wrapping the rope around their hand for a better grasp.

"You used to be the captain of your scavenging team, didn't you?" Sax cocked zyr head in mock curiosity.

"Mm-hm."

"I can tell. But the thing is, on this boat, I am the captain. You are a passenger. Not even a crew member. Just someone who I am taking from point A to point B, and someone who on occasion has to help out a *little bit* so that we don't all die at sea. You are not a captain anymore. So you're just going to do as you're told. Do you understand, Chavi?"

"Yes," Chavi said, and Jasmine could tell they probably thought this was the greatest indignity of their life.

"Yes *Captain*," Sax corrected, and Jasmine was now certain *this* was the greatest indignity of Chavi's life. They cast Jasmine a pleading look, as though begging her to intervene. She was about to speak when Sax abruptly shifted the topic.

"And don't hold the rope like that"—zey adjusted Chavi's grip—"unless you want to break your hand. Which I'd prefer if you didn't, because I'm going to need your hands later for other things."

Captain Saxifrage stalked off to steer the ship, and Chavi watched zem go with what Jasmine guessed was blossoming disdain.

Jasmine rubbed the spine of her new notebook delicately. A week out here, and she'd had nothing to fill it with. All she could see was open ocean. She'd never encountered a vastness like that before. Even in the dusts, she could look out in the distance and see something. Some rocks or a cave or some plants or, if they were particularly unlucky, a desertwalker. Was there a marine equivalent to desertwalkers? What would they be? Oceanswimmers? The name sounded silly to her.

"Have you ever encountered any creatures out here?" she asked Sax when zey were poring over some maps.

"Fish," Sax answered. Jasmine laughed despite herself, and she thought she saw a whisper of a smile on zyr face—a rare sight.

"You know what I mean," she said, twirling her new pen in her hands. "Anything...dangerous?"

"Fishers don't often go far enough from the coast to encounter anything odd," Sax said, and Jasmine found herself strangely disappointed. "But," zey continued, "that doesn't mean there is more varied marine life this far out. *I* haven't actually encountered anything interesting myself, but..." zey turned to look at Jasmine. "Let's just hope this trip stays pretty boring, okay?"

Jasmine nodded. A boring trip wouldn't be fun, but if something dangerous rose from the depth and gave them trouble, she was sure the trip would be even less fun very fast.

* * *

Harvard stood at the bow of the boat at night, when the rest of the Ivies were asleep in their cramped quarters below deck. Sax steered the ship alone. Jasmine had offered to help, but zey said it was actually easier to have everyone below deck and out of the way "where they couldn't fuck everything up further than they'd already fucked it up today." Harvard had to admit he could understand the logic there. He couldn't help the feeling that despite his best efforts, he made a pretty lousy seaman, and at best he was only a middling passenger.

Satisfied that he was alone, he removed Speedy from his satchel and held the little creature cupped in his hands.

"Are you doing alright?" he asked. Speedy had been near silent for most of the journey thus far, to the point that Harvard often feared he'd been accidentally crushed by a falling crate or loose boating supplies. Every so often he would peek into the bag, afraid to find only crab gore.

To his great relief, Speedy appeared entirely whole.

I am well, came Speedy's laconic answer.

"Do you need...exercise? Food? Anything? I feel bad keeping you trapped in my bag all day." Harvard would much prefer to allow Speedy to roam freely. At least that way the rest of the passengers would be aware of his presence and know not to hurt him. But whenever Harvard had whispered this idea quietly into his satchel the first night aboard, Speedy had swiftly shut it down. Even now, Harvard wrung his hands, wondering if he should just tell the others about their diminutive stowaway.

I require nothing, Speedy said, *though I do appreciate your efforts to allow me a bit of freedom each night.*

Harvard placed Speedy gently on the boat's railing. He wasn't sure what worried him more: the possibility of Speedy tumbling off the railing into the abyss of the ocean, or the idea of Speedy wandering the deck freely and getting crushed. He was larger than when Harvard had first encountered him, but he still seemed so painfully small.

You worry for my wellbeing too much, Speedy said, reading Harvard's concerns on his face.

"I just don't want anything to happen to you. You're very small—"

So are you.

"Not as small as you!" he gestured to Speedy's objectively tiny body.

I have my carapace to protect me. You have nothing but weak flesh.

"I guess," he conceded.

You doubt my abilities of self-preservation. This vexes me the same as it vexes you when others doubt you.

"What do you mean?" Harvard asked, and edge of defensiveness creeping his voice. Harvard wasn't vexed. He was...distinctly unvexed. No vexation here.

I can tell you feel conflicted about the way they treat you. You relish that you are important enough to care for, but resent that they don't seem to think you're able to care for yourself.

Harvard frowned. "Is 'they' the whole crew, or just Chavi?"

What do you think, Harvard?

Harvard looked out at the ocean, stretching out in every direction over the curve of the Earth. Speedy's words grated at him. In a way, the crab was right. At the same time, it didn't feel like he had any right to say those things.

"Do you not like Chavi?" Harvard finally asked.

Speedy waited a fraction of a second too long to answer.

I didn't say that, was his reply.

"Why don't you like Chavi?" Harvard asked, and he couldn't help feeling hurt at the idea.

My thoughts on your relationship are of no concern to you.

"Well actually they do kind of concern me. If you—"

"Harvard?" came Sax's voice from behind him. Harvard gasped quietly and shoved Speedy back into his satchel. He whirled around to see Sax approaching, holding up a lantern.

"What are you—" zyr face changed when zey saw Harvard was alone. "Oh," zey said. "I thought I heard you talking to someone."

"Talking to myself," Harvard laced his hands behind his back innocently.

"Well, you shouldn't be up here alone, especially at night. If you fell overboard and none of us knew, we'd just leave you behind and you'd drown." Zey said this with the same casualness that one might warn the fruit will go bad if you leave it out for too long. In fact, Harvard wondered if Sax found the possibility of him drowning a welcome one. Not that Harvard worried Sax bore him any malice, but that would be one fewer annoyance that zey had to deal with.

"Right, sorry," Harvard said, glancing out at the ocean that, this time, had failed to drown him. "I'll be more careful."

Sax nodded approvingly. "See that you do."

* * *

August would have loved sailing if the boat hadn't been piloted by Captain Buzzkill.

"It would be cool if you made the floor of the boat glass," he said as he scrubbed the deck. "So we could see fish and stuff?"

"It would not be 'cool.' It would be a leakage hazard. And do you know what the ocean looks like, August?"

"Um, no. That's why I want a boat window."

"It looks dark. Very dark. Your 'boat window' would see nothing but a deep dark abyss."

"Stop talking about that please," Chavi said abruptly, whom August hadn't even realized was listening.

August thought he made a pretty great sailor. He'd never considered trying to join the Fishers' Union as a kid—besides, it was a job mostly passed down through families, just like the corps—but maybe he should have considered it. This was way better than life out in the dusts. For one thing, he wasn't always worried about monsters eating him, which was pretty awesome, in his opinion. Second of all, he hardly had to do any work at all! Sax would ask him to do some chores, like, sometimes, but they were usually really easy. Fix this thing. Tape this up. Hold this rope. August, it turned out, was great at holding ropes. He could hold ropes all day. He was a bit of an expert, actually.

"Do fishers do any fishing songs?" August asked Sax while the two of them scraped organic buildup from the hull of the ship. Since there was always some kind of chore to do on the boat, they couldn't very well play games to pass the time. August figured songs were the next best thing.

"Yes," Sax said.

"So..." August prompted, "will you teach us?"

"No," Sax said.

August's heart shrank. "But like...we're all boating together."

"Fishing hymns are for the Fishers' Union only. They are not meant for you."

"Fine. I'll come up with my own boat song," August decided. So he did. His boat song went like this:

We are riding on a boat
We never sink and we always float
Lots of water all around
Makes a kind of whooshing sound

August thought this song was pretty good. He taught it to Harvard, who seemed weirdly touched that he had been asked to join in the song. They sang it together as they moved the crates Sax told them to move until zey commanded them to stop because it was too annoying.

"If it will make you stop singing that ear-bleeding tune," zey said through zyr teeth, "then I will teach you a fishers' hymn. *Just* one."

So much to August's delight, that night all the Ivies gathered in a circle on deck around Sax to hear zyr song. It wasn't what August expected, though. It wasn't a happy working song. It had a kind of sorrowful sound to it. The words went like this:

Sweat and seawater
Both are salt
To live is to toil
It's not our fault
Come the waves
And come the rain
I pray to no god
That I'll reach home again
August didn't understand those lyrics at all.

* * *

"We should be getting close to the island," Sax announced on the sixth morning of their journey, which Chavi was immeasurably thankful for. The past six days had been virtual agony. Sax's overbearing presence, the horror of existing on the open ocean, and the slow return of the smoldering pain that choked their veins all conspired to make Chavi's life miserable. They had hoped, at least, that maybe the voyage would be a distraction from the encroaching threat of Crab Disease, as they had dubbed it. An unpleasant distraction, but if they were focused on being terrified of the ocean then maybe they would be less terrified of dying (maybe?) slowly and painfully from the sickness that was burning them from the inside out. Instead they were just doubly terrified, which made it even more difficult to hide. And they *would* hide it, there was no question about that.

"Hey Sax," August said as he was tying the sail into position—a task that Sax had reluctantly bestowed on him when everyone else was otherwise occupied. "What's the deal with, uh, creatures in the water?"

Chavi looked up from where they were tying the rigging Sax instructed. They were actually getting pretty good at it. They heard a distinct note of concern in August's voice, one they hadn't heard since the dusts.

Sax gave an exasperated sigh from where they stood at the front wheel. "What do you mean 'creatures,' August?"

"Well, ya know, like desertwalkers, but in the sea?" August tied off the knot he was working on and pressed himself against the boat railing, looking out at something in the distance.

"Do you mean fish, August?" Sax asked. "Yes, there are fish in the ocean."

"Are they usually that big?" August pointed. Chavi put aside their work and moved to join August at the railing. Something was stirring up the waters not far from them. If it was a fish, then August was right—it was a big one. It must have been about two meters wide, the size of a large megacrab, but Chavi couldn't make out any of its features. Beneath the surface of the water, it was just a shimmering pale blob.

Sax appeared beside them, and Chavi hoped they'd dismiss August's concern, probably with a rude comment, then go right back to work.

The dismissal, and the following rude comment, were not forthcoming.

"Huh," was all Sax said, and coming from Mx. "I know everything about the ocean," this was deeply concerning.

"Do you know what that is?" August asked.

"No," Sax admitted, moving back to the wheel with a touch of urgency, "but there's no harm in getting away from it."

"Will that take us off course?" Chavi asked.

"Will moving off course take us off course?" Sax asked over zyr shoulder. "Yeah, a little!" Zey shook zyr head and muttered, "Collective, save me..."

"Should we be worried?" Chavi pressed.

"You could be. Or you could not be. Either that thing attacks us or it doesn't. Doesn't matter whether you worry about it or not."

Jasmine climbed out of the lower deck hatch with Harvard trailing behind.

"What's going on?" she asked.

August pointed out into the waters. "There's a creature," he said.

"A creature?" Harvard repeated, gripping his satchel closer to him.

Jasmine looked where August was pointing, frowning. "Sax?" she called. "Do you have some kind of..." she searched for the word, "scope? For distances?"

Wordlessly, Sax tossed her a metal tube. Jasmine caught it deftly and extended it to reveal long metal...eye? Thingy? Jasmine closed one eye and held the cylinder up to the other.

"Why didn't we get to use the eye thingy?" August complained.

"It's hard to see underwater," Jasmine said, "but it looks it has some kind of...tentacles? Like the crabsquid. Are there squid in this water?"

"Squid don't come near the surface," Sax called from zyr post. "They're deep-sea creatures."

"What's a squid?" August asked. "Is that like a crabsquid without the crab?"

Harvard stood beside Chavi at the railing, already beginning to tremble. Chavi gave his hand a reassuring squeeze, but they weren't feeling particularly reassuring. It wasn't as though they'd loved running into desertwalkers back in the dusts, but at least they had a sense of the kinds of creatures they would find. And they had vapor which—most of the time—was a guaranteed defense. Now they had no idea how to kill this thing if it became a danger; they didn't even know what "this thing" was. Chavi decided that they hated fish, and they hated the ocean.

"It looks like—" Jasmine cut off, gasping. Chavi didn't need the aid of the scope to see what she was seeing. The creature's tendrils broke the surface, reaching out for the boat, and they could see the arms were pink and ruffly, like gelatinous lace. The lacy appendages were connected to the central disc floating just beneath the surface of the water.

Sax came rushing over to the railing to join them. For the first time since Chavi had known zem, Sax's eyes widened in surprise—and perhaps fear. The fact that Sax was afraid made Chavi think the rest of them should be terrified.

"Sax, do you know what that is?" Harvard asked.

"Well, I would call it a jellyfish," zey said, "except it's quaking *huge*."

Interlude Three: Avi

Avi Taheri had made a promise to herself. She had made it so long ago she didn't quite remember doing it, but she knew that at some point in her early years she had seen her cousins and relatives and distant relations all busying themselves with complete nonsense, and she decided she would never allow that to be her. She would never allow herself to sit around doing nothing.

That was why young Avi threw herself into her studies, and that was why adult Avi decided she would turn her hostage situation into a productive experience. With a bit of careful research—and research was, after all, Avi's greatest skill—she was determined she could figure out what exactly was going on. She wished she could have explained this to Chavi, but saying, "don't worry, I'm gonna do some spying," in front of the people you were trying to spy on seemed like a pretty terrible idea.

And if she came up with nothing, at the very least she could use her time for schoolwork, which she was pretending to do regardless.

"Good morning, Ms. Taheri!" Devrin greeted her as he peeked into her workspace, which felt silly to her, like she was just a house guest.

"You can just call me Avi," she said, looking up from her work.

He looked over his glasses at her. "Feels a little wrong to call a daughter of one of the big six by her first name."

"I call you by your first name," she pointed out.

"No, you call me by *a* name. It's not a first name nor a last name. It's not even mine."

Avi reared back, narrowing her eyes. *What does that even mean?*

Pierce stayed with Avi in her little side-office each day, ostensibly to keep watch of her, though he didn't seem to be putting much effort into it. She had made it clear that she had no intention of running away, so in return he had made it clear he had no intention of bothering her.

Avi couldn't figure the man out. He seemed so tranquil, so reserved, sitting in the corner and reading idly. Could this really be the man who looked Chavi in the eyes while he broke Harvard's fingers? What was he doing here?

She surreptitiously peeked at the book he was reading. She was surprised to see it was a history book about pre-Quake religion. She chided herself for judging him. Just because he was a brutish man who seemed to be hired muscle by trade didn't mean he wasn't also an intellectual. Perhaps he knew more than she gave him credit for.

"What is this all about?" she asked. He looked up.

"Hm?"

"Surely you can tell me something," she reasoned, gesturing with her pen. "I'm harmless, right? And I'm a captive. So can you give me a sense of what all this is for?"

Pierce shook his head.

"Even if I knew, I couldn't tell you. But the truth is, I don't. Devrin is a very paranoid man. I know he's got everything all planned out, that everything he does is part of a larger scheme, but he's afraid that if it ever gets out of his own head, someone will come along and ruin it."

Avi twisted the pen in her hands. There were a lot of adjectives she might have used to describe the man in the office next door, but "afraid" was not one that would have come to mind.

"But surely you know more than me," she pressed. "There isn't anything you could tell me?"

"The way I see it," he sighed, putting aside his book, "we're just doing our best to keep our city safe. The way he sees it"—he nodded toward the wall that separated Avi's room from Devrin's office—"he'd say he's fighting a war."

"A war?" Avi laughed. Now that had to be a joke. "War" was a pre-Quake concept that had died with the rest of humanity during the Great Quakes. "There are no more wars. There are not enough people." This was fairly basic Bastion history. Everyone knew war did not exist. Had he not been to school?

"There are still wars," Pierce insisted. "They're simply fought behind closed doors."

"Well, then they're not really wars," Avi said, "because no one's getting killed."

"People are getting killed," Pierce said with an air of finality. He raised his eyebrows as if to say, *"You're smart. Can't you figure it out yourself?"*

Avi thought of her friends. She didn't know what going off to explore some island had to do with Bastion politics, but surely it must be related somehow to this "war" Pierce was so determined was real. Would her friends die as pawns of a war they didn't even know they were a part of? Would she?

Avi also made a few attempts at eavesdropping, but none were very fruitful. It wasn't that she couldn't overhear Devrin's conversations with Pierce—in fact, she could hear just about everything. They made no effort to hide anything from her. It was just that as Pierce had mentioned, he never actually told Pierce anything that seemed like it was much of a secret. Did he really just keep it all in his head? That seemed like poor planning—what if he was killed? Then again, would anyone be able to kill the Head Enforcer? Maybe he just took it for granted that no one would be foolish enough to try.

Avi did catch one thing that she knew must be important, but she couldn't figure out how. Devrin kept mentioning something called the Underground City. Things like, "Oh, the Underground City is going to love this!" or "How do you think this will play out with the Underground City?"

Only once did she ask Pierce what the Underground City was, but he only shrugged and said, "It's the city but it's underground." Avi rolled her eyes and made a mental note to explore Bastion's architectural records once she had access to the University library.

The thought of records, though, gave her a different idea. She could access public records from here, couldn't she? Corporation transactions were public information since, in theory, the corporations worked for the people and worked together in perfect harmony, so, in theory, they wouldn't have anything to hide. For that reason, of course, no one ever bothered checking them. She was able to access them via a reconstructed computer monitor, built with a chip scavenged from the dusts. She always thought it was a little ironic that those who had access to luxuries like computers were always those who looked down upon scavengers, even though scavengers were the ones responsible for just about all the technology they used.

Avi scanned the data, trying to glean some kind of information from it. A lot of business with the Bells, but she supposed that was to be expected. The Delian Group had prisons, and they needed someone to build them. And of course, the Satsukis supplied firearms—until, suddenly, they didn't. Avi furrowed her brow and scrolled through the file to ensure she hadn't misread. No, that was definitely correct. Transactions with the Satsuki group had definitely dwindled over the past few years. Which made no sense, because didn't a security force need weapons? If they weren't getting any new shipments, how would they replenish their arms stores?

In fact, now that she was really looking, she saw that the past few years had seen a significant uptick in transactions with Bell Enterprises? And though there was no additional information in the records except the note "services rendered," she could see that each one of these new purchases was signed off by Saoirse Bell herself. So the Delian Group was building something. But what? Wouldn't she know about any important construction projects in Bastion? Her family, after all, were the ones to sign off all land use. Then again, there was no indication of an interaction with her family over the past few years.

Avi tried to reconcile the information with her understanding of the way Bastion worked. The corps were supposed to work together. That was the idea that the city was founded on. But if these records were any indication, alliances were forming. And in order to be allied, one needed something to be allied *against*. Devrin was competing with someone. Who? Why?

She wondered how this fit with the "Underground City." She searched the term in the database and found no results. Well, she'd keep listening for anything useful. In the meantime, she had another research project she needed to work on—a personal one.

"If I'm going to be working on my research..." Avi reasoned to Devrin the following day. "I could use some of the books I left back at the university. Would you mind if I went back to pick up some things?"

Devrin raised an eyebrow.

"While I appreciate your commitment to your work, Ms. Taheri," he said as he idly spun a pen in his hand, "you do realize you are still technically a hostage?"

"Of course I do. But you've been such an accommodating captor. Besides, what harm could it do? Pierce could accompany me, I'd grab a few things from my dorm, and I'd be on my way."

Devrin considered her proposal, then shrugged.

"I suppose it couldn't hurt. Pierce!"

The hulking assistant appeared near-instantaneously at the enforcer's side.

"Would you kindly escort Ms. Taheri to her dorm room? She has some reading materials to pick up."

Avi smiled to herself, feeling like this was the first victory she'd achieved in her time as a captive. She put a hand in her pocket to ensure her find was still there, the card she'd found on Chavi's dresser when she was dropping off the sweatshirt. Something had been *off* about Chavi ever since their return to the city, something she was certain they were trying to cover up. The card bore only a name and address, but that at least gave her a place to start. Perhaps she couldn't unravel the city's secret, but she had another mystery to investigate. She couldn't do it on her own, but she could at least drop the card off with someone who could.

CHAPTER EIGHT

The Depths

Chavi watched the gelatinous floating disk with growing apprehension. They knew from their time as a scavenger that most beasts were harmless so long as you didn't draw their attention. But this wasn't a desertwalker. This was a creature from the depths. The desert was at least something they could see and understand. But the ocean was deeper than they could fathom, and home to beasts that dwelled so far below the surface that no light ever reached them, lurking in darkness forever.

Even though they knew it was a stupid thought, they felt as though the ocean had belched up this creature specifically to punish them. Jasmine once taught them a pre-Quake word for that.

"How do you usually deal with a jellyfish?" Jasmine asked.

"Well usually they're not that big!" Sax said, already bustling back toward the wheel. Zey gave it a firm spin, and then threw open the hatch and ran below deck. Zey emerged with—

"Is that a harpoon gun?" August asked. "Sick! Can I try—"

"No," Jasmine and Sax said in unison.

"Where have you been keeping that?" Chavi asked.

"Far away from the rest of you, that's where."

Chavi felt a little prickle of indignation. A *good* captain wouldn't hide things from the rest of the crew.

"You should have told us," they said. "What if we got attacked and you weren't around and—"

"Well, we are being attacked, and lucky for you, I am around, so it's fine," Sax said as they leveled the weapon at the encroaching beast.

"We're not being attacked," Jasmine laid a hand on Sax's shoulder. "We're only being...approached."

"This is my ship, and I'm not taking any chances," Sax squeezed an eye shut.

"Don't hurt it!" Harvard cried, launching himself at Sax. Zey gave a grunt of surprise as he threw zem off balance.

"Get away!" Sax shouted, shoving Harvard back. He stumbled and fell onto the ship deck. "You wanna make me misfire? Are you trying to get someone killed?"

Chavi ran over to help Harvard up. They opened their mouth to chastise Sax, but Harvard beat them to it.

"It's not hurting anyone!" he said. "You can't hurt it unless—"

The boat jolted, suddenly inclined toward the stern, and all five passengers struggled to keep their footing.

Wrapped around the back end of the boat was one of those frilly tendrils, along with some other, smooth tentacles that looked to Chavi like thick, wet pasta. It dropped a sharp beak onto the deck, the edges jagged like sharp teeth. The beak opened to give shrill whine.

"This is not a normal jellyfish," Sax said, which meant nothing to Chavi, who had never even heard of a jellyfish until like a few minutes ago.

Still, they spat, "We got that, thanks."

August unsheathed his hunting knife and moved to cut the boat free, but Sax grabbed his arm and held him back.

"Don't touch that thing!" Zey cried.

"What, it's gonna kill me to touch it?" August asked, waggling his knife way too casually.

"Yes!" Sax said, wearing a facial expression that clearly read as *"wow I knew you were stupid but I didn't actually think you were this stupid."* August stared at Sax. "The tentacles have venomous barbs. Even a tiny one could kill you. One this size? Who knows what it could—"

The creature yanked on the stern with its frilly tendril, and the boat bucked in the water. Jasmine yelped as she lost her footing. She slammed against the deck before sliding down the water-slick surface toward the monster.

"Jas!" Chavi cried, instinctively lunging for her. She reached out to them, and they clasped hands for only a brief moment before her wet skin slid out of their grasp. She gave a terrified shriek as she slid further toward the monster's gnashing beak.

With a ping, Sax released a harpoon.

It zipped so close to Jasmine's head that it might have grazed her had she not managed to roll out of the way in time. It struck the floating disk with a wet thud. Chavi expected some kind of roar, but the creature only gave a small, high-pitched squeal. It released the stern and retreated into the depths, and the boat righted itself, bobbing in the water.

Jasmine took as shaky breath as she righted herself, still staring at the water where the jellyfish had disappeared.

Sax whirled on Harvard, gripping his shirt.

"Next time," zey said, "don't get in my way."

"I'm s—"

The wood beneath them groaned.

"Hey, so, not great news," August said from the railing, where he was using the scope to look directly below him. "The thing didn't actually leave, it's just, under us now? And—"

With a wet slap, a tendril wrapped itself around the bow railing. Another lacy tentacle returned to the stern, and the two pulled, making the boards of the ship groan.

"Great, now you've pissed it off," Chavi said, shoving Sax's shoulder.

"What, should I have let it kill Jasmine?" Sax retorted, reloading zyr weapon.

"I was helping her!"

"You were useless!"

The boat jolted beneath their feet, and Sax swore. Leaning over the railing, zey fired off another harpoon. It hit the water with a wet smack, and Chavi thought maybe the heard the creature's muffled wail from below the ship, but maybe that was wishful thinking and actually that sound was just the ship's death rattle before it succumbed to the pull of slimy tentacles.

"It won't go away!" Sax said, marching over to the opposite side of the boat and peering over the edge. "Why is this thing so quaking persistent?"

"Because you made it mad!" August said, running his hands through his hair.

"Jellyfish don't get mad," Sax said, lining up another harpoon shot. "Then again, they don't usually have beaks. Or scream. Or grow to be that big. So who knows."

Before zey could fire, the boat leapt so violently that they all crashed into the deck, drenched in a spray of seawater.

Jasmine scrambled for the bow. "The island is not that far!" she said, pointing to any island that looked pretty fucking far. "We could make it on our own from here. If the jellyfish wants to boat, it can have it. *We* can swim to safety."

Chavi's whole body went cold. *No no no no no.*

"Um, no it cannot have it!" Sax protested.

"Wait, you want us to jump in the water? With the poisonfish?" August asked.

"Jellyfish." Sax corrected.

"Not calling it that. It's a stupid name," August said without turning to face zem.

"But poisonfish isn't?"

"We're at more risk if we stay. It's about fluid dynamics," Jasmine explained. "If this thing pulls us under, when the boat sinks, the air that's displaced creates a vortex and—"

Chavi grabbed her shoulders and shook her. "Jas, normal words!" they begged.

"If the ship sinks, we'll get pulled down with it. So we have to get far away before that happens."

"But the island is—" Harvard started to protest.

"Not that far," August cut in, who was now using the scope to look ahead. "I can see it! We can swim the last bit."

"No!" Sax shouted. "I'm not abandoning the *Solidarity*."

"It's that or drown," Jasmine said.

"What about the—the thing?" Harvard asked, pointing down. "Won't we be easy to kill once we're off the boat?"

"The thing's probably not that smart," August said. "I don't see much room for a brain. It probably doesn't even know we're on this thing."

Jasmine nodded. "And that means it probably won't notice if we leave."

"That's a few thousand meters away!" Sax protested, gesturing toward the island.

"We can swim a few thousand meters," August asserted.

"I can't," Chavi said. Everyone whirled around to face them, and they found themself feeling *embarrassment* of all things—not mortal terror, which was definitely what they should be feeling.

"What?" August asked.

"I can't swim."

August's hands flew to his head. "Don't you think you should have told us that before we all got on a boat?"

"I didn't think I'd have to swim! Isn't that kind of the point of a boat? Not to swim?"

"Swimming is easy. It's like this." August mimed something that was presumably swimming.

"Yeah great thanks that helps a lot," Chavi said drily.

The wood beneath them creaked and splintered.

"We have to go now," Jasmine commanded. "Chavi, it'll come naturally to you. I promise. Especially when—"

The boat jerked, and the wood beneath them gave another warning groan.

"Everybody go!" Jasmine shouted, shoving August toward the railing. August looked down at the jellyfish, then nodded resolutely. He hoisted himself up onto the railing, sucked in a breath, and leapt in the direction of the island.

Sax shook zyr head. "I'm not leaving my boat," zey asserted, but Chavi could tell zyr determination was fading fast. "This boat is my *life*. This is all I have. I can't just leave it."

"Then you can die on it," Jasmine spat. "*We* are leaving."

Sax murmured some kind of prayer to the Collective, kissed zyr fingers and laid them to the deck, then followed suit.

Harvard wrapped his arms around Chavi.

"I'm not leaving Chavi!" he cried.

"No, you're not," Jasmine said, "because Chavi is coming too. We're all coming. Okay?" Jasmine looked pleadingly at Chavi.

"Jas—"

Boards began to spring up from below the paint as the two halves of the boat were wrenched apart.

"We're going," she said, wrapping her arms around Harvard's waist and prying him off Chavi.

"Wait!" Harvard cried, but Jasmine was already towing both of them over the railing. Chavi willed themself to follow, but when they heard Harvard and Jasmine hit the water with a sickening splash, they were hit with a wave of nausea so powerful their knees buckled. Gripping the railing, they pulled themself to their feet and looked out toward the island. August was already shrinking in the distance. He'd been right— the creature didn't seem to notice the fleeing humans.

Chavi peered over the railing. And staring down the churning depths, they heard their own voice. They were back in detention, locked in the dark basement, fists pounding at the door, crying, "Let me out!" And they were back in the dusts with a tentacle wrapped around their leg pulling them underwater. And they were in the wooden casket with sand pouring down, sunlight blocked off, scraping at the panels until their fingers bled. And they knew that no force on Earth could make them jump into that water.

Behind them, boards snapped as the boat slowly began to split in two.

I'm gonna fucking die, they thought, and turned the other way.

CHAPTER NINE

Landfall

"Chavi!" Harvard cried, the billows lifting him then pulling him below the surface. Jasmine grabbed his arm and pulled him toward shore.

"They're right behind us," she assured him. The waves were too choppy for him to get a good view of the boat—every time he managed to get his eyes on it, he found himself dunked underwater. All he could do was believe Jasmine as she guided him toward the beach.

He wasn't sure how long they'd been swimming for—it might have been ten minutes, or it might have been an hour. He was only aware of the burning of his lungs, and the ache of his splinted fingers every time they pushed up against the water. He kept trying to look back to see if Chavi was with them, but between the waves and Jasmine's pull, he couldn't see anything but the saltwater splashing up to spray him. He hadn't even realized he was nearing land when the surf deposited him on the rock, the tide gently nudging him further ashore. The moment he felt solid ground beneath his palms, his body gave out.

He jerked awake to the sensation of water lapping against his face, unsure how long he'd been unconscious. Beside him were August, Jasmine, and Sax, all in various states of exhaustion. No Chavi.

He bolted upright, his aching body belatedly protesting the sudden movement. He didn't care if he barely had the strength to walk. He would throw himself back into the ocean to find Chavi if he had to. Once he managed to get his wobbling legs under him, he began wading back into the ocean. He held a hand over his eyes to shield against the sun, and when he squinted, he could just make out a figure appear on the horizon, kneeling on a broken scrap of wood, paddling awkwardly toward beach.

Harvard laughed, falling to his knees with a splash, and then his laughter became tears, and he buried his face in the heels of his hands.

Beside him, Sax and Jasmine helped each other stand. August lay on his back, staring blankly at the sky, chest heaving. Harvard watched Chavi's less-than-ceremonious approach, until they leapt off their makeshift-boat and waded the rest of the distance.

"That looked so stupid," August breathed.

"Well, I'm not dead," Chavi said, taking Harvard's hand. They both dropped back down to the rock, heavy with relief and fatigue. Harvard threw one arm across them, and satisfied that they were all alive, he allowed himself to slip into unconsciousness.

* * *

Harvard had never seen land like this—land that went *up*. Aside from the occasional ruins or crevice, the dusts were relatively flat in comparison. The mountains looked as though someone had pinched the Earth and pulled it up to a point. Not that he could see the point—all he could see was the canopy of darkness created by the sprawling plants. And what strange plants! The trees had no leaves, only *needles*, like a giant cactus. And the rocks gave way to soil, where other types of plants were abundant, even flowers. Except for the occasional desert bloom in the dusts, Harvard had never seen flowers growing on their own without having been planted intentionally. Here, the ground beneath the trees was dotted with them, these peculiar specks of white and purple.

"If we're looking for the center of the island," Jasmine addressed the crew as the sun peeked over the horizon, "it's going to be just beyond there."

"We have to climb the mountains?" August groaned.

"Mountain, singular," Jasmine corrected. "We only have to climb one, and from there we should have a high enough vantage point to determine the center of the island."

"I didn't even know mountains were real," August whined. "I thought they were just made up for stories."

"You're about to find out just how real mountains can be," Sax said, as though zey were already a seasoned mountain expert.

Sax had been right, though. Mountains were very real, and Harvard's aching legs attested to that. Harvard never had to fight against gravity itself, and certainly not such uneven terrain. The spongy ground was littered with branches and leaves and other debris, as though the trees had lazily dropped their trash and neglected to pick it up.

"Do you think the animals will be different?" Harvard asked Jasmine. "Will there be—" he cut himself off. What would you call a desertwalker that wasn't in the desert? Mountain...walker?

"Almost certainly," Jasmine warned.

So far, though, they hadn't encountered much of anything except the bugs that kept buzzing around them in a sort of cloud, and those seemed more or less the same as the bugs in Bastion. The air smelled different, though. It smelled…wet and smokey.

The first actual obstacle they encountered was a stretch of water flowing down the mountain, cutting through their path. Aside from the ocean, Harvard wasn't sure he'd ever seen this much water at one time. The stream looked wider and deeper than any of the water deposits they'd seen in the dusts, and it *moved*, swiftly and forcefully, which was completely alien to Harvard.

"Whoa, who left all this water lying around?" August asked.

In the dusts, it would have been a treat to encounter natural water—especially running water. Here, it was an annoyance. More than that—a danger.

"We can wade across, I think," Jasmine said, eyeing Chavi warily. "It looks like it gets pretty deep, but not so deep that we won't be able to keep our heads above water."

"Yeah, that's fine," they said abruptly in a manner that made Harvard think maybe it wasn't fine.

Sax surveyed the torrent.

"Current's pretty strong," zey said. "We should minimize weight on our bodies. It'll make it hard to get across."

"What, are you some kind of water expert?" August asked with his hands on his hips.

Sax eyed him. "Quite literally, yes. Now everyone strip so you can carry your clothes and belongings on your head."

Without any further protest, everyone but Harvard complied. Harvard squirmed. Did he have to do that, too? He remembered when Skrack had watched him bathe. But that was different. Harvard was fairly certain that no one in his entire childhood had ever seen him naked after the day he was born. In his adult life, it was only Chavi. But…that was also different. That was private. Now Jasmine was here, and August, and Sax…even Speedy, technically.

Speedy! Harvard hadn't checked on him since the whole crisis with the boat. He tore open his satchel, afraid of what he'd find.

The crab was toying with Harvard's switchblade.

How does this work? he asked. His claw closed around the spring button and the blade snapped out. *Aha!* he cried, *I have done it! I wield a blade!*

Wordless, Harvard closed the flap of the satchel. Clearly Speedy was fine.

"Um, Harvard?" Chavi prodded gently. Everyone else was already descending into the water, clothes bundled and safely stowed atop their heads.

"Right. Yes." Harvard dropped his satchel into Chavi's waiting hands so he could strip. To his great relief, no one even looked at him. Most of them were already making their way across the water.

He placed a tentative foot in the stream, the frigid water sending a shiver up his spine. The rocks beneath the stream were slick, and Harvard wobbled as he waded deeper, his arms flailing in an attempt to balance. By the time he made it to the center of the stream, he had to walk on his toes, his chin pointed upward, just to keep his face above water.

Jasmine held up a hand, and the party ground to a halt.

"No one move," she hissed. Harvard froze, fighting against the current to stay upright. He scanned the edge of the river for danger. A few meters downstream from them was a furry beast, lapping up water with a long, pink tongue. It looked a bit like a dog with long, slender legs and a craning neck. Well, two. And two heads. The head to the left had a branching structure protruding from its skull, like a sprouting tree trunk. That head stayed upright, looking out into the woods as if scouting for potential danger, while the other drank from the river.

"What the fuck," August murmured. Harvard was thinking more or less the same.

The drinking head whipped up to face them. Its eyes were wide and completely black, like a desertwalker's. The creature's muscles tensed as the other head swung down to face the five naked humans standing in the river. Harvard heard Jasmine draw in a quick breath.

"Do you think it's going to attack?" Chavi asked.

"I don't think it's a predator," Jasmine whispered. "If you look at the skull structure—"

"No science please," August begged.

"The point is, I think it's safe. I think...I think it's afraid of us."

As though proving Jasmine's point, the furry thing bounded off into the woods, springing over a log on its thin legs. Harvard watched the ripple of its muscles, and was struck with a sudden sense of loss. He'd never seen a creature so beautiful, and after his time on this island, he never would again.

Fascinating, he thought, *that a spindly creature like that could look so fragile, but at the same time be so strong.* The beast had leapt over its obstacles with unexpected power for a thing so frail. Maybe there was hope for him yet.

Lost in thought, Harvard didn't notice the current picking up until his feet lifted off the mossy rock. Before he could even call for help, the water whisked him away. He yelped, water splashing into his mouth and down his throat as he struggled to keep from going under. For a brief, terrifying moment, Harvard thought the rapids would carry him away.

A hand closed around his arm to haul him back, much to his relief. Trembling, he managed to get his feet under him again. He turned around to thank Chavi, but to his surprise, it was August who'd saved him.

"Careful, little dude!" was all he said before turning back to the shore. Harvard could see Chavi just behind him, and they looked pale.

Sax and Jasmine had already made it to the opposite shore. Sax dried off while Jasmine extended a hand to a stunned-looking Chavi. August gripped Harvard's for the rest of the way across, which was probably for the best. He realized when he was safely on the other shore that his clothes were now soaked. It wouldn't be comfortable, but he was just thankful that in his terror he'd managed to hold onto his clothes at all.

"What were you going to say? About that animal?" Sax asked.

August groaned. "I said no science!"

Sax pointedly ignored him. "I've spent my life studying sea creatures," zey continued. "Land creatures are a bit of a mystery to me."

"Well, I've never seen that particular land creature before," Jasmine said, "but on the whole, prey animals have eyes on the sides of their heads to keep watch for predators."

"So that's a good thing?" August asked. "That means that little furry dude wasn't a predator?"

"Well, yes," Jasmine said, "but that means that there are predators on the island, which is not a good thing. So...stay alert, I guess is what I'm saying."

As the rest of the group trudged forward up the mountain, Harvard looked back to Chavi, who was still standing by the edge of the water, trailing behind. He reached out hand to them. They turned away.

"I'm so sorry about that," Chavi said. "I should have been there."

At first, Harvard didn't understand what they were talking about. Oh, the stream?

"It's fine," Harvard laughed uncertainly. "It was nothing. I just slipped."

"But it could have been not nothing. You could have gotten swept up in the current, or you could have fallen and hit your head, or you could have—" they cut themself off, still refusing to meet Harvard's gaze.

"I could have drowned," Harvard said as it clicked into place. "You're trying to say I could have drowned."

Chavi bowed their head. "Yeah."

"I can swim." He didn't mean it to sound like a barb, but he worried they might have taken it that way. If they had, Harvard couldn't tell. They didn't even look like they'd heard him. They were staring off into the distance.

"I shouldn't let you get hurt," they said absently.

"I didn't get hurt," Harvard said, feeling like he was missing something. Why was *Chavi* guilty about *Harvard's* mistake? *He* was the one who had gotten distracted, and he was the one who had needed rescuing. "You know you're...not responsible for me, right?"

"Yeah, I know that," they said.

I do not believe them, Speedy's voice piped up in the back of his mind. Even though he sort of agreed, he still wanted Speedy to shut up. For a Guardian-in-Training, he hadn't really done much guarding. All he'd done was sit around in Harvard's satchel and provide unnecessary commentary. He wanted to tell Speedy he wasn't helping, but then he'd reveal his secret crab stowaway, and it would be a whole thing. So he answered both of them by simply saying: "Okay."

* * *

It was cold.

Chavi hated the cold.

They hadn't *known* that they hated the cold, because they'd never *been* this cold. The dusts had gotten *chilly* at night. This was the kind of cold that bit their skin and pierced their bones. Now that they spent each night shivering, nothing to shield them from the cool night air but their ragged clothes, they were quite certain that the cold was easily their least favorite thing.

In fact, Chavi hated this whole island. They hated how the plants were alien, how ground felt too soft beneath their feet, and how the unfamiliar sounds always kept them on edge. They hated that they didn't know what to expect, which left them always feeling helpless, at the mercy of the elements.

And they especially hated the water.

Chavi kept replaying that moment in the rapids over and over in their mind—Harvard had slipped, and they froze. They knew Harvard was right—it really wasn't that important. He'd been fine, and even if August hadn't helped him, he'd probably have been able to pull himself to shore. But they still couldn't help the nagging feeling that they should have been the one to help him.

Maybe they wouldn't feel like the river was such a big deal if it didn't feel like it was just the most recent in a string of failures. Their graceless exit off the boat was a residual source of embarrassment, but far worse was what Harvard had told them before they'd even departed. As Chavi dressed Harvard's head wound, asking him why he'd try to run away when he knew they were coming back for him, he'd said: *I started to get afraid. I started to think maybe you'd changed your mind.* Did he really think so little of them? That they would just abandon him on a whim? Did he see their failure to follow him off the boat as another abandonment? Or their inability to catch him in the river? They knew he was too kind to admit it, but Chavi couldn't help the feeling that Harvard was entirely losing his faith in them. Maybe he was right to do so. Whatever was happening to their body, it was becoming increasingly difficult to ignore.

The pain was getting worse. The thing that felt like searing tendrils wrapped around their bones. Crab disease. There was no explanation other than the fact that Skrack had not saved their life, but instead condemned them to a much more slow and painful death via whatever parasite or sickness or condition was killing off the desertwalkers. They'd brought some dazzle in the hopes it would help, but the few times they were able to sneak off and smoke a little, it didn't seem to do much. It didn't feel like anything anymore.

The higher they climbed, the colder it got. They tucked their nose into their shirt to shield their face from the biting wind, only to find it fogged up their glasses. Rather than risk blindly stumbling over a cliff's edge, they resigned themself to the sting of the wind on their cheeks. Chavi hadn't realized until now that cold could be a *danger*. They had no tents, no blankets. Everything was lost with the boat.

How would they survive an actual threat if even just the weather could kill them?

At night they dreamt of that same cavern, the one they'd dreamt of the night after the aquarium. After they'd spoken—or at least, thought they'd spoken—to a desertwalker.

Chavi used to have nightmares about being underground. Ever since their first day in detention, they'd wake up gasp after a dream about choking on dust, crushed beneath the sand.

The cavern did not scare them the way they thought it should. Nor did it inspire any comfort. The cavern just...was.

It appeared as though the walls were shifting, moving forward, desertwalkers of all shapes and kinds heeding the same call. They couldn't not see what was at the end of the tunnel, but they knew it was something warm and nice and they wanted to get there as badly as all the other creatures did.

They started to walk with the crabs, and soon they couldn't tell where they ended and where the crabs began.

* * *

Chavi groaned inwardly when they saw Sax approaching them at camp. "August, would you collect some dry wood? I'm hoping to actually start a fire tonight." August, hearing his name, looked up from where he was unpacking rations. Chavi blinked at zem.

"Did you forget my name?" they asked.

Sax rolled zyr eyes. "Listen, there's four of you and one of me. It's harder on my end you know."

"That's Chavi," Jasmine said, and Chavi knew she was trying to de-escalate a conflict before it started. "And *that's* August. And—"

"Yeah, the little one is Harvard. I know that."

Harvard flushed and ducked behind a tree, out of view.

"But those two"—Sax gestured between Chavi and August—"are basically the same. Well one of you go collect wood. Or both. Whatever."

"Basically the same?" Chavi bristled. How could anyone think they were like August?

"We're totally different!" August protested at the same time, which didn't really bode well for their argument.

"Sure. Okay. One of you get the wood, alright?"

"I'll do it," they both said, shared a frustrated glance, and stalked off.

For the first few moments of the walk, they were both silent. Chavi couldn't stop turning it over in their head. It's not that there was anything wrong with August, it was just...he was annoying. And a little stupid. And even though he'd changed a lot since the time when they were scavengers together, Chavi couldn't forget the time that August had slammed Harvard against a wall and screamed at him for almost getting them all killed. Chavi might have a bit of a temper, but they definitely wouldn't do that, right?

"We are not the same," August grumbled.

"Of course not," Chavi agreed, and then belatedly wondered why August would care so much, anyway.

"You're all...broody," August said.

Chavi reared back. "What? No I'm not."

"Yeah you are," August insisted petulantly. "You're brooding right now."

"Am not," they brooded.

"I see it in your face."

"This is just what my face looks like," they said, stomping away, but August trotted after.

"Exactly. You have no whimsy."

"I have no whimsy?" Chavi asked. Did they even *want* to have whimsy? If "whimsy" was whatever brainrot August had, they were probably better off without it.

"Yeah. I think that's the main difference between us. You have no whimsy. Me"—he indicated himself—"I have whimsy for days."

"*That's* the main difference between us?" Chavi asked, incredulously.

"Yeah. I think so."

They stopped walking, because this was an important misunderstanding that they needed to set straight. "August, we are *nothing* alike. There are...there are way more differences between us! There is a—an ocean of differences between us!"

"Yeah but I think it all boils down to the fact that you're grumpy."

"I'm not grumpy!" they said, and even they had to admit it sounded a little grumpy.

"Just...pick up some wood, okay?"

August didn't appear to be listening anymore. His eyes were fixed on something in the distance. He gripped their arms and yanked them back, pointing just ahead of them.

"The thing!" he hissed.

"What thing?" Chavi asked, with less urgency than August's warning probably warranted. It was just, well, August, as he'd just established, was so "whimsical" that it was hard to take him seriously.

"The thing!" August repeated, pointing more aggressively.

"That doesn't help!"

"Bird!"

"You're pointing at a bird?"

"Look!"

They looked, and yeah, sure, there was bird. Except—oh.

"OH."

It wasn't a bird, exactly. It was bird-sized and bird-shaped, but with feathers and a sharp beak that it was using to peck at the ground, but its tail was almost reptilian, and its wings were like a bat's...and Chavi realized they had seen a much, much larger version of this same animal out in the dusts.

It had nearly killed them, before Harvard and Skrack had come to their rescue.

"How is that possible?" they asked. August tugged on their arm.

"We gotta go tell Jasmine. She been keeping track of all the animals we see."

"Do you think it's dangerous?" Chavi asked, watching the little avian pick at the dirt. It spotted an insect with an eager squawk.

"Nah, it's just a little baby!" August said.

Chavi backed away, watching the beast warily. Sure, this one was a baby...but what if there was a much, much bigger one somewhere around here? They'd be dead for sure. "Let's leave it alone. You're right. We should tell Jasmine. She'll know what to do."

Jasmine did not know what to do.

"If I had to guess," she said, "I would say that the creature is native to the island, and either they migrated—which seems highly unlikely—or the one we met was brought across the water."

"So someone brought the little guy back to Bastion?" August asked. "How? I thought Devrin said no one else had been here."

"No he didn't," Jasmine scribbled in her notebook, which she was slowly starting to fill up. "In fact, he more or less said the exact opposite."

"He did?" Chavi asked.

Jasmine snapped the notebook shut. "He said he had reason to believe there was a piece of pre-Quake technology at the center of the island. How would he know that if he hadn't already sent someone here and had them report back?"

"Well if he already has a 'going to explore islands' team, why would he send us?" August asked.

Jasmine looked out into the forest, which was rapidly growing dark as the sun set on another day. "I'm going to guess that the first expedition here didn't go well."

"Why?" Harvard asked.

"Well, Delian guards have only ever lived in the city," she reasoned. "They've never known anything else. But Devrin was very specific about choosing scavengers. We've survived outside of the city before. We already know how."

Chavi shook their head. "That's not it," they insisted. Jasmine raised an eyebrow.

"What do you mean?" she asked.

"He wants to use scavengers for dangerous missions because he doesn't believe scavengers are people."

Jasmine adjusted her glasses. "I...find that hard to believe."

"He told me himself," Chavi crossed their arms. "At the Galvin Conference. He thinks being a scavenger is...subhuman." It was such a visceral memory, that simmering rage they'd felt when they'd first met him, burning so hot that Harvard had to drag them away. They turned to Harvard so suddenly that he jumped. "You remember, right?"

Harvard nodded. "He did say that."

Jasmine spun a braid on one finger, biting her lip, but said nothing. Chavi knew she didn't believe them, and admittedly they wished they didn't believe themself. But they remembered what Devrin had said that day at the conference. *Scavengers aren't people.* That's why he was perfectly fine having Chavi shot. That's why he was perfectly fine breaking Harvard's fingers. And that's why he was ready to toss them out onto an alien island completely unprepared.

* * *

They reached the top of the mountain the next morning.

Chavi watched from below as Jasmine climbed up a rocky outcropping once they reached the peak, hoping to get a view of the rest of the island.

"Careful!" they shouted, instinctively holding up their arms to spot her.

"I'm fine!" she called back down. She reached the peak and looked out at the horizon, holding Sax's scope up to one eye.

"What do you see?" August asked.

"Well there's—" Jasmine cut herself off. She froze.

"What?" Chavi asked, already starting to climb the rocks themself.

"Guys," Jasmine breathed, "you have to come see this."

August clambered up the rock beside her. Harvard struggled to get a foothold on the boulder, and Chavi lent a hand to pull him up. Sax climbed up behind them easily. Jasmine pointed down into the valley.

Harvard gasped quietly, covering his mouth with his hands.

Before them, down in the basin of the mountains, was a city.

Interlude Four: Avi

Only once did Avi see Devrin genuinely upset. Even then, "upset" was a strong word for it. She saw him at his desk wearing a frown, his forehead creased ever so slightly, which on anyone else would have been normal. But on him, someone who was all smiles and clapping and excitement, a frown looked deeply wrong.

Pierce stood across the desk from him, scratching his beard in clear worry. They both stared down at a piece of paper on Devrin's desk, as if neither knew what to make of it.

Avi knew this would be a terrible time to interrupt, so she decided to do just that.

"What's going on?" she asked innocently.

"Nothing," Devrin said absently, which again seemed strange to Avi, because he only ever said things with great intentionality.

"Doesn't seem like nothing," she pressed.

"A fire," he said. "In one of the Zuri medical labs. They want us to investigate it."

"Uh-huh," Avi drew out the words, guessing that if this were just some petty arson case, it wouldn't have been brought up the Head Enforcer.

"Probably nothing," he waved her away. "Those labs are full of all kinds of chemicals. Anything could catch on fire. Probably an accident, and the Zuri people are just being overly cautious." He flashed her a forced smile, and it was like seeing a smile haphazardly painted onto a doll. "Nothing to worry about."

Avi nodded and retreated into her room, feeling like she'd just made her biggest breakthrough so far.

He didn't know that her specialty was medical innovation. That meant he didn't know that she spent much of her time in a samples lab, so she was fully aware of the fact that flammable chemicals were forbidden in such areas for fear of damaging rare specimens.

He'd lied to her. This left her with a few key pieces of information.

One: the fire in the lab was no accident.

Two: Devrin wanted to hide that.

Three: Devrin wanted to hide that *from her*.

This led her to her fourth most thrilling conclusion: Despite his nonchalance, Devrin considered her a threat.

CHAPTER TEN

Descent

The city was unlike anything Jasmine had ever imagined. It had none of Bastion's concrete roads or steel towers or anything like that, but she knew it was still a city. Suspended in the trees at the foot of the mountain were wooden houses, connected by rope bridges to platforms full of huts, streets, and animal pens. They were too far up to make out the features of individual people, but she could still see them bustling about—walking, talking, leading animals. A structure that large could probably hold thousands of them, and she wasn't even certain she was seeing the whole thing. Humans outside of Bastion! She'd thought it was impossible—no. She'd been *taught* it was impossible, and she'd never thought to question it. Stupid! Here was a whole new society outside of Bastion's walls.

"Incredible," she breathed, watching the people—small as insects down below—traversing their system of ropes, ladders, and bridges.

"But...no one can live outside of Bastion," Harvard marveled.

"We did," Chavi said.

"Do you think they've been here...you know, since the Quakes?"

"If that's the case..." Jasmine mused, "their society would have evolved completely differently than ours. Different language, different beliefs, different values...who knows if we'd even be able to communicate with them!"

Sax held out a hand for the spyglass and Jasmine proffered it, feeling oddly numb. Zey held it up to one eye and whistled quietly.

"What if they're not human?" August asked.

"They look pretty human from here," Chavi said.

"We're too far to tell. Like you said, humans can't survive outside of Bastion. So, what if these guys are something different?"

Jasmine didn't respond, she only shook her head.

"I'm not certain," she said, gaze still fixed on the elevated city below, "if everything they taught us in Bastion is true."

She glanced over at Harvard, who was staring absently in the direction of the city.

"We have to go talk to them," he said. "We can be...like diplomats. We'll teach them all about Bastion and all the...all the stuff we have."

Jasmine shook her head again. "I don't know if that's a good idea. I mean, imagine. If Skrack walked into Bastion with the intention of making peace, what would happen to him?"

"He'd get destroyed," August answered.

"But these are other humans!" Harvard protested. "They can't be scared of us! They'll be happy to see us!"

Jasmine looked down at Harvard, wishing she could share his optimism after everything they'd been through. "I'd love to live in a world where that's true. I just don't know if that's the world we live in."

Harvard looked to Chavi pleadingly, but they shook their head.

"Jas is right. They might be hostile."

Sax looked between them, aghast. "Do you really have so little trust in mankind?"

Chavi shrugged. "We're just practical. Not everything is as magical as your fish cult."

"It's not a fish cult," Sax bristled.

"You actually *want* to speak to them?" August asked.

"Why not?" zey asked.

"Um, were you not listening when Jas said that they're a whole different culture that might *kill us*?" August asked.

"I didn't say that," Jasmine said.

"You implied it."

"No, I didn't," Jasmine said, letting a bit of frustration seep into her voice. "I'm with Sax, actually. I would like to meet them too."

"After you just said that they might try to murder us?" August asked, patently ignoring the fact that this was not what Jasmine had said.

"I said I'd *like* to meet them," she clarified. "Not that we necessarily should."

"We're not doing anything until we have more information," Chavi said.

"And who put you in charge?" Sax asked.

Jasmine could tell Chavi was fighting back their old captain's instincts.

"I'm not in charge!" they said, suddenly chastened. "It just...seems like a good choice."

Regardless of whether or not they chose to make contact, they still had to get to the foot of the mountain. They all clambered down from the rocky outcropping and started their descent.

They didn't get far before the sun began to set, and Jasmine declared that they should probably make camp. She sent Chavi to collect firewood again. She probably could have found some herself just fine, but she would take any excuse to keep Chavi away from Sax. She was about to ask August to go with them, but Harvard was already interlacing his fingers with Chavi's. Jasmine frowned, wondering if this was going to be an issue. Were the two of them getting too close? What did getting "too close" even mean? Jasmine wasn't sure, but it worried her anyway. Something about the way the two had become so infatuated with each other seemed dangerous. Maybe she was still stuck in the dusts mindset—no personal attachments, no grief when someone inevitably gets killed.

But that wasn't their life anymore, so none of them were inevitably getting killed. Right?

"'Fish cult,'" Sax grumbled as they started preparing a meager dinner. "The Union is not a fish cult."

"You have to admit it does have the...trapping of religion." Jasmine always felt as though she were walking a tightrope between defending Chavi and commiserating with the people they'd unintentionally wounded. In this case, though, she had to admit they'd had a point. The Fisher's Unionists were cagey. They had their own songs and beliefs, they didn't swear by the Founders. It did sort of feel like a religion unto itself.

"And what's wrong with that?" Sax demanded.

"Well it's just...don't you think that's a little antiquated?"

"No. I think Bastioners just have a hard time understanding spirituality."

"Most Bastioners believe in science."

"The two are not mutually exclusive. Jasmine, you're smart. Smarter than the rest of them, that's for sure. You of all people should be able to sort through all the garbage they filled your mind with, and understand what's real."

Jasmine opened her mouth to speak, but discovered she had nothing to say. Sax was right. Her whole childhood she'd learned that Bastion was the final city, and now she knew for a fact that wasn't true. How much else had she believed without question? How much else was a lie? She knew logically should be angry about this, but she couldn't fight back the weight of the shame that settled on her. She should have *known*. She had dedicated herself to her studies. Did those studies mean nothing now, if none of what she'd learned was even true?

"What are you working on?" Sax asked.

"Records," she explained. "Everything we've seen so far. I'm trying to keep a list. I could do with some pictures, though..." Jasmine wasn't much of an artist. She'd have to ask Harvard to do some sketches for her when he got back. She sighed. She wished he'd at least asked before going off with Chavi. She needed him here.

"Hey guys! Look at this thing I found!" August hobbled into camp, carrying something round and wet. He dropped on the ground with a squelch, and Jasmine noticed two eyes staring back at her.

"Is that thing alive?" she gaped.

"Yup!" August crossed his arms, looking pleased with himself.

"August!" Sax chided. "You can't just bring wild animals into our camp!"

"This guy isn't wild!" August gestured to the wet brown mound at his feet. Jasmine studied it. It was about the size of a small dog, but that was where its canine features ended. It was so rotund that it was nearly spherical, and its thin little legs looked like it could barely hold its weight.

"I named him 'Blobby' cos he's so blobby," August gave the creature a playful tap with his foot.

"That's a frog, August," Jasmine sighed. "Albeit a big one."

August blinked. "A what?"

"Do you seriously not know what a frog is?" Sax balked. "We do have them in Bastion, you know."

"Oh, I'm sorry I'm not a *nerd* like you guys, so I didn't know what a frog was!"

The giant frog named Blobby had no interest in the conversation, and leapt so suddenly that both Jasmine and August yelped in surprise. The creature launched its jiggling weight a good ten feet in the air before landing outside of their camp.

"Blobby! No!" August called after it.

"You can't go around treating this like a joke," Sax spat. "You're going to get us all killed."

"It was just a frog," Jasmine said quietly.

"But it could have been something else. Something dangerous."

* * *

Chavi and Harvard walked by the edge of a cliff, snapping off twigs from branches. They were pretty high up the mountain by now, and the higher up they got, the more perilous drops they encountered. Chavi found every time they glanced up at Harvard, they had the instinct to warn him not to get too close to the edge.

Something was off between them.

They worked in silence, which scared them. They didn't like silences, which is why they'd spent a lot of their young life trying to fill them. What made it worse, though, was that they knew that the silence probably meant Harvard was thinking about something, and that scared them even more.

"What do you think it is?" Harvard finally said, to their relief.

"What do I think what is?" Chavi asked as they snapped a branch off a fallen tree.

"The thing we're looking for. At the center of the island."

"Oh, I have no idea. I just figure we'll know it when we see it."

"So you haven't wondered about it? At all?"

Chavi shrugged. "Not really. Why? Have you?"

Harvard nodded. "All the time. I just...I'm so scared that we're not going to be able to find it. And we'll have to go back to Bastion with nothing. And Avi will be killed and"—he wrung his hands, looking out through the trees—"and it'll be all my fault."

"Harvard," they said, placing a tender hand on his shoulder, "none of this is your fault."

"You could have just left me," he said. "But you didn't. So this is my fault."

"By that logic, it's my fault," Chavi said. "Maybe even Avi's for showing up. Definitely not yours, though."

He didn't look convinced, but he went back to picking up branches, which made them think—

Chavi froze. They found themself staring into two pure white eyes that watched them intently, eyes set in a face that seemed to be constantly shifting in a haze of smoke.

"Harvard," they said levelly, "do you see that?"

"See wha—" Harvard cut himself off when he turned to face the creature, perched delicately on a branch with black paws that looked strangely like miniature human hands. Its tail flicked, and Chavi somehow couldn't tell if it had one tail or five. It was a shifting mass of grey and black fur, like shadows layered on top of each other, and markings around its reflective eyes that looked like a mask. They couldn't look away, even though they weren't quite sure what it was they were looking at.

"What is that thing?" Harvard wondered aloud, which Chavi found a relief, because they were beginning to wonder if they were imagining it.

The creature launched itself at them, and suddenly it became painfully real. Those little black claws, it turned out, were sharp. The creature was surprisingly heavy, and it knocked the breath out of Chavi when it hit them, knocking them to the ground. They tried to grab it as the claws raked at their face. They grabbed a fistful of fur and tried to dislodge it, but it seemed that the creature's many wispy tails had already wrapped around them, holding the creature in place.

The creature reached a claw-like hand toward their throat, and they could feel something like talons pierce the skin at the edge of their neck. A sudden cool sensation spread from their neck down their spine and into their extremities, and they gasped, their back arching convulsively. Their hands fell away from the creature, useless. Their legs stopped kicking. As much as they willed their body to move, to push the creature off, to unlatch its claw from their neck, they couldn't do it. All they could do was stare up at the treetops as the creature...pulsed. With each pulse, Chavi's chest heaved, and the colors of the world seemed to dim. Was it sucking their blood? Was that what it was doing? But Chavi now knew what it felt like to lose blood, and it wasn't this. They groaned involuntarily at the sensation of something being siphoned away from them, as the sunlight began to dim and the world started to fade.

* * *

Harvard stood motionless for longer than he should. The creature was just so hypnotic, an impossible flurry of shadow and fur, he could hardly comprehend what he was seeing. Chavi's screams pulled him out of his stupor. He lunged to where they'd fallen, hoping to pry the thing off of them, but it kept shifting in his vision, so he struggled to place a hand on it.

Harvard managed to grab onto one of the creature's tails with both hands and pulled with a cry of determination. The grip hurt his injured fingers, which weren't much help anyway, but still he forced them to close around the wispy, furry tendril and pull it back. The animal howled, leaving bloody scratches on the side of Chavi's neck as it was ripped away. Dragging it across the mossy ground, Harvard pulled it to the cliff's edge before swiveling to fling the thing into the foliage below.

He turned to find Chavi staring vacantly at the sky, and an icy knife of panic shot through his stomach. He knelt by their side, feeling for a pulse in their neck. He found it, and breathed a sigh of relief.

It's a state of paralysis, he heard Speedy's voice in his head as the crab crawled up onto his shoulder. *It should wear off shortly.* Harvard found that comforting, until suddenly he didn't. How did Speedy, a desertwalker, know anything about the creatures on this island?

"Speedy?" he whispered. "What's going on?"

I...did not know creatures here were capable of doing such things, Speedy said, which didn't do much to answer the question.

"You mean, you know that thing—" he looked over his shoulder, as if that shadow creature would return. "You know what it did to them? You've seen this before?"

I've...never seen it done on a human.

"What is it?"

There are...no words in your language to describe it. I am at a loss.

"Wait...can *you* do this?" Harvard asked, suddenly terrified of the little crab he'd carried with him in his pack as a companion.

No. Few have the ability.

"So what can I do?"

Wait for the venom to run its course. They should be back to normal in a moment.

So Harvard squeezed Chavi's hand, willing them to move again, for them to stop staring absently at the sky looking so disturbingly dead.

* * *

Jasmine jumped as Harvard burst out of the underbrush, his eyes wild, Chavi trailing behind him.

"Guys!" he cried. Jasmine leapt up when she saw the blood on Chavi's face, and dribbling down their neck onto their shirt.

"What happened?" she demanded. "What's wrong?" She waited for Chavi to respond, but they only stared forward absently.

"Chavi got attacked," Harvard panted. "It was—" he cut himself off, as though searching for words and coming up short.

August scoffed. "Did it actually attack you, or did it just jump out of the bushes and scare you a little?"

"It wasn't nothing!" Harvard cried. "It was...I don't even know how to describe it."

"I'm sorry, you're saying you got attacked by one of the dogs?" August asked Chavi. They looked at him, but still didn't respond.

"It wasn't a dog!" Harvard's face was growing red. "Not everything on this island is a dog! It had...venom..."

"Okay, sure, got it, scary 'venom.'" August sneered. "I'll try to remember that."

"August!" Jasmine snapped, with more ferocity than she'd intended. August recoiled. "Will you go do something useful? Anything useful. Just...just go away."

August nodded slowly, then retreated to go help Sax with whatever they were doing.

"Chavi," Jasmine said, drawing closer to examine their injuries, "do you want me to look at those cuts for you?"

They shook their head. "It's fine," they whispered. It was the first thing they'd said since they returned to camp.

"Are you sure?" she asked. She could see Harvard watching them with the same concern written on his face. Chavi nodded.

"I'm going to go lie down, okay? You guys eat dinner without me. I'm...I'm not hungry."

They pushed past Harvard and Jasmine to get to the corner of camp that they shared with Harvard.

Jasmine took Harvard's hand.

"Will you tell me about it?" Jasmine asked. "Partially for the records, and partially because...well, you seem a little shaken up, and maybe talking about it would be good for you."

Harvard only nodded.

"And…" Jasmine added. "I was hoping you would add some sketches to my notes. You can draw all the creatures we've seen better than I can. Maybe drawing would be nice?"

"Yeah," Harvard said, watching Chavi go, "it would be."

* * *

"Are you okay?" Harvard asked when he finished working with Jasmine. Their tents had been lost with the boat, so he and Chavi had laid some branches against a tree in a sort of lean-to to give themselves some semblance of privacy. Shielded from the eyes of the others, Harvard sat beside Chavi, who sat against the tree staring absently at the makeshift wall, their face only illuminated by the slivers of moonlight that made it through the branches.

Chavi nodded. Then started to sob.

For a fraction of a second, Harvard was stunned. He'd never seen them cry before—which he admittedly had felt a bit strange about, since he'd cried in front of them so many times. Technically there was the time he'd seen them have a drunken breakdown back at the Commission but…well, that was *Yale* and not *Chavi*—who were of course the same person but also no they weren't—so it felt entirely different. Besides, he hadn't been supposed to see that, and Yale hadn't even remembered it the next morning. Now that Chavi was crying in front of him for the first time, he felt completely ill-equipped to deal with it. What did they need right now? How would he know?

"Oh," he said, and immediately felt silly about it. He decided maybe he shouldn't say anything, yet. He just wrapped his arms around them, and placed a hand on the back of their head to direct their face into his neck. He could feel their body shaking in his arms. He rubbed their back.

"It's okay," he said. "You're here with me, now. Everything is okay."

Chavi pulled away.

"I'm sorry," they said.

"Don't be," Harvard smiled. He was actually relieved not to be the one who needed comfort for a change.

"I don't know how to describe what…what it felt like," they said. "Like…like everything I was, slowly being pulled away."

"I'm sorry." It wasn't enough, but he didn't know what else he could say. "It…it's over now. And it won't happen again."

"How do you know?" they rasped.

"I'll make sure of it."

He worried they would laugh at him for this, but they didn't. It actually seemed to comfort them.

"Thank you, Harvard."

Chavi fell asleep with their head resting on Harvard's chest. Harvard watched them, running a hand through their hair, unable to sleep. He took pleasure in having the chance to soothe them that night. Was that bad? Was he evil for enjoying Chavi's pain? Of course he wished none of this had happened to Chavi...but since it had happened, he felt good that he got to be the one they were vulnerable with, the one who was allowed to hold them and tell them it was okay. And when he said he would protect them, they actually believed him, which might have been the best part of it all. Was he some kind of twisted maniac for enjoying that?

Speedy crawled up on his shoulder, nestling in the crook of his neck.

I am deeply sorry for what occurred today.

Harvard, not wanting to wake Chavi, simply nodded.

I truly wish there was more I could do. But you did well, Harvard. Had you not acted, they would have died an excruciating death.

Harvard nodded again.

You should rest. This day was not kind to you, and while I hope tomorrow will be kinder, there is no guarantee. You need not maintain your vigilance. I am here, and can warn you of any danger.

Harvard thanked Speedy, though admittedly he didn't think the little crab's warning would be particularly helpful. After all, thus far Speedy hadn't managed to do anything except make Harvard increasingly anxious. Besides, Harvard's trouble sleeping had nothing to do with keeping watch, but it was still comforting to know Speedy was looking out for him. He allowed his head to droop, Speedy still perched on his shoulder like the excellent Guardian he seemed to want so very badly to be.

CHAPTER ELEVEN

City of Leaves and Wood

"Can you tell me more about that thing that attacked Chavi last night?" Harvard asked Speedy as the Ivies continued their descent down the mountain. Going down was faster than going up, and Jasmine had speculated that they would make it to the valley by the following day.

I do not know much about that creature in particular, but...Siphoning is something the world has not known for centuries.

"Siphoning?" Harvard repeated. "What's that? I mean, it looked like the thing was sort of...drinking their blood?" He remembered the crimson holes left in the side of their neck all too vividly.

No. It did put its venom in their bloodstream, yes, but it was not after their blood.

"So...what was it after?" Harvard asked, running his hands along to rough bark of the trees to keep his balance.

I...don't know that there is a proper translation into your human tongue.

"Do your best."

It was eating...Essence.

Harvard was doing his best not to get frustrated with the little crab, but it was proving difficult when Speedy spoke in terms he had no hope of understanding. "And what *is* Essence?"

Well, it's sort of like... are you familiar with the concept of a soul, Harvard?

"Yeah, sure. Like the...the stuff inside you that makes you you. Er, metaphorically?"

Right. Well imagine if it wasn't metaphorical.

Harvard's brow creased. "So you're saying...souls are real?"

No. Souls are naturally imaginary. They are, after all, a human invention, created in order to conceptualize forces beyond your comprehension. No offense meant.

"None taken," Harvard said with a shrug. A lot of things were beyond his comprehension. He knew that. Or rather, he *didn't* know that, but that was alright?

Souls are not real. Essence is.

"And...we have Essence?" Harvard guessed.

No. Desertwalkers have Essence.

"But...you said Chavi had Essence."

Yes. That's why I'm so confused.

Harvard suppressed an exasperated breath. "I don't understand how this works."

It is not something humans were meant to understand. I will attempt to explain. Imagine...a stream. The stream runs through a forest. The water in the stream sees the forest, and knows that it is beautiful. Below the stream is a cave. In the cave, too, is a stream. But the cave is dark, so that stream does not know it runs through a forest, let alone that the forest is beautiful. Are you following me so far, Harvard?

"Er, no? How can streams know things?"

The streams are made of souls.

"I thought you said souls weren't real."

They are not. This is a metaphor, so I used metaphorical language. I thought I was pretty good at it.

Harvard couldn't tell if Speedy was being needlessly obtuse, or if the problem was his own ignorance. Maybe both? "Um. Well. I sort of get it. Keep going."

The upper stream terminates in a lake at the end of the forest. Only then will the water know sunshine. The lower stream terminates in a deep pit that nourishes the roots of the trees. Do you see?

"I see." He did not see.

The upper stream is Essence. The lower stream is...everything else. The lake in the sun is The Serenity.

"What is the pit?"

We do not speak much of the pit. We call it Oblivion. It is possible for a creature with Essence to fall to Oblivion. If there are cracks in the land the water from the upper stream can fall to the—

"But how does that happen in real life?" Harvard asked, getting increasingly impatient with the figurative streams.

If a desertwalker—or any creature with Essence—is killed before they have achieved Serenity. But it only goes one way. Water flows down. It can never flow up.

"So what you're saying is—"

Chavi...contains water from both streams. And this should not be possible. It...frightens me.

"How do you know all this? I mean, did you learn it in, like, crab school?" He suddenly found his knowledge of the carcine education system woefully inaccurate.

All those who are born with Essence simply know. It is an instinct.

"Chavi doesn't know."

Chavi was not born with it.

"But they do have it? You're sure?"

Yes. I can feel it. It is as if my connection to every creature is made of different kind of string—

"Let's maybe take a break on metaphors for today," Harvard said, idly picking at the wrappings on his splint.

My connection to Chavi is different. Different from my connection with others of my kind. And different to my connection with humans. It is simply...different.

"What does that mean?"

We have yet to see.

Once the group reached the foot of the mountain and took a moment to rest, Jasmine gathered them in circle to discuss their options.

"We've got to make a choice." she said. "That city is the center of the island. And Devrin said that the tech we're looking is at the heart of the—"

"Wait," August said, "you think that the thing we have to take back to Bastion is a whole city?"

"No, that's not—"

"You want us to take the whole city"—August gestured upward—"and *push it somewhere else*?"

"I'm saying that whatever we're here for might be *in* the city," Jasmine clarified.

"Oh," August deflated. "Well, that's dumb. It might be any place else on the island."

"We're running out of food," Sax reminded him. "We're freezing every night. We have no protection from the creatures on the island."

"Which are not that dangerous," August said.

"Yes, they are!" Harvard said. Chavi said nothing. Harvard looked up at them expectantly, and finally they said, "It might be a good idea."

"Just...give us one more day, okay? I'm sure if we try, we can find enough food," August said, setting his jaw. His obstinacy reminded Harvard of the way he used to act back in the dusts, always contrary seemingly for the sake of being contrary. It was strange, because Harvard was growing to like August, but every once in a while a bit of Princeton peeked out, and it made him nervous.

"Jas and Sax are smart," August continued. "They can recognize edible plants, right?"

"Some," Jasmine conceded. "But it's doubtful that the flora here will resemble—"

"And we"—August gestured to the rest of them—"can hunt."

"Hunt?" Harvard asked, paling.

"Well there's really only two things to eat: plants or meat. Besides, my dad was a neo-butcher. I know all about how synth meat in Bastion works. I bet it's not that different."

"Yeah, except one comes from a living animal," Chavi said. "I mean, that's gross."

"Our options are pretty limited when it comes to food. Do you have a better idea?"

"I do," Sax said, indicating the direction of the city.

"Do you *want* to get killed?" August asked.

"I want to not starve to death."

"They live in trees, for Founder's sake!" August said with a wild gesture toward the city. "They're obviously not, like, at Bastion levels of progress."

Harvard thought it might be nice to live in a tree, but he didn't argue. The group had agreed to let August have his one day to prove that they could get by without the city people, so Harvard had no choice but to help...kill animals. To eat them.

"So, how do we do this?" August asked as they trekked through the woods.

"August!" Chavi said. "This was your idea! I thought you suggested hunting because you knew how to hunt!"

"Um, why would I know that?" August asked. "I just—"

Harvard heard something moving in the underbrush.

"Listen!" he said. The other two froze. Harvard pointed to a fallen log where they could crouch and get a better look at the creature. Peering over the wood, he could see it was another one of those two-headed tall-dog-things with the rocks for feet. One head grazed while the other glanced around with wide, black eyes, on the lookout for predators.

"Good job, Harvard!" August patted him on the back. "Now go kill it with your bare hands!"

"What?" Harvard asked.

"He's joking," Chavi said.

"Am not," August muttered.

Joking or not, Harvard didn't like the idea of such a sweet, gentle creature dying. He frowned. "We can't do this. I'm not going to kill—"

With a thunk, something planted itself in the beast's eye. One head slumped forward, dead, while the grazing head shot up, giving a cry of panic. It started to flee, but another projectile pierced its second neck, and the creature fell to the ground with a thud that made Harvard nauseous.

"Whoa!" August breathed. "Harvard, you killed it with your mind! How did you do that?"

"What? I didn't—"

"Sh!" Chavi clapped a hand over Harvard's mouth. They pointed to where the beast had fallen. A figure crept out of the underbrush—a woman, Harvard guessed—her hair so blond it looked silver, tied in a braid to keep it out of her face, wearing a thick cloak against the cold, a knife in one hand, a bow in the other. She placed a hand on the carcass, closed her eyes as she whispered something inaudible, then used the knife to carve the meat off the beast with remarkable ease.

"An islander," Chavi breathed.

"Yeah, and a merciless killer, too," August said, despite the fact that this was probably the most merciful way to kill the beast. Harvard wanted to point out that August had been more than happy to kill animals a few seconds ago, but given the fact that he had just seen this woman shoot two arrows cleanly through her prey, he decided it was best not to draw her attention. He pulled away, and the others followed.

"See!" August said as soon as they were out of earshot. "I told you the island people are bad news! She could have sliced us up just like she did that...that...that tall dog!"

"I never said you were wrong," Chavi said, but Harvard knew them well enough at this point to know that their tone meant, *"I did think you were wrong though, even though I didn't say it."*

"Whatever. We'll find something else to eat. Like—" August's eyes widened. "Like that thing!"

Harvard followed his gaze to a creature weaving its way through the leaves. At first he thought it was a giant worm, but upon closer inspection, he saw it had scales like a lizard.

"Look at that stupid thing!" August said. "I could kill that, no problem. Where are its legs?"

"Maybe it doesn't have any," Harvard said.

"Everything has legs, idiot. It's like a crabsnake, but minus the crab."

"So..." Chavi huffed out an exasperated breath. "A snake?"

"Is that where the word crabsnake comes from?" Harvard asked.

"Maybe," Chavi shrugged. "Ask Jas. She knows more about the pre-Quake world."

"It's so stupid," August said, wiggling a finger at it. "It's like a little noodle. *That's* dinner right there. I just gotta grab it."

"Princeton! Do not do that!" Chavi lifted an arm to hold him back.

"Princeton?" August gave a sideways grin. "It's been a while since I heard that one. Did you forget you're not captain anymore?"

The befuddled look on Chavi's face told Harvard that they had, for a moment. At the thought of danger, they'd briefly switched from being Chavi back to Yale.

"Look, I'm just trying to be resourceful here," August defended. "You're gonna be thanking me tonight when we're eating a giant worm and not getting killed by island people." He reached down and gripped the serpent with both hands. "See? Hunting is easy! You guys gotta feel this. It's so smooth it feels wet. Everything is so wet in this place."

The creature shot out its head and sunk its teeth into August's hand. He wailed in surprise, dropping the snake. It opened its jaw as quickly as it had clamped down, landed on the dirt with a soft smack, and slithered into the underbrush.

"Ow ow ow! Okay, not good! I don't like this thing anymore!" August cradled his bitten hand.

"August, you idiot!" Chavi said. "Let me take a look at it."

"It's fine!" August protested, clutching his bleeding hand to his chest, flushing.

"We don't know anything about the animals around here," Harvard held out a hand. "This could be dangerous."

August sighed, placing his hand in Harvard's. Harvard was no medical expert, not like Avi, but he'd seen enough injuries at the Shack to know when something would heal on its own, and when something was really serious. The site of the bite was already turning red, which wasn't so surprising, but the swelling worried Harvard, along with the purple bruising beginning to spread.

"I think that snake might have been venomous," Harvard said, trying to think back to anything O'Neill had taught him about venomous creatures. He didn't like to think back to his days trapped in the research pod, but during that brief period of his life he learned more about biology than ever before. "Venom can be really serious. We have to—" He cut himself off. He didn't actually know what they had to do.

Chavi covered their face in their hands.

"Founders, August! How are you so stupid?"

Harvard frowned. Admittedly, he was thinking the same thing, but he didn't think this was the best time to bring it up.

"Guys, I'm fine!" August scratched the back of his head with his uninjured hand. "You're totally overreacting. That was just, like, a little guy."

"August, if you die because you thought it would be funny to play with a snake, I'm going to kill you," Chavi said.

"Relax!" August said, wobbling a little as he pulled his hand out of Harvard's. Harvard could see he was beginning to sweat, and he wondered if it was just embarrassment or something more. "We just all need to chill and—" His eyes widened. "Hold on."

August swiveled around and vomited into a bush.

Chavi nodded. "Yeah, he's gonna die."

"No, no!" Harvard ran a hand through his hair, feeling himself get flustered. "We can figure this out. We can—Wait!" he grabbed Chavi's arm, eyes wide. "The hunters! From the city in the trees! They must know how to deal with this, right? They must know the animals better than anyone else!"

"Harvard, we can't talk to them! Didn't you see that girl with her"—they mimed a bow and arrow—"shooty thing? We're trespassing on their island! August is only maybe dead, but if we let them know we're here, we're all dead for sure!"

They turned back to face August, who was now leaning on a tree, wiping his mouth with the back of his uninjured hand. He used the other hand to give a weak thumbs up, and it dribbled blood down to his elbow.

"I wish Avi were here," Chavi said.

"Honestly, I'm not sure she would know what to do either. But these people might," Harvard looked up at Chavi pleadingly. They sighed.

"Okay," Chavi said. "I'll take August to the hunters. But you stay hidden, alright?"

"But—"

"I'm not going to have you getting hurt. Understand?" Harvard recognized the same tone of voice they'd used when they were captain.

"I have to do something!" he said. He wasn't going to stand idly by when a crewmate might be dying.

"Go find Jasmine and Sax. Tell them what's going on. If we get into trouble with the hunters, maybe the three of you can get us out of it."

Harvard opened his mouth to protest, but before he could speak Chavi grabbed his face and kissed him.

"If I die, make sure everyone knows it's August's fault, okay?" they said before dashing to August's side and wrapping his arm around their neck. Harvard watched, stunned.

"Go!" they said, and Harvard ran.

* * *

Chavi half-led, half-dragged August through the wilderness.

"Walking is crazy, right? Like, whoa, where's the ground? Why is it moving like that?"

"Please shut up."

Chavi breathed a sigh of relief when they spotted another hunter. He wore the same cloak as the woman, and bore the same weapons, but judging by the way he kept pushing his messy brown hair out of his eyes and fumbling with his bow, he wasn't nearly as skilled. He crouched beside a tree, pulling an arrow out of the pouch strapped to his back. Chavi figured they'd best catch him before his weapon was loaded. They burst from the underbrush, dragging August behind.

The man yelped, eyes wide, scrambling backward.

"Hey, okay, so sorry about this," Chavi began, struggling to express the situation to someone who didn't speak their language. "I know you probably can't understand any of this, so I don't know why I'm even trying, but—we're new here, and this is my friend, and he's dying. There was a...a snake?"

Chavi mimed a snake biting August on the hand. The man continued to stare at them blankly. They held out August's injured hand and made an exaggerated biting movement.

"Are you serious?" August slurred. "I'm dying and you're playing charades?"

"He doesn't speak Bastion Common, August!"

"I know what a snake is," the man on the ground said in perfect Bastion Common. Chavi stared at him.

"What?"

"I said, I know what a snake is," he repeated, standing. He slung his weapons over his shoulder and strode up to August, taking his injured hand.

"Awesome," August said, then collapsed.

Chavi watched, stunned, as the hunter took August's other arm and wrapped it around himself to keep him steady. Not only was he *not* trying to kill them. He was actively trying to help them, without hesitation.

"Looks like seed viper," the man said, gently running a finger over August's wound. "There should be seed viper stores in the med house, so if we're fast enough, we should be able to neutralize it."

"How do you—what—" Chavi stammered.

"Come with me," the hunter said, and Chavi obeyed.

* * *

Jasmine was happy to forage in silence, and Sax seemed just as content with it. Only when their search became both figuratively and literally fruitless after an hour of scouring did Sax deign to say something.

"I don't understand how you deal with them."

Jasmine felt a surge of defensiveness for her crew. "Look, I know they don't seem—I know they don't come off as the smartest people around—"

"Oh, that's not what I mean. I don't feel like I'm in a place to judge anyone's intelligence."

"Oh." Jasmine found herself at a loss for words. Admittedly, she thought that was what Sax had against her crewmates. She thought zey thought they were just stupid.

"I never went to school, Jasmine," Sax said.

"Never?" Jasmine gaped. "At all?"

"Nope. My mother was a fisher, and she taught me when I was very young. No need for schooling."

"But you're not—"

"Stupid?"

"I mean, I wasn't going to say it like that. But yes."

"Because I, unlike a lot of people in that city, I know that education and intelligence are not the same thing. I know that I'm smart—when it comes to my field of expertise. And I'm sure your friends are smart in their own areas of expertise too, whatever those may be. So I make no judgments there."

Jasmine frowned. "So then what's your problem with them?"

"Honestly? I find them annoying. Not Harvard, actually. He's fine. The other two, though...You'll excuse me if I say that I don't really think highly of Chavi."

"I don't think I will excuse you, actually," Jasmine said acidly. She knew Chavi sometimes got on people's nerves. She'd seen it hundreds of times. That didn't mean she was going to tolerate slander of her best friend.

Sax sighed. "I know you're very fond of them."

"I'm more than—look, do you know why Chavi and I became friends?"

"No, I don't."

"Every person who's ever become my friend only did it because they had to. Harvard and August would never have talked to me if we weren't on a scavenging crew together. Even Avi—we were tiny when we first met, and kids that age are still too young to judge their relationships. By the time I got to school and met Chavi, we were old enough to choose friends for ourselves. And they could have picked any of the kids in the Academy to make friends with. And they picked me. Do you know why?"

"Why?"

"Because they liked me. And they're the only person to ever become friends with me for that reason, and that reason alone."

Sax looked away from her, and she realized that for the first time, she was seeing them embarrassed. "I see. I'm not used to meeting people outside the Union. I know I can lose patience for non-Unionists quickly."

"And I know it's not easy being ripped away from your life to do something you don't want to do," Jasmine said, pushing aside a branch. "I've been there."

Sax leaned back and stared at her.

"I volunteered for this," zey said.

"You did?" Jasmine asked. "Why?"

Sax shrugged. "I wanted to know what was out there. I was sick of Bastion. I wanted to know if there was another way. And as it turns out...maybe there is."

Harvard burst through the underbrush, making both Jasmine and Sax jump. He bent over, panting, hands on his thighs.

"What's wrong?" Jasmine asked, but he was still struggling to catch his breath. He gestured vaguely upward, toward the suspended city.

* * *

The hunter led Chavi and August deeper into the woods. They wondered if they'd actually get to see it was like up there, in the city in the trees, or if they'd be killed first.

The woman from before, her bow now slung on her back, was leaning against a tree with her arms crossed, as though waiting for something.

She caught sight of the two dragging August, and she took up a defensive stance immediately, her eyes alert.

"Who is this?" she asked, pointing to August. For a moment, Chavi seemed to escape her notice.

"He's snakebit. Seed viper. We have to help," the messy-haired hunter said. When Chavi heard the pleading tone of his voice, they realized he probably wasn't much older than they were.

"Blaire—" the woman's brow creased with...concern? No, *disappointment*.

"We have to help!" he repeated.

The woman exchanged a glance with Chavi. They gave her a weak wave.

"Hi," they said. She bit her lip. Her hesitant look reminded them of Jasmine. She exchanged a long look with the hunter supporting August, and this reminded them even more of Jasmine, because it was the same look they had shared with her when they were scavengers when they wanted to communicate something that they didn't want to say out loud. The two hunters had that kind of silent exchange only two people who have known each other for a very long time can have before the woman seemed to lose the battle. She hissed, putting her face in her hands.

"Alright," she said. "But Marcel isn't going to like this."

"I know, I know," said Blaire. "But what are we supposed to do? Let him die?"

The woman winced as if to say, *"Well, yeah, honestly,"* but she stayed silent. She strode over to a tree and grabbed a rope Chavi hadn't noticed wrapped around a branch. She looked up, giving it two firm tugs. Chavi followed her gaze, and in the canopy above they could see the edge of one of the suspended city islands.

The woman untied the rope from the branch, allowing it to shoot upward. Chavi heard a wooden creaking and the hiss of moving ropes as a box descended toward them.

"Whoa," they marveled. "Is this, like, an elevator?"

Blaire gave Chavi a befuddled look. The box thudded on the dirt. Chavi tugged August's inert body forward, but Blaire held up a hand for them to wait. A gate on the wooden box unlatched, and Chavi saw two people step out, clad in similar tunics and belts. A shorter, weaselly looking boy led, with a hulking, scar-faced man trailing behind.

"This better be important," the small man said. He caught sight of Chavi and August, pinched the bridge of his nose, and sighed. Again, this was not the response Chavi had been expected. The islanders didn't seem so much shocked to discover trespassers on their land as they were *irritated*.

"Blaire," the man groaned, "have you brought outsiders again?"

Again? Chavi thought.

"No!" Blaire said hurriedly. "I mean, yes, but it's not like last time, because—"

"This one is hurt, Marcel," the woman strode to the two newcomers, gesturing to August. "We at least need to get him medical attention. Then we can proceed from there." She had the kind of voice that you couldn't very well say no to, even though it looked like Marcel desperately wanted to.

"Fine," he grumbled. "Get them in the gondola."

"Wait," Chavi said, and the man named Marcel shot them a look that implied it wasn't their time to speak. Chavi didn't care much. They were used to speaking out of turn. It was more important to them that they not leave Harvard and Jas stranded below while they were with August up in the city.

"Our friends will be looking for us. You take August, and let me wait here for—"

"You're coming with us," Marcel said. "We have strict procedures to follow."

Procedures? Chavi wondered. How often did outsiders end up here?

"Sylvania," Marcel gestured to the woman, and she stood at attention. "You wait and see if anyone turns up looking for them. Oleg and I will deal with this situation."

"And me?" Blaire asked.

"You," Marcel swiveled on him, "will answer to Rosenea. But we clean this up first."

Chavi wondered what "cleaning this up" could mean. If they were planning on killing the two of them, it would be a waste to put in all the effort getting August's wound seen to. So that was a good sign, wasn't it? But they didn't feel exactly welcomed.

The big man, who Chavi gathered was Oleg, ushered them into the wooden gondola. Blaire helped Chavi sit a barely conscious August on the floor, propping him up against the planks. Oleg turned a wooden crank, and the box rose haltingly into the air, swaying. Chavi watched the ground jerk farther and farther away with each turn of the wooden pulley, feeling a wave nausea wash over them and hoping that they hadn't just done something incredibly stupid.

It didn't matter. It was too late now.

* * *

Jasmine listened to Harvard's story with mounting panic. Sax only seemed mildly irritated.

"Unbelievable," zey muttered.

Jasmine gripped Harvard's arm. "Do you know where they went? Or can you take us back to the place where you last left them?"

Jasmine had hoped that Harvard's navigation skills would again come to their rescue, but he looked doubtful. "I don't know," he admitted.

"I mean, I was so focused on finding—I wasn't really paying close enough attention—I was worried—"

"It's alright," Jasmine said, even though the dread settling in her stomach informed her that it definitely was not. How would they find Chavi and August if they couldn't even find a way into the city?

"There you are!"

Jasmine turned to see a girl with a halo of sunlight, perched delicately on a fallen tree. She gracefully leapt off, her silver hair streaming out behind her. Her skin was paler than Jasmine had ever seen—as white as paper. Her pale blue eyes glittered, and for maybe the first time in her life, Jasmine was at a loss for words.

Angel, she thought, then immediately felt stupid for thinking it. Angels were an ancient myth. They weren't *real*. But Founders, this girl seemed to have descended from the skies in their hour of need like an ethereal savior, which did sound pretty angelic.

"Come with me," she gestured, and entranced, Jasmine moved to follow. Sax held her back.

"Where are you taking us?" zey demanded.

"To your friends," the girl said over her shoulder, then lifted a hand pointing skyward. "To Haven."

* * *

"How do you know Bastion Common?" Chavi asked.

Blaire opened his mouth to speak, but the big man shushed him.

"Don't speak," he said. "Don't tell them anything."

"But—"

"Sh!"

"Okay," Blaire looked chastened.

Chavi couldn't help finding Blaire a bit endearing. Maybe he reminded them of Harvard.

The gondola docked at the edge of a wooden platform.

Chavi had seen the city from afar, but it was nothing compared to seeing it up close. The only city they'd ever known was filled with asphalt and glass and noise and smoke. They'd never known that a city could be so...organic. The ground itself was built around tree trunks, the wood delicately carved to accommodate the branches. The thatched huts seemed so seamlessly connected, it looked as though they'd grown out of each other, as though the whole city had sprouted from the same plant.

And it was quiet. Besides the quiet conversation of passersby, and the giggle of children playing somewhere in the distance, there was no sound but the wind in the leaves.

Chavi wondered if this even qualified as a city at all.

A hand shoved them forward.

"Move," Oleg said.

"Blaire," said Marcel, "see the injured one taken care of."

"I'll go with him," Chavi said, gripping August's arm. "He's my friend. I'm not leaving him."

"He'll be fine," Marcel said. "We know how to deal with a simple snakebite."

"I'm not leaving him," Chavi repeated. August might be an idiot, and he might be the reason that they were involved in all this in the first place, but they still weren't going to hand him off to a group of strangers when his life was in danger. Unfortunately, they didn't have a choice. Oleg pried their fingers off August and pulled them away, leading them toward a hut by the gondola dock.

"You stay here. We'll figure out what to do with you later."

* * *

"I'm not sure what I'm allowed to say, I'm afraid." The girl massaged her pale braid as the wooden box ascended. "But I'll try to help you, if I can."

"Help us with what?" Jasmine asked. The girl frowned.

"Everyone in Haven has been a bit wary of outsiders after the last ones," she said, eyeing Jasmine. "But somehow I'm not too concerned about you all."

Jasmine found herself smiling.

"We don't mean you or your people any harm," Jasmine assured her.

The girl laughed. "I guessed as much." She held out a hand for Jasmine to shake. "I'm Sylvania."

"Jasmine."

They held each other's gaze for a moment.

"Um," Harvard said. "Also, I'm Harvard. And this is Sax."

"Oh. Right," Jasmine gave a nervous laugh. She glanced over at Sax, who didn't seem to be paying any attention to the conversation. Zey leaned on the edge of the gondola, looking out over the woods.

"It's incredible," zey breathed.

"It is, isn't it?" Sylvania said with a smile, and Jasmine guessed she took some pride in the island. Her face fell as the gondola docked.

"I'm...not sure anyone else will say this to you all, so let me say it now." She opened the gondola gate. "Welcome to our home."

Sylvania led them along the wooden platform, which—although logically Jasmine knew was perfectly stable—felt dangerous. If a person was going to be this high up, they should be in a nice, firm concrete building, not standing on a thin wooden island. She tried not to think about the fact that only inches of wood separated her from a deadly drop as Sylvania led them into a hut, constructed from what looked to Jasmine to be mud and straw.

"Chavi!" Harvard cried.

Chavi stood at the sound of their name, and Harvard wrapped his arms around them.

"You're okay!"

"Yeah, yeah, I'm fine." They looked beyond him at Sylvania, Jasmine, and Sax. "They didn't do anything to me except be kinda rude."

"They do that," Sylvania laughed.

"Is August okay?" Jasmine asked.

Chavi shrugged. "They took him away. Said he'd be fine, but I don't know if I trust that. These people seem pretty antsy to have us gone."

"Sylvania?" Jasmine turned to the girl at the doorway, who was kneading her braid with her fingers nervously.

"Not every Havener is like Marcel, I promise!" she said. "He just wants to protect the city, is all. I'll go get Rosenea. She'll...she knows what to do."

Sylvania scurried out, and the way she moved reminded Jasmine of the graceful creatures they'd seen drinking from the stream.

"What is this place?" Chavi asked. "I mean, how does it even exist? And how do they speak our language? Why do they hate us so much?"

Jasmine stared at them blankly. "Is it not obvious?" she asked.

Chavi sighed. "Jasmine, I wish I was as smart as you. I wish that every day. But I'm not, so please tell me what you've figured out, because I'm definitely not gonna figure it out myself."

Jasmine looked around at the others, trying to gauge if this was in fact that general opinion. Harvard nodded that yes, she was definitely the only one who had an inkling of what was going on.

"They're defectors from Bastion," she explained.

"What?" Chavi asked. "What do you mean, defectors?"

"These people must be from Bastion originally, and they left, and founded this place. A Haven. The answer's right in the name."

"So, people from Bastion just showed up here and built this place?"

"Yes."

"That's..."

"Beautiful," Harvard said at the same time that Chavi said "stupid."

"Why would anyone leave Bastion for this Founders-forsaken place?" Chavi crossed their arms. "Bastion has running water and electricity and no—whatever that thing was that tried to kill me. What's wrong with Bastion?"

"Are you joking?" Sax asked from where zey reclined in the corner. "Everything is wrong with Bastion! I'm sorry, weren't the four of you scavengers?"

"Yeah? And?" Chavi prickled.

Sax looked appalled. "Bastion treated you like scum!" zey said. "And now you're licking its boot?"

"You don't know anything about what happened to us," Chavi snarled, getting too close to Sax for Jasmine's liking. She put a hand on their shoulder to hold them back, but they shook her off.

"I don't need to know," Sax said with a dismissive hand wave. "Every scavenger's story is the same."

"I don't see what *you* have to complain about," Chavi shot back. "You had it pretty good, from what I could tell."

"Hey—" Jasmine started.

"Yeah, because the Fisher's Union members are the only people in Bastion with any common sense!"

Chavi took a step closer. "Oh, well I'm sorry I didn't have the common sense to be born into the Fisher's Union. My mistake."

Sax seethed, but thankfully August swaggered in before zey could respond.

"Sup gang!" he said. "Look at my cool glove!" He showed off a hand wrapped in bandages.

"So you're not going to die?" Chavi asked, their anger seeming to ebb.

"Nope!"

"That's a shame," they grumbled. Jasmine nudged them. She started to chide them, but she cut herself off when the door swung open, revealing a woman with grey hair woven with leaves, her face creased with age. She was draped in a burgundy cloak, and perched on her nose were half-moon glasses. Sylvania stood behind her like an attendant.

This, Jasmine realized was someone very important. Rosenea, who likely held the Ivies' fates in her hand. *Please*, she begged her crew internally, *please behave.*

* * *

Harvard wondered if Haven had corporations like Bastion did, and if so, which one did this woman run? He wondered if her role in this world was something like his mother's. She carried herself with the same intensity and poise as Saoirse Bell.

Rosenea smiled congenially, something his mother never did. And it was a genuine smile, so it was doubly unlike Saoirse Bell.

"It is a rare joy to encounter outsiders," she said warmly, "but please understand, many here view it as a rare danger as well. We do not mean to be inhospitable, only cautious. We've had to revise our policy regarding outsiders over the past few years. Haven, as you may have guessed, was once a refuge. We welcomed anyone who stumbled upon our island. Now we must be a little more discerning."

"Why?" Chavi asked.

"There are a few things"—she fixed Chavi with a cold look—"that we do not speak of in Haven. That is one of them. We have many customs that you are going to have to get used to if you're going to stay here. I must insist that you follow them to the letter."

"We're not going to stay here, though," Chavi said. "We're going back to Bastion."

"I'm afraid," Rosenea sighed, "that's simply not possible."

"We don't have a boat, for one thing," Sax pointed out.

"What's more," Rosenea continued, "is that we cannot allow you to leave. Not now that you know we're here. We can't risk further hostilities from the outside world. Surely you understand."

"No, we don't understand!" Chavi said. "You can't hold us prisoner—"

Jasmine held up a hand to stop them.

"We understand completely," she said sweetly. "You need to take care of your own people, just like we want to take care of ours. We can't thank you enough for seeing to August's injury for us. We are in your debt. In fact, we're very lucky to have found you. We left Bastion in hopes of building a new life elsewhere, but we ended up stranded on your shores. This sort of community is exactly what we were hoping to start, away from the city. We had no idea something like it already existed. We'd been more than happy to learn your ways. We only ask that you're patient with us."

Chavi gave her a wide-eyed *"What in the name of the Founders are you saying?"* kind of look, but stayed silent.

"Excellent," Rosenea said. "We'll have your citizenship ceremony at the Full Moon Festival in two weeks' time."

"Citizenship ceremony?" Chavi asked. Rosenea pointedly ignored them, which irritated Harvard. They'd only just arrived here, and under dire circumstances. Now suddenly they were expected to be citizens? This was moving too fast.

"In the meantime," Rosenea continued, "we'll teach you our ways, and see how well you fit in. And at the ceremony, you'll be welcomed into the community of Haven."

"But—"

"We understand the need for discretion," Jasmine said before Chavi had a chance to protest further.

"I'm pleased to hear you understand. We have a rotation for newcomers, you see. We'll cycle you through each of our roles until you find an occupation that suits you. In Haven, we believe no one should be forced to do labor that does not become them. You will find your place here, and grow with us."

"That sounds wonderful," Jasmine nodded.

"Where will they stay?" Blaire asked. Rosenea turned to him.

"I would have thought," she said, "that was obvious."

"Oh. You mean—I'm supposed to—"

"It is the responsibility of all Haveners to look after each other, which is why we will welcome these newcomers accordingly. But you are the reason they are here, so seeing to their needs is your responsibility alone."

"Alone?" Blaire repeated. "I mean, last time—"

Sylvania put a hand on his shoulder. "You won't be alone," she assured him. He relaxed.

"Okay everyone," he said, "um, I guess we're going to my place."

"You may report to the Meeting Hall tomorrow for job assignments," Rosenea said. "In the meantime, Blaire will be your host."

"Cool. Yeah. Host," Blaire said as Rosenea turned to leave. "It might be...I mean, it'll be a little cramped."

Jasmine stepped forward and took his hand.

"Thank you," she said, "for bringing us here. You could have turned us away. But you didn't, and that means everything to us."

Blaire blushed. "Oh. I mean, I couldn't really not do that, so—"

"No, you could have. And I'm grateful that you didn't. We all are." She turned to the others, and they took their cue to nod in agreement.

"Well. Thanks. I'm sorry about all of this. But I think you guys are really going to like it here! And I'll do my best to make you feel at home."

He gestured for the others to follow him. Jasmine shared a glance with Sylvania, who gave her an appreciative smile.

* * *

Blaire's "house," as it turned out, was another one of those huts August had seen after they'd fixed his hand, made of a combination of wood, clay, and dried grass. It was mostly a single room, complete with a wooden table, a few chairs, and a hearth at the back. Beyond that was a little bedroom, a washroom, and a closet that Blaire said could be repurposed into a very small bedroom. The whole place was even smaller than Chavi's mom's living room, which was already so tight that the four of them always sat on the rug for Sunday dinner. Apparently, Sylvania's was right next to it, and there was even a door inside. August actually thought that was pretty nice—kinda like the way the Ivies were all living together now.

Blaire had been right: it was cramped. They hardly all fit sitting on the ground by the hearth as he boiled water in a stone bowl.

"Isn't this a fire hazard?" Jasmine asked, looking up at the thatched roof.

"Oh, we have very firm rules about fire," Blaire smiled, indicating the stone that lined the inside of the hearth. "Only in hearths and lanterns. We haven't had a serious fire in years. Besides, that's part of the reason we've got so many platforms. We cut bridges to keep a fire from spreading—the bridges are actually pretty easy to cut down for that exact reason. As long as the central platform doesn't burn, we're fine."

Jasmine looked skeptical, but she only nodded, cupping a clay mug in her hands as Blaire poured in some steaming water.

August blew on his, and tried the tea when it was cool enough. He didn't know if he liked it. It kind of tasted like dirt, but in a good way somehow. He glanced at Chavi out of the corner of his eye. They were still mad at him, weren't they? They gave him a withering glare before turning away. Yeah, they definitely were. And who could blame them? August couldn't. He was the reason they were trapped here. His chest tightened.

"I'm sorry I was such a dusthead about the venom thing," he said, testing the waters as they settled near the hearth beside Jasmine. "I guess I thought...I don't know. It sounds dumb to say out loud. But if I could convince myself not to be scared of any of the island creatures, then I could be the brave one and maybe like save all of us or something. At *least* get us some food. But it turns out...venom kinda sucks."

"It's okay," Chavi said, much to August's surprise. "I mean, you were right. The creatures here are...different from the dusts. It was easy not to be scared of them, even though maybe we should have been."

"Whatever happened to you with the..." August didn't know how to bring this up. He hadn't realized how affected Chavi had been by the attack until the days after. "Whatever that thing was, I'm sorry. It must not have been fun."

Chavi shook their head, the flickering light of the flame illuminating their face unevenly. "No, it was not."

"I imagine you all would like to bathe?" Blaire asked.

Jasmine nodded. "That would be very nice, thank you."

"I just refilled the cistern, so you should have enough. It's not heated, though."

"That's okay."

"So, my washroom is just there. And Sylvania's is on the other side of that wall, so you can use that one too. What pairs do you want to go in?"

"Pairs?" Jasmine asked.

Blaire paused for a moment, as though he wasn't sure how to respond to this. "Yeah, like...one person bathing, one person to pour?"

They stared at him blankly.

"Do you guys...is that not how you take baths?"

"We have running water," August said.

Blaire cocked his head to the side.

"Like...a river?"

Jasmine laughed. "Pairs will be fine," she said, and before August could say maybe it actually wasn't fine, Chavi was already pulling Harvard to his feet and toward the washroom. August glanced at Jasmine to get a read on her feelings about this. Was this actually fine? She was okay with taking a bath with him? In the same room? And not totally grossed out? She just shook her head and laughed at the other two's eagerness.

"I guess you're with me, August," she stood, waving for him to join her as she fetched the water from the cistern.

"You're sure you're okay with this?" August asked Jasmine as she poured the water into the wooden basin.

"Sure," she shrugged, leading the way into the washroom Blaire had indicated. "We've been on a scavenging team together long enough, I think."

August's face flushed, and he wrung his hands. He followed her into the small, dark room. In the center of the floor was a large tub, and beside it a chair.

"Um. Okay," he said, letting out a shaky breath. "But before we take baths, can I tell you something?"

Jasmine looked up at him, and concern creased her face.

"Of course," she said, but that almost made it worse, because that meant he had to tell her, and he didn't really know what words to use. He'd never tried to explain it to anyone before. He shouldn't have said anything, should he? But now he'd dug himself a hole so he might as well commit and...and dig all the way.

"I just wanted to tell you—in case you were worried—in case you thought this would be weird—"

"I really don't think it's weird," Jasmine laughed.

"I know, but I guess I wanted to clarify—I just feel a little uncomfortable, since that's happening over there"—he cocked his head to indicate all the sexy-bathtime that was no doubt happening on the other side of the wall—"and so I just felt like I should tell you, that, uh, I'm not gonna be looking at you that way. I don't, uh, I don't really think of people that way. Like, at all."

Jasmine nodded slowly, eyeing him, as though she was trying to parse his meaning. "August, are you trying to tell me that you're asexual?" she asked.

He scratched the back of his neck. It hadn't occurred to him that there was a word for it. "Um, yeah. I think so."

She laid a gentle hand on his arm, smiling sweetly. "I appreciate you telling me that. But...you know you didn't have to, right?"

"Yeah, I know," he said, though admittedly he *didn't* know. He wasn't sure how any of this worked for anyone else. Was this not the kind of thing you were supposed to disclose to someone before taking a bath with them? "And it was probably weird that I did, so I should just shut up, I think."

She laughed. "No, I'm glad you did. Not because I was uncomfortable bathing with you. I really don't mind as much as you seem to think I do. But...it's nice to know that you feel comfortable telling me about yourself. It's nice to know that—that we're friends, I guess."

"Yeah." August let out a sigh of relief. "That is nice to know." He recalled their conversation in that crab den back in the dusts, when Jasmine—Columbia, as she'd been called then—had allowed him to open up to her. He hadn't felt that he'd had someone to really listen to him in years, certainly not since joining the Commission. Perhaps they *had* become friends then, and he didn't even notice.

"So, would you like to go first?" Jasmine gestured to the tepid basin, which honestly looked wholly unappealing.

"No, you go."

Jasmine shed her clothes and lowered herself into the basin. August sat in the chair by her head and watched her carefully pressing soap suds into her braids.

"Would you give me a rinse?" she asked, and August used the pitcher by the basin to pour some water over her.

"So, what about you?" he asked. He wasn't sure if it was appropriate, but he figured that since he'd had the opportunity to share, she should have it too.

"What about me?" she asked, not unkindly.

"Are you, like, into people?" It seemed like a weird question. He'd never asked it to anyone before. Jasmine froze in the process of scrubbing her arms, and he worried he'd offended her until he realized she was thinking.

"I...don't know," she admitted. "I've never given it much thought."

"Oh," August leaned back in the chair. He'd figured it was the kind of thing that you'd just *know*. He certainly had. When his sisters got all interested in kissing people and whatever, he'd been very certain he just *wasn't*. Even when they'd told him he was just too young, he knew that wasn't it.

"I've just...I've never had time to think about it, to be honest," she said, almost sounding mournful. "I spent my whole childhood so focused on school, I never had a moment to consider sex or dating or anything like that. And then we were in the dusts—"

"And the only thing you could think about was crabs," August nodded and Jasmine laughed.

"Yeah. Just crabs. So...I don't know. Maybe I will think about it." She dunked her arm in the water to rinse it off.

"August?" she looked up at him.

"Yeah?"

"Thanks for asking," she said with a smile.

"Sure," he said, reaching for a towel to hand her, "any time."

* * *

Blaire dropped a bag of dried grass in the backroom, and he called it a mattress, so Harvard assumed this was just what a normal mattress looked like. If he and Chavi curled up, they could sleep semi-comfortably. August and Jasmine could sleep in the main room, by the now-dark hearth.

To Harvard's pleasant surprise, their room had a window. After Blaire bid them a good night and closed the door, Chavi nestled next to him and Harvard leaned on the windowsill, watching the wind in the trees. He hadn't been able to see trees from his window since Bell Manor, but even those trees had been short, spindly little things compared to these bushy giants. The way the leaves rippled in the wind, a susurrus of whispers, reminded him of the ocean. Like the Earth itself was breathing.

Chavi's breathing turned slow and even sooner than Harvard had expected. He guessed they were probably exhausted after the events of the day. He was too, but he knew he had something to do before he fell asleep. He spoke their name a few times to see if they stirred, and when he felt confident that Chavi wouldn't wake, he pulled Speedy out of his bag and placed him on the windowsill.

"So, what do you think?" he asked.

The place fascinates me, Speedy said. *I would like very much to explore.*

"You can," Harvard said. "I mean, not that you need my permission. But it seems like we may be here for a while..." he trailed off when he remembered that according to Rosenea, they were supposed to stay here forever. "What I'm saying is, we'll be here, so you're free to go and explore."

I will do this, Speedy said. *Perhaps I will find something to assist you in your quest.*

Harvard doubted this, but he didn't want to hurt the little crab's feelings. He just wasn't sure that such a small creature could have anything to contribute. Still, he appreciated that thought.

"Alright," he said. "Go explore."

With that, Speedy leapt off the windowsill and scuttled along the wooden floor into the city, moving with the very swiftness that he had been named for.

* * *

Chavi dreamt of the cavern again. It felt so natural, to be back in that place, moving with the rest of the creatures toward some unknown, unseen goal.

You, a voice said.

No one had ever spoken to them in the dream before.

The voice didn't sound accusatory so much as it sounded confused, like the speaker couldn't tell if they were making a statement or asking a question.

Chavi knew this voice, they realized. They'd heard it in a memory that had been locked away.

This cavern. They'd been here before.

They were here when they'd been shot, and before they awoke they'd existed in a nowhere-space where they dissolved into nothingness. They'd heard this voice then, and it had said to them, *You will be changed. Do you still wish to live?*

Why hadn't they remembered that until now?

You are not supposed to be here, the voice continued, and now Chavi realized that even though it was a voice they felt instead of heard, they knew it was coming from behind them. They turned, though they weren't entirely sure how because they didn't think they had feet in this cavern, or any body at all.

A megacrab towered over them, watching them with glimmering black eyes. They'd seen this crab before, they realized. He was the one that Harvard had befriended, the one that Harvard claimed he could speak to. The one that had apparently saved their life.

What was his name?

Skrack? Chavi asked. They didn't know how they were able to speak without talking, without a mouth or a tongue, but somehow they managed it. Just like before, with the scorpioncrab. Instinctively, they knew how to *send* the words without sound.

What are you doing here? Skrack asked, and Chavi didn't have an answer, so the two just stared at each other in befuddled silence as the creatures swarmed around them. Chavi didn't know when the dream ended, but when they awoke they remembered staring into those carcine eyes so vividly that it felt as though it were real.

Interlude Five: Speedy

Speedy had made it all the way this way without being trampled or discovered. It would be such a shame for him to kill himself now.

There was nothing for it, though. If he was to pursue his ultimate objective, and protect Harvard and his friends from harm, he would need to gather intel, even if the pursuit of knowledge proved to be his downfall. He was one of many Guardians-To-Be. Their role was not to survive, but simply to be one of many. Of that many, one would survive, and if one survived, they all survived.

Speedy knew this.

But he also did not want to die.

Nevertheless, he clambered his way through the darkness, following the sickly sweet trail of a creature that had just gorged itself on the Essence of another. He dared not draw too close, sequestering himself in the shadow of a tree root where he could not be seen.

Make yourself known.

He received no response. He needed to be more commanding, like his father.

Face me. Make yourself known.

A voice, wicked in its smoothness, slithered into his mind.

Do you think I make a habit of bending to the whims of inferior beings?

Only when the creature replied did Speedy realized he had hoped it would not engage with him. Now that it had proved it was open to parley, he would actually have to speak to it, which both repulsed and terrified him.

You are here, are you not?

The creature materialized from the shadows, perched delicately on a tree branch, only visible as a roughly shifting outline and a pair of stark white eyes.

Only to see if you're worth drinking from. One so young, however, is hardly a meal. Should I taste your Essence, I would only manage to reawaken the ancient hunger, and it may drive me to do something...unwise.

So he was safe. Speedy lowered his defensive posture—for all the good his miniscule claws would do him against a legendary beast. He knew he could not trust the word of the foul thing, but its logic was sound enough.

We have legends of your kind.

Translucent tails flicked. *As you well should.*

The legends say we exterminated you parasites.

What carelessness, then, to allow a few of us to escape.

Speedy skittered back in horror. *There are more of you then? On this island?*

Some. Not enough. Many starved.

There's food enough on the island, is there not?

None like you. Your kind was uniquely satiating. It was a great tragedy to be driven away. The memory of Essence still gnaws at our appetites. The mere sip I took from your companion...it nearly destroyed me.

How?

Foolish little sandbreather.

Speedy did not enjoy being called foolish, nor little, for that matter, even if it was objectively true. He was still barely more than a hatchling, yes, but even surviving long enough to tap into the Essence stream was a feat. He was a mature desertwalker and he would be treated with respect. And if this vile thing would not show him that respect, then he would sort it out for himself.

You're afraid, he guessed. *You enjoyed Siphoning so much you fear you will be driven to seek Chavi out again, which would mean revealing yourself to humans.*

The beast turned its gaze out into the darkness of the woods. *There are too few, too few of us to risk. Too many starve, too many killed. I must resist. We all must resist. But we were born to feed. It is not simple thing, resisting your very nature for the good of your kind.*

Tell the rest of your kind to leave the human alone, Speedy commanded, tilting his shell up with pride. *There will be swift and violent consequences.* Yes, that was something a real Guardian would say. Very threatening. Even a little dramatic.

And what will you do, little sandbreather? Pinch me? I'd like to see you try.

Not me. The rest of them. The humans preserve their kind the same way you preserve yours. If you hurt one of their number, they will hunt you. And I will tell them where to find you.

The creature recoiled. Evidently it hadn't considered this. The only defense a desertwalker had against a creature that could Siphon was the ability to track it in the Essence stream. Knowing the creature was upon you didn't necessarily help defend against it, but with an army of humans, Speedy expected he and Harvard could wipe the beasts off the island if they wanted to.

It was satisfying, to see the pompous thing scared.

Warn them. Warn the rest of the parasites they had better give the humans a wide berth.

I cannot guarantee they will heed it.

Make them.

I may not heed you either.

You'll regret it if you don't.

Speedy thought this was an excellent line to end the conversation on, and twitched his claws in annoyance when the thing tacked on one last thought.

They came once before, you know.

He should have ignored it, but as his father often told him, his curiosity was a dangerous trait. He paused, just for a fraction of a second, but just long enough for the creature to see it had piqued his interest.

The humans. You believe they are allies to your kind, but you are wrong. They will betray you.

Speedy wished he could dismiss the creature, but he hesitated. He knew it was not wrong. Humans already had betrayed the desertwalkers, years ago. Speedy had not been alive when Myrk was captured, but every hatchling of the Southwest Plains knew that it was human trickery that allowed the Empress' heir to be imprisoned.

Not these humans. Not Harvard.

They were kind to us. They fed us, allowed us sacrifices from which to Siphon, promised us impossible sweetness. Then they took one of us away.

Speedy did not respond. Instead, he clambered back up the tree from which he'd come, hoping to fool the beast into believing that he gave its warnings no mind. It likely spoke false. In its duplicity, it sought to sow the seeds of distrust between Speedy and Harvard.

Speedy would not allow such wicked sprouts to grow.

Speedy trusted Harvard as Harvard trusted Speedy. And that was simply the way it had to be.

CHAPTER TWELVE

Job Assignments

"You'll freeze if you keep wearing the clothes you arrived in." Blaire handed Harvard a bundle of thick, pale green fabric. "This'll keep you warm. And you won't look so...out of place."

He shifted uncomfortably, and Harvard realized that Blaire must be worried about his guests being obvious outsiders. Harvard wondered why that was a problem.

"Thank you," he said, unfurling the bundle to see it was a cloak with a little wooden hook as a fastener. He examined the material. It was heavier than any fabric he'd held in Bastion, and softer.

"How do you make fabrics if you don't have textile factories?" he asked.

Blaire stared at him.

"You shear a sheep. You spin the wool into thread. You use the thread to make clothes."

"Oh. Okay," Harvard nodded slowly. "And what's a sheep?"

"An animal."

Harvard dropped the cloak reflexively, recoiling.

"This came from an animal?" he balked. "You want me to wear animal clothes?" he asked. He worried he might have hurt Blaire, but he only looked confused, scooping up the cloak.

"I mean, you don't have to, but...that's what most of clothes are made of."

"From animals?" Harvard didn't want to be rude, but the thought made his stomach turn. He imagined trying to make a shirt out of dog hair, or crab shell. Ew. It seemed not only disgusting, but cruel. To strip a crab of its shell and then wear it like a trophy? Was that not painful for the crab? Surely the sheep, whatever that was, wouldn't be very pleased about having its shell stolen from it either. However, Blaire seemed very insistent that the Ivies should try to fit in, so he owed it to his host to try his best to adhere to Haven customs. Harvard guessed he was afraid of getting in trouble with that security liaison—Marcel—and admittedly, he would be too.

He screwed his eyes shut, as though that would make it more bearable, and held out his hand for the cloak. Blaire handed it back to him. Harvard slung it over his shoulders and struggled to clasp it, what with his splinted fingers.

It was the most comfortable article of clothing he had ever worn.

He was glad he'd relented and accepted the garment, because the morning air was crisp and cool on the walk to the meeting house. Harvard rubbed his reddening nose as they walking, Blaire explaining a Haven concept called "choring."

"We know how having a job works," Chavi brushed him off.

"Well, it's just, it's not exactly like that," Blaire said. "Because you can do more than one thing if you—"

"You work a job and you get points. I get it."

Blaire winced. "Well, not really, because we don't have points."

"You don't have points? How do you pay for things?" August asked.

"You don't! You just—sorry, it's really hard to explain to Bastioners."

"You've had to explain it to Bastioners before?" Jasmine asked. Blaire flushed.

He rubbed his already tousled hair, looking away. "Once. Yeah."

The Meeting House itself was on the far end of the city's central platform and was by far the largest structure in the city. Round like an impossibly thick tree trunk, Harvard was shocked to see that some living saplings and vines had woven their way into the actual structure of the building. The Meeting House was alive.

Rosenea appeared in the doorway, moving with such grace it almost appeared as though she levitated. She ushered them in with an inviting gesture. The entrance led directly into a wide-open space, a dais at the back of the room with a podium serving as a stage.

"This is the Central Hall," Rosenea explained. "We hold all our community events here. That will include your citizenship ceremonies."

Harvard tensed at the word "citizenship." It reminded him that their whole presence here was founded on a lie.

Rosenea gestured to a carved wooden plaque that hung beyond the dais.

"If you're going to live here, then you're going to have to accept the Haven Principles, our governing document. Think of it as the...oh, what is the name of that event you celebrate in Bastion?"

"The Bastion Summit," Jasmine said. It was the event that Bastioners celebrated with the Founders Festival each year.

"Yes, that. This is our equivalent. *Our* founders laid out these principles for us."

The plaque read:

1. *We renounce the wrongs of pre-Quake humans.*
2. *We renounce the ways those wrongs have been replicated in Bastion.*
3. *We put the community over the individual.*
4. *We care for each other.*
5. *We accept these words as holy.*

"Um...I'm a little confused by the last one?" August glanced sideways at Blaire, but everyone seemed to ignore him. Harvard wished someone would answer. The word "holy" made him uneasy. In Bastion, which was founded on the principle of science and innovation, religious language was taboo. Wasn't calling anything holy kind of...sacrilegious?

"What wrongs of the pre-Quake world?" Jasmine asked.

"And what's wrong with Bastion?" Chavi added on, crossing their arms. Harvard remembered some of what Sax said the previous day, and wrung his hands. Chavi was getting oddly defensive of Bastion, weren't they? Well, they'd had a home there. He'd seen it. Harvard never really felt he'd belonged there, but maybe if he'd grown up in a home like Chavi's with a mom like Rivka, then he'd be defensive of Bastion too.

Rosenea only shook her head. "I can't expect you all to understand on your first day here. Blaire will guide you, and soon the light of the Haven Principles will shine through you."

"That was like...a really weird thing to say," August whispered. Harvard agreed, but he didn't dare say so for fear of offending anyone. Their language reminded him of the strange words Speedy had used to describe desertwalkers concepts that he couldn't understand.

"Now, every citizen contributes to the community," Rosenea said, lacing her fingers together. "What can each of you contribute?"

"I was in the Fishers' Union," Sax said. Rosenea smiled knowingly.

"If that's your vocation of choice, you may continue that work here. The gondola that leads to the shore is just to the west of the Meeting House. You can't miss it."

Rosenea turned to the rest of them.

"And what about the rest of you? What did you do back in Bastion?"

"We were scavengers," Chavi said. "We used to—"

Rosenea held up a hand.

"I know what scavengers do," she said. "While most of today's Havener's were raised here, the memory of Bastion is still...salient." She frowned deeply, as though the memory of Bastion was one she avoided as much as possible, and she did not appreciate the reminder.

"Unfortunately, that skill set does not translate well to Haven. Do you have any other skills to recommend you?"

"Before scavenging," Jasmine said, "I was student, and I had been hoping to continue my studies. Do you do any kind of...I don't know, research? Record keeping? Maybe that's a long shot."

Rosenea nodded.

"You'll find the library on one of the southeast platforms. Blaire can point you there."

Jasmine's eyes lit up at the word "library." Harvard was jealous of her. She knew exactly what she wanted to do with her time, and it was actually something *useful*. It always seemed that the only things he was good at were things that nobody wanted.

"And the rest of you?" Rosenea looked to Harvard, August and Chavi. "What can you contribute?"

Harvard massaged the fabric of his new cloak.

"I don't think I have much to contribute," he admitted. Rosenea gave a kindly smile.

"Everyone has something to contribute. We just need to find the right work for you." Harvard's heart fluttered at the thought. Did he dare believe there was something in him worthy of being valued? Perhaps Rosenea only thought this because she didn't know him yet. If Kathy were here, she would have scoffed at the notion that he could manage a *job*. "We'll set you up on a rotation, alright? You can see what work is available, and maybe you'll find something that speaks to you. Blaire?"

"Yes!" Blaire stood at attention.

"They can start at the Cultivation Center."

"Right! Yes! Cultivation. Sounds good."

Rosenea nodded. "Now if you'll excuse me, I have my own contributions to make. I promised the woodworkers that I would meet with them regarding new projects." She started to leave, then turned back to face them one last time. "I know this place must seem strange to you. But please trust that you will find joy here. All of us do. Otherwise, we wouldn't have made it our home. You'll learn to live by the Haven Principles, and you'll find peace in them, just as we all have."

She turned to enter the Meeting House, and her burgundy cloak billowed behind her as she closed the wooden door.

"Great," Chavi grumbled, quiet enough that Blaire couldn't hear, "so we've stumbled upon some weird forest cult."

"It's not a cult," Sax corrected. "The sandheads are a cult. This is just a religion."

"What's the difference?" Chavi asked.

Sax opened zyr mouth to speak, but Jasmine cut zem off.

"A crowd," Jasmine said, looking pensive. "A cult becomes a religion once it's considered socially acceptable. The only difference is numbers."

Sax gave her a *"I can't believe you're siding with them over me, I mean come on, you're supposed to be the smart one"* kind of look.

"I think that's an over-simplification," Sax said.

"Yeah, well I think your little Union is a cult too," Chavi said. "A Fish Cult."

"It's not—ugh!" Zey buried zyr face in zyr hands. "There's no use arguing with you. You don't have enough brain cells for it. Look, everyone has a belief system. Some are just more grounded in facts. The sandheads have some...far-fetched ideas. But Haven's religion doesn't seem that different from Bastion's."

"Bastion doesn't have a religion!" Chavi said. As far as Harvard knew, they were right. The closest thing to a religion he was aware of was that way that some of the big six families still wore symbols of spirituality, like the Rubiras with crosses and the Taheris with headscarves. But that wasn't about religion, that was about ancestry, which was a totally different thing, wasn't it?

"Haven't you been paying attention?" Sax laughed, and Harvard could see it made Chavi bristle. "Of course, Bastion has a religion. It's just that Bastioners would never call it that. Bastion worships the abstract ideas of science and progress."

"That is not religion," Chavi said. "It's not religion to believe in something everyone believes in."

"But not everyone does believe in all that. I doubt the people of Haven care very much about industry. It seems to me they only care about being happy, which seems like a much better way to live."

Chavi crossed their arms.

"Go catch your fish in your stupid fish cult."

"Not a cult."

"Whatever!"

Sax gave a satisfied little smile and followed Rosenea's directions toward the shore.

"I'm going to try the library," Jasmine said. "Will you all be okay on your own?"

Probably not, but Rosenea's faith in them had given Harvard a little more faith in them too. He nodded emphatically.

* * *

Jasmine had hoped the Library might provide a first clue as to the tech the Ivies had been sent here to find, but when she actually arrived, she assumed she must have entered the wrong building. She knew that buildings on Haven weren't going to look like those on Bastion—all wood and thatch instead of concrete and steel—but she would at least have expected to see some bookshelves. Instead, the building called a "library" looked more like a science museum, filled with display cases. Well, "display cases" was the best analog Jasmine could come up with. The fragments of stone and bone and other natural materials were placed on wooden pedestals with no protective glass, and even more strangely, no placards to tell of their significance. In fact, Jasmine couldn't find any written words anywhere. How could she do research in a place with no words? What kind of library was this?

"Jasmine?" asked a soft voice behind her. She whirled around to see Sylvania, carrying a box of what looked like bone fragments. "What are you doing here?"

Jasmine suddenly found herself embarrassed, but she didn't know why.

"I've been assigned to work in the Library," she said. Sylvania's face lit up, and seeing her smile made Jasmine's stomach flutter. *Oh, be rational,* she told herself. *You don't know this girl at all.*

"Oh good!" she exclaimed, setting her box on a table with an unceremonious clatter. "I didn't want to get my hopes up or anything, but I was really hoping that they would send you here. We could use another specialist around here and you seemed like such a good fit. I mean"—she brushed a stray strand of white-blond hair out of her face—"from what I saw of you yesterday, that is. Which, uh, I guess was not that much. But still."

Jasmine found herself smiling, but she wasn't sure why.

"I'm happy to be here," she said, and Sylvania grinned.

"So! What do you think of the Library?"

Jasmine glanced around at the sea of unlabeled pedestals. "It's not entirely what I expected from a library."

Sylvania cocked her head. "What were you expecting?"

"Well, books for one thing."

Sylvania laughed.

"Do you know how hard it is to make paper?" She asked. Admittedly, Jasmine didn't. Sylvania waved a hand. "On the whole, it's not worth the trouble. We have a few books upstairs, and some are just Bastion relics. Any records we really need to save, we scratch into metal. But what's the point of printing a book when you could just remember?"

"Remember?" Jasmine repeated, incredulous. "Remember everything in a book?"

"Why not? We have the bards to keep our songs and stories and poems. So we have the library to keep our records and research."

"You know all of Haven's records?" She gaped.

"No, of course not," Sylvania laughed. "We've all got specialties."

"What's yours?"

Her eyes lit with excitement. Jasmine knew that feeling—the high of getting to share information that fascinated you. "Wildlife."

Jasmine eagerly pulled her notebook from her pack, and Sylvania gasped quietly.

"You've got a book?" she asked, reaching for it reverentially. "You brought one with you?"

"It's really not all that special, where I come from," Jasmine smiled. *But this one* is *special, given how nice it is*, she thought, before remembering where she had gotten it. She flipped to the pages where she'd had Harvard sketch the beasts they'd come across on the island.

"Do you know about these creatures?"

Sylvania drew her fingers across the pages, and Jasmine wondered how often Sylvania had the simple pleasure of turning a page. She wondered if Sylvania had ever had the opportunity to read a book in her life.

"The sketches are incredible," she breathed. "Did you do them?"

"I wish," Jasmine said. "Harvard did. He's somewhat of an artist."

Sylvania nodded dreamily, then touched Jasmine's arm lightly to indicate that she should follow her.

"This is my wing of the library," she said as she pushed open a door. Jasmine gasped despite herself.

Before her was a room full of skeletons.

Each one was suspended from the ceiling with string, pieces tied together delicately to mimic life. The peculiar floating creatures, though skeletal, were positioned so as to look as though they were alive—running, hunting, or eating. It gave the uncanny impression that Jasmine was looking at a menagerie of levitating skeleton creatures.

"This is the anatomy lab," Sylvania said, beaming. Jasmine was too awed to speak. Sylvania gently took the notebook and pointed to the creature Harvard said had attacked Chavi.

"This one is a procyon," she explained, leading Jasmine to one of the skeletons hanging in the corner of the room. "They're pretty rare. I'm amazed you were able to spot one. They're also dangerous, so I'm even more amazed you were able to spot one and live."

"Chavi almost didn't," Jasmine said.

Sylvania's eyes widened. "You mean it actually *attacked* them? I don't think there are any recorded cases of someone surviving a procyon attack. They're timid creatures so they rarely approach humans, but when they do, it's always deadly. How did they manage it? Can I interview them about it?"

"Um..." Jasmine twisted a braid in her fingers. She hated to let Sylvania down, especially when she looked this eager, but she knew Chavi wanted very much to forget about the incident. "I don't think they'd like that," she said.

"Oh." Her face fell. "Right. Of course. It must have been—I'm so sorry!" She placed the heel of her hand against her forehead. "I shouldn't have even asked! What was I thinking?"

"I get it," Jasmine laughed. "It's always enticing to learn something new." She flipped the page in the notebook, hoping to distract Sylvania with another drawing.

"Oh! This is a hydradeer." She led Jasmine to the skeleton of that two-headed dog thing the Ivies had seen a few times. "Harmless, and very skittish."

"And none of this is written anywhere? You just keep it memorized?"

Sylvania blinked. "Don't you keep things memorized?" She did. She'd memorized as much of Bastion history as she could fit in her head. "If you can remember it, then it seems like a bit of a waste to go through the trouble of writing it down."

"You're incredible," Jasmine said without thinking, then chided herself. She *never* did anything without thinking.

Sylvania blushed and looked away.

"Would you like to see the observation tower?"

Jasmine hadn't heard a more thrilling question in her life.

* * *

"So let me get this straight." August studied soil in one of the Cultivation Center's raised beds. "You eat dirt?"

"No," said Jerricho, the leathery gardener who had begrudgingly taken August on as a protege. "We grow food in the dirt."

"So, you eat out of the dirt?" August poked the soil, disturbing a worm. As the son of a neo-butcher, August knew a fair bit about food. Namely, that food was made in a lab and then people like his father sold it. He was pretty sure it did *not* come from dirt.

"No. We grow our own food. The food grows in the dirt."

"Why do you grow it in the dirt? That's gross." He'd just found a worm in there, hadn't he? Did these people seriously not realize there were worms all wriggling up against their food?

Jerricho gave him a flat stare. "That's where the nutrients come from," he explained.

"Well just give it nutrients!" August said—rather wisely in his opinion. "You don't need dirt to do that."

Jerricho gave an exaggerated sigh. "Will someone please explain the basics of agriculture to this boy?" he asked. The other gardeners either ignored him, or were too involved in their dirt-tasks to care.

What were the other gardeners doing, anyway? August glanced around at the other raised bed. He wasn't stupid. He understood that plants grew and sometimes you could eat the plants. But that happened in labs and stuff. Not outside. In the dirt. With bugs.

Also, why was this dirt so weird? It was all soft and wet and like...August shuddered. He didn't even have a word for it. It was just *wrong*.

These Haveners, though, they didn't seem to mind pulling their food out of the ground. August saw a group of them, harvesting potatoes, chatting and laughing. The dirt food was making them happy. Others were planting seeds, some were repairing fences and setting up trellises. Some he didn't know what they were doing. It looked like they were stirring the dirt like soup.

What would it look like, he wondered, *if we could grow all our own food? If we didn't need to rely on the corps? What if we just made stuff for each other, and we didn't need to pay points to get things in return?*

August couldn't imagine it working, especially not in a city as big as Bastion. But it definitely seemed to be working for Haven. Maybe it would work for him too.

He turned back to Jerricho.

"Okay. Explain it to me one more time."

Jerricho gave another exaggerated sigh, but when he launched into his explanation again, teaching August how to plant a tomato, August could tell that he was secretly enjoying it.

* * *

"*That's* a sheep?" Harvard clung to the fence railing, watching the creatures amble around their pen. "They're like...they're like clouds with legs!"

Very dirty clouds, admittedly. But Founders, he didn't know an animal could be that fluffy! Most of the animals he'd seen in his life were some form of crab, and the rest had been pets, which only had a thin coat of fur. How else could they manage the Bastion heat? Blaire laughed.

"I guess they kinda are, huh?" He unlatched the gate. "Do you want to meet them?"

"I can meet them?" he gaped. He'd never been able to get close to an animal other than the crabs. He'd never even been allowed to pet a stranger's dog.

"Sure. In fact"—Blaire pushed through the sea of fluff, and Harvard followed tentatively—"Ellie just had a lamb, and Abigail is feeding it now. Do you want to name it?"

"*I get to name it?*"

Blaire led Harvard to the back of the pen, where another Havener in a coarse brown tunic held the tiny creature in her arms like she would a human baby, wrapped in a quilted blanket. She even held a bottle to its mouth, and it drank milk. Harvard imagined swaddling a crab like that, and he laughed. What would Skrack say if someone tried to wrap him in a blanket? *Release me, human! Unhand me! Or, um, unblanket me! I refuse to be blanketed!* Animals were so strange on Haven.

"Back in Bastion, me and my friends were discussing what to name our dog," he said. The memory of that night warmed him—all his friends, seated on Rivka's floor, playing games and laughing. Chavi's mom had invited him into their family. He had a family. One that wanted him. He missed that time, however brief, when everything had felt alright.

Abigail looked up and smiled, but she didn't say anything.

"You cared for a dog?" Blaire asked, rubbing a sheep's head.

"No," Harvard said, "it's too expensive. But we'd like to have one, one day."

Blaire wore a look that Harvard was beginning to recognize—it meant Harvard had said something about Bastion that didn't make any sense to him.

"Well, in Haven, you can't really have a dog," Blaire explained. "But you can care for one and everything."

Harvard stared at him. "How is that different from having a dog?"

"Well, you don't *own* it. The dog is just another community member."

Abigail laughed, and Blaire flushed. "Well, not exactly. I mean, it's not like the dog can vote."

Harvard cocked his head.

"Vote?" he asked.

"Like, in Council Meetings?" Blaire said. Abigail placed the bottle down on her bench and laid a hand on Blaire's shoulder.

"You're just confusing him even more," she said, then turned to Harvard. "So, Bastioner. Would you like to name the newest addition to our community?"

"Yes please!" Harvard ran up to her to look at the creature in her arms.

"I switch to fishing duties at midday, and Blaire goes off to hunt, so you'd better pick a name quickly."

For a moment Harvard worried she was annoyed with him, but he heard no frustration in her voice. Strange. Every other time in his life some had told him to hurry up, they'd done so because they were angry with him. Well, how could anyone be annoyed when they held such a precious creature in their arms? It watched him with wide, black eyes, and bleated quietly. What name for such a sweet, soft, little thing?

"Floppy," he said.

"Floppy?" Blaire laughed. Harvard nodded definitively.

"It's what I was going to name our dog. Er, not our dog. A dog. That we would take care of. Even though it couldn't vote."

Abigail laughed again, and Harvard felt a little embarrassed—but oddly, only a little. He had a sense that she wasn't laughing in a mean way, which, again, was sort of a shock to him. This was a day of many firsts.

"Floppy is the perfect name," she said, flicking the lamb's small ear.

"What do you think, Ellie?" Blaire ruffled the ears of the sheep standing by as he leaned on the fence.

Ellie bleated, and Blaire nodded to Harvard. "Floppy it is."

* * *

Jasmine covered her mouth with her hands when she and Sylvania emerged onto the wooden platform at the top of the observation tower. From this height, she could see over the tops of trees. To the west, the mountain they'd crossed to get here. There was a narrow valley to the north where she could make out a little glimmer of ocean. To the east, more forest, and the island's opposite shore.

"You like it?" Sylvania beamed. Jasmine only nodded—she couldn't summon any words to describe what she was seeing. She pointed out everything she could make out, and Sylvania nodded along, even though she must have seen these sights hundreds of times by now. Eventually Jasmine got a bit dizzy, and Sylvania led her back down the stairs.

"I always try to get Blaire to come up here," Sylvania said as they arrived in the library's entrance hall, "but he's too scared."

"Right. Blaire." Jasmine felt a spike of jealousy, which she immediately tried to logic herself out of. What right did she have to be jealous? She'd only just met Sylvania! And yet the thought of Blaire still made her angry, and she hated that. She could feel that anger gnawing at her stomach, and despite the fact she knew that *rationally she should not be feeling it*, it wouldn't go away.

"How long have you been friends with Blaire?" she asked, hoping to force herself to feel some kind of affection for him.

"We grew up together. Babies born on Haven are paired with companions at birth."

Jasmine pushed down disappointment. "So you're...companions?"

"Not like that," Sylvania blushed. "It's more like...a work partner. But a partner in everything. When we hunt, we hunt together. When we cook, we cook together. We care for each other, because on Haven we believe that no one should ever be alone."

Jasmine's envy evaporated. That sounded...well, incredible, actually. In fact, it made her envious for an entirely different reason—she wished Bastion had a system like that. "That's beautiful," she said.

"I think so," Sylvania said with a proud smile. "I love Haven. Truly. I guess that makes sense, though. It's easy to love the place where you grew up."

"I don't think that's true."

"Really?"

"I don't love Bastion."

"No?"

"No. There was nothing to love. That's not to say it was bad. It just...was. There was no alternative. We were always told it was the only city, so I never imagined what my life could be outside of it. Compared to Haven, Bastion is..." Words failed her. She'd never allowed herself to reflect on Bastion's failings because it would have been pointless. There had been no alternative. But now? She didn't know what to think. She was beginning to wonder if they should just tear Bastion down and start over.

"I've only heard about Bastion," Sylvania admitted. "My parents were born in Haven, too. My grandparents immigrated from Bastion, but they never talked about it much."

"And they didn't keep any records, or—" Jasmine cut herself off. "Right. You don't do records here."

"Memory is generally good enough for us."

"But memory is so...unreliable," Jasmine said. She loved to memorize information, but she wouldn't trust herself to get everything *correct*.

Sylvania laughed. "I think writing something down is so much more unreliable. Just look at the Great Quakes! So many records were lost because everything was written down. No one bothered to remember anything."

Jasmine supposed this made some sense. Much of the information that had been preserved came not from records but from language. Documents were lost, but many remnants of culture passed down verbally—stories, names, words, concepts—had remained.

"But I mean...what if you die?" She winced, hoping this wasn't too dark a question. Sylvania, luckily, didn't seem offput by it.

"It's not like there's only one record keeper. And if something happened to all of Haven...well, then it wouldn't really matter if we kept records or not. There would be no one to keep records for."

Jasmine considered for a moment.

"Do you know what it means to be a scavenger, Sylvania?"

The girl nodded gravely. "I've heard the stories. And I know that you and your friends—" she cut herself off, biting the inside of her cheek as though she were unsure how to word this.

"Yes, we were scavengers. And we scavenged for pre-Quake tech. Actually, pre-Quake anything. Anything we found that could be useful, we brought back to Bastion."

Sylvania's demeanor shifted dramatically. "Pre-Quake reverence is a sin on Haven," Sylvania said quietly, looking away. Dusts, had she said something wrong? She had forgotten about the Principles they'd learned this morning, and the ecclesiasticism of it. She just wasn't *used* to people being religious. She wasn't prepared to anticipate the taboos.

"We didn't revere the old humans," Jasmine explained. "If anything, we stole from them, which was probably disrespectful."

Sylvania shook her head. "Based on Haven's doctrine, using their work counts as reverence. Even excavating their ruins would be sacrilege. That's why none of us are allowed to view the Relic."

Jasmine inhaled sharply, tensing. Her heart hammered.

"What's that?" she asked too eagerly. She couldn't help it. Was this the mystery they were after? She buried her excitement, afraid it would scare Sylvania, a devout believer in Haven's practices. Jasmine wondered if even this very discussion felt like blasphemy to her.

"Just off the edge of the city"—Sylvania gestured in the direction of the Meeting House—"is the remainder of a pre-Quake...something. I don't really know what it is, to be honest. I've never seen it, obviously. It's off limits."

Jasmine nodded, choosing her words very carefully so as not to come off as blasphemously curious. "If it's so offensive to the people of Haven, why leave it there?"

"At this point it's become part of our tradition, and no one's really sure why the first Haveners decided to leave it. Maybe they just couldn't move it. My theory is that it's a test of faith."

"Test of faith?"

Sylvania nodded.

"Everyone *wants* to know what the Relic is. Of course they do. It's the biggest mystery in Haven. But those who truly have faith in the Haven Principles know that it doesn't matter, because it's only a testament to the folly of pre-Quake mankind."

Jasmine guessed from the wording that this was a quote of some kind, and she made a mental note to do some research on the Haven Principles in hopes it would give them some kind of clue about the thing they were searching for.

"If you truly believe the ideas that Haven was founded on," Sylvania said, her eyes downcast, "then you don't care what the Relic really is."

At first Jasmine was thrown by her sudden solemness, then it clicked. Sylvania was a scholar. Of course she was curious about the Relic. It was her nature. But according to her religion, that curiosity was a crime. Jasmine couldn't imagine it. If she were a Havener, the curiosity would eat her alive. She just had to *know* things. She thought better of saying this aloud.

"What happens? If someone is caught viewing the Relic?"

A cloud passed over Sylvania's face. "They're banished."

"Isn't that harsh?" Jasmine marveled.

"Haven is based on a social contract," Sylvania explained. "If you prove you can't honor that contract, then you can't be trusted."

Jasmine nodded, though she hardly understood. Theoretically it made sense, but to run a society this way? To Jasmine, it was absurd. Then again, she imagined Sylvania would feel the same way if she tried to explain the big six corps of Bastion. She would have to be very circumspect with how she chose her next words.

"If one of us," she started, "being outsiders, breached the social contract, what would happen to us?"

"I don't know," Sylvania said, shaking her head. "I guess we couldn't really banish you. I mean, I don't think we could trust you enough not to take word of us back to Bastion—if you ever made it back."

Jasmine nodded, hoping to mask her mounting panic. The thing they had been sent here to do was *punishable by death*? This mission was suddenly so much more dangerous than searching for an artifact on an uncharted island, which was already pretty dangerous.

"I mean, I do trust you!" Sylvania added. "I trust you, Jasmine. But in the eyes of the rest of Haven—"

"I understand," Jasmine said.

"If it were a regular Havener, it would be different. They probably wouldn't even try to cross the ocean, and even if they did, they wouldn't be welcomed into a city where no one knew them. But if outsiders were to leave, it would be dangerous for all of us. And we can't put the whole city in danger like that."

"So..." Jasmine prompted.

"It would be up to Rosenea," Sylvania evaded. Jasmine inhaled deeply, then pushed through her last question.

"To your knowledge," she asked, "has anyone in Haven ever been executed?"

"Not officially," Sylvania said, "but...I don't know. I sometimes feel like security takes their job a bit too seriously."

Jasmine nodded slowly, hoping Sylvania couldn't tell that she was terrified.

That night, she debriefed the rest of the Ivies in Chavi and Harvard's cramped closet while Blaire and Sylvania were busy preparing dinner.

"So this Relic," Chavi said, "is what Devrin is looking for?"

"It may be," Jasmine said. "I think our best bet is to bide our time. They seem to take these Relic rules very seriously. I say we lay low and do our best to fit in, then we make our move after our citizenship ceremony."

"And then we have to steal it?" Harvard asked.

"I don't know," Jasmine admitted. "I think we need more information before we make any plans. Which means for the time being, we need to focus on following their rules and making them like us. *You* don't have to like this place," she gave Chavi a sidelong glance. "You just have to behave until the next full moon, when they'll make us citizens. You can do that, right?"

She locked eyes with Chavi, and they shared one of those moments of silent understanding, a skill they'd perfected out in the dusts.

"Yeah, of course I can do that," Chavi said, and though their face told her they didn't want to, she knew they would try. She heard a bit of Yale in their voice—a leader, who would do what needed to be done. Or, at least, would like the rest of the group to believe that. She wished she did.

* * *

Harvard watched in a combination of amazement and horror as Blaire and Sylvania chopped vegetables that had come from the ground and meat that had come from an animal.

"How do you get the legs from the bird without hurting the bird?" Harvard asked. He knew the Haveners hunted, but this kind of bird was one he'd seen in pens at the Cultivation Center, so he figured it must be more like a pet. Blaire shifted uncomfortably and glanced to Sylvania.

"The bird is dead," she said without looking up. "I killed it."

"You killed it?" Harvard gaped, appalled. "Why? What did it do wrong?"

Sylvania set aside her knife and looked at Harvard. "Think of it this way. We need to eat meat because we have to get the nutrients, right? So either we die, or the bird dies. And we choose to kill the bird. But to thank it, we raise it well and make sure it lives a good life, and we make sure it dies painlessly, and we don't let any part of it go to waste."

Blaire handed his knife to Harvard, and he examined it.

"That handle is made of bone," Blaire told him. Harvard yelped and dropped the knife.

The hut wasn't built to house this many people, and it was crowded as they gathered around the hearth and Blaire ladled out the stew. Despite the fact that it had dead animals in it—real ones, not synth ones—it smelled good. He was kind of excited to try vegetables from the ground, and though he didn't want to admit it, he was kind of excited to try meat from an animal. He blew on the bowl, cupping it in his uninjured hand, and the steam billowed away.

He took a dainty spoonful, sipped it, and surreptitiously spit it back onto the spoon, gagging. He tried to hide it, but a gag is pretty difficult to hide. It *burned*. And not in a hot way. In a different way. He didn't want to be rude, though, so he sipped the soup until tears welled up in his eyes and started to spill over. He glanced around at the other Ivies to see if they felt the same. Jasmine took tactful little sips, almost managing to hide her distaste. Chavi grimaced. August sipped directly from his bowl, and spit it back up theatrically, spraying everyone with orange specks.

"Why does your food hurt?" he asked, grimacing.

"What?" Blaire asked.

His face was scrunched in a way that reminded Harvard of the time he'd once seen a stray cat sniff a pile of discarded, rotting fruit. "Like, it's spiky in my mouth?"

Blaire and Sylvania shared a look.

"Is it the spices?" Sylvania asked.

"No, we have spices," August said. "Those are the little powders you put in food to make it taste good. But they don't make it spiky. Why would you put something in your food that makes it taste like pain?"

Sylvania sighed. She set her bowl aside and stood, walking toward the counter. She returned with what looked like a shriveled red berry.

"Try this. Tell me if it's 'spiky.'"

August eyed the berry, then the rest of the Ivies. "Anyone else wanna try it?"

Chavi and Jasmine shook their heads. August shrugged. He accepted the berry and popped it in his mouth.

He made a choking sound, spitting it back up.

"Why would you invent berries that are full of pain?" he cried.

Sylvania gave Blaire a look that lived somewhere between pitying and amused.

"So," Blaire said, "I'm guessing you guys don't have hot peppers in Bastion?"

* * *

Jasmine wasn't sure when she and August had gone from being crewmates to being friends, but she knew the change had happened, because as she strolled through the streets of Haven with him, chatting and joking and laughing, she realized it was so easy, almost like how she felt with Chavi and Avi. When Jasmine had arrived at the Cultivation Center, they had taken a break from gardening, and Jerricho was teaching August how to braid dyed reeds into cords.

"Jas!" August had waved when he saw her approaching, holding the ugliest braid Jasmine had ever seen. "I'm learning crafts! I'm crafting!"

As they meandered through the city, she fidgeted with the ugly bracelet on her wrist, smiling fondly.

"You like the city?" she asked as they stopped at a railing, looking over the forest. The view wasn't as incredible as the one from the observation tower, which had given her a high enough perspective to see over the tops of trees and mountains all the way to the water beyond, but it was still unlike anything they'd ever seen in Bastion. From here, they could see the lush greenery that surrounded Haven like an ocean of sighing leaves, dancing in the wind. In the distance, they could see the slopes of mountains before their peaks reached up into a blanket of mist.

"It's beautiful," August said, gripping the railing. "I...never thought a city could be beautiful."

Jasmine nodded. "I didn't either." She couldn't see the eastern shore from here, but she knew it was out there, beyond the dense woods.

"What are you looking at?" August asked.

"If this place exists," Jasmine mused, "what else must be out there?"

"Well, Bastion is the only city that survived—" August started.

"I'm not sure I think that's true anymore," she cut him off. "Growing up, they taught us all desertwalkers were evil, but the Empress proved that wrong. They also taught us no one could survive outside of Bastion. And here are the people of Haven, surviving. Who else survived the Quakes? What are they like? What kinds of advancements have they made? What does their culture look like?" *How many assumptions have we made,* Jasmine added internally, *about the way that human existence is* supposed *to be?*

"Do you...do you think we should look for them?" August asked hesitantly, as though he thought it should be done, but was reluctant to do so himself.

"I'm not sure," Jasmine admitted. "I don't know if the right thing to do is to seek them out, or let them be. I just wonder...if they exist at all." What would that look like, though, to encounter a city that had developed entirely independent of Bastion? Would those people even want them there? And would the possibility of being unwelcome guests alone make it unethical to even try?

August frowned, following her gaze.

"I don't know," he said, forlorn in a way that she'd never heard from him before. No, not forlorn. Pensive. For the first time, she was witnessing August thinking, *really* thinking, about something he'd never considered before.

Jasmine laughed, but it felt hollow.

"It's almost silly," she said, "that we ever imagined we were the only survivors. What proof did we ever have? How narcissistic of us to ever think that we were important."

For once, August didn't say anything. It reminded Jasmine of the time the two of them had stood in silence in the dusts after their encounter with the sandheads. But this was so different, wasn't it? The dusts were hostile, and the people in the dusts were even worse. The island was not their enemy, and the people on the island had shown them nothing but kindness.

"There could be a million Bastions out there," August finally said, "and each of them would look totally different."

Jasmine nodded, and the two of them stood together in silence, imagining the millions of alternate Bastions that might exist miles away.

Interlude Six: Speedy

Again, Speedy stole out into the night, this time more confident he was not at risk of having his Essence torn from his shell. He would know if the avian could Siphon. The creature was no threat to him—unlike the monstrous version that had nearly killed Harvard and his companions back on the mainland.

Unlike the parasite, he had no way of tracking the winged rodent menace, so he wasted a great deal of time scouring the island in hopes of running into one. Finally, he came upon one rubbing its bulbous body in a puddle of water. The creature contentedly chirped, either unaware of Speedy's presence or uncaring.

What are you? Maybe this was not the best way to open a line of questioning, but Speedy had never interrogated an unfamiliar creature about its own existence before. The avian looked at him curiously, gave a defiant squawk, then continued poking at the grass with a menacing beak.

Speedy thought this incredibly rude. At least the vermin had been willing to speak to him. This creature flicked its scaly tail in what Speedy thought to be an irreverent, even sassy manner, patently ignoring him.

Respond when I speak to you, he commanded in his best impression of his father. Unfortunately, Speedy did not resemble his father much at all, save for the fractal markings on his shell. He certainly hadn't yet mastered his father's forceful voice.

Do you spurn me, you base creature? Speedy asked, again aiming for his father's diction, though even he thought this was a bit much.

The avian raised its rat-like head, scratched behind its ear with a talon, and Speedy wondered if that was another insult, intended to display the creature's feathered cloaca.

You insult me! Speedy declared, though he wasn't entirely certain that he had actually been insulted. He huffed. Or, at least, he tried to. He did not actually have the lungs required to huff, but it was a thing he'd noticed humans did when they got annoyed, and he had decided to adopt it because these days he found himself increasingly annoyed.

Useless, Speedy chided as he skittered off, but he wasn't entirely sure whether he was referring to the creature or himself.

CHAPTER THIRTEEN

Fitting In

Harvard wished he didn't love Haven as much as he did. It had only been ten days or so, but he had grown so accustomed to the communal meals and the friendly animals and the crisp air he kept forgetting that they were going to leave it all behind. Since they'd all agreed that their plan was to become citizens *before* pursuing the Relic, he hardly remembered the Relic existed at all.

It was a painfully beautiful day, refreshingly chilly compared to Bastion's sweltering heat, when Harvard and Chavi went out to the water pump to refill the cistern. Jasmine had marveled at it when she saw it for the first time—a belt with hundreds of little buckets attached to it, affixed to a crank so anyone could pull up fresh water from the river below. They'd started taking turns fetching water for the household, in effort to do anything they could to make Blaire's life easier.

Harvard pulled on Chavi's arm.

"What?" Chavi asked.

He pointed. Sax was already at the water pump. Chavi groaned. The Ivies had barely had any contact with their escort since they'd arrived in Haven. Sax had fallen in with the fishers—in fact, zey were living with one of them, last Harvard heard—so zey rarely had occasion to cross paths with the other four. The idea of encountering zem again after zey'd clearly made the intentional choice to drift apart from the Ivies made running into zem feel very, very awkward.

"Should we wait for zem to leave?" Harvard asked. Chavi was already pulling away from him, standing behind Sax to wait their turn at the pump. Harvard ran after them, really hoping they weren't about to start a fight for no reason.

"Haven't seen you in a while," Chavi said amiably—or, at least, as close to amiably as Harvard thought they could manage.

Sax shrugged without looking up from the water pump. "Well, you know. I've been busy."

"The *rest* of us have also been busy," Chavi said, stepping closer. "Figuring out how we're going to do what we were sent here to do."

Please stop please stop please stop, Harvard begged internally.

Sax refused to be distracted from zyr task. "Okay. Well. Good luck with that."

"You're not gonna *help*?" Chavi prompted.

"Why would I?" zey said absently.

"Um, because you need to get back to Bastion too?"

Sax let out an exasperated huff, then pulled zyr full bucket away from the pump, turning to face Chavi. "I'm not going back to Bastion. I'm staying here."

"What?" Harvard asked, his eyes wide. He didn't know that was *allowed*. "Why would you do that?"

Sax turned to him, and zyr expression softened a touch. "What is there back for me in Bastion?" zey asked.

"You really want to do that?" Harvard asked. "You don't have people you'd miss at home?"

Sax shook zyr head. "Bastion is a corrupt, dangerous place. I've always known that. Now I know there's something better. A place where—"

"You've been here for like a week!" Chavi interrupted. "I guarantee you it's just as bad as Bastion."

"Why are you all *defending* Bastion?" Sax laughed humorlessly. "You were scavengers! That city treated you like garbage! That city threw you to the crabs! If it weren't for the Union and the power of the Collective, I would have been just as bad off as you. And you actually think it's better than this place? Are any of these people poor? Are any of them struggling for food? Hell, are any of them even unhappy?"

Chavi glared at zem but said nothing. Harvard looked between the two of them, wondering if he should grab the bucket and start filling it, just to fill the silence. He hated how much sense Sax was making, and he wanted something else to occupy his mind. He couldn't afford to think like that.

"Face it," Sax finally said. "You can defend Bastion all you want, but that city will never love you. If anything, it'll use you up, and then it'll kill you."

"Well," Chavi said, "we have a friend to save. And we're not leaving her."

"I'm not asking you to. I'm just saying, my role in this is done."

"Okay, Sax," Harvard said hurriedly.

Chavi gave him a wide-eyed glance.

"It's what zey want," he whispered to them. They let out a frustrated breath, but said nothing.

"I've already spoken to the Council about it," Sax continued, jutting out zyr chin. "I've already got a companion, so they're doing my citizenship ceremony tomorrow. It's all decided. I'm going to be a Havener, whether you all like it or not."

Harvard nudged Chavi gently.

"Congratulations," they said, and Harvard liked to think that it wasn't sarcastic, but he couldn't be sure. "That's great news."

"I...hope you all will come?" Sax said, and for the first time since Harvard had known zem, zey looked a little sheepish.

"I think we have to," Chavi mumbled.

"We'll be there!" Harvard said, and surprised even himself by walking up to Sax and giving zem a hug. Zey made a surprised grunt, struggling to keep zyr water bucket from spilling.

"Thanks for getting us this far. And I think it's great that you've found a place here. I'm really happy for you."

He was, actually, and found himself a little irritated at Chavi for *not* sharing in that happiness. In fact, he was jealous of Sax. He would love to feel like he'd found a place for himself. He didn't feel that way in Bastion, and he didn't think he'd feel that way in Haven either.

Maybe he would, though. He'd been wrong before.

Harvard had expected anything with "ceremony" in the title to be a somber event, but it seemed that citizenship ceremonies in Haven were just an excuse for a party. Almost the whole city gathered in the Meeting House, and someone played an instrument Harvard couldn't see but it sounded like bells, and people were dancing and drinking and singing and genuinely celebrating welcoming a new member to the community. It was so nice Harvard found himself looking forward to his own citizenship ceremony, before remembering that he wasn't going to stay here, which sent a pang of regret into his stomach.

The ritual itself happened at dawn, as the sun peeked over the eastern shore. Rosenea stood at a podium and held up her hands for silence. Sax sat at a table on the dais next to her, hands folded. Zyr chosen companion, a lanky girl named Ziva whose former companion had passed away, sat beside zem with a hand on zyr back. Watching Rosenea and leaning into Ziva's touch, Sax allowed a subtle smile to crack zyr veneer. Harvard wasn't sure if he'd ever seen Sax smile before. It was nice.

"The Haven Principles teach us that change is all around us," Rosenea began. "When we change as people, we grow. Community facilitates that growth. In return, we lend our hands to help foster the community." She turned to Sax with a matronly grin. "Our community will grow tonight, and with that growth, our community becomes stronger."

She lifted a wine bottle delicately painted with vines and poured it into the wooden cup before Sax.

"A symbol," she said, "to show that you are one of us. That the blood of Haven runs through you as well."

Sax drank the blood of Haven, and became a part of its beating heart. Harvard's own heart ached with longing. He hoped one day, he could be come a part of something, too.

The afterparty was even more raucous. It seemed to Harvard that the only thing they cared about on Haven was surviving and having fun. Given that for most of Harvard's life he struggled with just the surviving part alone, the fact that fun was even a possibility was novel to him. The only person present not engaging in the festivities was Marcel, the security liaison, who was pacing around the border of the meeting house as though he anticipated a disaster at any moment.

Blaire weaved through the crowd to make way for the Ivies, helping them get to the bar.

"Get a drink!" he said. "You'll like it!"

Harvard hopped onto one of the stools at the bar to get a better look at the place. Bodies were packed so tightly together that he was already beginning to sweat in his woolly Haven attire. The air was thick with unfamiliar scents, woodsy and floral. Harvard spotted a stage at the back of the room, and on it the instrument he'd heard at the ceremony. It looked sort of like a piano, but instead of keys, it was made of planks of wood at different lengths.

"What's that?" he asked.

"That? A vibraphone," Blaire said, and then added eagerly, "Can you play it?"

Harvard wrung his hands. "I don't know."

If he were anywhere else, he wouldn't have had the courage to try. But they'd been in Haven a long time now, and no one had chastised him or criticized him or told him he was doing things wrong. So what was the harm in giving it a try?

He wove through the crowd and climbed up on the stage. He didn't think he could pluck the wooden planks with his fingers like keys on a piano, but he found some mallets hanging from a sack on the back end of the instrument. He turned the mallets over in his hands. He wouldn't be able to use these to play something as complex as what he'd played on the piano, but then again, with his broken fingers, he wouldn't have been able to do that anyway. With these he could at least pluck out a basic melody, maybe even some counterpoint if he got the hang of it.

He gave one of the wooden planks an experimental thump with one of the mallets, then another. The wood rang out with a satisfying, ethereal hum. He identified the location of each of the notes, surprised to find that a scale in Haven was the same as in Bastion. *Maybe music is universal,* he thought. Once he got used to the instrument, he started to play a simple melody—a nursery rhyme about the Creatures of Ruin, the first song he'd ever learned to play on the piano.

It was an uncanny experience to hear such a familiar melody coming from such an alien instrument. But it was an instrument that he had *never played,* and here he was, making music! He wasn't sure if he'd ever been good at something that quickly. He smiled, speeding up his tempo, his pulse matching the rhythm of the song. His mind achieved that pleasant emptiness, allowing the music to flow through him without thought, without intention. The world melted away. Nothing was left but Harvard and a song.

He struck a wrong note.

The discordance made him dizzy. Suddenly he was a child hiding in the bathroom of a concert hall.

His mother strode in and banged on the door.

"What was that?" she demanded.

"I'm sorry!" he cried, wiping tears away with the heel of his hand. "I messed up, and then, then I got nervous, and, and I started to get shaky and I tried to stop but it only made it worse—"

"You ran away!" she chided. "I saw it. We all saw it."

The shame washed over him like a duststorm. He hugged himself tighter. "I'm sorry!"

She banged on the door so hard it rattled in its hinges. "You open this door right now, Ronan!"

He cowered. She wouldn't hurt him. He knew that she wouldn't hurt him. But...there was always a part of him that worried she wanted to. He took a shaky breath and slid the lock open. His mother towered over him, her hands on her hips. He'd never felt so small in his whole life. And that's what he was destined to be, wasn't he? Small. Always small.

"A Bell does not run away."

"I'm sorry," he said again, this time in a chastened whisper.

"If you can't do something well..." She shook her head. "There's no point doing it at all. There's no reason for me to continue paying for these piano lessons if you can't perform."

His stomach dropped. "But I like playing piano!" Ronan protested. "I'm good at it! I promise!" Music was everything to him. It was all he had.

His mother raised an eyebrow. "Can you prove it?"

He cringed, then shook his head solemnly. He knew he couldn't.

"Well, keep going!"

Chavi's voice pulled him out of his memory. He turned to see that the rest of the Ivies and Blaire were standing at the foot of the stage, watching him almost reverently. In fact, he realized the whole tavern had quieted a little to listen to him play. He started to shake, but only a little.

That familiar shame squirmed in his stomach. "I messed it up," he whispered.

"Sounded fine to me," Chavi shrugged, beaming. "Keep going!"

Harvard turned back to the vibraphone, willing himself to forget that people were watching him. It didn't work. He took a deep breath, and tried a different approach. He knew he was going to mess it up. He'd never played the thing before, and he could hardly expect himself to play perfectly with everyone watching him. Chavi didn't care if he made a mistake, so he shouldn't care either.

Oddly enough, his trembling went *down*.

He laid the mallet against the plank and started to play again. People started to cheer—cheer for *him*—and he found himself smiling. Chavi went to get them drinks, August started dancing with some of the people in the crowd, and Jasmine disappeared into the crush of people.

The song was clumsy and halting and full of errors that made Harvard cringe, but no one seemed to notice. They were too busy drinking and dancing and cheering him on. At some point, he even heard Chavi lean into one of the Haveners and drunkenly shout, "That's my boyfriend!"

He wasn't sure how long he played for, but after a few songs he found himself sweating and tired. He didn't realize how exhausting the performance would be—he hadn't performed anything since he'd told stories to the children at the Shack. This actually felt strangely similar; he was performing for a group of people that didn't care about the quality of the performance, only that he was giving them something to listen to.

As he stepped off the stage to find Chavi, a girl with leaves braided into her blond hair stepped in his path.

"That was incredible!" she said, and her smile was so warm and genuine that Harvard melted a little. She held out her hand for him to take. He shook it gingerly.

"I'm Ira," she said. "And I lead the Music House."

"The what?" Harvard asked.

"It's right by the Library!" she explained. "We're the ones in charge of Haven's music."

"That's—that's a job? To play music?" Harvard asked. The only people he'd ever seen make a job of playing music were street performers in Bastion, and he'd figured they only did that because they couldn't get something better. Music was nice and all, but in Bastion it wasn't something that anyone should aspire to, and certainly not something one could do as a career.

Ira laughed. "Of course it is! And I hear you don't have a choring track yet. Would you like to join?"

His heart leapt. "I—um—yes! That sounds wonderful!" Harvard stammered.

"Great! I'll see you there tomorrow, then!" Ira gave him another warm smile and disappeared back into the crowd, like a friendly apparition. When he finally managed to locate Chavi by the bar, they pulled him into a hug so tight it lifted his feet off the ground.

"You did great up there!" they said.

"Thanks," Harvard said, and to his surprise, he wasn't even blushing. He *had* done great up there, hadn't he? That was just a fact. "I just got invited to do music. Like, as my job."

"That's great!" Chavi released him and summoned someone behind the bar to bring drinks.

"You know what's nice about Haven?" Harvard said, scanning the crowd. "People are allowed to just have a good time. In Bastion you have to be worth something. And you have to prove that you're worth something. But here, as long as you care for everyone and you do your work, you can do whatever you want. You can be whatever you want. It's not like that in Bastion."

He grimaced the moment he said it, fearing that he'd provoke Chavi's defensive side if he spoke ill of their home city. Instead, they nodded, lifted their wooden mug. "That's like what my mom always told me."

"What?" Harvard cocked his head. It was the first time since they'd arrived that Chavi had actually agreed with criticism of Bastion.

"She said that in Bastion there were all these rules that we were supposed to follow, about how we were supposed to live. And that it was all fake, but most people don't want to admit it's fake, so they just go along with it. She called it our little secret." They looked at him and grinned. "So now I guess you're in on the secret too."

A pleasant ache blossomed in Harvard's chest. It wasn't really a "secret" like Chavi said it was, but still, he had just entered into some kind of special family bond. He remembered what Rivka had told him at that first dinner—that he could be part of the Chakrabarti family. Maybe he really could. He used to think no one would ever welcome him into their family, but here in Haven, everyone seemed to accept him. They seemed to *want* him, even.

"It would be nice, to actually become a citizen here," Harvard said. "I bet the ceremony will be fun, at least." Again, he chastised himself for saying something that he was sure would ruin the moment. Chavi's smile faltered, but didn't disappear entirely.

"I know," they said, eyes distant.

"You know?"

"Look, don't tell anyone I said this," Chavi said, leaning in conspiratorially, "especially not Sax. But it's not so bad. I just..." they huffed quietly, searching for words. "Do you know how often people told me I was a waste of space when I was growing up?"

Harvard's brow knit. "I...no?"

"A lot. And every time someone talks about how perfect it is here...it makes me feel like my whole life has been a waste. All because I was born in the wrong place. And it doesn't feel good." They took a swig of their wine.

Harvard bit his lip, uncertain how he was supposed to respond to that. "Well...I don't think you're a waste," he tried. Apparently, this was the right thing to say, because Chavi laughed.

"Well, thanks for that," they said, handing him their mug. "Want some?"

Harvard took a tentative sip, and to his surprise, it was warm. It was full of leaves and specks of spices, and it smelled like cinnamon, like warm apple cider, but he knew that the plants that made this wine were real plants grown in the actual ground. He downed the whole mug, and he slammed it down on the bar to find Chavi gawking at him.

"Damn! Okay! Want another?"

Harvard felt warm from his chest to the tips of his fingers, and sure, maybe it was the fact that he'd just downed a mug of wine—or it was because Chavi's approval was so delicious, and it was what he'd been craving ever since...well, ever since he'd met them, to be perfectly honest.

"I wanna try the ceremony wine!" Harvard declared, looking up at the painted bottles above the bar.

Chavi chuckled. "I think they're saving it for the ceremony."

Harvard leaned in conspiratorially. "Let's steal it!" he hissed, surprising even himself. He felt feral, out of control. And he *loved* it.

Chavi's eyes widened. "Yeah!" they agreed. "Let's steal it!"

"I think I can sneak behind the bar," Harvard said, peering at Marcel to see if he was looking their way, "but I need you to distract the servers for me. Then we run?"

"Oh yeah," Chavi said. "I can be very distracting."

* * *

Harvard had forgotten what a simple pleasure it was to *run*. More importantly, to have a reason to run wasn't just staying alive. The cool night air kissed his skin, and though he had to admit he was a lot faster when he wasn't staggering, he decided the pleasant buzz in his brain and looseness of his limbs were absolutely worth it.

Chavi caught up to him, placing a hand on his back as they ushered him behind a hut. Harvard leaned against the wall, panting. Chavi joined him, and they shared a breathless, smiling moment, hearts racing. Harvard lifted the wine bottle from where he'd concealed it in his cloak.

"Got it," he breathed, and Chavi laughed, taking the bottle from him and pulling the cork. They took a swig.

"Founders, it actually is good," they said, then handed it back to him. Harvard shook his head. "You'll like this. Trust me."

And he did trust Chavi, so he accepted the bottle and took a sip. His tongue burned with an explosion of fruit flavors, but not an unpleasant one. Maybe he did like wine after all. The trick, he realized, was to have more of it. The more he had, the better it tasted. Chavi sank to the ground, leaning against the back of the hut. Harvard joined them, handing the bottle back as he wiped wine from his mouth with the back of his hand.

"Well?" Chavi asked.

"Worth it," Harvard smiled. He realized suddenly that he wasn't shaking at all. He felt utterly and completely calm. More than calm. He was happy. Maybe alcohol was good for him.

"You know, it's been a long time since I stole anything," he said. "I forgot how good it feels. I used to do it all the time." He remembered those times...fondly. Strange. He never expected to be fond of his childhood. He thought childhood fondness was for people who'd grown up with family and friends and home where they felt happy. Not him.

Chavi nearly spit out the wine mid-sip.

"You used to steal? All the time?" They sounded impressed, and Harvard swelled with pride. He nodded, beaming.

"I used to take things from my parents when they weren't looking. I used to steal my mom's jewelry and give it to the birds."

Chavi laughed.

"That's great. I never would have guessed."

Harvard shrugged like it was no big deal, but actually it was a big deal. It was a huge deal. Chavi thought he was cool, and that was the biggest deal Harvard could imagine.

"I used to swipe stuff too, at school. Like, there was this teacher who just hated me—every time she put down her glasses, I'd hide them. She'd have to stop the whole lesson to find them again. I think she knew it was me, but she had no proof, so she couldn't do anything about it. Looking back, it was kinda mean. But, I was a kid so..."

Harvard giggled harder than he should have, wine dribbling down his chin. He'd never had enough wine to feel the effects of alcohol, but he figured he must be feeling it now. His whole body was warm all over, and the world sloshed around lazily, and also Chavi was the most beautiful thing he'd ever seen—that wasn't really new, but the wine definitely enhanced the effect.

"After I ran away," he said, scooting up next to them so their bodies were touching, "I used to steal food where I could get it. I lived with some other kids and we liked to help each other out that way." He'd never told Chavi about the Shack. In fact, he'd never mentioned it aloud to anyone. But the words just spilled out.

"You were feeding the other kids?" Chavi asked, and maybe this time more concerned than impressed—Harvard couldn't really tell—but he continued because he couldn't stop himself.

"It was...I mean, it was fun, honestly. I knew I could get in trouble, but when I was running away, I felt like no one could stop me. I felt—"

"Free?" Chavi guessed.

"Yeah," Harvard said, leaning back. "I felt free. And I felt useful. And, like, sometimes, I would get just so sad about my life and the world and everything, and it was just like...like..."

"A little way to fight back," Chavi said. Harvard nodded. They understood it. They understood *him*.

He took a swig of wine. "I haven't felt free in a long time," he added, "but I feel free right now."

Suddenly Chavi's hands were cupping his face, and their lips were on his and their tongue darted into his mouth, and Harvard made no protest. He wrapped his arms around them, wine bottle still clutched in one hand. It was all a little bit messy and drunken, but Harvard didn't care because he ran his fingers through Chavi's hair and realized it felt different when he was drinking wine, and he wondered if the rest of their body did too. He decided that he would find out.

* * *

Giggling and tripping over brambles, hands tightly clasped, the two of them stumbled through the woods. Somewhere in the back of Chavi's mind, they were vaguely aware of the fact that this was a bad idea, but they had plenty of practice silencing that part of their consciousness.

They emerged from the woods at an isolated section of beach, the rocky shore stretched out in front of them, the ocean lit by the rising sun.

"This is perfect!" he cried, running up to the water's edge as he pulled off his shirt. Chavi followed behind, staring out into the watery expanse, and Harvard finished stripping and dove into the water. He stood, waist deep in the ocean, and turned back to Chavi, who still stood a few strides away from the water's edge.

He looked at them expectantly. "Are you coming?" he asked.

Chavi didn't answer. They just looked out at the water that seemed to go on forever and ever.

"It's so...big," they said.

"Well, sure!" Harvard said. "It's the same size as when we were sailing."

Chavi grimaced. "Yeah, but...then we were in the middle of it. We didn't have a choice. It was just like the desert, then. This..." they were at a loss for words. When they were on the boat, they were stuck in the center of the ocean. Now they had the opportunity to turn away, which was becoming a tantalizing thought. They took a step back, toward the safety of the woods.

"I think..." they said, "I think I'm just gonna stay here, okay? You swim. I'll watch."

Harvard's face fell.

"The whole point was that we were gonna go swimming together," he said.

Chavi's stomach twisted. They hated to disappoint Harvard, but they were beginning to think that maybe they hated the ocean more. "I changed my mind."

It's so vast, they thought. How did Sax get used to it? How does anyone get used to the vastness of the ocean?

Harvard looked out at the open sea, then back to Chavi. He stepped toward them, splashing, and Chavi shied away a little for fear of getting wet. Harvard extended a hand.

"'I won't make you do anything you don't want to do," he said, "but I'd like you to just put your feet in. For me."

Chavi's gaze was still fixed in the expanse of water behind Harvard. He used his outstretched hand to gently hold their chin and face them toward him. They looked in his eyes, and realized they were almost the same grey-green-blue as the ocean had been from Sax's boat. The ocean itself was intimidating, but the two little oceans on Harvard's face were not.

Slowly, they took off their shoes and laid them aside. They took Harvard's hand. And with a sharp intake of breath, they stepped into the water.

Chavi cringed at the sudden cold, maintaining Harvard's hand but leaning away from the water that lapped at their feet. They stayed like that for a moment, face scrunched up in discomfort, as they got used to the sensation.

"It's so cold," they said.

"You get used to it."

"And it's always...moving." They looked down at the little waves washing over their feet. "It's like it's...an animal."

"I've always liked that about the ocean," Harvard said. "It has a rhythm of its own. I've always thought of it as a heartbeat."

Chavi's head snapped up.

"Always?" they asked. "What do you mean 'always?'"

"When I was little."

"Did you...did you see the ocean when you were little?" Chavi didn't understand how that was possible. From most of the city, all you could see looking east was the elevated platform of Upper Bastion.

Harvard looked away abruptly, toward the beach that stretched out before him.

"No," he said. "But...I always imagined it." Ah, that explained it. Chavi could picture a little Harvard, sequestered in his parents' home, dreaming of the ocean. Drawing it, maybe. The two stood there for a little longer, hands clasped, until Chavi inched a little closer.

"I'll get my pants wet," they said.

"You can take them off!" Harvard laughed. "There's no one around."

"Right. Yeah. Totally." Feeling stupid for not considering that, they stepped back and pulled off their pants. "Do you, uh, keep your underwear on?"

"Whatever you like!"

"Okay. I just wasn't sure, like, what the rules are. For swimming in the ocean."

Harvard laughed. "There are no rules. It's the ocean."

Chavi took Harvard's hand again, and this time they summoned the courage to stand next to him, where the water was up to their knees. They shuddered.

"This is nice," they said, and sort of meant it.

"It is," Harvard said, and they knew he meant it wholeheartedly. He stepped forward, pulling them along. Soon they were far enough that when the waves came, they were both lifted off their feet. Chavi laughed, but they weren't sure if it was a sound borne of joy or fear. Probably both. It really was like an animal—one that could scoop you up and put you down wherever it pleased. Or devour you, like it had Sax's boat. They gripped Harvard's hand tighter.

"Are you okay?" he asked.

"Yeah, um...just don't let me go, okay?" they said shakily.

Harvard smiled.

"Of course."

The setting sun lit his hair like a beacon, and he seemed to glow, and Chavi wasn't sure if they'd ever seen anything so beautiful in their life.

"You look..." they started, searching for the right word. Otherworldly. Magical. Divine. "Like an angel."

Harvard laughed. "An angel?" he asked. Chavi nodded.

"You know, like Jasmine was talking about. The little gods. That's you."

"What does an angel look like?"

Chavi shrugged.

"Like you, probably."

"What if we stay?" Harvard asked abruptly, grasping their arm. "I mean, what's in Bastion for us anyway? We were on the verge of starving, we're still criminals, the Commission is probably still after us for our debt...we could make a new life here. We could really be Haveners. You and me. We could...we could run away!"

Chavi's smile faltered. Despite their reservations about Haven, it was a tantalizing thought. To run away with Harvard, and leave everything behind. But what would they have to sacrifice?

"What about Avi?" they asked.

"We'll send Jas and August back to make sure she's okay," Harvard reasoned. "And we could stay here! And...*reinvent* ourselves. And—"

"What about my mom?" Chavi cut in. Founders, they would love to reinvent themself. Just fade away into nothing and start anew. But they wouldn't—*couldn't*—abandon their mother, and they hated to be in a position where they had to choose her over Harvard.

He must have read their discomfort on their face, because he withdrew, brows creased. "I—I'm sorry. Did I upset you?"

"No, no, I mean—I get it. It's nice to think about. But, I mean, we have to go back to Bastion."

"Right. No, of course," he backtracked hastily, reddening. *I've ruined it,* Chavi thought. *We were having such a nice time, and I crushed him, and ruined it. Just like I ruin everything.* "I wasn't being serious, obviously. I was just saying...it's nice to think about."

"It is nice to think about," Chavi agreed, but they couldn't mean it, and they suspected Harvard could tell.

A scream from the forest pierced the air.

It cut off abruptly.

"What was that?" Harvard asked, but Chavi was already wading toward the shore to investigate. They both threw on their clothes without bothering to dry off and went in search of the source of the sound.

"Do you think someone's hurt?" Harvard asked as they pushed through the underbrush.

"I don't know," Chavi said, "but that definitely sounded like a person. I think—"

They cut themself off when the two of them stumbled across the body.

Harvard yelped, covering his hand with his mouth. Chavi had never seen a dead body—at least, not a fresh one—but they were pretty sure it was supposed to take some time to grow cold and pale. This woman's skin was already as white as milk, her eyes staring vacantly up at the sky, her body twisted as though she had been in the middle of a fight and given up halfway through.

"Abigail," Harvard murmured. "I...know her. She was feeding a lamb I—" He inhaled sharply. "I named it Floppy."

Chavi knelt down to inspect the body, placing a hand on her neck.

"Is she dead?" Harvard whispered, but the answer was clear. The shell of a person they saw in front of them was so vacant that he could hardly imagine she was once a living, breathing woman.

Gingerly, turning the dead woman's head, Chavi found what they were dreading—puncture wounds, still dripping blood onto the forest floor. Puncture wounds almost identical to the ones that were still healing on their own neck.

Before either of them had a chance to speak, Marcel and his security retinue came charging through the underbrush. Chavi didn't have time to panic, only to think, *oh fuck this looks bad.* Marcel took only a second to take in Chavi kneeling beside Abigail's corpse before grabbing them by the arm and hauling them up.

"What did you do?" he demanded, a hand discreetly placed on the hilt of his knife, partially covered by his cloak.

"Me?" Chavi asked. "I didn't do anything! We found her like this."

Marcel glanced at Harvard, who still stood a few paces back, and he looked as though he were puzzling something out.

"Then what were you two doing down here?" he demanded. "Everyone else is still at the meeting house."

"Are you serious? You're thinking about the *party* right now? This woman needs help!" She didn't, of course. She was beyond helping.

"Lyle," Marcel commanded to the boy next to him, another security worker by the looks of it, about Marcel's age. "Go check the body."

Lyle crouched down next to Abigail the way that Chavi had, inspecting the bleeding holes in her neck. Chavi watched, and the woman's vacant eyes seemed to seek them out. *I didn't do this*, they thought, but the eyes watched them anyway. Soulless.

"Procyon," Lyle confirmed, standing.

Chavi whirled on Marcel. "See? We couldn't have anything to do with that!"

"We haven't had a procyon attack in years," Marcel said. "They almost always stay away from people, and especially people in groups."

Chavi laughed, and the sound was filled with so much anger that they scared themself. Harvard winced.

"I don't understand why you're acting like this is my fault," they said. "Ever since we got here, you've been looking for a reason to kick us out. What's your problem with me and my friends?"

"Oh, I don't have a problem with your friends," Marcel said. His stance shifted, like he was getting ready to fight. Well, that was just fine with Chavi. "I have a problem with *you*. Just you."

"Why?" Chavi demanded.

"It is my *job* to be suspicious of outsiders," He hissed, closing the distance between them. "Until they prove they can be one of us. Your friends, they're starting to convince me, but you're not even *trying*. There is no place for someone like you on Haven," Marcel concluded.

Chavi wasn't sure what they would have done next if Harvard hadn't stepped in between them.

"Abigail was my friend," he said. "She let me name a lamb. She was kind to me. I can't stand to see her like this. Can we take care of her, please?"

Marcel's face softened a little, and his shoulders dropped.

"Fine," he said. "Lyle, help me with the body. Everyone else...I think we can take the rest of the evening off."

* * *

The funeral was the first truly somber event that Harvard attended on Haven. It was held that night, by the meeting house. The body was burned, and the ashes cast over the railing, into the darkness of the forest. Abigail's companion gave a tearful eulogy, and the rest of the city listened in reverent silence.

Harvard was surprised at how quickly the city was able to organize itself for the service.

"They don't have a morgue," Jasmine explained, "so they have to dispose of bodies quickly."

With Abigail died any chance the Ivies had of truly belonging here. Even though they had nothing to do with the death, people would associate them with it, would blame them for it.

But what if they did have something to do with it? What if Speedy was right about Chavi being some kind of anomaly? Had that brought the creature to Haven?

It had been a lovely dream, imagining that the Ivies could fit in here. But it was time to wake up. They had a job to do, and that job involved betraying the trust of everyone in the city. They would find no welcome here.

That night, Harvard had his usual evening debrief with Speedy in the privacy of their closet, while Chavi explained the events of the days to the rest of the Ivies, Blaire, and Sylvania in the main room.

"So since the procyon also attacked Abigail, that must mean nothing's wrong with Chavi, right? This must mean that they're normal."

Not entirely, no.

"Why not?" Harvard asked. He had been hoping for a simple answer, and a silver lining to Abigail's sudden death.

Because what happened to Abigail is different.

"How can you tell?"

I can just tell. To eat a creature's life is not the same as to eat a creature's Essence. Abigail's death was abrupt but painless.

"What's the difference?"

Allow me a metaphor. Imagine a stream—

Harvard frowned. "No more stream metaphors, please."

As you wish, Harvard. But my point is, no, this is not proof that Chavi is "normal" as you say. In fact, this is only more evidence that something about them is decidedly…off.

Harvard could hear their voice in the other room, muffled through the wall. He didn't want to imagine that something about his partner was "off." He was finally truly getting to know them, understand them, and if they were going through some kind of…transformation, would it change who they were? Speedy could be wrong, right? But his instincts told him that Speedy must be onto something, even though he didn't want to admit it.

* * *

Chavi awoke to Harvard shaking them.

"Hm?" Chavi opened one eye. Harvard's head was resting on their chest, and their arms were wrapped around him. He gestured to the doorway, where Blaire was peering in through the doorway.

"Chavi! Hi!" he said, practically vibrating with nervous energy. He had rings beneath his eyes, and his hair unkempt and tangled. "Rosenea is here. She, uh, she wants to talk to you."

Chavi groaned, their head lolling to the side.

"I'm guessing you…know what this is about?" Blaire asked, and judging by his edginess, he did too.

"Maybe. Kind of. I don't know." They gently moved Harvard aside so they could stand up and begin dressing. Blaire gave an embarrassed squeak and disappeared from the doorway.

"You think you're in trouble for last night?" Harvard asked from where he lay on the mattress.

Chavi shrugged, pulling on a shirt.

"Are you worried?" Harvard asked.

Yes, Chavi thought. *I might have quaked up our chances of getting accepted here, which in turn quakes up our chances of stealing from them, which in turn quakes up our ability to save Avi.* But if Chavi was worried, then Harvard would be worried, and they didn't want that. They only shrugged again.

Once they were halfway presentable, they stepped out the door into the early-winter sun. Before Haven, Chavi hadn't known that winters were supposed to be cold. Now they knew that winter sucked. Rosenea was waiting for them, hands clasped, silver hair tied into a braid that cascaded over her scarlet cloak.

"What is this about?" Chavi asked. Rosenea smiled, but her smile was tight and unreadable.

"I prefer to wait to discuss business until we reach my office," she said, then gestured for Chavi to lead the way toward the Meeting House. Chavi moved ahead of her, warily. They walked in silence for a moment.

"Lovely weather we're having, no?" she asked.

"It's quaking cold," Chavi said. They hadn't meant it as a complaint, more as an observation, but it came out more bitter than they intended.

Rosenea nodded. "Well, it's pretty nice weather for us," she said.

Chavi grunted noncommittally. They could feel Rosenea's eyes dart toward them.

"Are you not enjoying your time here, Chavi?" she asked.

"I thought you said we weren't going to talk about business until we got to your office."

"We're not talking about business," she said levelly. "I'm just asking you if you enjoy Haven."

"Haven is great," Chavi said, and they meant it, but they knew they didn't sound it. It *was* great. It just wasn't great for *them*. Rosenea seemed satisfied, though, and she stayed silent for the rest of the walk. She led them up the wooden stairs of the Meeting House to her office. It was a round room atop the building that Chavi guessed must have been hollowed out of a much larger tree. It had large circular windows carved out to view the city from every angle, though it was high enough that much of the vista was blocked by tree branches. Chavi chose a chair around the table in the center. It looked like it had been made of a wide tree stump. Rosenea stood across from them.

"It has come to my attention," Rosenea said, "that you have been having some trouble fitting in with the Haven community."

Chavi tried to remain impassive, and hoped Rosenea couldn't tell that their heart was hammering. What would she do to them if there was no "role" for them here? Would she really have them disposed of? The memory of their conversation with Jas the other night was all too salient. Haven presented itself as a paradise, but based on what Sylvania had said, dissenters were liable to disappear. They regretted everything they'd said to Marcel last night. But in that moment, all that had mattered was Harvard. Harvard and...that *thing*. The procyon scared them far more than they wanted anyone to know.

"I'm trying," they said. "It just seems like people around here don't like me very much."

Rosenea laughed good-naturedly. "Don't let Marcel fool you," she said. "He's very protective of this place and these people. He's wary of outsiders, but that's only because he cares."

Chavi didn't believe this, but they thought better of protesting. They glanced out one of the wide windows into the swaying leaves.

"Your friends, it seems, have all found roles that suit them," Rosenea continued. "Sax with the fishers, August with the gardeners, Jasmine with the record-keepers, and Harvard with the bards. Strange, then, that we've found nothing for you."

Chavi shrugged, but they guessed that Rosenea could see past it. They sank into a deep well of shame, and suddenly this meeting felt discomfortingly close to the days when they were summoned to the principal's office at the Academy. During their school years, they could never figure out who they were supposed to be, and it ate at them. At least out in the dusts, they understood their job.

"It's my understanding that back in Bastion, you all were a scavenging crew? Minus Sax."

Chavi nodded.

"And on that scavenging crew, you were the captain?"

Chavi turned to face her.

"How did you know that?" they asked. Rosenea gestured to their wrist, and Chavi saw that they still wore their captain's band.

"We may be an old city," she said, "but we still remember a few things about Bastion. I know what that thing means. You would not be the first scavengers to come here seeking asylum from the Commission."

Chavi opened their mouth to ask who else had once been a scavenger, but before they could get the question out, Rosenea continued, "Chavi, I'd like to encourage you to join the Haven leadership track."

Chavi's mouth remained open. Rosenea waited, smiling.

"What?" they finally asked.

"You kept your team alive out in the dusts. I know enough about that place to know that that counts for something."

"I don't—I mean, if anyone of us is a leader, it's Jasmine. She was always the smart one."

"You know," Rosenea said, "I've noticed a trend in the groups of scavengers that have joined our community over the years. The captain was never the one making most of the decisions, and not even the one that the team deferred to. You could tell who was the captain even without the band because they were the one with the most obvious protective instincts over the crew. Because they were the one who bore the responsibility. And often, they had grown so used to that responsibility that they sought it out again."

Chavi fiddled with the captain's band. They wondered if they missed being a captain. They never thought they would miss anything about being a scavenger, but perhaps Rosenea was right. Perhaps they missed being in charge, feeling like people depended on them. They could *be* Yale again. Confident, collected Yale.

"I'm...I'm touched that you think I'd be good at leadership," they said, "but after last night, I don't think that anyone would accept me. The people here just don't like me."

"Actually, Chavi"—Rosenea walked around the table to their seat, and sat daintily on the edge—"I suggest this because you were recommended to me."

"Recommended?" Chavi's head snapped up.

Rosenea nodded. "Three different people on separate occasions have encouraged me to invite you into the leadership track. And to be honest, I agree with them. You care about your friends, and I can see that. I like to imagine what you could be if you cared about Haven with the same passion. Besides, a variety of perspectives is important for any governing body. And your perspective is certainly a unique one."

Chavi stared forward, savoring the image of themself as a leader. Could they really care for Haven the same way they cared for the Ivies, defend the city with the same ferocity that Marcel did? Yes. They could. If—

What were they thinking? None of this mattered. They weren't going to stay here. This was all fake, all for show. As long as they didn't get kicked off the island or killed, none of that mattered.

"Sure," they said, looking back up at Rosenea. "I'd like to join Haven leadership."

"Wonderful," Rosenea held out a hand, and Chavi shook it. "We'll put you on the training track within the next few days. You do have a lot to learn, I'm afraid, but after a few years, you'll be on the Council."

"I'm a quick learner," Chavi lied, but they figured as far as their lies went, that one was only a drop in the ocean.

Interlude Seven: Speedy

While the humans were off doing human things (Speedy did not know what they got up to regularly and had no desire to find out) he took a moment to sequester his corporeal form in the safety of Harvard's room so that he could drop into the Essence stream. There he could meet his father and report back as instructed.

His consciousness dipped down to a level humans could not fathom, and he was surrounded by the warmth of his kind, brushing gently against the awareness of their presence.

Your report is late, his father chided. *What have you learned?*

A great many things! Speedy informed him eagerly. *I learned of snow. I saw a fish. I learned many interesting words by listening to August.*

Fool child! his father boomed. *What of your purpose? What have you learned that is pertinent to us?*

Were he in his physical form, Speedy would give a deferential bow. *Well, my purpose has not yet proved to be relevant as of yet, but I have learned much of the creatures beyond the mainland.*

Explain.

The ancient parasite lives on the island.

Skrack was silent for a long moment. *I feared this was the case.*

You knew?

I doubted. But a creature like that is not easily eradicated.

This should not have stung. Skrack was only doing his duty as guardian to the Empress Myrk, and Speedy was only doing his duty as a Guardian-To-Be. It did sting, though, because his father had knowingly sent him into the domain of a creature that would drink his very lifeforce, and given him no word of warning. It was only to be expected of him, but did his father bear him no love? Or, rather, was his faith in Speedy his manner of showing his affection?

I spoke with it, Speedy said, hoping to prove his bravery.

Good, his father said, and Speedy felt as though he could burst from his shell with pride. *What have you learned?*

From the parasite I gathered very little. Few of their kind remain. Without access to Essence, they barely have enough sustenance to keep their kind alive. Soon I expect they shall be extinct. Speedy decided he need not mention that the temptation of Essence had drawn the parasite out of hiding, resulting in an untimely human death. But surely that wasn't *his* fault, was it? So, no need to report it.

Skrack gave a skeptical click. *For many years with thought we had eradicated that threat. A shame to learn some managed to elude us.*

They shall soon be dead, Speedy assured him. *Except...*

Except?

The parasite told me that one of its kind had been taken by humans. I do not know if it spoke true, but it is possible that one such beast exists in the city?

Doubtful. This was boasting, a tactic to frighten you. There is no threat to our kind present on the Southwest Plains. That is certain. What else have you discovered?

I spoke to the intruder! Speedy reported.

Intruder?

The creature that was wrong, he explained. *The one that did not belong. The non-desertwalker that trespassed on our plains.*

You spoke to it?

Yes, but it ignored me.

Fool child! The beast is not Essenced.

Oh. Speedy *was* a fool. He should have known. His connection to the Essence was still new and fragile. He did not yet fully understand it— though he doubted any of his kind truly did. Still, he should have sensed that there was no tether between him and the flying rodent. It was only a mindless animal, no different from a baby or a pseudocrab.

I am sorry, father. I now see I was in error. I will do better.

See that you do. I did not send you on this quest so that you could muck about, playing with rodents.

You did not, Speedy said, chastened.

Or have you forgotten your purpose?

Were he in his physical form, he would have lifted his claws in a gesture of supplication and shame. *I have not.*

Then see to it that you have something new to report to me next time. The situation worsens, and somehow I manage to collect more information than you, my sole scout.

I apologize, Father.

None of your groveling. Off with you now.

Speedy summoned himself back to his own diminutive body, relieved to have his being contained again in the confines of chitin.

CHAPTER FOURTEEN

Holy War

"Whoa," Harvard breathed, taking in the suspended skeletons. "This is amazing!" He had just gotten off work at the Music House. He'd tried out some of their instruments, none of them things that they had in Bastion. Everyone there had been so welcoming and encouraging, especially Ira, who seemed particularly proud that she had "discovered" him. She'd had to leave early for a meeting with leadership that she seemed pretty excited about, so he had some time to go visit Jasmine at the Library.

"I'm glad you like it," Sylvania smiled with a bit of self-satisfaction. Harvard glanced at Jasmine, and saw she was watching Sylvania, beaming.

"Is there anything in the library about the Relic?" Harvard asked.

Jasmine's smile faded. "Harvard, I don't think they like to talk about—"

"No, it's okay," Sylvania said. "Before the Haven Principles were established, a few Haveners did try and study it. Their work is off limits, of course."

"What kind of work?" Harvard asked.

"I...I don't really know," Sylvania said, stroking her braid. "I don't ask those types of questions."

Harvard cocked his head. He didn't understand why such a curious person would *avoid* asking questions.

"You probably shouldn't be asking either, Harvard," Jasmine chided, but he could tell that she was secretly pleased. It felt good to impress Jasmine. Seeing a little smile on her face made him feel like he'd won a medal. He knew she was just being super careful about what she said so she didn't ruin anything before the citizenship ceremony the following night.

"So—observation tower?" Sylvania asked.

"Harvard, you're going to love this," Jasmine gestured for Harvard to follow them. They led him up a wooden spiral staircase and—

Harvard gasped.

"I take back what I said before," he murmured, looking out over the whole island, painted pink and orange in the glow of the sunset, "*this* is actually way more amazing."

"Do you think you could map it?" Jasmine asked.

"Yes!" Harvard cried, positively giddy at the prospect of doing something useful. "Yes, I'd love to! Jasmine, may I have your notebook?"

"Of course," she handed him the book. "I thought you'd like it."

"This is incredible," Harvard indicated the tower itself. "What do you use it for?"

"We used to use it as a beacon, to signal to newcomers," Sylvania explained. "Haven used to welcome everyone."

"That was before—" Jasmine started.

"Yes."

Harvard paused his sketch. He didn't fully understand what it was that had happened in Haven before they arrived. Something bad, he knew. But the Haveners wouldn't talk about the outsiders that had somehow betrayed them.

"What do you mean by everyone?" it occurred to him to ask. "I mean, isn't it just people from Bastion?"

"Well, not everyone is from Bastion," Sylvania said.

"What? Where else could they be from?"

Sylvania laughed. "It's a big world out there, you know!"

Harvard looked up at Jasmine expectantly, but he could tell her thoughts were occupied. She looked out at the ocean, toward Bastion, and he wondered what she was thinking. Then he saw her eyes land again on Sylvania, and he knew exactly what she was thinking. He gingerly touched her hand, and they shared a silent truth. It would be lovely to stay here. But they couldn't.

"Thank you for taking us both up here," she said.

"Of course," Sylvania said.

As the three descended the steps, Sylvania and Jasmine struck up a conversation about the history of the island and the founding of Haven. Harvard found himself forgotten. The two girls made for the Library entry hall, leaving Harvard on his own.

This is the perfect opportunity to search for information on the Relic, Speedy said from his satchel.

"We can't do that," Harvard whispered. "It's illegal. Or. I mean, they wouldn't like that."

They won't know.

"They're right there," he said, pointing down the hall.

They are distracted.

Harvard paused, and Jasmine and Sylvania kept walking. Sylvania said something and Jasmine threw her head back and laughed. Harvard had never seen her do that before.

"I guess they do seem pretty distracted," he conceded, shifting his weight.

Come. We will search. We will find the records of the Relic and we will learn its nature.

Harvard inhaled sharply, his resolve hardening. He darted in and out of the libraries many archival rooms, not totally sure which ones he was and wasn't allowed into, but he assumed he wasn't allowed into any of them. Mostly he found stores of items like those on display in the entry hall—shards of rock, dried plants, worn wooden tools and woven fabrics. Relics, he guessed, but none of them *the* Relic.

He knew he was getting closer when he found the room lined with drawers, each containing metal plates. Jasmine had mentioned that Haven's only written records were etched, so if he was going to find any written information, it would be here. The language was alien and written in a peculiar, jagged script, but it was close enough to Bastion Common that he could understand it.

"Here!" he exclaimed, kneeling at a bottom drawer in the corner. "This one is about the Relic. Um, I think." At least, he thought he saw the word Relic, but maybe it said relish or relevant.

Speedy climbed onto his shoulder.

Well done. Now, does it help us?

Harvard scanned the metal sheet. This one was written in a more rounded script, and it reminded him of some of the images he'd seen over pre-Quake texts. It must be an old one, maybe inscribed shortly after Haven was founded. It chronicled the discovery of some explorers, who found a pre-Quake *something* stuck in a tree as they were constructing the city.

"So the Haveners didn't put it there. They found it there," Harvard mused aloud. He'd imagined that the room holding the Relic would look like a museum, that the thing would be under glass, but this made it sound like it had always been in that tree, and the Haveners had simply never bothered to move it.

"I wonder if—"

He cut himself off at the sound of footsteps outside, a jolt of panic running through his body.

He shoved the metal plates back in the drawer and darted for the door, only to slam right into Marcel.

"Watch it!" he shoved Harvard aside, before taking him in. Harvard realized that from the perspective of the security liaison who already hated Chavi, he must look very, very guilty right now.

"What are you doing here?" Harvard asked with attempted casualness.

"Our normal rounds. What are *you* doing here?" Marcel narrowed his eyes. "You elected the bard track. Why would you be in the library?"

"Well, Jasmine works in the library," Harvard explained. Tremor aside, he'd always been a pretty good liar, and he knew that the best lie was just a pared-down version of the truth. "She asked me to come with her so that I could use the observation tower and make a map of the island."

He started fishing around in his bag for the map to give some evidence, but Marcel waved his hand.

"I don't need to see your useless map," he said, then added, "Any true Havener doesn't need a map, anyway."

Harvard's jaw clenched. "Well, if I'm going to become a Havener, then I'll have to learn somehow, right?"

Marcel ignored him. "The girls are downstairs, talking about history or something." Harvard simmered at the dismissive way he spoke of "the girls," but he masked it with wide-eyed innocence.

"Oh, that's where they are? Thank you! I've been looking all over for them!"

He brushed past Marcel as quickly as he could, and saw a few of his security underlings were just behind him—including Lyle, Marcel's companion. They all watched Harvard with the same hawkish suspicion.

Harvard decided that perhaps he should leave now.

He tread down the stairs and peeked into the entry hall. Jasmine and Sylvania were animatedly discussing their knowledge of the evolution of language in both of their respective cities. It would be a shame to interrupt them. Besides, they didn't have much longer in Haven. He should let Jasmine enjoy what little time with Sylvania she had left.

He found a side entrance to the library and slid out before Jasmine and Sylvania would even realize he was gone. Oddly enough, that only hurt a tiny bit. Mostly he was just happy that Jasmine had found such a good friend. If anything, it hurt knowing that she'd have to leave Sylvania behind when they all went back to Bastion.

Once he made it out of the library, he started running. The more distance he could put between himself and the security team, the better. He paused to look over his shoulder. No one was pursuing him. Which meant no one knew he'd been peeking around where he wasn't supposed to. Good. He smiled. Maybe he'd managed to commit sacrilege without any nasty consequences.

A hand descended over his mouth and pulled him backward, into the shadowy gap between two huts, where only a few shafts of moonlight pierced through the thatched canopy above them. Someone grabbed his arms, roughly forcing them behind his back as they dragged him into the shadows. He was shoved up against the wooden slats of the Music House. His injured hand slammed against the wall, and he gave a muffled cry of pain. He could hardly see, but he knew it was Marcel standing in front of him, silhouetted by the glow of lanterns out on the street.

"Where is it?" he hissed.

Harvard's panic mixed with confusion. Where was *what*? For once in his life, he hadn't actually stolen anything.

"I don't know what you're talking about," he said, hoping he was keeping his voice firm and brave despite his hammering heart and trembling...well, trembling everything.

"We all saw you leave the records room looking like you were up to something. There was no one else in the building. We know it was you."

"Yeah, I was in the records room," Harvard said, forcing down his mounting panic. "Looking for my friends! But I didn't *take* anything."

Marcel unsheathed a knife, and the severity of the situation struck Harvard like a charging pinchdragon. He wasn't just in *trouble*, he was in danger. He gasped in horror, pressing himself against the wall to put as much distance between himself and the blade. Harvard yelped as Marcel swiped, but the boy only grabbed at the strap of his satchel and cut it loose. He tossed it to someone standing behind him.

"Des, empty it," he commanded.

Harvard felt a stab of panic when he thought of Speedy. Was he still hiding in there? Would they hurt him? Had they ever seen a crab before?

"Wait!" he cried, pulling against his captors.

"Krisha, Lyle—hold him back," Marcel commanded, and the two security workers at his side pushed him back up against the wood with a thud.

The boy named Des dumped the contents of his bag, almost exclusively items from what felt like eons ago, things he'd scavenged in the desert. The broken shard of mirror wrapped in fabric. A switchblade. Dust scarf and goggles. He hadn't even thought to take those out. Luckily, no Speedy.

His moment of relief was cut short by a fist jammed into his stomach. A sickening *snap* in his gut forced him to double over, gasping. His mind was racing, frantically trying to grasp the situation. He'd never particularly liked Marcel, but he didn't actually believe the boy would hurt him. What could he possibly have done that could merit *this*?

"Where is it?" Marcel asked again, his voice taut like a coiled spring.

"I don't...even know...what it is..." Harvard panted.

"The fragment!" Marcel cried, reddening. "The Relic fragment!"

"You have...a piece of the Relic?" Harvard asked.

"*You* have it now."

"I don't understand," Harvard regained his breath. "Is it really that dangerous?"

"Oh, it *is* dangerous! The *idea* of it is dangerous!" Marcel said. "Anyone who touches the Relic fragment is...is tainted with ideas of the pre-Quake world!" He was trembling with fanatical rage. "The only crime worse than you stealing it"—Marcel drew in close, fist clenching, and Harvard prepared for another strike—"is that fact that you *wanted* it."

"What's going on here?" said a voice from the mouth of the alley. It was too dark to see more than a silhouette approaching across the wooden planks, but he would recognize Chavi's voice anywhere. Harvard had completely forgotten Chavi was supposed to meet him at the Library after he'd drawn his map.

"This doesn't concern you," Marcel said without turning around.

"It does concern me, actually. It concerns me a lot."

"What, is he your boyfriend or something?" taunted the boy holding Harvard's left arm. Lyle, the sycophantic companion.

"As a matter of fact, he is."

Marcel's face changed almost imperceptibly as he realized who was behind him. His eye twitched. Was he afraid of Chavi? Harvard couldn't tell. But something changed as Marcel whirled around, striking a defensive pose.

"Well your boyfriend has stolen something very important from us, and we are kindly asking for it back."

"He stole from you?" Chavi asked, still just an inky shadow backlit by lanternlight. "That doesn't sound like him. Did you do that, Harvard?"

He shook his head frantically.

"See? He says he didn't do it."

Even up close it was hard to make out Chavi's features, but the thin rays of moonlight that made it into the alleyway glinted off their glasses. The effect put Harvard in mind of a black cat, stalking its prey. Harvard suddenly couldn't blame Marcel for being scared, even though he had the advantage in numbers. If Harvard didn't love Chavi, he'd probably be scared too.

"This is what's going to happen," Chavi said, and Harvard could see them shift slightly in a gesture he'd seen them do hundreds of times before—resting their hand on the hilt of their hunting knife. "You're going to let Harvard go, and we're all going to go home feeling happy that everything is sorted out and no one got hurt."

Marcel laughed, but it wasn't an evil laugh so much as it was a *"That's a joke, right? You're joking?"* kind of laugh.

Marcel took a step forward. A challenge. "Now, I'm not sure if they taught you to count back in Bastion. Or if they tried, maybe you were too thick to pick it up. But there's four of us, and one of you. And beyond that, we're the ones in charge of keeping Haven safe. You're not even a citizen yet. If you wanna start a fight, then start it. But there's no way it ends well for you."

Chavi didn't move. Harvard didn't know what that meant.

Marcel continued, "My turn to tell you what's going to happen. You're going to go home, and we're gonna find what we're looking for. If Harvard cooperates, then he'll be just fine. But that decision is up to him."

Chavi remained motionless, like a predator lying in wait.

Thunder rumbled overhead, and Harvard realized a storm must be approaching.

Marcel sighed theatrically. "Alright, fine. But I want you to keep in mind that this is a choice the two of you are willingly making. Lyle." He nodded to the boy on Harvard's left. "Go ahead."

As Lyle launched himself at Chavi, Harvard screamed, but he found it muffled by a hand descending over his mouth. He squirmed in hopes of wriggling out of Krisha's grip, but she still held his arm and wrenched it behind his back, pressing him against her chest. Lightning flashed overhead, and Harvard saw a snapshot of Lyle's fist connecting with Chavi's jaw.

* * *

Okay, so they didn't think this Lyle guy was gonna be that fast. But they'd get the upper hand. They knew that. This was how they defeated a scorpioncrab! That and the fact that they may have been able to speak to it telepathically, but now was not the time to delve into that.

Chavi made a big show of reeling backward, letting Lyle think this would be easy. Lyle took a step forward, raising his arm for another swing, and Chavi took the opening to ram their shoulder into his stomach. He crashed into the wall of the library with a grunt, air forced from his lungs. Chavi allowed themself to be shoved back. Now that they had their footing, they were confident that this would be a swift victory. With renewed determination, Lyle swung at them again, but they pushed the blow aside easily. He was still trying to catch his breath, and he was off balance. He would be easy to knock over. Chavi swung their fist upward and connected with Lyle's chin, and he stumbled backward but didn't quite fall. While he was bent forward, gripping his jaw, Chavi planted a booted foot on his shoulder to knock him to the ground.

Lyle landed heavily on his back, and before he could scramble to his feet, Chavi planted the knee on his stomach. They were intending to stop there, but the cocktail of adrenaline, the weight of their repeated failures to protect Harvard, and...and something else propelled them forward. They drew their knife before they realized what they were doing, and when lightning flashed overhead, they could see Lyle's eyes go wide with panic.

A foot connected with their chin, sending them backward. The knife clattered out of their hand on the wood floor.

"Did you forget there's more of us, idiot?" Marcel shouted as Lyle pounced on top of them. They probably could have thrown him off easily, but the other boy came and placed a booted foot on one of their arms, and Marcel came to step on the other.

For the first time during the fight, Chavi's confidence faded, and they thought: *Hey, this might have been a bad idea.*

* * *

Harvard screamed and thrashed against Krisha's grip, watching Marcel and Des hold Chavi down as Lyle laid into them, landing blow after blow on their face. Chavi didn't cry out, only made little grunting noises as they struggled to get free.

"Are you ready to give up yet?" Marcel asked conversationally. Chavi didn't answer. Harvard couldn't tell if this was stubbornness, or if they physically couldn't answer.

"Alright, if you insist," Marcel said with a shrug. Lyle landed another blow, and Chavi went limp.

No no no no no no. It was all Harvard could think as tears welled up in his eyes, blurring his vision. He couldn't tear his gaze away from Chavi's inert form, motionless. This was his fault. They'd only been trying to protect him, and now they were—

Harvard squeezed his eyes shut and screamed, thrashing. Marcel, Des, and Lyle were already surrounding him.

"As you can see, Harvard," Marcel began, "we take matters regarding the Relic very, very seriously. So I'm going to ask you again: where is the fragment?"

"Stop."

Now the voice was too raspy and labored, Harvard almost didn't recognize it as Chavi's. But when Marcel whirled around, he could see them struggling to their hands and knees.

"Stop," they said again, weakly.

Stay down, Harvard willed them. *Please. They'll kill you. Stay down.* But by this point he knew Chavi better than that.

"By the name of the Principles," Marcel laughed, "do you really not know when to quit?"

Chavi made a shaky attempt to stand, but only managed to flop forward, decidedly unconscious. When lightning flashed, Harvard could see a growing crimson pool of blood on the wood. He screamed into Krisha's palm.

Marcel turned back to Harvard, looking amused.

"You know you two are actually perfect for each other. You are both impressively stupid." Harvard's arm jerked with the impulse to strike him, but Krisha's grip was too strong.

"Now," Marcel said, "I will give you one more chance to tell us where the fragment is, before we search you."

Krisha removed her hand from his mouth.

"I hate you," Harvard hissed. Marcel rolled his eyes.

"Well duh." He turned to Lyle. "Search him!"

A new panic blossomed in Harvard's stomach. His body recalled that same visceral humiliation he'd felt when he'd had to strip down to wade across the stream. To have his clothing forcibly removed was so, so much worse. He'd rather Marcel hit him again than that.

"No!" Harvard cried, but Lyle had already grabbed the cloak Blaire had given him and yanked it off, ripping it at the wooden hook, and Harvard felt painfully exposed.

* * *

Chavi's eyes opened.

There was something burning in their chest.

They knew there was pain, but they couldn't feel it. That kind of pain was on their skin and muscle and nerves, and the only thing they could feel now was their blood, and it was hot, like molten stone.

There was something inside them that wanted to get out.

Chavi stood, but it wasn't really them that was standing, it was the thing inside them that was standing, the thing inside their blood. It guided Chavi's flesh and bone like a puppet, and maybe they should care, but they didn't care, because they were angry, and they couldn't tell the difference from the heat of the creature that lived inside them or the heat of their own rage.

They saw the four people pulling at Harvard's clothes, running their hands over him as he begged them to stop, and all they could think was how small and weak and fragile these humans were, and how easy they would be to kill.

The wood creaked beneath them. Marcel turned at the sound.

"You *still* won't give up?" he sneered.

"I'll deal with it," Lyle said from behind him, placing himself protectively between Chavi and Marcel.

The human thought he was a threat. But he was wrong. This human was prey.

The beast inside Chavi's blood broke free.

* * *

Harvard couldn't make out anything in the darkness, but he heard Lyle gasp and let out a gurgling shriek.

Lightning flashed, and for a fraction of a second Harvard saw something that could not possibly be real.

Lyle was impaled on a thick crab leg.

There was a wet sliding sound, and Lyle's body thudded to the ground. Even in the sparse moonlight, they could all see the gaping hole in his chest, and his wide, glassy eyes.

Krisha screamed. She threw Harvard to the ground, and when he hit the wood, his ribs screamed in protest. He heard the pounding of footsteps on wood as the security team fled. Des was calling out that there was an animal attack.

The rain from the impending storm began to pound down.

Harvard pulled himself to his knees, searching for the creature that had attacked Lyle. It must have fled into the night. He saw Chavi on the ground in the middle of the alley, inert.

"Chavi!" he cried, scrambling over to them, one hand gripping his aching chest. Their face was badly cut and bruised from Lyle's attack, but they were alive. The heavy rain was already starting to wash the blood away.

Harvard felt that familiar sinking sensation he got when his body betrayed him. If he were the one unconscious and Chavi needed to get him to safety, they could easily scoop him up and bring him home. He knew he couldn't do the same for Chavi. Even if he weren't in a shaking, aching mess, he was just too weak.

But there was something else Harvard could do that Chavi couldn't: he could ask for help.

Thankfully, Sax's door swung open after Harvard pounded on it a second time.

"Harvard?" zey asked when zey opened the door. Zey didn't seem upset to see him, which was great news, but zyr brow creased in confusion. Zyr eyes widened as zey took in Harvard, already soaked in the rain, Chavi lying limp in his arms. He'd managed to drag them this far with his arms beneath theirs, their head resting against his stomach, but he knew he wouldn't make it the rest of the way.

Despite the way things had ended between them, Sax looked genuinely concerned as zey took the pair in.

"What happened?" zey asked.

"I need you to help me get them home. I know you don't like us, and you don't even want to be associated with us anymore, but—"

Sax was already closing zyr door and picking up Chavi's legs.

"Let's go."

* * *

The bone dice clattered on the table. August still didn't fully understand what each of the symbols meant, so he looked to Blaire for an interpretation. He leaned over the table inspecting the combination.

"That's two hydra deer!" Blaire said, giving August a pat on the arm.

"So...is that good?"

"Pretty good, yeah! You get four points for getting a pair, but you get minus one for rolling a prey animal instead of a predator."

August picked up the die and examined the carvings, surprisingly intricate. Blaire said he'd carved them himself. So much nicer than the flimsy playing cards he usually used when he invented games.

"If we made these dice on Bastion, it would just be like, crabs on every face," August said. Blaire laughed.

The door swung open, and Jasmine and Sylvania entered, so deep in conversation they didn't notice the other two until Blaire said, "Took you too long enough! Soup's already ready."

Sylvania started. "Sorry! We got a little caught up with research," she said, tucking a white hair behind her ear and glancing sideways at Jasmine.

"Sure," Blaire said, giving Sylvania a friendly touch on the arm.

August peered behind them, into the night. "Where's Harvard?"

Jasmine's eyes widened. "Harvard!" She cried. "We left him at the library!" She blushed, twisting one of her braids in her fingers. "We should go back—"

"He knows the way," Blaire shrugged as he ladled out soup. "He'll be b—" Someone banged on the door. Blaire set his ladle down. "That's probably him now."

Jasmine opened the door, revealing a rain-soaked Sax and an even more rain-soaked Harvard, trembling. Between them they carried—

Jasmine gasped. August stood so abruptly his chair clattered to the floor, then ran to help the two at the door carry a bruised and blood-soaked Chavi inside.

Blaire leapt into action. "Clear the table!" he said.

"I'll grab my medical supplies," Sylvania disappeared into her own hut.

August helped Blaire clear space on the table so Harvard and Sax could lay Chavi down. Jasmine examined their cuts on their face, and when Sylvania returned with rags and alcohol, she started to clean them.

August took a step back, noticing Sax, who remained by the door, observing.

"What did you do?" August demanded.

Zyr face was stony as they replied, "Harvard needed my help. So I helped him. That's the Union way."

It would have been a lot simpler to just blame Sax, the traitor who had abandoned them, for whatever had gone wrong this time. But it actually sounded like zey were being nice, so August supposed he couldn't really blame zem for that. He eyed zem suspiciously but said nothing.

Harvard, who was now trembling violently in his soaked clothes, pushed between Jasmine and Sylvania to hold Chavi's hand. With his other hand, he grasped Jasmine's arm. He was babbling incoherently about the Library and Marcel and a creature that had attacked them and a fragment and a lot of other things August couldn't make out. He took a moment to gasp for air before another torrent of words came out.

Sylvania gently nudged him away from the table.

"August, why don't you take Harvard into the other room?" Jasmine suggested.

"But I want to stay here! I want to be with Chavi!" Harvard cried as August wrapped a hand around his shoulders.

"No offense, little dude, but you're kinda freaking out right now, and that's probably gonna make things worse. Let Jasmine handle this, okay?"

August guided Harvard to the closet-bedroom and shut the door.

* * *

A combination of terror, cold, and adrenaline had turned Harvard into a trembling mess. He was shaking so violently that he needed August's assistance just to walk, lest his legs give out. August sat him down on the straw mattress, placing his hands on both of his shoulders and looking him in the eyes. Harvard breathed deeply, and his shaking subsided a little. *Don't panic,* he told himself forcefully, as if his body would actually listen.

"Are you alright?" August asked.

"I'm fine," Harvard said instinctively. He wasn't the one who needed help. He didn't *deserve* help. This was all his fault.

"Really think about it," August insisted. "Are you hurt?"

Harvard took stock of his body. After the security team had fled, all that mattered was Chavi. He didn't have the presence of mind to feel pain. He couldn't afford to. Now that he was alone with August—

His hand glided to his stomach, which seemed to suddenly remember that it was supposed to be hurting. August gently moved Harvard's hand aside and prodded the area. Harvard hissed in pain.

"Yeah, that's a broken rib," August concluded. "What happened?"

"He hit me," Harvard said through gritted teeth.

"Who?"

"Marcel."

August squinted, like he was trying to place the name. "The police guy?"

"Yeah."

August's expression darkened. "He did that to Chavi?"

"Him and two others."

"*Two* others?" he repeated.

Harvard nodded. At the time, he'd only felt raw, animalistic panic. Now that he recalled events to August, hot rage seared his chest. How *dare* they do this to him. How *dare* they hurt Chavi. "They said I stole something," he said. "They lied. Just so they could have an excuse to hurt me." He gripped the fabric of the mattress in two tights fists, trembling again, the time with fury.

August squeezed his shoulder. "You're gonna be fine, okay? Both of you."

Harvard didn't feel like he was going to be fine. He was so full of anger he could explode—anger at Marcel, but also himself. If he'd been able to get out of that situation on his own, then he'd never have put Chavi in danger. If he'd just been able to take care of himself like he always insisted he could, this wouldn't have happened. When would he learn how to protect himself? Would he ever?

He looked to August, who watched him with intense, worried eyes. August, who had once lifted him off his feet and slammed him against a wall, now showing him a tenderness he wouldn't have thought possible only a few months ago. August, who was bigger and stronger and scarier...

"August?" he asked. "How do you know what a broken rib feels like?"

August shrugged. "I used to wrestle with my sisters all the time."

"And you'd break each other's bones?" Harvard gaped.

"I mean, not on purpose. But, ya know, sometimes an elbow hits a nose and there's tears."

"Did that happen often?"

"Oh yeah," he snickered. "All the time. But it's the kinda thing where it's always funny a year later. Once June threw a cookie at me and I tried to catch it in my mouth, and I fell on May, and I broke her collarbone. We still laugh about it."

"Oh," Harvard said, not comprehending why breaking your sister's collarbone was funny.

August seemed to sense Harvard's confusion. His brow furrowed. "You never played like that as a kid?"

Harvard looked down. "I mean..."

"Right, right, the whole blood thing," August looked guilty for bringing it up. "But you didn't even have siblings?"

Kathy's face flashed in Harvard's mind—the look she'd worn when they locked eyes at the Galvin conference.

"No. No siblings."

"Well, as your honorary brother, which I decided I am, let me teach you something about siblings," he with a fraternal pat on the back. "Sometimes play gets rough. But I guess the benefit is that I really learned how to hold my own, ya know?" He laughed. "You missed the whole thing with the Chocolates, but I took two of them down at once!"

"Can you teach me?" Harvard asked.

August cocked his head. "Teach you what?"

"How to hold my own." He kept his gaze fixed on his feet. It felt so stupid to say. Most people didn't need to be taught. They just knew.

"Um, sure? Why?"

"I just keep thinking," Harvard explained, "if I'd been able to get away on my own, this never would have happened to Chavi. If something like this ever happens to me again, I don't want someone else to have to come save me."

"Oh, yeah. What to do if you get grabbed is, like, total basics. Rule number one." He held up his elbow and patted it. "This thing is your best friend. Hardest bone in the body."

Harvard placed a hand on his elbow. It didn't seem *that* hard. "Is it really?"

August shrugged. "Dunno. But it definitely feels that way when someone jams it in your ribs, I'll tell ya that much. Rule number two: the power of a punch actually comes from your leg. And don't tuck your thumb, and unless you want even more broken fingers..."

* * *

Jasmine took a step back and exhaled. Sax had already gone before she had a chance to thank zem. Blaire stood back, ready to help the two women if they needed anything. He wrung his hands, looking nauseated as he stared at Chavi.

"I think that's all we can do for now," Sylvania said. "At least, until they wake up and we figure out exactly what happened to them."

Jasmine sighed. They'd patched up the cuts on Chavi's face, and luckily they didn't seem to have many other injuries. There was a sizable cut on the back of their head that looked like it was from impact, though, and Jasmine worried about brain trauma.

She gripped their shoulder, starting to roll them onto their side to get a better look at the head wound. Something warm and slick wet her fingers. Did they have another injury on the back of their shoulder? She lifted their arm up to check just behind their shoulder blade—

Oh.

Oh no.

"Sylvania!" she said, straightening as she rolled Chavi onto their back again.

The girl gave her a concerned look. "Yeah?"

"I think—Maybe—" Jasmine stammered. She didn't know what she had just found, but her instincts told her this was something the Ivies should discuss in private. She had to get the Haveners out of the room somehow. "This is a lot, for all of us. I think the four of us might want to spend some time together. Alone."

Blaire and Sylvania shared a glance, then Sylvania nodded.

"Of course," she stepped away from the table. "We understand. We'll be in my hut, if you need anything."

Once Sylvania and Blaire were safely on the other side of the divide, Jasmine called, "August? Get in here."

Her voice was shaking.

* * *

August froze at the sound of his name. He had his arm wrapped around Harvard's neck, showing him how to bury his chin in the crook of someone's elbow if they ever tried to choke him from behind. August released him, which Harvard was thankful for, because he wasn't quite getting the lesson and he was starting to black out a little. He couldn't believe this was the kind of thing that August had done for fun as a kid. No wonder he was like that.

"Uh, just a minute little dude," August said, moving for the door.

"Let me come too!" he said.

August shook his head. "You stay here. Let me deal with it, okay?"

Harvard's two greatest fears wrestled within him—the possibility that he was neglecting Chavi in their time of need, and the possibility that he was getting in the way. Eventually, the latter won out. He stepped back.

"Okay," he said.

"Everything is fine," August said, before slipping out of the room. Harvard doubted that.

Harvard?

"Speedy?" Harvard cried, searching for the crab. He found him perched on the windowsill. Harvard scooped him up and nuzzled him. "I was so worried about you!" he cried. "I'm so happy that you're safe!"

Not only am I safe, I also procured something that may help you.

Harvard pulled back to look at Speedy in his hands.

"What do you mean?"

Speedy leapt down and pulled something from underneath the mattress, where he'd hidden it.

I retrieved this for you in the records room. I thought you might find it useful.

Harvard's stomach sank as he saw the paper-wrapped package in Speedy's claw.

"Oh, Speedy. No."

* * *

"What's up?" August asked. Jasmine waved him over.

"What does this look like to you?" she asked, lifting Chavi's right arm so he could see the back of their shoulder blade. It glimmered with blood, and the skin looked ragged, like something had ripped through it, and at the edges of the skin—

"Whoa!" August recoiled. "That's the crab stuff!"

"Chitin, yes," Jasmine took a wet cloth and started to wipe away the blood. "I suppose I just wanted to make sure I wasn't losing my mind."

As Jasmine cleaned the wound, August could see it more clearly. The hole in Chavi's skin was a handspan wide, and underneath was what looked like crab shell. August stepped forward and ran his fingers along the smooth surface. In the flickering candlelight, he could even make out a bit of a pattern—green fractals against maroon.

"Okay Jasmine," he breathed. "I have a stupid thought. I'm gonna say it, and you're gonna tell me it's stupid, just so, like I don't have to be thinking it anymore. What if...when Chavi got shot and you took to them to the crabs to heal them...what if they got turned into a crab?"

Jasmine said nothing.

"Jas!" He pleaded. "This is the part where you tell me that's stupid!"

She stared blankly forward. "I don't have an explanation."

"They can't be turning into a crab!" he said, slamming the back of his hand onto his other palm for emphasis. "That's stupid!"

"They have chitin under their skin. I don't know what could cause that."

August ran his hands through his hair, starting to pace.

"This is crazy, dude. Like this is totally crazy."

Jasmine remained completely still, looking vacant.

"Harvard?" she called. "Get in here."

* * *

Harvard was relieved to finally be invited back into the main room, which hopefully meant everything was alright. He hurriedly stuffed the package in his boot and hurried out. He still winced seeing Chavi lying on the table, but the situation definitely looked less dire with the wounds bandaged.

"Do you know what this is?" Jasmine asked, indicating something on Chavi's back that looked like—

Harvard inhaled sharply, slapping a hand over his mouth. He'd been so caught up in getting Chavi home safely, he'd forgotten that horrible moment when he'd thought he'd seen a crab leg sprouting out of them. He'd chalked it up to adrenaline and the thunderstorm and the darkness. But that spot on Chavi's back...it reminded him of Skrack.

The whole story came pouring out of him, this time coherently, everything about Marcel and the Relic and the fight with Chavi, right down to the part where he thought he saw them impale a boy with a crab leg.

"And I thought maybe I was just seeing things," he tried to catch his breath, "but I guess...maybe...I wasn't."

August shook his head.

"I can't believe this," he said, turning to Jasmine. "You turned Chavi into a desertwalker!"

"Me?" Jasmine turned so sharply her braids whipped around. "I didn't do this!"

"You were the one who gave them to the crabs—"

Jasmine's fists clenched. "What was I supposed to do, let them die?"

"I'm just saying, we wouldn't be dealing with this—"

She took a step toward August and he leapt back.

"You don't get a say," she hissed, jabbing a finger at him. There was a ferocity in her voice that Harvard had never heard from her before. "You weren't there."

"No," August conceded, holding his hands up in defense, "I wasn't."

Jasmine took a deep breath and centered herself. "Tell us more, Harvard," she finally said.

Harvard looked between them. "That's...that's all."

"This is just a chitin plate. You're sure it looked like a whole leg?"

"It...it went right through one of the guys. I think it killed him."

"Did you leave the body?" Jasmine asked.

"Yes," Harvard said. It hadn't even occurred to him that he should have gone back for the body. "I'm sorry. I just—I was worried about Chavi—"

"It's okay," Jasmine said, holding up a hand to stop him. "You did the right thing."

Chavi groaned.

"They're waking up," Jasmine said. "Harvard, get some—"

Harvard was already running to get some soup for them, and a glass of water from the cistern.

Chavi jerked up, but Jasmine lowered them back to the table with a gentle hand on their shoulder.

"You're fine," she said. "Harvard is fine."

On cue, he reappeared next to her.

"Soup?" he offered.

Chavi's frantic eyes darted around, taking in the three Ivies standing over them. "What...is...going on?"

"Well, you're not gonna believe this—" August started, but Jasmine held up a hand to silence him.

"Let's get you someplace more comfortable, alright?" Jasmine suggested.

Harvard and August each took an arm to help steady Chavi, then guided them to the floor by the hearth.

"What's the last thing you remember?" Jasmine asked, lowering herself beside them. Harvard grabbed one of Blaire's woven blankets and draped it over their shoulders.

Chavi shook their head. "That Lyle guy beat the shit out of me," they said. "Last I remember, they were trying to search Harvard, and I just...I blacked out."

Harvard could hear the shame in their voice, and he placed a hand on their knee.

"But then you got back up," he reminded them.

Chavi turned to face him.

"I did?" they asked.

Harvard blinked. "You...don't remember that?"

"No," Chavi said, and their voice shook. Harvard wondered if he should say the next bit. It would upset them, but...well, they should know.

He swallowed, then took a deep breath. He forced himself to meet Chavi's gaze. "You got back up and you...you killed Lyle."

"I *did*?" Chavi's eyes widened. "I don't—I don't remember that." They curled up with their knees against their chest, heels of their hands pressed into their temples. "I don't remember—I don't remember—"

"That's normal," Jasmine laid a hand on their back. "With head trauma, it's normal for some memories—"

Chavi whirled on her. "I killed someone, and I don't remember it!" Harvard jumped at the sudden intensity of their voice, ragged with confusion and terror. He'd never seen them this panicked before. He didn't know what to do.

"Also, you're turning into a crab!" August said from where he stood behind them.

"I'm *what*?"

"August!" Jasmine and Harvard both cried.

"What?" he said with an open-armed shrug. "They should know!"

"What do you *mean* I'm turning into a crab?" Chavi demanded of Jasmine.

"August is exaggerating," she shot August a look, "but you do have...a patch of chitin on your back that appears...carcine in nature."

"Also," Harvard added, knowing it would only make things worse but unsure if he should hold back, "when you killed Lyle—it sort of looked like you grew a crab leg?"

Chavi stared at him. They looked sickly pale, and Harvard wondered if they were about to cry, faint, scream, vomit, or some combination for the four. Admittedly, he didn't know what he would do in this situation. Well, probably cry. But that was just how he was. He was a crier. He knew that.

Chavi didn't cry. They just stared at him. Then, slowly, they raised their hand to their shoulder and felt the chitin with their fingers. They gave a little whimper.

"We'll report this," Jasmine said hurriedly, seeming eager to change the topic. "Marcel and his gang should never have attacked you like that—"

"Especially when Harvard didn't even steal anything!" August added. "Right, Harvard?"

Harvard flushed. "Um," he said.

August's face dropped. "Oh, Harvard," he said, "please tell me you didn't actually steal anything."

"It was an accident!" he blurted out, unsure how he could explain that it was in fact an accident without revealing Speedy's existence. He looked at Chavi, afraid they'd be angry with him, but they only stared absently into the fire, fingers still tracing the edges of the carapace that peaked out of their skin.

"Well, let's make sure all this wasn't for nothing," Jasmine said, holding out her hand. "Let's see it."

Gingerly, Harvard removed the package from his boot and proffered it. Jasmine unwrapped the paper, revealing a jagged piece of rusted metal.

"That's it?" August exclaimed. "All this, for some scrap metal? That doesn't help us at all! What are we gonna get from a piece of metal? This tells us nothing!"

Harvard cowered instinctively. Whenever he was angry, August became Princeton again, and while it was hard to reconcile the two in his mind, his body remembered what Princeton had done to him.

"No," Jasmine said, holding the piece of metal reverently toward the fire, and it glinted in the light of the flames. "This tells us everything."

"Um, hello?" August said. "What do you mean?"

Her eyes flashed with excitement. "This tells us that the Relic is some kind of machine."

"So?" August asked. "We still have to steal it."

"No, we don't. What is important about a machine is not the machine itself. It's how it works. If we can just get in there and figure out how it works, we don't need to steal anything at all."

"But how will we do that?" Harvard asked. Jasmine grinned mischievously.

"I have an idea."

* * *

Are you mad at me, Harvard? Speedy asked. Harvard faced him, resting his head on his arms folded on the windowsill.

"I don't know," he admitted.

Harvard was confident speaking aloud to Speedy even though Chavi was sleeping next to him. Blaire had given them some kind of draught to help them sleep through the pain from their injuries. It smelled familiar, like the tea O'Neill had given Harvard what felt like ages ago.

Why would you be mad at me? I don't understand. I helped you and your friends.

"But stealing that fragment almost got me and Chavi killed."

I had no way of knowing that would happen.

"Still. You should have asked me."

I do not need to ask your permission to act. I am a free crab.

"I know. You can do what you want. But you should ask me if I need help before you try and help me."

Very well. Next time you need help, I will ask you. I am...regretful about what happened to you and Chavi.

"Yeah..." Harvard glanced over at Chavi. "I am too."

The next morning, no one was surprised when a messenger arrived to summon the Ivies to the Meeting House for a meeting with Rosenea.

"Good luck," Blaire said as the four of them left, but Harvard could tell that he didn't think they would be having any good luck that day.

They walked in solemn silence, the air thick with moisture and unspoken fear. Even August didn't make an attempt at humor, like he had before the Galvin Conference. By unspoken understanding, their prospects were bleak. What would it mean for the Ivies to be banished? If the Haveners feared being revealed to Bastion, would they even allow the four of them to leave? Harvard kept his gaze fixed on the still-wet planks beneath his feet, but that reminded him of seeing blood seep into those planks, and his head snapped up.

When they entered Rosenea's office, Marcel was already seated at the wooden table, his eyes red and puffy. Seeing him so distraught was strangely humanizing, and almost made Harvard feel bad for him. Almost. He still looked as though it was taking all his restraint to keep himself from giving Chavi another beating.

Rosenea, on the other hand, looked placid as always.

"Have a seat," she gestured for the four of them to sit. They did, across the table from Marcel.

"I trust you all know why you've been summoned here today," Rosenea said.

"We do," Jasmine confirmed quietly. August looked pointedly out the window.

"I want to hear your side of the story."

Marcel opened his mouth to speak, but Rosenea raised a hand to silence him.

"You will have your turn as well," she told him, then turned to the Ivies. Harvard looked to Chavi to indicate they should go first. The way Harvard saw it, Chavi was lucky. They didn't have anything to hide. They told their whole story just as it was. They'd gone to inspect a noise in the alleyway and found Harvard being attacked. They'd tried to help him, but they were far outnumbered and were knocked unconscious in the scuffle.

"And that's all I remember," they concluded, and Harvard envied the fact that they got to tell the truth.

Rosenea nodded.

"And you, Harvard?"

Harvard swallowed. He told the story to the best of his ability, sticking to the truth as much as he could and skirting around key details that would have been incriminating. When he got to the part about Lyle, he discovered it was actually hard to recount. His throat tightened.

"Take your time," Rosenea said.

"They hurt Chavi," he rasped, staring down at his folded hands, "Badly. And it was dark so I couldn't really see but I saw that they were not moving and I thought they might be dead." Harvard tried not to let himself cry, but then he realized the tears might be more convincing, so he let himself cry just a little bit. Marcel tensed, and he could tell that the tears were making him angry, so he cried even more.

"And then they tried to search me and...something attacked Lyle." And now for the only true, honest-to-Founders lie of his whole speech. "I don't know what it was."

"It was Chavi!" Marcel cried, shooting up out of his chair and slamming his palms on the table. "I saw it! They killed him! I saw!"

"Sit down, Marcel," Rosenea laid a hand on his arm. "I'm sure it was very disturbing to see your friend killed—"

"My companion!" Marcel shouted, his face contorted with rage. "And he was murdered. I saw my companion murdered!" He pointed at the Ivies, now speaking directly to Rosenea as if they weren't there. "I told you! I told you not to let them into the city! I told you they were a threat! First, they steal the fragment—"

"I didn't steal it!" Harvard protested.

"You lying little whelp!" Marcel cried.

"You will have," Roseanea said levelly, "your chance to speak. But that time is not now. So sit down. And be quiet."

Marcel sat heavily in his seat, glaring at Harvard, but remained quiet as Jasmine and August gave their account of events: Harvard showing up with Sax and Chavi, a rundown of Chavi and Harvard's injuries. They didn't have to lie, though they did conveniently omit the chitin patch they'd found on Chavi's shoulder.

Marcel smoldered the whole time.

"Marcel—" Rosenea started.

"I'll tell you what really happened," Marcel seethed. "We knew that Harvard had stolen the Relic fragment—which is sacrilege, in case you've forgotten! We went to question him—and we only used force when he wouldn't cooperate. Then Chavi showed up and picked a fight. And then they killed Lyle right in front of us! Des and Krisha were there too. They'll back me up."

"Actually, Des and Krisha have already given their accounts," Rosenea said. Marcel glanced at her.

"They have?"

"Last night, they came straight to me. You, on the other hand, took your time. Where did you disappear to?"

Marcel fidgeted in his seat. "I stopped to see Oleg. As head of security, I thought he was the most important to notify."

"Very well," Rosenea nodded. "I see the logic there."

"So? Did they back me up?"

"You compatriots did corroborate most of the story. They agree that Harvard seemed to have stolen the fragment, and that you all were justified in apprehending him."

Harvard began to tremble. His pulse thundered in his ears. If Rosenea agreed he was guilty, would she take Marcel's side? This could be it for them. If Rosenea decided Chavi really did kill Lyle, would they be executed for it?

"They did not, however, seem to believe that Chavi was responsible for Lyle's death. They both say it was too dark to see what happened, but it appeared to be some kind of wild animal." Harvard's stomach twisted. *Wild animal.*

"That's sheepsdung!" Marcel said, throwing his hands in the air.

"It's also consistent with the medical examiner's reports on the body. The hole in Lyle's chest looks more like something an animal would have done than a person."

Harvard looked over to Chavi. They looked like they would be sick.

"Besides, according to all three of your stories, Chavi only had a hunting knife. This knife in fact."

She placed Chavi's knife on the table.

"It was found near the body, without a trace of blood."

"It was raining!" Marcel protested.

"It was, but the knife was found under this."

Rosenea produced Harvard's cloak.

"This, I believe, belongs to you." She handed it to Harvard, who accepted it wordlessly. He checked the clasp to inspect the damage. Someone had already mended it. He heard the rustle of fabric and saw that she'd placed his broken satchel on the table in front of him as well. He tied the broken strap and put it over his shoulder, at least comforted to have his bag back. It felt somehow protective, like a crab shell. He peered inside to confirm that all his belongings had been returned. It was all there—switchblade, dusts gear, and even the mirror shard.

"If Chavi had been able to use that knife on Lyle," Rosenea continued, "there would have been blood on that knife, and it would have soaked into the cloak. According to all accounts, it didn't start raining until after the three of you had fled. Besides, the wound doesn't appear to be a knife wound. It's unclear what could have inflicted it."

Chavi groaned quietly, but Harvard was pretty sure he was the only one who could hear it.

"Still," Rosenea continued, "punitive action must be taken."

Harvard's body went rigid and cold. Out of the corner of his eye, he saw Chavi tense. Jasmine bowed her head, and August stared blankly forward.

"Ha!" Marcel slammed his fist on the table.

"Against you, Marcel."

The boy paled. Harvard sagged with relief.

"What?"

"All accounts acknowledge the fact that you injured Harvard. Something you never should have done, even if he had stolen the fragment. You've been in this role for years now. Surely you know proper protocols for justice, and you didn't follow them."

"I knew he was guilty." Marcel shrank like a chastised dog. "I just knew it."

"That doesn't justify you hurting him, and it certainly doesn't justify what Lyle did to Chavi." Rosenea gestured to the bruises on Chavi's face. "I'm not saying this justifies Lyle's death, but we simply don't have the evidence that Chavi had any part in that. By all accounts, it seems like an animal."

"Procyon attacks don't look like that," Marcel shook his head.

"Procyons are not the only predators on this island."

"But—"

"We will discuss your punishment later. For now, you are dismissed."

"Rosenea!"

"You are dismissed."

Marcel stood so abruptly, his chair scratched on the wooden floor. He stalked for the door, and as he was leaving whispered, "This isn't over," quiet enough that Rosenea couldn't hear him.

"Did you guys hear that?" August asked. "He did, like, a creepy whisper thing going out the door. You guys heard that, right? That's like, classic villain move, right there."

Rosenea wasn't paying attention. She pinched the bridge of her nose.

"We do our best to be kind and good people in Haven," she said, her eyes closed, "but the four of you test my patience."

"We didn't do anything wrong!" Chavi said.

"I never said that you did," Rosenea opened her eyes to look at them, "but it seems that you've brought all the ills of Bastion with you."

"That's not—"

"Look," she held up a hand silencing Chavi. "By the Haven Principles, you have done no wrong. That's why I can shield you from formal procedural consequences. But I cannot shield you from other consequences."

August cocked his head. "What do you mean?"

Rosenea only shook her head.

"Your ceremony is tonight. Perform well. Prove that you are ready to become true Haveners. Then, perhaps, the people will accept you. I will do my best to placate Marcel and the others, but I cannot guarantee that they will not try to seek some kind of retaliation."

Jasmine spoke for the group. "We will be the perfect Haveners at the ceremony. We promise."

Rosenea nodded. "I'm sure you will," she said. "But in the meantime..." She lifted Chavi's hunting knife and handed it to them. "You'll probably want this back."

The Ivies walked back to Blaire's with a peculiar sense of relief and dread hanging over them. There had been no repercussions yet. And maybe there wouldn't be, once they were accepted into the community. But that wouldn't be until tonight.

"Rosenea is right," Jasmine said as the four of them walked back. "Just because you're not in trouble with the Council doesn't mean you're safe. People will talk about what happened, and even if we do become citizens, we won't be welcome." She gave a sorrowful sigh, massaging a braid in both hands. "We really do have to leave tonight, after the ceremony."

"Right, so this Relic-stealing plan you mentioned," August said. "Do you wanna share it?"

Jasmine pushed the braid behind her ear. "It's not a plan so much as it's an idea, but it's an idea that I think will work. We don't need to bring the whole Relic back to Bastion so long as we have all the details. Which means a detailed diagram should be enough. And we happen to have a very skilled artist with us." She glanced at Harvard with a sideways smile.

Harvard's stomach dropped. "Me?" he asked. "*I* have to go draw the Relic?" He wasn't sure if he should be proud or terrified that Jasmine's plan rested entirely on his shoulders.

"Everyone else will be at the ceremony"—Chavi laid a hand on his shoulder—"and we can make sure to keep them distracted."

"You can't distract a whole city!" Harvard protested. August cracked his knuckles.

"Challenge accepted," he said.

"We won't need to distract a whole city," Jasmine clarified. "At the beginning of the party but before the wine-pouring, you play a song on the vibraphone. Everyone will love it, and since you'll have made a memorable appearance, no one will wonder where you are."

"So you want me to perform and *draw* the pictures of the Relic?" He was beginning to feel like this wasn't a plan so much as it was a *"Harvard does everything."* And given last time the plan relied on him...

"I know it's a lot," Jasmine admitted, looking away, "but you're the only one with the skills required."

Harvard opened his mouth to protest, but then snapped it shut. Skills? Him? He had valuable skills?

"It shouldn't be too hard," Jasmine added hurriedly. "From what I understand, the Relic is on its own platform right behind the Meeting House, and there's a bridge. You should be able to get there and back pretty quickly without anyone noticing that you were gone. Besides, the wine-pouring isn't until dawn, so you've got plenty of time."

"Okay, so, listen," August cut in. "Me and Harvard are buddies now. You know I'm very pro-Harvard. He's like a brother to me. So it's with brotherly love that I remind you all that last time we had a plan that relied on Harvard stealing something, he famously did not steal it. Like that was a very important part of what happened at the Galvin conference was that he did not steal it. And then Chavi got shot. So I'm asking us to all think very carefully about whether we want to rely on Harvard again. Ya know, so Chavi doesn't get shot again. No offense, Harvard."

"None taken," Harvard said, flushing. He didn't think any of the Haveners had a gun, but his track record with getting Chavi shot was so bad that he didn't want to risk it.

"Would *you* like to draw the Relic?" Chavi asked, elbowing August. "I'm sure Harvard isn't a fan of the idea either—"

"I'm not," he admitted.

"But he's definitely the best candidate to draw diagrams."

"Look," Jasmine opened her notebook and flipped through the pages. August's eyes widened when he saw the drawings of creatures Harvard had penned for her, and on the last page, the map of the island. "You have to admit that if any of us can draw those diagrams, and fast, it's Harvard."

August scanned the drawings, then looked at Harvard.

"Yeah," he deflated, "I guess you're right."

August clapped a hand on Harvard's back.

"Well, don't fuck it up little dude!"

"I wasn't planning on it," Harvard murmured, but knowing his luck, he guessed he would find some way to fuck it up anyway.

CHAPTER FIFTEEN

The Citizenship Ceremony

Jasmine should have guessed what to expect on the night of the Full Moon Festival based on the celebration she saw at Sax's ceremony and in the tavern, but she still found herself shocked by the sudden outpouring into the streets that night, musicians all playing their own tunes, everyone dancing to a different beat, colorful lanterns illuminating the path that led to the Meeting House, where the citizenship ceremony would be held. It reminded Jasmine a bit of the Founders' Festival, but without the costumes. And without the sense of otherness she felt when the people of Bastion proper were allowed into Upper Bastion for one day each year. She could hardly believe they did this every month.

"Come on!" Sylvania waved the Ivies forward, toward a railing at the edge of the platform. "You'll miss the show!"

"Is this not the show?" August gestured to the musicians in the street. Sylvania laughed.

"They're just having fun," she said. "This is the show."

The crowd quieted. The sun now hovered over the water at their backs, perfectly illuminating the woods that they looked into.

"Um...is something going to happen in the woods?" Harvard asked.

"Just watch," Blaire said.

A bright flash of *something* flew through the leafy canopy, then disappeared. Jasmine yelped in surprise. For a moment, she thought that was a *person*. But that wasn't possible. How could—

Two more figures shot out from the leaves, did a flip in the air in perfect unison, and grabbed onto ropes that Jasmine hadn't even realized were hanging from the trees.

"What is this?" she marveled. "Is it...a kind of dance?"

"Sort of?" Sylvania said. "You don't have performers in Bastion? No acrobats?"

Jasmine shook her head. She couldn't imagine anyone in Bastion would have enough free time to learn to do something like this. She watched in a combination of amazement and horror as another performer launched themself out of the leaves, just barely catching a rope with their feet before they plummeted to the ground.

"What if they fall?" Harvard asked, gripping the railing tightly, as though he feared that he too would end up falling through the leaves.

"There's nets!" Blaire said, pointing down below, though it was so dark below that Jasmine just had to take his word for it. "Besides, they do this every month. No one ever falls."

Jasmine allowed herself to relax a bit when she knew no one was in danger. When her shock wore off, she found the movements of the airborne dancers—acrobats, as Sylvania had called them—breathtaking. Why didn't they have anything like this in Bastion? The moment she wondered, she knew the answer. In Bastion, anything that wasn't productive was a waste of time. She thought of Harvard, a talented musician and artist who still ended up as a scavenger. How could someone like him ever hope to find happiness in a city that didn't value what he had to offer? Here in Haven, people could do something that was beautiful just for the sake of beauty. And because they wanted to.

Jasmine remembered that tonight they would be leaving Haven, and the profound sadness pressed a heavy weight into her chest. She pushed that thought aside and did something she rarely did: she allowed herself to enjoy this one night.

Sylvania silently slid her hand into Jasmine's, and their fingers intertwined.

* * *

Harvard was shocked to find how easy it was to slip out of the ceremony without being noticed. He'd given a little performance on the vibraphone in the Meeting Hall, and the already wine-addled ceremony attendees cheered and danced and clapped. Blaire had even given him a big hug afterward. At first Harvard thought he was drunk too, but when he pulled away Harvard realized that he was actually just really happy. In fact, Harvard was shocked to see tear tracks on his cheeks.

"You are so, so special, Harvard," he said, squeezing his shoulders. "I'm so glad you've come here. I'm so happy I found you. I'm so excited that we get to make you citizen of Haven."

"Me too," Harvard said, and already guilt roiled in his chest. It was so nice to be accepted, and it felt like a waste to be throwing that away. Here he was, at a party all about welcoming him and his friends into the community, and here he was about to go commit sacrilege. Again.

He made a surreptitious exit through the backroom, where they stored extra chairs, food, and the ceremonial wine. He found a door around the corner and slunk out. According to Jasmine, the tree with the Relic should be just around here, accessible via rope bridge just like the rest of the city. He located the bridge in the darkness, the only corner of the platform that the lantern light didn't reach. Shrouded in shadows was a thin, weathered rope bridge.

Harvard set one foot on the first plank, and it creaked in protest. Harvard guessed this bridge didn't get as much upkeep as the rest. It was probably rarely used. He wondered if it would even support his weight.

Trembling, he took a deep breath and pushed himself forward. Everyone was counting on him, after all. He would not let them down because of a stupid bridge. Besides, he'd been living in Haven for two weeks now. He was used to these bridges.

A gust of wind swayed the bridge in the wind. The other bridges didn't sway like this. All the bridges in Haven that saw regular use had ropes that were pulled taut. This bridge had been allowed to sag with the weight of fallen branches and time. Harvard inhaled sharply and gripped the ropes tight. He squeezed his eyes shut and willed himself forward. When he opened them, he hazarded a glance down at the abyss below him, a wave of nausea rolled through him, and instead he looked at the abyss in front of him. There were no lights illuminating the Relic. He walked toward a featureless shadow.

When he made it to the platform without tumbling into the void below, he collapsed with relief. He shakily pulled himself back on his feet and fished around in his bag and pulled out Chavi's lighter. He flicked it on, ready to search for the Relic. He didn't need to search. It towered over him.

Harvard tried to make sense of what he was seeing. First of all, it was big. It reminded him a bit of O'Neill's pod, but it didn't have any legs. He knew it must have been meant to have people inside it, though, because the remains of its sole occupant still sat inside. The skeleton, strapped in place, had been picked clean by the island's wildlife. Was that some kind of restraint? So what had the pod done to this person? Had it killed them? Tortured them? And why?

Harvard shuddered, and suddenly he understood why the Relic was forbidden. This thing...it felt evil. He'd seen human remains in the dusts a few times, and the sight never got any less unsettling. But the bones he'd come across while scavenging at least, seemed at peace. Most had received a partial burial, sand deposited on top of them by wind to form a sort of shallow grave. Those pre-Quake humans were those who had succumbed to the whims of nature, so the land had reclaimed them.

The skeleton in the Relic was different. There was no peace for this corpse, strapped forever into a tableau of violence, jaw hanging open in a perpetual scream. The trunk of the tree seemed to be fighting to swallow the machine, tree branches had begun to weave their way into the corroded metal of the pod, like a body working to combat an infection. The infection, however, stubbornly remained, rooted to the spot. The Haveners probably couldn't dislodge it if they tried.

Harvard had always chosen to believe that the corpses he came across in the dusts had died quietly, slowly, and calmly. He had no doubt that this person had died afraid.

To bring this thing back to Bastion—even just to bring the idea of it back to Bastion—felt...well, it felt sinful. But Avi had sacrificed herself for him, and he wasn't going to let that sacrifice be in vain.

He pulled out Jasmine's notebook and began sketching.

His work was quick but detailed. He didn't dare enter the pod, but he got close enough that he could peer inside and sketch the interior. He drew the seat and the restraints, even the corpse. Lastly, he stepped back and drew the entire thing. There were spikes jutting out of the top.

This is a weapon, he thought. *Devrin must be trying to build a weapon.*

He wondered if his sketches were going to get people killed. He took a deep breath. He kept sketching.

Satisfied that he'd taken down everything, he slipped the notebook back in his satchel and made his way across the rope bridge to the ceremony.

When he pushed open the back door, hushed voices gave him pause. They were just around the corner. The room had been empty when he'd first left. If anyone saw him sneaking back into the party, they'd ask questions. He'd have to wait until they cleared out. He closed the door silently behind him and pressed his back up against the wall.

"I still think it's a shame," a voice said. "I like Jasmine. I think we could have been friends."

"I know, I know," said a higher-pitched voice. "But we don't know who gets which cup, so it has to be the whole bottle."

What were they talking about? What was going to happen to Jasmine? Or the rest of them?

Neither of the voices were Marcel's, but Harvard guessed these must be his people, and they must be planning something.

"Do we know which crate they're pulling from?" asked a gruff voice. That must have been Oleg. Harvard inhaled sharply before clapping a hand over his mouth and nose to stifle the sound of his breathing. Marcel had mentioned going to visit Oleg after Lyle's death. Was this somehow related?

"We'll just hand off the wine ourselves," said the higher voice. "It'll be easier that way."

"No good," said Oleg. "It's not our job to select the bottle. If we're suddenly pretending like we're wine experts, they'll know we've done something. We pick a crate, we do the whole batch, and then we come back here and get rid of it after the ceremony is over."

"I still think it's a bad idea," said the first voice. Harvard thought he recognized it—it was the boy who had gone through his bag! Des, he remembered.

"If you don't want to have a hand in keeping our city safe," Oleg grunted, "then you can leave the security force now."

"I'm not leaving the security force, I just don't like this," Des whined.

"Then open the crate and hand me the venom."

Venom. Like from the snake that bit August. They were poisoning the ceremony wine.

His mind raced. He had to do something, didn't he? He couldn't stop them from doing it without exposing himself, which he guessed would be a risky move. *But I can warn them*, he thought. *They can't be poisoned if they don't drink it.*

Slowly, deliberately, silently, Harvard placed a foot in the direction of the door he'd come in through. He shifted his weight soundlessly. Again, he placed his foot ahead of him, shifted his weight—

The board creaked.

The movement around the corner stopped.

"What was that?" Krisha asked.

"I didn't hear anything," Des said.

"Hold on," Krisha said. "I don't think we're alone."

Harvard's breath caught in his throat. He lunged for the door, but before he could get there, someone grabbed the hood of cloak and yanked him backward. He yelped, falling hard on his back. He saw Krisha, Des, and Oleg all standing over him.

"Maybe he didn't hear anything?" Des asked hopefully.

Krisha shook her head, and her long copper earrings jangled. "Look at his guilty little face. He heard everything."

Harvard struggled to his feet, but before he could try and explain himself to cry out for help, Oleg grabbed him by the throat and slammed him against the wall. Harvard gasped—or at least, he tried to. He instinctively grabbed Oleg's arm, but he remembered he still had a knife in his bag. He fumbled for the open of his satchel.

"His bag!" Des pointed. "Get the bag!"

Before Harvard's hand could close on anything useful, Krisha leapt for him and yanked the bag off him. It broke at the same place it had when Marcel had cut it off the previous night—he'd only managed to tie it loosely back together.

The bag fell to the ground, out of his reach, and Harvard's only hope of defending himself was dashed.

"He's spying," Oleg hissed.

"No!" Harvard wheezed. "Wasn't spying. Got lost."

"Lost?" Krisha laughed. "And you ended up here? Yeah, right. The only entrance is the one near the Relic and—" she paused. "Wait. Did you go look at the Relic?"

"No!" Harvard squeaked.

"Don't lie," Oleg growled.

Harvard winced. "Yes," he rasped before he could stop himself.

Krisha stepped up to him, her hands balled into fists. "Kill him, Oleg."

Harvard's eyes widened. "No! Please! Pl—" The word was choked off as Oleg's grip constricted. As Harvard gasped for air that wouldn't come, pawing weakly at Oleg's hand.

"Wait!" Des cried. "Not yet! Wait for Marcel at least."

"He has heard what he cannot hear and seen what he must not see," Oleg said. "He must die."

"But Marcel said not to—"

The wood outside the door groaned under the weight of footsteps.

"Someone's coming," Des said.

"Hide him!" Krisha demanded.

Oleg released his grip on Harvard, and he dropped to the ground. He grabbed at his throat, gasping. He barely had time to catch his breath when he was roughly bound and gagged, and he was still too weak to protest as three pairs of hands shoved him in an empty wine cask and closed the lid. The space was so cramped he couldn't even knock on the wood in front of him to alert anyone he was there. He bumped his shoulder against the lid, and it didn't budge. He wondered if someone was sitting on it.

"Oh. Um, what are you all doing here?" he heard a familiar voice say. Blaire.

Harvard tried to scream, but between the gag and the wooden cask, all he could manage was a muffled yelp.

"Preparing for the ceremony. Obviously. What are you doing back here, Blaire?"

"Rosenea sent me back to get some extra chairs. Is...everything alright?"

Please help me. You have to help me, Harvard willed, tapping against the wood with what little room he had. *If I can't get out of here, I can't save everyone. My friends will die. Chavi will die.*

"Everything is fine. Get your chairs and get out of here, alright?"

"Um...okay."

Harvard heard the clacking of wood, and a door opening. Blaire's footsteps stopped.

"What's that?" he asked.

"What?"

"That bag."

The satchel. He'd seen the satchel. *Please,* Harvard begged internally, *please put it together Blaire. Please.*

"Dunno," said Oleg.

"I recognize it. I...think it's Harvard's."

Yes! Yes, Blaire!

Harvard heard movement, and the rustle of fabric.

"Well," said Krisha, "then you better go take it to him, huh?"

"Yeah..." Blaire said, "I guess I should."

The door closed behind him. Harvard, trembling in the confines of the box, gave a terrified wail. No one, not even his captors, could hear him.

* * *

Chavi liked to think they did a pretty good job of making people like them. Whatever stories Marcel was spinning about what happened last night, people either hadn't heard them, or weren't buying them. They'd chatted a bit with August's gardening mentor, Jerricho, and some of Jasmine's research companions from the Library, and some of the music people that Harvard had worked with. They were pretty sure that after doing their rounds at the party, at least three different Haveners had a crush on them.

And Chavi wasn't even the most distracting of the distraction. August had organized a big card game in the center of the floor, and people were getting pretty riled up about it.

"That's the three of dirt, everyone!" he shouted. "And the round goes to the woman in the pink tunic! Congratulations, pink lady!"

This announcement was met with some cheers and shouts, especially from the people who had placed bets. Of course, in Haven there was no money, so they bet things like string and acorns.

"Alright people," August shouted as he shuffled the cards, "time for the next round!"

Someone strode up next to Chavi, and they almost jumped when they saw it was Marcel. They decided not to let the boy know how much he'd startled them. They opted for casualness.

"Hey man," they leaned back against the bar. "What's going on?"

Marcel smiled congenially. "Just enjoying the party." He laid a hand on their shoulder, and they fought the urge to shrug it off. "I'm sorry about earlier today. I know I got a little...riled up. I was just...shaken, you know? I know you don't have companions in Bastion, but it's hard to lose one."

Chavi didn't fully understand the companion system in Haven, but they knew enough to know that Lyle must have been important to Marcel somehow, and they'd accidentally taken him from him. They felt a stab of guilt in the pit of their stomach. For a moment, it hardly mattered what they'd been doing to Harvard. Chavi had killed someone, someone with a life, someone who would be missed. And they didn't even remember doing it. They'd somehow lost control, and...that was it. Just like with Carter back at the Academy. Just like with Minty on the Cookies. Somehow, bodies just kept falling around them, and they knew it was their fault but they didn't know how to stop it from happening.

"I am...really sorry about what happened to Lyle." And they meant it. "I got attacked by a procyon before and it was...well, it was horrible. I wouldn't wish that on anyone."

Marcel nodded somberly.

"I imagine you're...not thrilled to hear that I'm on the leadership track," Chavi ventured.

"Actually," Marcel said, "I'm fine with it."

Chavi reared back. "Wait, really?"

"I trust Rosenea, so I trust whoever she chooses. In fact"—he gestured with the drink in his hand—"I think the leadership training will be good for you."

"You do?" Chavi frowned. They knew a backhanded compliment when they heard one.

"Maybe one day we'll learn to get along. I'm looking forward to working with you, Chavi." Marcel held out a hand. Chavi took it tentatively.

"Yeah," they said, "me too."

Oleg appeared behind Marcel so suddenly Chavi almost jumped again.

"Marcel," he said, "we need some help with the ceremony preparations. Right now."

Marcel rolled his eyes.

"Can you please deal with it on your own?" Marcel asked.

Oleg shifted awkwardly, and Chavi thought it was ironic to see the hulking man looking so nervous in front of weaselly little Marcel, like a scuttler scared of a bird.

"I—I think you'd better come have a look," Oleg gestured toward the back room. Chavi snorted. How much preparation did the ceremony really need? And was it really *that* urgent? This whole thing was stupid.

"Fine," Marcel grumbled, turning to go. "I'll be seeing you, Chavi," he said over his shoulder.

"So that's good news, right?" August sidled up next to them, evidently taking a break from his gamemastering. "Marcel doesn't hate you anymore. That's—I mean, that's cool."

Chavi shook their head.

"I don't buy it," they said, then took a sip of their drink. "It's just like, the weird diplomacy rituals they have around here. Something super shady is going on."

August shrugged.

"Did you have the cheese dip? It's like, really good. I didn't know cheese was supposed to taste like that."

Chavi watched Marcel go.

"I think cheese dip is the least of our problems."

* * *

Harvard heard the door again, and his heart leapt.

"This better be important," Marcel said.

Dusts. It was *him*. Was this it, then? His breath came fast and shallow, his heart hammering, his mind racing. What could he do? Could he do anything? He heard creaking above him as the cask lid was lifted. He squinted into the candlelight, silhouettes peering in on him.

"Why is he here?" Marcel asked levelly.

"He heard—well, he heard everything, we think."

Harvard pushed himself up, but Marcel easily shoved him back. The cask lid slammed closed so quickly it hurt Harvard's ears.

"How did you let this happen?" Marcel hissed.

"We didn't know he was in here! He was—He was spying on us!"

"I can't believe you people are so stupid."

"I said we should kill him."

"Well thank the Principles you didn't! What if someone had walked in?"

"Blaire almost did, actually."

"Did he see anything? Do we need to get rid of him as well?"

The "get rid of him" part made Harvard worry about Blaire, but then he remembered the "as well" part, and he worried more about himself.

"I don't think so, no."

"Alright. Good."

"And...the kid?" Harvard simmered.

"Come with me."

Harvard felt the cask lift, and he was jostled around, his face bumping up against the wood. He couldn't get a sense of where they were taking him, but when he heard the sound of wind and insects, he guessed they'd gone outside. The din of the party faded, and soon the only sounds were the rustle of leaves, the chirping of bugs, and the clomping of boots.

"Listen," Marcel said, "we gotta do this fast before anyone misses us. Oleg, you hold him. Krisha, kill him quick. Then we dump him over the edge, problem solved."

Harvard's heart hammered. He wasn't sure if he was more scared for himself or the rest of the Ivies. He didn't want to die. Not now. Not here. But if they did kill him, no one would warn the rest of his crew about the fate that awaited them. He had to get out. He knew he had to get out. He pushed at the wood, he pulled on his bonds, but there was nothing he could do.

"I don't—" Krisha started.

"What? He was gonna be dead by the end of the night anyway," Marcel said. "We're only speeding things along."

"It just feels more...personal."

"You know what was personal, Krisha?" Marcel asked, his voice breaking like he was near tears. "When Chavi killed Lyle right in front of us."

"Look we—we don't know exactly what happened—"

"We do. I saw it. You all may not know what you saw, but I do. If you can't think of this as a service to Haven, that's fine. You can think of it as payback."

"Alright. Fine. I just..."

"Do you think he can hear us?" Des asked.

"I don't care if he can. He'll be dead in a minute."

"I feel bad, talking about killing him when he can hear us."

"Alright. Fine. If you all don't wanna handle this, then I will."

Harvard recognized the sound of a knife being unsheathed.

"Oleg, you hold him. I'll be quick."

The cask lid swung open again, and two hands roughly pulled him up. He squirmed, desperately fighting to get away, but Oleg's grip was iron.

"You're a wriggly one, huh," he laughed, and Harvard knew he had no hope of breaking free. He caught sight of Des and Krisha, looking away, and Marcel stepping forward, wearing a hard look of determination.

"It's nothing personal, Harvard," he said. "Though to be honest, I never did like you all that much."

Harvard screamed, and he could see Des flinch away, covering his ears with his hands.

Elbows are your best friend, Harvard remembered August had told him.

Fueled by primal terror, Harvard rammed his elbow into Oleg's ribs. He grunted, caught off guard, and his grip on Harvard weakened, just enough to allow Harvard to escape.

Marcel slashed at Harvard just as he jerked to the side, missing his throat but biting into his cheek. He was aware it should have hurt, but in the moment pain didn't register. His mind, body, and whole being were all consumed with the single impulse: *run run run run run.*

Harvard darted toward the nearest rope bridge he could find. He had to find people. Anyone who could help him. But everyone was still at the party, weren't they? In order to alert someone, he'd have to run back in the direction he'd come. Well, he'd just have to lose them, then he could sneak back.

He'd have to run fast. And Harvard was nothing if not fast.

Harvard could hear Marcel cursing behind him.

"Get him!" Marcel demanded, followed by the pounding of boots. The world swung dizzily around Harvard as he surveyed his options. He made for the Cultivation Center. At least he knew the territory there, as opposed to the vast sections of the city that he still hadn't seen.

He slung his legs over the sheep pen and dove in with the ambling creatures, crawling by their legs so their ample wool hid him.

"Sheepsdung. Where'd he go?"

He padded silently on his hands and knees, gently nudging sheep out of his way. He bit down the urge to say "excuse me." The opposite end of the pen was so close. If he could just—

Ellie, the sheep whose lamb he'd named, stepped in front of him. He held his finger to his lips, as though she could understand him. She only nuzzled him affectionately. He wished he could communicate with her like he could the crabs, tell her he was in danger, tell her not to make any—

"Baaaaahhhhh!"

Dusts.

"In the sheep pen!"

He bounded over the opposite end of the pen as he heard his pursuers clomping into the enclosure behind him. Sheep bleated in protest. He worried they were getting hurt because of him.

Harvard rounded a corner and came across a rope bridge. Maybe if he left the central platform of the city, he'd be harder to catch. He started across the bridge, and it only swayed a little.

He hazarded a look over his shoulder, and saw that his pursers hadn't followed him onto the bridge. They stood at the edge of the platform, watching him. His stomach dropped. Something was wrong.

Only a moment too late did he see Krisha, Des, Oleg and Marcel all had the knives drawn, and each gripped the frayed edges of the ropes that had held up the bridge.

Marcel gave a sweet smile as the four of them dropped the rope, and the bridge fell from under Harvard. He barely had time to scream before he plummeted into the darkness below.

* * *

"Would you like another drink?" Sylvania asked.

"I probably shouldn't," Jasmine said, her face heating. "I mean, I do have to drink a whole cup of wine as part of the ceremony, right? And that's actually—what time is it? That must be soon."

As she said it, she felt a pang of worry. The ceremony was about to start, wasn't it? Where was Harvard?

Chavi must have been thinking the same thing, because Jasmine could see them pushing their way through the crowd toward her.

"I need to speak with Jasmine. Alone," they said, hardly even glancing at Sylvania. Sylvania's face hardened, and for a moment Jasmine thought she was irritated, but then she realized she was jealous. Jasmine wanted to laugh. She knew how her relationship with Chavi must look from the outside, but for Sylvania to worry that Chavi might be a threat to her? It was actually hilarious.

Jasmine reached out and gave Sylvania's arm a squeeze. She flashed her a reassuring smile.

"It'll only be a moment, okay?" she said, and while Jasmine had never been particularly good and flirting, she tried to make it the most romantic thing she'd ever said. Sylvania seemed to get the message.

"I'll be waiting for you," she said, and slipped away back into the crowd.

"Harvard should be back by now," Chavi said.

"I was just thinking the same thing."

"I think he might have gotten into trouble. I mean, if someone caught him—" they glanced over their shoulder. The room was too crowded for them to risk being overheard. "If someone caught him doing what he's doing, it could be serious. I'm going to go look for him."

Jasmine twisted one of her braids in her fingers. "I'm not sure that's a good idea. One of us sneaking off is fine, but if you disappear too, don't you think people will notice?"

A cheer rose from August's game at the center of the room.

"And this round goes to the person with the feathers in their hair! Neat head-feathers! The winner of the next round gets the prize of bringing me more cheese dip!"

"I think August has them pretty distracted," Chavi said. "Besides, I won't be long."

"You don't know that," she shook her head, but she already knew she wasn't going to convince them. If Chavi was stubborn before they were with Harvard, then she didn't have a word for what they were now. When it came to their boyfriend, there was no talking them down.

"Just keep doing what you're doing here, okay?" they said, though all Jasmine had been doing was talking with Sylvania about theoretical evolutionary biology.

"I'll be right back."

* * *

Harvard awoke on the forest floor shocked that he woke up at all. His whole body screamed with pain. He wondered if he would be able to get up, or if he'd just die here. Surprisingly, he was able to bring himself up to a sitting position and prod himself for wounds. Nothing broken. He looked up—how far had he fallen?

Above him he saw the net from the acrobat performance, and he realized he had been very, very lucky. The net must have broken his fall, but he still hit the forest floor hard enough that he'd been knocked out. He rubbed his head and wondered how long he'd been out.

The party. The poison.

Memories flooded back to him, and he struggled to his feet, only to fall back to the ground on a twisted ankle. He dragged himself across the forest floor until he found a branch sharp enough to saw off the bonds on his hands. Once he'd freed his wrists, he tore off the gag and took a deep breath. He looked up at Haven, glowing with lanternlight. How in the name of the Founders would he get back up there?

Harvard? He heard Speedy's voice in his head. *You're awake. I can sense it.*

"Speedy!" he cried, searching the forest floor for his carcine companion, "Speedy, where are you?"

I cannot find you, Speedy said, *I can tell something is wrong. I can tell you are hurt.*

"Speedy! You have to help me. The others are in danger. The ceremony, the wine at the ceremony—"

I cannot find you.

"Forget about me! Go to the ceremony and—"

I am searching for you.

"But—"

Speedy couldn't hear him. Of course. That was always how it had been with Skrack and the Empress. The crabs could speak into his mind, but he couldn't do the same for theirs. He had no way of communicating the direness of the situation. All Speedy knew was that he had suddenly disappeared.

"Speedy! I'm down here!" he cried.

I can sense you. You are far away. Just a moment.

Harvard waited, looking up at the city silhouetted in moonlight, and every second was agony. What if the ceremony was over? What if his friends were already dead? What was happening up there?

You are below?

Thank the Founders for the crabs and their inexplicable sense of location!

"Yes!" Harvard cried. "I'm down here!"

You have fallen? I cannot reach you. But I...I will find a way to help you.

"Please!" Harvard shouted, though he knew he couldn't be heard, "Help me, Speedy!"

He waited for something, anything to happen. Maybe Speedy would find a way to send down one of those gondolas.

Unless...you do not want to be helped?

"No, Speedy! I need your help! Please help me!"

This is a conundrum indeed.

"No, it's not! Help me, Speedy!"

What to do...

"Speedy! Help me!"

If you are below, I must assume you are in danger. Therefore, I must assume you need my help. And if I assume wrong, then I suppose I will endure your ire at a later point.

Something fell in front of Harvard with a thud. In the darkness, he could hardly see it. He moved closer, and saw a rope dangling from a platform of Haven. The end was frayed, as though roughly severed by a claw.

I'm afraid this is the best I could do, Speedy said, and even in Harvard's mind he sounded apologetic.

I could not send down a box for you without ruining the apparatus that would bear you to safety. But I've loosed one end of a rope, which is fastened to it.

"Speedy..." Harvard said, looking up the rope, and suddenly distance felt infinite.

I'm sorry, Harvard, Speedy said, *but you're going to have to climb.*

* * *

Chavi pushed open the door into the backroom of the Meeting House. This was the path Harvard was supposed to take to get to the Relic. All they found were wine casks and chairs. And...Blaire?

Blaire was seated on a cask, trembling. He was holding something—Harvard's satchel.

"That's Harvard's bag," Chavi said, already holding out their hand for it. Blaire jumped.

"Where did he get this?" he asked, holding up Jasmine's notebook.

"That? That's just Jasmine's notebook. Why—" Chavi looked closer. Scrawled on the pages were hurried sketches of some kind of machine. It was unmistakably Harvard's work.

The Relic, they thought. So Harvard had managed to take down the diagrams, and get the notebook back to the party. But then where was he?

"Why does he have this?" Blaire asked, and Chavi realized he was near tears. Did their stupid little island religion really mean that much to them?

"I don't know," Chavi lied. "He likes to draw. He probably just stumbled on it—"

"You don't just stumble into the Relic!" Blaire cried. "It's...it's evil. It...messes with your mind. And it makes you evil if you see it!"

"Blaire." Chavi held out a hand as if to calm him. "You realize that sounds totally crazy, right?"

"It's part of the Haven Principles! And the Haven Principles are true!" he cried with the frenzy of a man who was grasping desperately at his belief system before it shattered.

Chavi dropped their hand. "Wait," they said, "how do *you* know what the Relic looks like?"

Blaire's grip on the notebook loosed, and it dropped to the floor. He fell to his knees and started weeping into the heels of his hands.

"When I was a kid," he sobbed. "I was curious. And I was weak. And that's why I'm like this. That's why I'm a curse on Haven. I was the one who brought those outsiders. And I was the one who brought you in, and now, now..." He sobbed again.

Chavi softened a little. He really was like Harvard, wasn't he? They'd heard Harvard articulate the same thing countless times.

"You're not evil, Blaire." They took a step toward him. "And you're definitely not a curse on Haven."

Blaire shook his head. "I am, I am, I am!" he insisted. Chavi lowered themself down beside him, placing a hand on his back.

"Of course you're not. You saved our lives. You didn't have to do that. And beyond that, you've cared for us, and given us a home, and more importantly, given us a friend..."

Blaire let out another sob, his face still buried in his hand. Chavi rubbed his back with one hand while reaching for the notebook with the other. It was just beyond their grasp. They bent forward, still with one hand on Blaire.

"Just seeing the Relic doesn't make you a bad person," they said, their fingers brushing against the edge of the binding. "You were just a kid—"

Blaire's head snapped up. He snatched up the notebook, clutching it to his chest, and leapt to his feet, backing away.

"No! No!" he cried, wearing a horrified expression. "You're...you're lying. You just want the notebook. But I can't let you have it. I can't!"

Chavi let out an exasperated breath, then tried to approach from a different angle. "Look, I—I just can't have you getting Harvard in trouble, alright? You like Harvard, don't you? You wouldn't want to see him get hurt."

"But—but—" Blaire looked between the notebook and Chavi. "You all are supposed to be initiated tonight! And that can't happen if Harvard isn't in line with the Principles—"

"He is in line with the Principles. He just got curious, just like you did, so you really can't blame him—"

Chavi took a step forward, reaching for the notebook, and Blaire scampered back.

"I have to report this," he said, wiping away tears with the back of his hand. "I'm sorry."

Chavi sighed, lowering their outstretched hand. They didn't want to have to do this. They looked at him and couldn't help but see Harvard, trembling and sobbing. But they may not have a choice.

"Are you sure?" they asked pleadingly.

Blaire sniffled. "Yes."

Chavi's heart sank. "Blaire," they said, "I was really, really hoping you wouldn't say that."

They drew their hunting knife, and Blaire froze, eyes wide with panic. Chavi's chest tightened, and they wanted nothing more than to back down and apologize for scaring him. But Harvard was more important than anything. Blaire watched them with the same fear and confusion that he had when he'd first encountered them on the forest floor as Chavi approached him. They gently pressed the tip of the knife to Blaire's chest, just above the edge of the notebook. Blaire's eyes locked with theirs, and the terror they saw there made them hate themself. They didn't want to be terrifying. But for Harvard, they would be.

"Give it to me," they said, "or I will kill you."

"I don't...I don't understand," Blaire said in a frantic whisper. "I was nice to you. I opened my home to you. Why would you...you couldn't. You *wouldn't.*"

Chavi laughed, and they didn't know why. It wasn't a sound they meant to make. It was cruel and cold and felt unnatural coming out of their mouth. "If you think that, then you don't know how far I would go to protect him. I would do anything to keep Harvard from harm."

"I thought we were friends," Blaire said.

"We *were* friends," Chavi said, drawing closer. Blaire squeaked. "And then you threatened Harvard. You have to understand that I can't allow that."

"But...I gave you everything," he said, trembling. Chavi willed him to stop, before it made them lose their nerve. "I housed you and fed you and taught you and—"

Chavi put a little more pressure on the knife, and a pinprick of blood wet the fabric of Blaire's tunic. He gasped.

"Notebook. Now."

With a little whimper, Blaire relinquished his grip on the notebook, and Chavi snatched it. They kept the knife level.

"This is what you're going to do," they said. "You're not going to tell anyone that this happened, and that way, you won't get hurt. That way we can keep being friends. Alright?"

Blaire stared blankly. "I—But I—"

A little more pressure. A little more blood. *Please, Blaire. I can't keep doing this.*

"Alright!" Blaire cried. Chavi withdrew the knife, and Blaire crumpled weeping.

Chavi surprised even themself to find in that moment, they hated him. Hated him for making them do this, hated him for making it so quaking hard.

They sheathed the knife, then hauled Blaire to his feet.

"Go," they commanded, shoving him toward the door, and Blaire scurried off like a scared animal.

* * *

For the third time, Harvard launched himself into the air, his injured ankle protesting at the effort. He managed to grip the rope, holding himself a few feet off the ground. He gripped the bottom of the rope between his shoes, which, again, did not please his twisted ankle. He willed himself to pull his body up, but his arms were just too weak. Besides, he struggled to grip the rope with his still-healing fingers. He trembled with effort.

Climb! he told himself, *Climb!*

His arms gave out, and he fell to the forest floor was a painful thud.

He wanted to scream. He wanted to cry. But he knew there wasn't time.

The Ivies needed him. Chavi needed him.

"Argh!" he cried, throwing himself at the rope again. The rope swung lazily with his momentum. He could barely catch it with his feet, the way it lolled back and forth.

"Stop swinging!" he shouted in frustration. He lost his grip again. *If the stupid thing would only stay still*, he thought as he picked himself up, *then I could—*

He froze, watching the rope continue to swing in the evening breeze.

He couldn't climb it. He knew he couldn't climb it.

But he could definitely swing.

* * *

"We've got a problem," Chavi said, thankful to find Jasmine and August already together by the food table.

"Is that Harvard's bag?" Jasmine asked, seeing the satchel clutched in Chavi's hand. The strap was broken a second time.

"We've got Harvard's bag but no Harvard?" August asked.

"Does he have the drawings?" Jasmine added.

Chavi pulled them both into a tight huddle. "Yeah, he's got the drawing. And Blaire saw them."

Jasmine's eyes widened. "Oh."

"I think I convinced him not to tell," Chavi said.

"How did you do that?" August asked.

Don't make me talk about it, they begged inwardly. *It was not my proudest moment.* "Um. I...said I would kill him."

Jasmine's brow furrowed, as though she were pleading with them to say that this was a joke. "Chavi..."

"What?" they hissed, suddenly on the defensive.

"Maybe people wouldn't believe Blaire even if he did tell," August offered. "I mean, he's not the most popular guy around. Who can prove those drawings are Harvard's?"

Jasmine bowed her head, rubbing her forehead. "Sylvania."

August turned to look at her. "What?"

"She knows what his art looks like. I...I gave her some of his sketches."

"You *did*?"

"She was interested in them!"

"Well great," Chavi said, "thanks to your crush, we're absolutely fucked."

Jasmine ignored them, which was probably for the best because they both knew that was totally unfair.

"But if you have the drawings," she asked, "then where is Harvard?"

"That's what I'm trying to figure out."

* * *

Harvard swung his legs out in front of him, gaining air with each journey back and forth. He guessed he was now a few meters off the ground, at this point. If he could only get himself high enough, he could launch himself onto one of the Haven platforms. Or he might miss, and launch himself into nothing, and then fall all the way back down *without* a net, and die for real. He decided, for the time being, to put that possibility out of his mind. He had to warn the Ivies. That was all that mattered.

He looked down as he swung backward. His arc brought him dizzyingly high up—maybe ten meters at this point? His grip tightened on the rope. Harvard had never been afraid of heights, but admittedly before this point he'd never had many heights to be afraid of.

He used all the core strength he had to swing himself forward again, gaining just a little more height.

"I'm coming!" he shouted to no one. "I'm coming!"

* * *

"Are you ready?" Rosenea laid a gentle hand on Chavi's shoulder, startling them. "The sun is almost up. We need to get started."

"Harvard isn't here," Chavi said, and Jasmine sighed. They weren't supposed to point that out. If someone did find the drawings, Harvard's absence at the ceremony would essentially cement his guilt. Well, what did it matter? If they started the ceremony now, they'd notice his absence anyway.

"We can start without him," Rosenea said.

"No, we can't," Chavi insisted. "It wouldn't be right. This is something we're supposed to do together."

Rosenea studied the three Ivies with a matronly gaze.

"I understand. You four feel that you are a team."

"We *are* a team," August said.

"Very well," she said with an impatient glance out the window at the horizon. "We can wait a bit longer. But only a bit."

* * *

Harvard might not have been close enough to land on a Haven platform, but he didn't think he had much time left. He could see the horizon beginning to glow, and he knew that dawn must not be far off. If he missed his chance, that would be the end of it.

This time, I'm gonna jump, he thought as he swung back. As he reached the top of his arc, he kicked his feet forward with as much strength as he could manage. He swooped down to the forest floor and back up again, up into the treetops, up toward the Haven platforms.

And then he let go.

For one exhilarating, terrifying moment, he was weightless, only aware of the whistling of the wind and the flailing of his limbs in the cool night air. He could see the platform coming up toward him, and it looked as though he would just barely be able to grip the edge. He reached for the platform. His fingers brushed up against the wood. And he started to fall.

Just before a scream was able to burst from his lip, a hand closed around his wrist, stopping his descent. He hung suspended for a fraction of a moment before someone pulled him up.

"Harvard," said Captain Saxifrage, "what the quaking fuck are you doing?"

* * *

"Harvard is still not here yet," Chavi said to Rosenea as she took her place at the podium, holding up a hand for silence. "Then we can perform his ceremony another day. The full moon won't be up all night, you know. And we always do wine-pouring as the sun rises. It's a Haven tradition. We cannot miss the sunrise."

"But—"

"We're starting. Now."

They frowned. "Fine."

Chavi allowed Jasmine to pull them into their seat. Harvard's chair was conspicuously empty next to them. Chavi wasn't sure if they heard confused murmurings in the crowd, or if it was in their head.

Rosenea launched into a speech about the Haven Principles, the power of community, and the importance of growth.

"And our community will grow tonight, and with that growth, our community becomes stronger."

The crowd cheered. Most of the crowd did, anyway. Chavi caught sight of Blaire at the back, leaning against the wall. He had his arms wrapped around himself, and he looked sick. Not angry, just deeply, deeply sad.

Chavi broke their gaze away when they heard the cork pop of the ceremonial wine. Rosenea poured them each a glass in turn.

"A symbol," she said, "to prove that you are one of us. That the blood of Haven runs through you as well."

* * *

"Have they had the ceremony?" Harvard gripped Sax by both shoulders.

"They're about to start," Sax said, looking befuddled. "I left. I didn't...it felt wrong to be there. Why? What is going on?"

Harvard grabbed zyr wrist and pulled zem along with him.

"We have to go! Now!"

"I just left!" Sax said, pulling back. "I'm not going back there!"

Harvard turned to face zem, stunned.

"But I—I have to—"

"Just go," Sax said, rubbing zyr wrist where Harvard had grabbed zem. "And whatever you're doing...good luck."

Harvard nodded his thank you, then whirled around, racing toward the Meeting House.

* * *

Chavi lifted the wooden chalice, looking into the deep crimson wine. The blood of Haven. It felt wrong, after what they'd done. They'd drawn the blood of Haven tonight.

Oh well. No turning back now.

They raised the chalice to their lips.

The door burst open.

"Stop!" Harvard appeared in the doorway, shoving Haveners aside. Held up his hand.

"Harvard!" Chavi cried, leaping up from their spot at the dais so abruptly their chair clattered to the floor. They dove into the crowd and ran for him, shoving their way through the stunned Haveners. To their surprise, Harvard wasn't shaking. But he was a mess. His clothes were caked in dirt, and there were leaves and sticks decorating his hair. On his cheek he bore a long cut, trails of dried blood painting a path down to his jaw. And from what they could see of his outstretched palm, the skin on his hands was blistered and torn. It reminded Chavi of their own hands after the sandheads incident.

"What's going on here?" Rosenea asked from the podium.

"Don't drink that wine." Harvard pointed to the cups on the table. "It's poisoned."

August spit out his wine, spraying some unhappy Haveners with crimson.

Chavi managed to fight through the crowd and reach Harvard, wrapping him in a hug.

"Are you alright?" they asked, examining the cut on his face.

"I'm fine," he shook them off, eyes still focused on the dais.

"That's a dangerous claim," Rosenea said levelly. "You imply that one of our own would try to hurt you?"

"Yes," Harvard said, and Chavi had never seen such fury on his face. "Him."

Harvard pointed a finger at Marcel, who looked stunned.

"What?" Marcel gaped, looking genuinely shocked. He was a surprisingly good actor. "I'm the security liaison! I would never let something like that happen! Rosenea, surely you trust me more than these outsiders?"

Harvard balled his bloodied hands into fists. "I heard about his plans to poison the wine—him and his underlings—and when they realized I knew, they dumped me off the edge."

A gasp rippled through the crowd. Chavi stared at him. How had he survived that? They turned their gaze back to Marcel. They would kill him for this—and this time they *wouldn't* have any reservations about it.

"Rosenea," Marcel pleaded, "you can't seriously be entertaining this."

Rosenea held up a hand to silence him.

"Anything is possible," she said. She reached forward and lifted Jasmine's cup. "May I?" she asked. Jasmine nodded.

"If this is all a lie," she said, handing the cup to Marcel, "surely you won't mind drinking some yourself?"

Marcel scoffed.

"I'm wounded," he said, scrunching up his sneaky little rat face. "You don't trust me? After everything we've built here together, you're going to trust these—these—people"—he gestured broadly at the Ivies—"over me?"

"I didn't say that," she said. "I'm merely asking you to drink the wine."

"I don't see how—"

"I understand that you must still be hurting from the death of your companion," Rosenea cut him off, "and I simply want to ensure that you haven't done anything...destructive in your grief."

Marcel accepted the cup. He glared at Harvard, who—to Chavi's surprise—glared back.

"Drink it!" they shouted, their grip tightening on Harvard's shoulder.

Marcel rolled his eyes, and lifted a cup to his lips. Chavi may have imagined it, but they could have sworn he was trembling.

"Wait!" someone shouted. Krisha stepped up to the dais. She pointed an accusing finger at Harvard. "*He's* only trying to cover himself because we caught him viewing the Relic."

A susurration of discontented whispers rose from the crowd, and Chavi's stomach fluttered. They saw Jasmine and August share a look, then start making their way through the crowd to join them. August still clutched the satchel.

"Is this true?" Rosenea asked. Harvard opened his mouth to speak, but Chavi beat him to it.

"Of course it's not," they said. "You just wanna accuse him because he's an easy target. Because of course everyone is gonna believe that the foreigners are part of some evil scheme, right? It's just a distraction. I can't believe you people are actually fooled by this."

"I wasn't talking to you, Chavi," Rosenea said coolly. "I was speaking to Harvard."

Harvard flushed. *Now* he was trembling. Chavi could feel hand shaking in theirs. They pulled him closer to them.

"Who cares about the Relic? He tried to murder us!" Chavi said. This elicited a murmured response from the crowd, but they couldn't tell if it was the response they wanted. "Make him drink the wine!"

"Not before I hear what Harvard has to say for himself," Rosenea said. The crowd gradually fell silent, all eyes expectantly fixed on Harvard. Harvard scanned the room.

"I didn't do it," he said.

Rosenea nodded, as though this answer was accepted. Chavi's muscles relaxed, and beside them Jasmine let out a relieved breath.

"He's lying," said a new voice from the back of the room. All eyes shifted to the man pressing himself against the back wall, hugging himself.

"Blaire?" August gaped. "What are you doing, man?"

"I'm sorry," he said through tears. "I didn't want to do this to you. I thought that I was friends with you. But—" He swallowed, looking to Rosenea. She gave him an encouraging nod. Chavi's hand closed around the hilt of their knife, and they wondered if they'd have to make good on their threat. They locked eyes with Blaire.

Stand down, they thought, *if you don't want to get hurt.*

But Blaire was no desertwalker, and he couldn't hear them. He pressed on.

"I found Harvard's bag," he said, "and he had...he had sketches of...the Relic. And before you say anything"—he held up a hand—"I know I've committed sacrilege myself. And I am sorry. And I will repent. But I welcomed them." He paused, holding back tears. "I welcomed them into my home. And they betrayed us."

To Chavi's surprise, their grip on their knife slackened. Blaire was right. They had betrayed him, and all of Haven. Out of the corner of their eye, they saw Jasmine glancing at Sylvania. They couldn't bring themself to look at either girl's face.

Rosenea, unflappable, watched the Ivies over the rim of her glasses. "Well?"

"Let's see the bag!" someone in the crowd shouted.

"Yeah!" someone else echoed, "Open up the bag!"

"I think you all are forgetting," Chavi seethed, "that *Marcel* tried to kill us."

"Maybe he should have!" someone shouted, and the crowd erupted into chaos. Hands reached out to pull the bag from August's grip, and Chavi shoved them away.

"That doesn't belong to you!" they said. "That's Harvard's!"

Rosenea gave a sharp, piercing whistle. Chavi winced, one hand instinctively covering an ear.

"*QUIET*." she commanded.

All at once the room fell silent, under Rosenea's spell. She stepped down from the dais, and the crowd parted for her. She strode toward the Ivies with a regal gait. She held out a hand.

"Give me the bag," she commanded, "and I will inspect its contents. If I'm satisfied that no crime has been committed, then Marcel will drink the wine. Then the truth will out."

"Fine," Chavi said, ripping the bag from August's grip with one arm and shielding Harvard with the other. "We'll give you the bag. But first I wanna say that I'm disappointed in all of you." They cast their eyes over the crowd. "We tried to fit in, you know. We really tried. And you all rejected us. And we can't be blamed for that."

Harvard slipped his hand into Chavi's and gave it a squeeze. They turned to look at the other three, watching them with quiet intensity. Back in the dusts, Chavi and Jasmine used to share meaningful glances that the other couldn't decipher so that they could have a silent, private exchange. This time, all four Ivies shared a moment of wordless understanding.

"Chavi. Bag."

Chavi sighed. They clutched the bag to their chest.

"I hated this place anyway," they said.

As one, the Ivies turned and ran.

Interlude Eight: Avi

When Pierce disappeared, Avi knew her time was running out. He wasn't reading in her room anymore, which she guessed meant he must be preparing for the Ivies' return. Whatever they were bringing back, it was important, and Devrin was getting pretty excited about it. She could tell because he'd often be humming to himself in his office, looking through papers or files or whatever it is he spent his time going through, and he'd pause and say, "oh, I'm just so excited!"

Avi, on the other hand, was not feeling particularly excited. She'd committed herself to researching what the Delian Group was up to while she stayed here, and now her time was nearly up, and it seemed she'd made no headway. She didn't understand the transaction records she found, she didn't know what the Underground City was, and she didn't know what the fire in the laboratory had to do with any of it.

She did, however, seem to have garnered Devrin's favor for some odd reason, so she decided to use this to her advantage.

As a last-ditch effort, she decided she might as well try being direct, even though she didn't expect it would get her anywhere. She strode into his office, arms crossed, and asked: "Who are you competing with?"

To her surprise, he answered, "Arch nemesis," without looking up from his work.

"You have an arch nemesis?" Avi snorted.

He shrugged. "Of course I do. Everyone does."

"I don't."

"You'll understand when you're older."

"It's not normal to have an arch nemesis." Avi insisted. Devrin put down his pen with a click and stared at her incredulously.

"You're in *academia*, aren't you?"

"Yes?"

He smiled knowingly. "Then you'll definitely have one, believe me." With that, he made a shooing gesture and went back to his work.

Avi couldn't decide if he'd told her nothing or everything. On the one hand, "arch nemesis" was a pretty useless way to identify someone. But this meant he had an enemy within the city. She had been correct about that. But who in Bastion was powerful enough to compete with the Head Enforcer of the Delian Group?

CHAPTER SIXTEEN

Flight

For the second time that night, Harvard was running for his life, but at least this time he wasn't alone. After being in the heat of the cramped Meeting House, the cold felt like a slap in the face. The wind stung the cut on his cheek. His injured ankle complained at every step. It didn't matter. He kept pace with the Ivies. He refused to be the reason they got caught.

He did, however, wish he knew where they were going.

"Jasmine," August panted, "you know how sometimes when Plan A doesn't work it turns out that you secretly thought of a Plan B?" He hazarded a glance over his shoulder. "Well now would be a super great time to pull out that Plan B."

Jasmine, however, was already running ahead of them, in the opposite direction of the lift that had first taken them to Haven. She led them to the fishing gondola.

"This one is less discreet," she explained, climbing into the box, "but I think the time to be discreet is over. Right now, what we need is something that will take us to the shore."

Chavi paused, looking from the gondola to the Meeting House, where people were already streaming out into the night in search of the Ivies. "We don't have enough time," they said. "We need to slow them down."

"We'll make it if we go now," Jasmine said, holding out a hand to them.

Chavi backed away, shaking their head. "You guys go," they said, "I'll meet you down there."

"Wait!" Harvard lunged for them, but they were already sprinting back toward the village. Harvard moved to follow but August held him back.

"Chavi!" Jasmine cried.

From a distance, he saw them withdraw something from the satchel, then reach up to one of the thatched roofs...

The lighter.

The flames caught instantly, leaping up into the night sky so abruptly that Chavi stumbled backward. The inferno spread hungrily from hut to hut. Haveners began shouting as they noticed the blaze. Chavi reeled back, and as they neared the gondola Harvard could see the naked horror written on their face. What they intended to be a distraction had instantly morphed into wanton destruction. Harvard pulled them into the gondola, where they fell into August. Jasmine slammed the gate closed and started to work the crank.

"I have a better idea," August said, pulling out his gardening shears. He cut the ropes with an elegant snap.

"Wait! That's not—" Jasmine cried, but she reached it too late. Untethered, the gondola streaked down into the forest below.

Harvard could hear nothing but the roar of wind, and see nothing but the silhouettes of tree branches nearly taking his head off. He dropped to the floor of the gondola, which lurched and rattled as they descended.

His face slammed down onto the wood when they came to an abrupt stop, the basket tipping to violently deposit them onto the rocky beach.

"Fishing boats!" August cried, pointing to the dock. Jasmine nodded.

"We're going to steal their boats?" Harvard asked. Hadn't they done enough damage at this point?

Chavi towed Harvard along with them, the other hand gripping the satchel. "I think we already stole something much more important than that." Harvard's gut wrenched.

August was already cutting the boat loose with his sheers.

"Everybody in!" He called. Chavi practically threw Harvard into the boat, then helped Jasmine in. Before they could insist that August board, he wrapped his arms around them and swung them into the boat ahead of him, then started pushing it into the water.

The din of voices grew closer. Harvard could hear the sound of another gondola careening toward the sand.

"They're still chasing us!"

"Yeah I mean that makes sense, we *break their one law* and *set the place on fire*," August grunted, now up to his knees in water. Harvard remembered the bows and arrows that he'd seen Sylvania use to hunt. Unbidden, the image of Chavi impaled on an arrow sprung to his mind, and he couldn't banish the thought. He climbed on top of them toward the back of the boat, partially to shield them, and to offer August a hand. August gripped Harvard's forearm, but weighed down with water, he wasn't strong enough to pull him. Jasmine and Chavi reached around him, grabbing August's other arm and dragging him into the boat.

"Row!" he commanded. Chavi took up the oars. Harvard remained at the back of the boat, watching the Haveners gather at the shore, lanterns in hand, hunting bows ready. Someone fired off a shot. The arrow planted itself in the wood of the boat just below Harvard's fingers, and he could feel the reverberation of the impact in the wood. Another arrow smacked the water next to them. Another whipped past Harvard's face so close he could feel the displaced air. Harvard wanted to duck, but Chavi was right behind him, rowing with their back turned. He wouldn't expose them.

On the shore, someone screamed.

It was hard to tell with the island already receding in the distance, but Harvard thought he saw silver-white hair glowing in the firelight. Sylvania cried something that he could not hear. The Haveners lowered their bows.

Harvard should have felt relief at this, but instead he just felt nauseous, watching the Haveners recede in the distance. The Ivies had broken their trust, and in the end the Haveners were willing to let them go in peace. It didn't feel right.

They didn't deserve it.

* * *

Jasmine thought perhaps she could see Sylvania on the shore. She wasn't sure. Perhaps she'd already seen Sylvania for the last time and she hadn't known it. She chastised herself for thinking such stupid thoughts. Wasn't she supposed to be the smart one? They were always going to leave. That was always part of the plan. There was no use feeling bad about it now. Nothing was ever going to happen between them anyway. But she had represented a possibility, a future where Jasmine could live for herself, be loved for who she was, and spend her days doing work that fulfilled her.

Well, perhaps if that future only ended in violence and flames, it was never meant to be. It had been nice to imagine, though. As she watched the glow of the fire that ravaged through Haven's central platforms illuminate the canopy of trees, she thought to herself, *It was nice to play pretend. But if this is the cost, I can't afford to do that anymore.* She hadn't realized how quickly the fire would spread, or how big it would get. Even though only a sliver was visible through the valley, Haven glowed like a beacon in the night.

Haven would never welcome outsiders again.

As the light of Haven faded in the distance, so did the shouts of the Haveners. Everything grew silent except the sounds of paddles against water. August lay on his back, panting. Chavi stopped rowing and leaned back, letting out a deep breath. Harvard was curled up in a ball at the stern, gripping his knees, staring absently ahead.

For a brief moment, they were at peace.

August sat up abruptly.

"What a damn minute," he said. "What do we do now?"

"We'll think of—" Jasmine started, but he cut her off.

"We're quaking stranded out here!" he cried. "We've got no food! We've got no supplies! We've got nothing!"

"We'll go back to Bastion," Jasmine said.

"In this?" August asked, indicating the cramped rowboat. "It took us a week with Sax, and zey actually knew what zey were doing! And which way zey were going! Even if we could get back in a week, we'd starve."

"Hold on," Jasmine said, raising a hand to stop him. If she allowed him to start panicking, she would never get him to stop, and they didn't stand a chance of making it out of this situation if they couldn't all think clearly.

August ran his fingers through his hair. "We are so, so fucked. All because Harvard got caught."

"Hey!" Chavi shouted. "Do not blame this on him!"

"Well, it's not like you helped much either!" August snapped. "I held up my part of the plan. I was the best distraction ever. All you did was piss them off! Also arson, which probably pissed them off more!" He slapped a hand against the water for emphasis.

"I was trying to keep us safe!"

"*Look around, Chavi!*" August gestured at the open ocean. "Does this look very safe to you?"

"August, stop," Jasmine pleaded. She knew this would escalate quickly if she didn't put an end to it—Chavi was unstable when they were emotional, and they'd just *lit a village on fire*, which kind of terrified her but she didn't have time to process that right now.

"The way I see it," August said, jabbing a finger at Chavi's chest, "we're all going to die because the two of you couldn't stick to a plan."

Chavi batted the finger away, taking their hands off the oars. They inched deeper into the water.

"Watch the oars!" Jasmine said. She looked to Harvard for help, but when she saw him curled up in the back corner of the boat, she knew he was elsewhere. His eyes were wide, but vacant. He said nothing.

"Shut up, Princeton!" Chavi seethed. Maybe Sax had a point, Jasmine wondered. Maybe the two of them were similar. Before Jasmine could say another word, Chavi launched themself at August. The boat swayed as the two of them grappled, sloshing water into the boat. The neglected oars slid into the water. Jasmine reached for them, but she was too late.

She watched the oars sink into the abyss, the last hope they had of saving themselves. She clenched her teeth, and her fury boiled over.

"STOP IT!" she screamed. The two of them froze and stared at her. She wasn't sure if she'd ever screamed like that before. "If you two don't stop right now, we are all going overboard, and we are all going to drown!"

Chavi and August shared a look, then unsteadily lowered themselves back to sitting.

"Harvard," Jasmine said, "are you alright?" The other two turned to look at him. He shook his head mutely.

"He was like this after the aquarium, too," Chavi said. "He'll talk when he's ready."

"I—" August began, but Jasmine held up a finger to silence him.

"No," she said. "No more, from either of you. You're both going to sit here and shut up and *calm down*, because we're not surviving this if the two of you can't *keep it together*."

Chavi opened their mouth to speak, and Jasmine guessed by their contrite expression that they were about to apologize, but she still wasn't having it.

"Silent," she said again. Chavi's mouth snapped shut, and they cast their gaze down. August rubbed his arm. The rowboat bobbed on the billows, and Jasmine forced herself to take a deep breath.

Why does it always have to be me? She wondered. *Couldn't someone else be the level one for a change? When is it my turn to panic? When is it my turn to feel?*

A bright light in the distance blinded all four.

"What the—" August shielded his eyes.

"A boat!" Jasmine breathed, pressing herself against the bow to get a better look. "Another boat!"

"Should we try to flag them down?" Chavi asked.

"It's not like we can try to get away," Jasmine said, squinting to make out figures on the deck. "We have no oars."

As the vessel neared, Jasmine could see that it was larger than Sax's ship, and a few crew members worked on the deck. The searchlight turned out, and as Jasmine's eyes adjusted, she saw someone at the bow holding a lantern. A battery-powered lantern. A Bastion lantern.

A rope ladder dropped down next to the fishing boat.

"What are the four of you doing all the way out here?" asked Pierce.

* * *

The rest of the night passed like a dream for Harvard, like none of it was really happening. He felt like an observer, watching his own life from the outside. He climbed the rope ladder with help from the others, and he heard Jasmine giving an explanation of everything that had happened at Haven, but her words felt muffled. Pierce explained that he'd gone looking for them when they didn't come back after two weeks.

No one asked Harvard any questions. He was thankful for that. He couldn't have answered even if he wanted to.

Pierce led them to a hatch to the lower deck, like the one on Sax's ship. Again, someone had to help Harvard with the ladder. The raw skin of his palms stung so much that he could barely grip anything.

The lower deck was too cramped for him to stand up, which was fine because he didn't feel much like standing anyway. In fact, a wave of fatigue washed over him. Now that he was safe, and more importantly, his friends were safe, he had a chance to feel exhausted. He wrapped his cloak around himself and laid his head against the metal floor. Chavi gently lifted his head and placed it on their lap. They ran their fingers through his hair. They felt so warm. The gentle pitching of the boat lulled him to sleep.

Maybe when he woke up, he'd be himself again. For now, he was no one, watching Harvard from the outside as he slipped into unconsciousness.

* * *

Jasmine wrapped the blanket tighter around her shoulders, her hands cupping a mug of tea from the thermos Pierce had provided. She sat beside August at the bow, Chavi at the stern, with Harvard curled up next to them, his head resting on their knee. Pierce descended the ladder.

"I've got some matzah, if you want it. It's not much, but it keeps well."

"Thank you, Pierce," Jasmine said, who by unspoken consensus was now the ambassador of the group. She handed some of the flat crackers to August, and another stack to Chavi.

"Has Harvard eaten?" Pierce asked.

"He's out cold," Chavi said, rubbing Harvard's ginger curls. "It's been a tough night for him."

Pierce nodded. "I'm sure it's been a tough night for all of you."

August snorted.

"Well, I'll let you get rest," Pierce turned to climb back up the ladder, when Chavi laid a hand on his arm.

They held his gaze silently for a moment, as though they were struggling to find the words they were looking for. "Thanks, Pierce," they finally said. The man gave a kindly smile.

"Don't mention it," he said. He started to make his way up the ladder but paused, turning back around to say something. He opened his mouth to speak, thought better of it, then ascended to the top deck.

The Ivies sat in silence, no sound but the waves outside and the gentle creaking of metal.

"I'm sorry about what happened on the boat," August finally said.

"I'm sorry too," Chavi said, petting Harvard's hair. "We were scared. We said things we didn't mean."

"Well..." August looked away. "I did mean some of it."

Chavi's head shot up. "What?"

"Some of the stuff I said," August said with a shrug. "I mean, I wasn't totally wrong. You have been...acting a little weird about Harvard lately. And I think it made things worse, back in Haven."

A cloud passed over Chavi's face. "What are you talking about?"

August shifted uncomfortably, refusing to meet Chavi's eyes. "Maybe Blaire wouldn't have told on us if you hadn't, I don't know, threatened to kill him."

"You think I shouldn't have said anything? That I should have just let him tell Rosenea everything the moment he found the sketches? We'd be dead right now!"

August gave them a skeptical look that verged on pitying. "You set the place on fire—"

"Yeah, so it would be harder to follow us—"

"Then there were the guys outside the Library—"

"They were going to hurt Harvard."

"You killed someone, Chavi!" August shouted. Chavi recoiled as though struck. "No one's wanted to say it, but that's what happened. You killed someone. I think we need to just...have that out there in the open."

Chavi stared at him, wide-eyed. "That was an accident," they whispered. They looked to Jasmine for support. "Jas, are you hearing this? Tell him he's being totally unreasonable!"

Jasmine looked between the two of them, picking her words carefully. August was right, but the last thing she wanted to do was make Chavi feel cornered. If they felt even their best friend had turned on them...well, at this point Jasmine was entirely sure what they'd do. She had to handle them like a volatile chemical that at any point might combust.

"You have been...very protective of Harvard," she said, working to keep her face neutral.

Chavi still looked at her incredulously. "Well yeah, did you miss the part where Marcel tried to kill him twice?"

"Even before that," August crossed his arms. "You two have been, like...in your own world."

"Oh. I see," Chavi laughed humorlessly. "So what this is actually about is that you two are jealous." Jasmine drew back. This felt...uncharacteristically cruel. Chavi could get defensive, but never *mean.*

"What?" August blushed bright red, and with a jolt Jasmine remembered their conversation in the washroom. Romance and sexuality was a sensitive topic for him. He wasn't *jealous*, he was *uncomfortable.* "That could not be further from the truth!"

"Really August? Cos you've been acting weird about me and Harvard ever since we got together."

"It's not—" August stammered, "You don't understand—"

"Chavi, you don't know what you're talking about," Jasmine cut in, hoping to deescalate the situation without outing August.

"No, you don't know what *you're* talking about. You don't know anything about our relationship!" Jasmine saw Chavi's hand tighten in Harvard's hair, as though they were afraid someone would try to snatch him away. They were treading into dangerous emotional territory here. Jasmine couldn't remember a time Chavi had been mad at *her*.

"No one is criticizing your relationship, Chavi," Jasmine said slowly. "We've all had a long day. We're all tired. There's no point in discussing this now."

"Yeah," Chavi said, eyes still fixed on August, "let's sleep." They crossed their arms, leaning against the metal of the ship. Their fingers stayed laced in Harvard's hair.

"Sure," August grumbled, and, thankfully, that seemed to be the end of it. For now.

Jasmine curled up on the metal floor to get some much-needed rest.

Despite her exhaustion, she couldn't seem to fall asleep. She glanced over at August next to her, and she saw that he, too, was awake, wearing an expression of concern. When he caught her eye, furtively peered at Chavi to make sure they were asleep, then hissed, "They set the place on *fire*, Jas."

She nodded. He didn't need to say more. It was extreme, even for Chavi, and she was pretty sure that it had scared all of them a little.

"I know," she whispered.

"On *fire*."

"I know." She didn't want to worry August further, but she had to acknowledge the pattern forming. Carter Vik, whom Chavi had permanently injured when they were only sixteen. Minty, their crewmate who Chavi had inadvertently gotten crushed. Now Lyle, whose death Jasmine still didn't fully understand. And then there was the fire.

She didn't know what this pattern meant, but she didn't like it. She knew Chavi never intended to hurt anyone.

Somehow, it happened anyway.

August shook his head, but there was nothing left to be said. He buried his face in the crook of his arm, trying to fall asleep. Jasmine wanted to do the same, but her thoughts still ate at her. Chavi was still her best friend. Nothing was going to change that.

But when your best friend starts to rack up a body count, you have to wonder if maybe they have problems you don't know how to fix on your own.

* * *

Harvard awoke to the gentle swaying of the boat underneath him. He rubbed sleep from his eyes. His whole body ached. The coat of dirt and sweat he'd accumulated felt like a new layer of skin. He sat up. The rest of the Ivies were still dozing peacefully. He found that he was strangely thankful the others weren't awake yet. He could use some time to himself, to get clean, bask in the sunlight, and appreciate the quiet of the ocean. He unlatched his cloak and gingerly climbed the ladder to the upper hatch.

The sun blinded him as he pulled himself onto the upper deck. Sailors bustled by him, paying him no mind. This boat had a crew, unlike Sax's. It pained Harvard to think of Sax. He missed zem, oddly enough. He hoped zey hadn't gotten in trouble after everything last night. He hoped zey were happy. Strange to think that he would never see zem again.

Harvard strode toward the stern and found Pierce sitting on a crate, whittling. The sight of Pierce still gave Harvard a visceral panic response, but he pushed through it. It was important to him that he speak to the man.

"What are you working on?" he asked. Pierce held up a little wooden hydradeer. Only the front half was done, and that gave it the appearance that it was leaping out of the wood.

"Did you sleep well?" Pierce asked.

Harvard shrugged. He had so many questions, but didn't know how to ask them. He started with a simple statement.

"You knew about Haven," he said.

"Yes," Pierce said matter-of-factly.

"Why didn't you tell us?" He knew, objectively, that Pierce was not his ally. But he still felt like he should be, so it was hard not to feel betrayed.

Pierce shook his head. "Devrin doesn't want news of Haven to spread. If you all failed on your mission, it would have been best if you'd returned *without* knowing what was out there."

"But *why*?"

He flipped his penknife in his hand, looking out at the water. "Things are...better for him if fewer people know that there are alternatives to Bastion."

"Then why let us find out?"

"Because he had a job for you."

"Is he going to kill us, then?" Harvard asked, surprised by his own forwardness. The question didn't scare him, oddly enough. He just wanted to know. "When we get back?"

"No."

"But we know about Haven."

Pierce went back to his carving, and Harvard noticed that he was avoiding looking directly at him. "Yes, but you may still be useful to him. He wouldn't kill you if he thought he could still find a use for you. And besides, you're only a bunch of scavengers. No one would believe you. I hardly believed it, until I saw it for myself."

Harvard's brow creased. "Have *you* been to Haven?"

"No," he shook his head. "But I've seen it."

Harvard watched him for a long moment, shucking wood flakes of his fledgling creation. "How do I know you're telling the truth?"

"About Haven?"

"About Devrin. That he won't have us killed when we get back. I mean, here we are on your boat, letting you take us right to him. Why should we stay with you? Why shouldn't we leave?"

Now Pierce looked up at him, and his expression was a cross between concern and pity. "How would you make it back to Bastion?"

Harvard didn't know, but that didn't matter. "We'd find a way," he said with a shrug.

"You can trust me, Harvard," Pierce said, and he almost sounded like he was pleading. Like he was pained by the idea that Harvard could ever believe he was lying. And that made Harvard want to trust him, but his fingers still ached, and that was all the reminder he needed that trusting this man was not an option.

"I can't trust you," he said, and it came out more regretful than he meant it. "You work for him. And he's evil."

"He's not evil," Pierce said, an oddly defensive edge in his voice. "He just has a different way of viewing the world."

"Why do you do it?" Harvard asked. "Why are you a part of this?" Harvard wanted to like Pierce. He wanted that desperately. And if he wouldn't be wrapped up in this, then maybe Harvard would be able to like him.

"Why are you?" Pierce asked.

Harvard cocked his head. Was it not obvious? "Because he made me."

Pierce shrugged.

"Well, there you have it," he said, standing. For a moment, there was no sound but the ocean.

"That's not your real name, is it?" Harvard asked. "Pierce?"

Pierce looked away again. "No."

"Where's it come from, then?"

He resumed spinning the knife, and he watched it twirl in his hand, as though debating whether or not to answer. "The Pierce-Arrow was a pre-Quake brand of car."

"It's a brand name?" Harvard gaped.

"Yes."

"So you were a scavenger?"

Pierce was silent.

"What happened to your crew?"

Pierce ignored the question, beckoning for Harvard to follow him. "How about we patch up you a little? Looks like you didn't make it out of Haven totally unscathed."

Harvard's hand flew up to the spot where Marcel's knife had cut him.

"No," he murmured, remembering the sensation of tumbling into darkness. "I didn't."

"Let's take care of you then, alright?"

Pierce was already walking away, so Harvard let the conversation drop, and followed.

* * *

Chavi awoke to the realization that Harvard was not there. They sat up abruptly, instantly panicked. August and Jasmine were still asleep on the other side of the lower deck.

Chavi clambered out of the hatch into the mid-morning sun to search for him. They preferred this boat to Sax's. Pierce had a larger crew, so they seemed to take care of everything. No one was telling them what to do or what not to do.

They found Harvard standing by the railing, looking out at the water.

"Hey," they said. Harvard turned around. The cut on his face had been bandaged, and Chavi could see there was gauze taped to his blistered palms. The grime and blood from the previous night was washed away, and he wore a clean set of clothes—Bastion clothes. Pierce must have given them to him. Harvard smiled when he saw them.

"Hey."

Chavi joined him at the railing, draping an arm around him. They both looked out across the water. It still scared Chavi, but not as much as it did when they were in it.

"How are you feeling?" they asked.

"Better."

"Are you going to tell us what happened to you?"

"Yeah. Eventually."

Shame washed over them. They shouldn't have let any of this happen to him. This time, Harvard had saved the rest of them. They shouldn't have let him be put in that position. Still, the fact that he managed it was impressive. "Harvard. You did a good job. You know that, right?"

"Did I?" He sounded skeptical. Chavi laughed, looking down at him.

"You got the pictures, and you saved all our lives in the process. That's incredible. You're incredible."

Harvard blushed, eyes still fixed on the water.

"I want to go home," he murmured.

"That's where we're going," Chavi said, and they pulled him in closer. For a moment, everything was alright.

Part Three: Harmony

Interlude Nine: Oman

Oman didn't like people. He made a point of avoiding them. After his retirement, he'd moved into a small ground-level townhouse in Upper Bastion, where it was nice and quiet and the people kept to themselves and didn't think to bother an old man like him. That was the way he liked it.

He was enjoying a particularly cozy night by himself; he'd just put up the kettle for tea, and he was starting to work on a puzzle. He liked to do puzzles. He liked the feeling that he was building something. This puzzle depicted a pre-Quake form of transit called a train. He was fascinated by them. No one needed long distance transit anymore, so they'd never been reconstructed. But how he wished they would be, just so he could see one in action. It was a quaking shame that no one traveled anymore. He didn't much care about where people would travel to, but how they traveled, that was interesting. There used to be so much more than just trains, he'd read. People traveling the world like blood pumping through veins. Whoever controlled transit controlled the flow of humanity. For a long time, he'd hoped that would be him. Now his only hope was that he would be left in peace.

There was a knock on the door.

Oman grunted and placed a puzzle piece down on the table with a crisp snap. He didn't usually get visitors at night—in fact, he didn't usually get visitors at all. He liked it that way. Any visitor was an unwelcome one, but he had a sneaking suspicion that his current visitor was the most unwelcome of them all. He took his time making it to the door, his gait uneven as he rested his weight on an understated metal cane. He opened the door to see a slender man in a sleek suit, with a hawkish nose and twinkling eyes behind round glasses.

"You again," he grumbled.

"Me again," Devrin said. "You're looking well."

Oman looked down at his fraying sweater.

"Am I? Hadn't noticed."

"Won't you invite me in?" Devrin asked.

"No," he said, placing both hands on the cane, "I will not."

"You do realize that I'm just going to keep standing here at your door until you do, don't you?"

"I do."

"Then surely you see there's no reason to keep both of us here standing in the doorway when we could both be inside, sharing a cup of tea?"

The kettle began to boil.

Oman grunted a sort of noncommittal acknowledgment and trudged over to the kitchen, cane tapping on the tile.

Devrin helped himself to a seat as Oman went to fetch the kettle.

"Something herbal for me, please!" He called into the kitchen. "I've been cutting down on caffeine."

"I'm not making any for you," Oman replied as he poured two mugs. When he re-entered the living room, he found Devrin working on the puzzle he'd left out.

"Don't touch that," he said, setting down the mugs. "I'm working on it."

"I'm helping you."

"I don't want your help."

Devrin accepted his tea and reclined in the chair. Oman sat heavily in his.

"So, how have you been?" Devrin asked.

"The same." Oman sipped from his mug. A silence passed between them.

"Are you going to ask how I've been?"

"No."

"I've got a lot going on."

"I'm sure you have. You always do."

"Yes, you do know that, don't you?" Devrin said fondly, turning his gaze to his mug and bobbing the tea bag up and down by the string.

"The answer is no, by the way," Oman said. Devrin looked up.

"Hm?"

"Whatever you've come to ask me, the answer is no."

He feigned wide-eyed innocence. "You don't know I've come to ask you anything."

"I do, as a matter of fact, because you only ever come to see me when you want something. And whatever you want, I won't do it."

Devrin wrapped the tea bag string around his fingertip, watching the steam curl.

"I don't want anything," he insisted.

Oman settled back in his chair, watching him. This one was always such a liar. Even when they'd first met, when he really *was* innocent, he'd still had his own private agenda—even though, at the time, his objectives were simplistic and selfish—and he managed to get exactly what he wanted from Oman. Oman hadn't even realized he'd been manipulated, and he often wondered if Rin had even been aware of what he was doing. It seemed to come to him by instinct.

"I think I know you better than that."

This seemed to satisfy him. "Of *course* you know. And I admit, it would be...nice to have you on board. But really, I'm only offering for your own sake. It's *your* vision I'm working toward, after all. You know that, don't you? You always told me that you believed a revolution was coming to Bastion, and you wanted to be in the center of it when it did. I'm offering you a spot in the center."

Oman raised an eyebrow, drumming his fingers on his cane. "Right, this visit is for my benefit? Because you're famous for your altruism?"

Devrin laughed good-naturedly.

"I'm not famous for anything, and I make a point of that," he said. Oman grinned despite himself. Maybe he'd missed this. A little.

"You know, I could really fix this place up," he glanced around the apartment.

"It's fine," Oman said with a shrug. He couldn't be bribed if he was happy with what he had, thank you very much. Then again, he was pretty certain Devrin didn't entirely understand the concept of a bribe. If your entire life was a series of quid pro quo, then a bribe wasn't underhanded, just another transaction.

"Are you sure?" he asked. "Because I'm overdue to pay Saoirse a visit regardless. I'm sure if I let her know you've been—" he cut himself off, smiling at a joke that only he could hear. "Do you want to know something funny?"

"No."

"I ran into her *son!*"

Admittedly, this piqued his interest a bit. "She has a son?"

"You remember, the other twin?" Oman nodded slowly. That's right, there were two of them, weren't there? "He's grown so much." Devrin shook his head, grinning. "It feels like only yesterday he was just a little thing cooing in my arms. At first, I didn't recognize him, and I accidentally—" he cut himself off again. "No matter. The point is, I'm sure

Saoirse would be happy to redo the place free of charge. And to be clear, I'd arrange this for you even if you said no to my offer—"

"I have said no to your offer—"

"Even if you said you never wanted to speak to me again."

"I have said that. Many times. Yet you keep showing up."

"Yes, I'm very persistent," he said, reclining. "It's one of my better qualities. You find it endearing, don't you?"

"I don't."

"You do, though. A bit."

Maybe. Maybe a bit. Founders, the man was annoying. But Oman had to admit it was pleasing to have him show up every now and then, even if only because it was so satisfying to turn him down. He had the power to say no, the only power he had in this world, and he liked to wield it. Oman wondered why Rin even tried. Maybe Oman represented a unique challenge, the one the only two people in the city that Rin couldn't control. Or, perhaps, on a deeper level, what he really wanted was forgiveness, but too afraid to ask for it, requested something else. Just to keep Oman around a little longer. Maybe that *was* a little endearing.

Then again, in order to receive forgiveness, one first had to apologize. Something Rin was never particularly good at.

"I often wonder what the three of us would have achieved," Devrin mused, "if we'd ever managed to work together. You, me, and Allura. Competition breeds innovation, sure, but would collaboration have pushed us even further?"

"We never would have managed it, Rin," Oman shook his head. "We'd have torn each other apart. Sometimes I think it would have been better that way. If we could have just torn each other apart to begin with, without dragging anyone else into it."

Devrin tsked. "Surely you don't believe that. Everyone will be better off once we've remolded the city. Safer, certainly, and happier. You should see the progress we've made."

"Yes, I expect you do think I should see it," he said, and with a skeptical glance added, "And I expect you *do* think it's progress."

"It is."

"I've made a bit of a breakthrough, actually. I've made a very interesting new friend." Devrin turned his attention back to his tea.

"Good for you. Still not interested."

"You will be," Devrin grinned.

"Well then, why don't you just contrive some way to corner me into it and I won't have a choice?" he asked, though he knew the answer.

"I'd never do that to you, Oman," Devrin shook his head. "Never you. This is a true, honest-to-goodness choice. And if you refuse me—well, I will be back, I won't lie. But I won't try to convince you."

Oman wished he could believe that. Maybe Rin did believe it, but Oman knew it was a promise he couldn't keep.

"Just let me tell you a bit about it, then you can make an informed decision."

Oman set his mug down on the table with a sense of finality.

"Fine," he settled back in his chair. "I'll still say no, but at least make your story worth my time."

So Devrin told him.

And Oman became the only person in the world to know how he planned to put an end to the Final City.

CHAPTER SEVENTEEN

Return on Investment

"Happy?" Chavi asked, dropping the battered notebook on the desk.

Devrin flipped through the pages, raising an eyebrow. Chavi struggled to maintain a neutral face while their heart raced. What if he *wasn't* happy? After all they'd been through to get these sketches, what if it didn't satisfy him? What would he do then?

Devrin nodded curtly, and Chavi let out a sigh of relief.

"Avi!" Devrin called.

"Yeah?" she peered out of the adjoining room.

"You're free to go, love," he said, snapping the book shut.

"Cool," Avi smiled, darting off to grab her things. From inside the room, she shouted, "Well, thanks Devrin!"

Chavi watched her in amazement. What did she just say?

"Oh! Before you go," Devrin stood. "I have a parting gift for you both. A token of gratitude, for your hard work and patience."

"I don't want a gift from you," Chavi snarled. Devrin only shrugged.

"Well, that's fine. Avi can have yours. Though I admit I'm a little hurt." He pouted coquettishly. Chavi rolled their eyes. "I thought," he continued, "that you might be wanting this back." He hefted Chavi's Commission-issue sledgehammer with surprising ease. He was surprisingly strong for someone so lanky.

Admittedly, there was part of Chavi that did want the thing back. Other than the captain's band they wore around their wrist, it was the last vestige of who they'd been out in the dusts. It wasn't as though they needed a souvenir of those years, but it was nice to remember that they could be a captain. They could be Yale when they needed to be. Well. They hadn't been feeling very Yale recently, but they'd recover soon enough.

Then again, they didn't want to accept a gift from Devrin. And now the hammer only brought back memories of Harvard's fingers snapping, and the scorpioncrab soundlessly wailing in agony for only Chavi to hear.

"No, I don't want it," they said, and they meant it to come out with more acid than it actually did. Instead it just sounded petulant. "I never want to see the thing again."

"They're just being difficult," Avi smiled, accepting the sledgehammer on their behalf. Chavi gaped at her congeniality.

"And for you, Avi dear," Devrin smiled, producing a glass vial from a suit pocket, "a little research sample to entertain you."

Her face lit up with genuine delight, and Chavi wanted to punch a wall. *Stop being happy!* they wanted to shout. "Thank you!" she said. *Stop thanking him!* Chavi pointedly did not say.

"It's a small fraction of the scorprioncrab venom that Chavi here helped to source," Devrin gave them an appreciative nod. They glared at him. *"Helped to source."* The venom that Chavi was *forced to kill for.* "As a thank you for your cooperation."

"Any time," Avi gave a little curtsy.

"Hello? Avi? Can we go now?" Chavi asked.

"Coming!" Avi gave Devrin a friendly wave before following Chavi to the elevator.

Chavi grabbed her arm possessively and pulled her into the elevator.

"Ow!" she batted their hand away. "What's this about?"

"You're thanking him?" they hissed. "After all he's put us through—after all he's put *you* through—and you're thanking him?"

Avi paused, eyeing Chavi, as though judging what answer would sate them.

"You never were very good at this, were you?" she asked, a touch of pity in her voice making Chavi bristle.

"Good at what?" they demanded.

"Playing along!"

She pressed the elevator button, and Chavi heard the smooth whirring of the mechanisms as it bore them to the ground level. They still didn't trust the thing.

"I could be good at it if I tried," Chavi defended, "but I just don't get the point. That man is—I mean, he's a killer! I can hardly stand to look at him without...I don't know, without wanting to hit him! How can you stand to be nice to him?"

"Because when I'm nice to him, he's nice to me. And that's how I get what I want."

"And what do you want?" Chavi asked.

"Well, while I was a hostage, I very much wanted not to have *my* fingers broken," Avi snapped, which shut them up for a moment. "How do you think it would have gone for me if I'd been as principled as you, Chavi? If I reminded him every second what I really thought of him? Do you think I would have come out of that doorway unharmed? Do you think I would have come out that doorway *at all*?"

Chavi opened their mouth to say something, but no words came. The elevator dinged to announce the end of their journey, and Avi swept out brusquely. Chavi trailed after.

"Okay, okay, I see what you mean," they trotted up to her. "But how do you do it? How do you keep up the, the...the act?"

She stared at them blankly.

"What exactly," she asked, "do you think I've been doing for my whole life?"

* * *

Avi loved her best friend. Truly, she did, and she wanted to think the best of them. Sometimes, however, Chavi was such a quaking idiot. Had they really tried to talk to her about Devrin while they were still in *his* building? The headquarters of city security? The single most likely place in the world to be overheard? She couldn't blame Chavi for their hatred of Devrin in the least, but surely they understood what a supremely stupid move that was.

She wished she had more information to share with them. She had a bunch of tidbits, puzzle pieces that didn't fit together. Who started the fire in the testing lab, and why did Devrin care? What "wars" was Pierce referring to? And what *was* the Underground City? Maybe it was useless to let her friends in on her espionage now. Maybe they'd think she was grasping at straws in a desperate attempt to feel useful.

Acting was exhausting. When she returned back to her apartment at the University, she wanted nothing more than a nap. She shouldn't be feeling so sorry for herself. She hadn't had it nearly as bad as Harvard had. Then again, if Harvard had known how to play along with Devrin's games like she had, maybe he would have been just fine. She worried about that boy. He didn't grow up like she did. He didn't know how to pretend.

The moment she tossed herself onto the bed, there was a knock on her door. She groaned. Another knock. Why now?

With great effort, she picked herself up and made her way to the door.

"What is this about?" asked an irate Simon Foster, holding out the card she'd left him.

"Some greeting," she grumbled, heading back to her bed. Simon followed her into the room, taking care to close the door behind him.

"Yeah, of course, welcome back and all that," he amended, "now tell me why you wanted me to research this for you."

Avi groaned, rolling onto her back.

"What are you talking about?" She just stared at him blankly.

He gave her an incredulous look before fishing out the card she'd left him and handing it back to her. She'd been so focused on her own espionage that she completely forgot she had Simon investigating the card she found on Chavi's nightstand.

Simon crossed his arms, his gaze darting away. "I had to do a lot of research, you know. The kind that involves asking around. Now everyone probably thinks I'm some kind of addict."

This caught Avi's interest. She sat up in bed.

"What?"

"This person," he indicated on the card, "is apparently a supplier for a drug called Harmony. The core chemical compound is a prototype depression medication from the Zuris. It's prescribed very rarely though because, well, people started using it to make this." He indicated the card.

"And 'this' is..." Avi goaded. She was way too tired to have to be pulling information out of him like this.

"Basically, a very potent version of the drug."

"A super antidepressant?" she said, tapping a finger to her chin. "That doesn't seem so bad."

"It's more than that. It's..." Simon paused, looking as though he were trying to remember the words that had been spoken to him. "Okay, you know what a performance enhancing drug is, yeah? This is like a personality enhancing drug. It makes you confident. Super confident. So confident you think you can read people's minds."

Avi's eyes narrowed. "You can't read people's minds with a drug."

"No, obviously not, but people realized if they could get a whole group to sit down and take it at once, they all start to think they understand each other, like this, this enlightenment—"

"Mm. A social narcotic," Avi mused.

"Exactly. Do you see now?"

"No," she admitted. "What's so dangerous about some delusions? Lots of people are delusional."

Simon sighed. "Imagine this: a group of people who are totally okay with breaking the law, since they're already using an illegal drug. Suddenly they all think they're connected on a spiritual level. Suddenly they have synthetic confidence—in themselves, and in each other. They start to think they can do the impossible."

Avi nodded. "I see where you're going with this."

"Oh, but I'm not done. You have a group of people who think they can do the impossible, but find themselves financially strapped thanks to getting hooked on a highly addictive drug."

"You've got a bunch of zealots who are desperate."

"Exactly. Things could get violent."

"And do they?"

"It's hard to say. If the Zuris are tracking street use of it, then that's certainly not public information. If anything, they probably sell it to the Delian Group, if it's somehow associated with crime."

Avi folded her hands, pondering this. Was Chavi *actually* involved in any of this? They certainly didn't seem like a desperate zealot. And while they weren't always the brightest, she couldn't imagine they could be duped into thinking that some drug had given them superpowers. Besides, they'd been away from the city for a month, hadn't they? She was still convinced they were hiding something, but a drug cult didn't sound like a likely option.

Then again, if they weren't at least interested, then why have the card?

"Avi." Simon drew close, his academic intensity melting into genuine concern. "Are you involved in something...illegal? Something dangerous?"

She recoiled, eyes wide. "No! Of course not!"

"Then why do you have this?" His initial anger had evaporated. Now all that was left was care for his friend, the only true friend he had. It made her heart ache a little.

Oh Simon, she thought, *I've been so unfair to you.*

"I'm fine," she insisted.

"You promised me, Avi," he pleaded. "You promised me you'd tell me the truth."

"About the Galvin Conference, yes," she evaded.

"This can't be a coincidence!" he exclaimed. "You suddenly abandon the conference—*your life goal.* Then you take a spontaneous thesis retreat even when you hardly have enough time to do your work as is. So you stuck me with the work, which is fine I guess—except you also stick me with a research project that could get me in huge trouble if anyone knew I was looking into it. Then you make a reappearance—looking like dusts, by the way, and you won't tell me a quaking thing. This—I mean, this has to stop, Avi! Not just for me. For you! Whatever you're involved in...it's bad. I mean...you're better than this."

She studied him—sad, lonely, desperate—and she *did* empathize with him. He'd never been adept at making friends, so she knew it must be isolating to have his only one keeping secrets from him. He almost had her for a moment, but something about that wording made her bristle. *You're better than this.* Better than what? Better than caring for her friends? Better than Chavi? Better than Jasmine? Simon, of course, didn't know the context, and she'd taken pains to keep it that way. Maybe she should just let him in on it...but Simon had an internship with the Satsukis, and the Satsukis wanted the Ivies dead. Was his allegiance to her stronger than his allegiance to his employers? She wasn't about to bet the Ivies' lives on it.

"I said I'd tell you eventually," she countered, "but not yet. I can't yet."

"But why?" Simon pleaded.

"I just. Can't."

"But—"

"Do you trust me, Simon?" she interrupted. His mouth made a flat line. She knew the line of questioning was unfair of her, but he'd left her no choice.

"Yes, but—"

"Then trust me when I say I will tell you. And I will not tell you now." Feeling guilty, she added, "Thank you, by the way. For the work you did."

"No problem," he shrugged. "I mean, actually, huge problem, 'cause if anyone found out I was looking into this stuff I'd probably lose my scholarship, but like...you're my friend. So no problem."

She winced. "I'm sorry, Simon. Really."

"It's fine," he sighed, making it very obvious that it wasn't fine at all.

"Let me make it up to you. Let me take you out to dinner or something. Buy you a drink."

He looked away. "You don't have to do that."

"I know I don't. But I want to."

"I don't have time to go out."

"How long has it been since you last left campus?"

He shrugged. "I don't know. Too long."

Avi smiled fondly. "Let's fix that. One night with no schoolwork. Dinner on me. We'll go to the arcade."

She could see Simon's defenses break a little. She knew the Bastion Arcade was his favorite place in the city. It wasn't so much the promise of the activity that wore him down as much as it was the pleasure of being known. He sighed.

"One night," he agreed. "I'm still not happy about this."

"I know, sweetheart," Avi put a gentle hand on his arm. "I know."

* * *

Harvard sat at the piano bench in the Academy closet, hesitating to put his fingers on the keys. He'd come here to take his mind off the fact that Chavi was back in Delian Towers right now, but as it turned out, showing up here only made things worse.

He hadn't tried playing the piano since his fingers were broken.

He clunked out some chords with his left hand, but without use of his right hand, he couldn't play a melody to go over it. He tried, but his fingers still hadn't healed enough. They screamed with pain when he put pressure on them, so he gave up. He settled for playing a sad, simple melody with only his left hand. It was pathetic.

He let his head fall against the keys with a discordant clang. He cried quietly, face pressed up against the piano.

The door opened.

Harvard stood, acutely aware of the fact that he wasn't supposed to be here. The piano bench screeched against the concrete floor. He whirled around, prepared to spin some kind of lie.

Standing in the doorway was Pierce.

The last time Harvard had seen him, he had been saving the Ivies' lives. The time before that, he had been holding a knife to Harvard's throat. So Harvard didn't know what to make of seeing him now. He tensed, and he prepared himself to flee. He wondered if he would be able to dodge if Pierce tried to grab at him.

Oddly enough, Pierce looked just as surprised as he did.

"Are you here to kill me?" Harvard whispered.

"No, no!" Pierce said, on the edge of laughter. "I didn't even know you'd be here."

"Then what are you doing here?" he asked.

Pierce held up a key. It matched the one Harvard wore around his neck. He reached up to touch his own key instinctively.

"Devrin has a thing about keys," Pierce explained. "When he saw you wearing one, he had a copy made. He checked it with his records and tracked it to this building. He sent me to figure out what it was for."

"Why?" Harvard asked. Pierce shrugged.

"I don't know why that man wants anything he wants. I just have to make sure he gets it."

Harvard stayed silent, wondering if he should try and leave. Pierce suddenly looked oddly embarrassed, and Harvard was surprised to see he actually blushed.

"I didn't mean to interrupt," Pierce gestured toward the piano. "Please. Keep playing."

"I...I can't," Harvard said, holding up his splinted hand. Pierce's brow knit, and he looked genuinely pained.

"I'm sorry, Harvard," he said. Harvard caught himself just before he said, "It's okay." It was an automatic response—but it wasn't okay, was it?

"Let me help you," Pierce suggested. Harvard didn't understand, but before he could protest Pierce stepped up to the bench to join him. Warily, Harvard sat back down beside Pierce.

"Just pick a key," Pierce said, "and I'll play along."

Harvard placed his left hand on the keys and began playing some broken chords in A minor. Pierce nodded, listening, then placed both hands on the keys and improvised a melody. Harvard couldn't help being impressed—he didn't know how to improvise. And Pierce's melody was such a beautiful, mournful tune that Harvard could hardly believe he was making it up on the spot. He touched the keys with achingly gentle precision, and Harvard could see his whole body moved as he felt out the different phrases. It felt incongruous to watch such a big man do something so delicate. They could both sense that the song was coming to an end, and they brought it to a close.

"You're really good," Harvard said when the song finished.

Pierce kept his eyes on the keys. "I used to play duets with my husband."

"You don't anymore?" Harvard regretted the question as soon as he asked it.

Pierce's face hardened. "He's gone. There was an accident. It was my fault." He said it was a kind of finality that let Harvard know they wouldn't be discussing the topic further.

The two sat in silence. Harvard looked back at his hand resting on the keys. His left hand. The hand that had drawn the sketches of the creatures on Haven, and the Relic.

"You knew I was left-handed," he realized.

Pierce shook his head. "I didn't."

"You did," Harvard insisted. "You knew I was left-handed because you were watching us, and you've been watching us since the Conference, so you knew and you broke the fingers on my right hand. You did it on purpose, didn't you?"

Pierce refused to meet Harvard's gaze. Harvard didn't understand. Was he embarrassed by his own kindness?

Finally, Pierce said simply, "I knew you'd have to draw."

"No, you knew I *liked* to draw," Harvard guessed. "You didn't do it for Devrin. You did it for me, didn't you?"

Pierce stared at the pale wood of the rehearsal piano. He nodded.

"I think," Harvard started, a peculiar realization washing over him, "that you're a good person."

Pierce only shook his head.

"You are," Harvard insisted. "I can tell. I'm good at telling these things. You are a good person. So why do you work for him?"

Pierce looked down at the keys, and for a fleeting moment Harvard wondered if he was going to cry.

"Because he asked me to," Pierce rasped.

"And you do everything he asks?" Harvard said.

"I do now."

Pierce stood, and Harvard knew the conversation, and the duet, were both over. Pierce made his way to the door wordlessly, but as his fingers closed around the handle, he looked back over his shoulder and said, "Do you believe me now, Harvard? That I'm only trying to protect you? Bad things happen to people who don't comply with the Delian Group. And I don't want you to end up like me."

"What happened to you?" Harvard asked after him, but Pierce was already out the door.

* * *

Chavi never planned on showing up at Ariel's door. It felt like years ago when Mellie had met them in the alley and told them about Ariel's community. They'd decided it sounded fun but expensive, and therefore wasn't a viable option.

The incident on Haven had changed that. Someone had died due to their inability to control their own...powers? It didn't feel like a power. It felt like a curse, and if anything it made them even more powerless, because as far as they could tell there was no taming the beast that grew inside them.

But they knew one thing: it had happened because they were angry and scared. If they could just get their emotions under control, then maybe they had a chance to keep the creature at bay.

The only problem with that was Chavi had a terrible track record with keeping their emotions under control. If they were going to manage that, they would need help. Artificial help.

Ariel's help.

Their fingers traced the edges of the chitin on their shoulders as they knocked on Ariel's door.

"Chavi! Hi!" Ariel seemed genuinely delighted to see them when they opened up, cupping a mug of coffee in one hand, dressed in a sheer billowing shirt with matching ribbons braided into their hair. "It's been a while. How have you been? Readjusting to life back in the city?"

"No," they admitted. That was kind of the whole reason they were here. Why lie?

Ariel gave a knowing nod. "Would you like to come in?" Chavi was about to refuse, but they realized they didn't entirely know if Harmony was an open secret, or something that was actually illegal. They'd never bothered to find out.

"Why don't you sit down?" they gestured to the cushions.

"I don't—I've never—" they stammered. This was distinctly different than falling back in with their old Academy friends. There had been a routine to that, a sort of script. Harmony was something that they didn't understand, and Chavi was so tired of not understanding things.

"I know," Ariel smiled sweetly, pressing a gentle hand on Chavi's back, urging them forward. "Sit down, Chavi."

Chavi lowered themself onto one of the cushions, unsure if they should feel relieved, or more uneasy than they had to begin with. Ariel lowered themself onto a cushion across from them, their legs crossed primly. They always had a way of moving that seemed so fluid, like vapor.

"Can I get you anything?" they asked. "There's still some coffee in the pot."

"I just want to know what to do," Chavi admitted, and they didn't like how desperate their voice sounded, but they couldn't seem to be able to mask it.

Ariel placed a hand on Chavi's knee.

"It's okay," they said. Realistically, they had no way of knowing this. Ariel, who presumably had normal human blood inside them, couldn't possibly understand the violent and brutal metamorphosis that Chavi was dealing with. But they had such a warmth to them, such confidence and effortless grace, that when Chavi met their eyes, some of their discomfort melted.

"Are you sure?" Chavi asked. Of course they couldn't be. But it *felt* so true. "I haven't even told you—"

"I already know," Ariel said sweetly. "There's only one reason anyone shows up on my doorstep. You want to join the circle. All of us joined this Harmonization circle because we have struggles in our lives we're trying to overcome. We understand that, and we support each other. You would not be the first member to seek out the circle in a time of personal struggle, Chavi."

"Really?" they asked, and the scale of their feelings started to tip toward relief. Ariel shook their head, sleek braid swinging, a shadow of a smile playing on their lips.

"Of course not," they said. "What is community for if not lifting each other up during our times of need?"

Community. That sounded nice. That sounded like Haven. Chavi hated to admit it, but there was a part of them that missed Haven. They'd never felt like they belonged, but what if they could have? The other three had found their place.

Maybe the Harmonization circle could be their place.

"What do I need to do to join?" Chavi asked.

"Just be present," Ariel gave a warm smile. "And contribute to the circle's funds. Harmony itself is not easy to attain, and our current supplier has been raising prices."

Chavi's stomach sank. After Haven, it was so easy to forget that currency existed. It was just an accepted fact of life that people would take care of each other. Now that seemed ridiculous. Of course you had to *pay for things*. That was how the world worked.

"I don't think I can do that," they admitted. They'd all agreed that the payment for the Haven mission should go toward legally renting the townhouse lest they be found out and evicted. It hadn't left them with much.

Ariel cocked their head. "You could always come work for us, if you would like."

"Work?" Chavi repeated. Actually, that was perfect. Figuring out what work they were best suited for was kind of the major issue that put them in this position to begin with. That and...well, it was easier to pretend that was all. "You've been able to find a job for some of the Harmonizers? How?"

"Not a job exactly," Ariel said. "It's nothing reliable. We do odd jobs, and it's enough to keep those suppliers that you're so worried about away from us. Would you like to join us?"

It was a tantalizing opportunity. Work was the thing that all of them had been chasing, and here it was, however...questionable.

"What would I have to do?" they asked.

"Nothing untoward, I promise!" Ariel laughed, setting their mug aside their mug. "Don't look so scared. We've got a job lined up at The Sand Crystal this weekend. You know it?"

"I've heard the name," they said. The Sand Crystal was one of the clubs on the Cusp. Some students at the Academy would try and sneak their way in, but Chavi always thought it was too dangerous for them to do something outright illegal. Any rich kid could get away with sneaking into a club, but if they'd gotten caught, then at minimum they would be expelled, and their mother fired. Which of course happened anyway, but they didn't know at the time what their future would hold, so they'd settled for house parties, which were abundant anyway.

"If you work the Sand Crystal with us," Ariel continued, "your first Harmonization will be free."

"Really?" Chavi asked. How much could this club possibly pay? Actually, that made sense. Cusp clubs were usually run by the absurdly wealthy, those who could certainly afford to live in Upper Bastion but found it more lucrative to live amongst the people they profited off of. Rich people had no concept of the value of money, so the owner of The Sand Crystal was probably paying a ludicrous sum for some basic promotion. That would be easy enough. Club promotion was just talking to people and looking attractive, two things Chavi knew they were really good at.

Ariel nodded. "The guy who owns the place is swimming in points. After this, we'll be set for a while. Meet us there around ten. Wear something nice, but not formal. Something you can dance in."

Chavi smiled at the thought. They hadn't revived their party wardrobe since high school. Maybe this would be fun.

"Okay. I can do that."

Chavi knew, on some level, as they bid Ariel farewell and made their way onto the street, that this was too easy. But they desperately wanted everything to be okay. If Mellie was right about Harmony, it could be the one thing to keep the thing inside them under control—plus it wouldn't hurt to make some money, maybe even a few friends. Slip off one night, go have a good time doing promotion or serving drinks or whatever it was they were getting paid to do, and then show back up the next morning before Harvard even realizes they were gone. *What's the worst that could happen?* they thought, pointedly not considered the worst that could happen.

CHAPTER EIGHTEEN

A Gift in Return

"Is this okay?" Jasmine asked after scribbling down a paragraph, twirling a braid in her fingers as she slid the scrap of paper to Avi.

"Well, it's well written," Avi said, "but it doesn't really show off your qualifications."

"I don't have any qualifications," Jasmine murmured, looking down.

"Being Jasmine Reyez is qualification enough. You just have to show them what exactly that means."

"I don't know how to do that," Jasmine said, and Avi could hear she was dangerously close to crying.

The front door burst open, and Jasmine gave a squeal of surprise. It was only Chavi and Harvard, coming back from wherever they had been. Chavi took a seat by Avi at the counter, and Harvard went over to the couch, where he'd left his sketchbook. Avi's stomach sank. It was probably time to have that conversation, as soon as she could speak to Chavi privately.

Jasmine fidgeted with her pages, seeming to try to cover them up so no one could see.

"Maybe if this doesn't work out, I should just try to work full time at your University after all. In person," she said. "Do you think everything's fine now? After the Conference?"

"I don't know," Avi admitted. "Simon says that Katherine Bell came to see him while we were gone, still asking about it."

Harvard's head shot up. "Who?" he asked.

Right, of course none of the Ivies would know who that was. "Kathy Bell. One of the corp heiresses. You wouldn't know her. But the point is, there's a lot of weird stuff happening with the corps right now, and for some reason the four of you are still of interest to them."

Harvard looked suddenly terrified, as though she'd told him giant lizards were attacking the city. Well, that made sense, she supposed. She probably would have been scared too if she thought a corp heiress was out to get her.

"I'm sure it's nothing to worry about. Yet," she added, which didn't seem to comfort him.

"What did—what did the girl from the Bell family want?"

"I don't know. She was asking about the Galvin Conference. Apparently, she said it was a personal project, but I don't buy that."

"I'm um—I'm really tired," Harvard stood abruptly. "I'm gonna go to bed now, I think."

Poor Harvard. He'd seemed like his nerves were fraying ever since—well, ever since Avi had met him, to be completely honest. He seemed to live his life like a teacup balanced on the point of a knife, any moment so close to completely breaking. Avi wished she hadn't rattled him so much, but she supposed that if she had only just started to live a normal life and then someone told her she was being hunted, maybe she would feel the same way.

"I'm actually going to go to bed too," Jasmine said, and Avi could tell she was shifting the papers on the counter to cover up the application materials. She scooped them up and hugged them to her chest. "Goodnight," she said, barely glancing over her shoulder.

Avi and Chavi were left alone—which, as much as Avi was dreading it, was what she was waiting for.

"I guess I should—" Chavi started. Avi grabbed them by the arm.

"No," she said. "I need to talk to you. Alone."

* * *

Harvard slammed the bedroom door behind him, shaking. He didn't know what he was going to do about this—he didn't know what he *could* do about this—but at the very least he needed to be alone before he accidentally revealed everything to everyone. Katherine Bell always got what she wanted, and for the first time in her life, what she wanted was him. Why? Why now?

Harvard? Speedy's voice made him jump. He turned to see the crab resting on the bedside table, where he'd first appeared before the trip to Haven. *Is something wrong?*

Harvard's instinct told him not to tell anyone—as though verbalizing the truth somehow made it more real—but he knew that Speedy was a safe confidante.

"My sister," he said, sitting heavily on the bed. "She's looking for me, for some reason. Maybe not. Maybe she was interested in the Conference for a different reason. I don't know. Maybe I'm getting upset over nothing."

Harvard wanted to put the lingering threat of his family out of his mind, but Speedy was inquisitive.

I do not understand, he said. *You are an adult. Your family has no bearing on you now.*

"It doesn't work like that, Speedy," Harvard gave a sad laugh. "If my family found me, they could force me to go back to living with them. I don't know why they'd *want* that, but, I mean, if Kathy is looking for me, there has to be a reason. And I...can't go back to living that way."

Do you think your family will try to make you return?

"I don't know. But even if my family doesn't do anything about it...what will the rest of the Ivies think? When they find out I'm from one of the big six families."

They don't seem to have any problem with Avi Taheri.

"Avi never lied to them."

Does it matter?

Harvard started at Speedy in abject horror. "*Yes!* If Chavi found out I had lied to them about who I was...would they leave me?"

He fiddled with the key that hung around his neck. Chavi was so kind to him. They took good care of him. And in return, all he'd done was pretend to be something he wasn't.

"I need to be a better boyfriend," he decided. "I need to get them a nice gift too."

I am confused. You think a nice gift...will prevent them from feeling betrayal at your deception?

"No, it just"—he ran a hand through his hair—"I need to make sure they know how much I care about them. Even if I'm lying about everything else. But what...what should I get them? It needs to be perfect."

I do not know what sorts of gifts humans like.

Harvard didn't either. He didn't have very much experience with humans, despite being one himself. But if he could ask someone—

He stood up abruptly.

Where are you going?

"I have to go see a human about another human. You know, human stuff."

Ah, Speedy said sagely, *Human stuff.*

* * *

Avi steeled herself for the inevitable, then placed the card on the counter.

"Can you explain to me what this is?"

Chavi's eyes widened. "Where did you get that?" they asked.

"You left it on your dresser. I found it when I was dropping off the sweatshirt. I *knew* something was going on with you that you weren't telling me." She tapped the card. "Is this it?"

Chavi glanced up at the steps, probably to ensure that Harvard wasn't somehow within earshot. "Not here," they said. "Let's walk."

Avi allowed them to pull away from her, and she followed them to the door. The sun was low enough in the sky that it cast an orange glow across the buildings of Lower Bastion, a patchwork of puzzle-piece homes all layered over each other like climbing ivies.

"Do you know what it is?" Chavi asked without looking at Avi, hands shoved in their pockets.

"Yes. I want to know why you have it." Avi watched them carefully. Their jaw clenched.

"I think I might need it."

"What do you mean, you need it?" Avi tried to keep her voice level, but a little bit of derision snuck in.

"I mean," they said, "that ever since the Conference, I've felt like there was something wrong with me. In my body. In my…in my blood. I thought maybe with time it would get better, but when we were away…it got worse. Out of my control. And if I don't do *something*, I worry I'll lose control altogether."

Avi went cold. Chavi stared forward, refusing to meet her gaze, and she knew that meant they were guilty, and now *she* suddenly felt guilty for making them feel that way. She was a medical student, after all. She shouldn't shame someone for seeking treatment for a condition, even if they were seeking it in the most misguided way possible.

"You should have told me," she said.

Chavi shook their head. "There was nothing you could do. Whatever is happening to me, I don't think it's something anyone knows how to cure. So maybe I don't need a cure, I just need to find something to make it bearable. I don't know if I'm going to join yet, but I'm going out with them tomorrow night."

Avi studied them.

"Really? Out?" she asked.

"Yeah, we're going to The Sand Crystal together. You know it?"

Avi had never been to The Sand Crystal or any place like it and she had no intention of going. She tried her best not to judge the...proclivities of others, but her parents had brought her up to think that places like *that* were hotbeds for all kinds of...distracting indulgences that a good girl like her should not be party to.

"Yeah, I know it," she said. "And how does Harvard feel about going clubbing?"

"He's not coming. He"—Chavi looked down at their feet and shuffled a little—"well, I didn't want to make him feel left out, so I didn't tell him."

"Why haven't you told anyone?" she asked. If Chavi truly believed what they said about Harmony, that it was just some kind of group therapy that helped them feel better, then they would have no reason to hide it.

"I just didn't want to worry anyone. If I can deal with it on my own, then I don't see any reason why I should tell anyone."

Avi nodded curtly. "Right. Well, I do. I'm telling Jasmine."

Chavi grabbed Avi's shoulders so abruptly she nearly pushed them away. Their eyes were wide with panic.

"Avi, no! You cannot do that."

"I can." She pushed their hands away. "And I should. It's the right thing to do."

"There's no reason to tell her about something that's not her problem!" Chavi protested.

"It *is* her problem, because if you end up joining this group, you'll have to pay with her money."

"It's *our* money."

"Then why are you using it for yourself?" She knew before it was out of her mouth that it would wound them, but she didn't expect it to break them in the way it did.

"Please, Avi!" they cried, gripping her shoulders tighter, and pleas sounded so alien coming out of their mouth. "I'm begging you. Please."

Avi's reason warred with her emotions. Chavi was not the kind of person who begged for anything. They were nothing if not proud. So whatever was happening to them, it must be pretty dire for it to come to this. They were also not the kind of person to change their mind once they'd decided what they wanted, and what they were going to do about it. So was there anything she could do?

"I'm not going to lie to my best friend's face, Chavi," she said as gently as she could manage. "It would hurt me too much."

Their face hardened frighteningly fast, their supplication melting into anger in an instant. "This isn't about you! This is bigger than you! I am asking for a tiny bit of help here, and you are actually selfish enough—"

"Don't you dare!" Avi said, words spilling out of her. She surprised even herself when she shoved them away. "I risked everything for you. I gave myself up for you, let them take me prisoner for you. And while I was there, I did my research. I worked hard. For you. I saved your quaking life, okay? And I don't even recall you *thanking* me for that. So don't you dare call me selfish. I have given *so* much of myself to you. If one of us is selfish, Chavi, it is *not* me."

Avi breathed heavily, surprised at how much the rant had winded her. She hadn't realized she felt that way until it all came tumbling out. Chavi stared at her, their brow creased, looking properly chastened. Well, good. That was what she wanted, wasn't it? Then why did it feel so horrible?

"I—I'm sorry, Avi," they said. "I'm so sorry."

Before Avi could respond, they sank to the ground, sitting on the edge of the curb, wrapping their arms around their head. Avi considered her movements carefully before sitting down beside them. She ached to comfort them. She also didn't like being manipulated, and while she was sure they weren't doing it intentionally, she didn't like the way Chavi seemed to be forcing pity from her.

"It's okay," she said. "I mean, you *were* totally in the wrong—"

"I know, I know," Chavi said, their voice muffled.

"But it's okay," she rested a hand on their back.

"Fuck, I'm such a monster," they whispered.

"*No*," Avi said sternly. "Don't do that. Don't pull that self-pitying shit, okay? You're not a monster and you know that."

"But I am," they insisted.

"Chavi—"

"No, Avi, listen to me," Chavi lifted their head and turned to face her. "There's something I need to tell you. I should have told you earlier, but—

fuck, it's just like, admitting it to you made it feel real. And I didn't want it to be real. I so, so badly didn't want it to be real."

"What are you talking about, Chavi?" she asked.

"I'll show you."

* * *

Chavi was dreading discussing the crab thing with Avi, but it was inevitable. She was probably the best person in the whole city to consult about it, and besides, they were friends. Sprouting a crab leg was the important kind of life update that one tells their friends about. Still, it wasn't easy. Every time they spoke about it with anyone, (which was not often because by unspoken agreement the Ivies were acting like it never happened) it was an internal battle trying to convince themself that what felt like a feverish nightmare was actually a real thing.

They took off their hoodie—it was the new one, the one from Avi, to replace the one from their mother. For Avi to really be able to see it they knew they should take off the shirt underneath as well, but that felt wrong. There was no one on the street, but somehow the little patch of chitin on their back felt like the dirtiest secret in the world, and they didn't want to risk a single other soul in Bastion knowing that it was there.

"What are you—" Avi started, but she cut herself off when they took her hand and guided it through their shirt sleeve, onto their shoulder blade. Avi gasped.

"What is it?" she asked.

"I don't know," Chavi said, and even though it was technically true, it still felt like a lie. Somewhere deep down, they did know. They just didn't want to admit it.

Avi pulled back the sleeve so she could take a look. Only a few slivers of sunlight remained, but the meager streetlights of Lower Bastion had turned on, bathing them in more orange light. Avi traced her fingers along the edge of their skin, and even though it was her, someone they loved, it still hurt to have her looking at it.

"It looks like—"

"I know," Chavi cut her off.

"Do you think it's because—"

"Yes," they pushed her hand away and pulled their shirt sleeve back down. "And I think that's what's been making me feel...wrong. I don't know how to describe it. It's like there's another creature living in my blood that wants to get out. And I have—" they swallowed. They hadn't told this part to anyone, not even Harvard. "I have dreams. About being in a cave with the desertwalkers, and I don't have a body but somehow I know that I'm one of them, and we're all going to the same place. And they don't feel like dreams, they feel—"

Chavi cut themself off. *They feel real,* they thought. *They* are *real.*

Avi stood up abruptly, holding out a hand to Chavi.

"Come," she said. Chavi took her hand, and they allowed her to pull them to their feet.

"Where are we going?" they asked.

"To the lab I work in. I'm going to do a blood test for you."

Chavi eyed her skeptically. "Will that tell us anything?" they asked.

Avi shrugged. "I've got no idea. But it will give us some place to start." She squeezed their hand. "Believe it or not," she said with a smile Chavi didn't realize they had missed until it appeared for the first time in the whole conversation. "I only brought up all of this because I care about you. And if I can figure out some way to help you without you needing to use Harmony, then we're going to find it."

Chavi doubted she could do it, but Avi Taheri was not one to be cowed, so they allowed her to guide them down the street, to where her car waited to take them to the east end of the city.

* * *

Harvard knew it was getting late, and this was probably stupid of him to do anyway, but fear of Kathy was a powerful motivator. If everything came crashing down, he needed Chavi to know that even if he'd lied about pretty much everything, he hadn't lied about loving them.

He knocked on Rivka's door.

"Is everything alright?" she asked the moment she saw him. "Is Chavi okay?"

"Yeah," Harvard said, stunned. "Yeah...everything is fine."

"Okay. Good," Rivka visibly relaxed. "Sorry. It was probably silly of me to worry. I'm sure you all just got busy with things. But, you know, you were coming over so regularly, and then you weren't..."

No one had told her about Haven, had they? "Right," Harvard said slowly. "We've just been busy."

"Good! Busy is good. So you all have found work?"

"Um. Sort of?" The Haven job had technically been work, and it had technically been legal work given that it was the security corporation that hired them. To steal. But again it was for the security corp, so it was legal stealing.

"'Sort of' is better than not at all," Rivka nodded, then abruptly added, "Come in! Can I get you anything?"

Harvard was about to say no, thank you, but even as he crossed the threshold Rivka was already going to pour him a glass of water and fetch some food. She returned with a little bowl of rice crackers, and she pulled out a chair at the table to indicate Harvard should sit.

"So," she said, sitting next to him, "what brings you here?"

"Well, it's kind of silly"—Harvard scratched the back of his head—"but I want to get Chavi a really nice gift, and I'm not sure what to get them? And that feels stupid. Like, I know them really well, I think, but I haven't actually known them that long, so..."

"That's not stupid," Rivka said. "Sometimes you get to know someone very well, even if you don't know *things* about them. And sometimes you know a lot of *things* about a person, but you don't know them well at all."

"Right," Harvard sighed. He hoped Chavi would see it that way, if the truth ever came out. "So I thought maybe you could tell me a bit about what they liked before they became a scavenger? Maybe something they were into when they were growing up?"

Rivka looked away. Harvard wasn't sure if she was aware of what she was doing, but she was looking toward Chavi's childhood bedroom.

It took her a long moment of contemplation before she spoke again. "They did teenager things, you know? They weren't exactly...academically inclined."

"Yeah, I kinda figured," Harvard laughed.

"They always had a bit of a thrill-seeking personality, I think. Life was never enough for them. They liked...spending time with their friends. Going to parties. Doing drugs. I assume. I didn't really ask about that, but when your kid comes home confused about who they are and what they're doing, it's generally a safe bet that they're high."

Harvard was surprised to hear her mention this last bit so casually. "It didn't scare you? That you knew they did drugs?"

"Of course it did!" Rivka laughed. "I don't think any mother likes the idea of their child messing with their brain chemistry. But I just figured...well, they were living at the Academy, so they could do whatever they wanted without me knowing. What good would it do for me to lecture them about those kinds of things? It would only drive a wedge between us. And that was always the last thing I wanted." She seemed to deflate a little, leaning back in her chair. She placed a hand on the table, fiddling with a cracker but not eating it. "Maybe I was always too lenient. Maybe I should have said something. But I always thought I was so lucky, you know, that we had a good relationship? I knew plenty of other parents whose kids went through a teenage rebellion."

"Chavi didn't?" Harvard asked.

"Well, I mean, they *did*, but they didn't rebel against *me*. And I was thankful for that."

"But was there anything they really loved doing? A hobby?"

Rivka sat back in her chair, drumming her fingers on the table. "Well, I mean...they worked out quite a bit, but not for a sport or anything. Honestly, I think they just did it to look good. They were a bit vain, as a teen. I don't know. They were kind of...directionless. Maybe that was part of the problem. Why they struggled so much in school. I don't think they really did know what they liked. Other than people. They've always loved people."

Harvard could see that now, though he never would have guessed it based on the sullen captain that Yale had been. Chavi and Yale seemed like two different people. But Chavi was the real one, right? Yale was just a role they'd had to play, the hardened scavenger they'd had to become in order to survive. But surely they'd left Yale behind in the dusts, where they belonged.

"Admittedly..." Rivka continued, "they didn't really have much time to grow, the way a kid should. They were sixteen when...you know."

"They went to the Commission?" Harvard wondered why she treated it like a dirty word.

"Yes. I always wondered...what could have happened if they stayed? Who would they have become? I mean, I'm so proud of them, of course, but...maybe they would have found themself. It wasn't possible, though. Even if it weren't for the money—me getting dismissed and all that—that poor boy's parents might have tried to take legal action if Chavi hadn't disappeared when they did."

Harvard's brow furrowed. "What poor boy?"

"Oh!" Rivka's hand jerked back as though she'd been burnt. "They...they didn't tell you?"

Harvard had no idea what she was talking about. "No?" Suddenly he was sweating. He'd been so concerned with his own secret, it had never occurred to him that *Chavi* had secrets, too.

She bit her lip, shaking her head. "It's...it's not really my place to say. I'm sorry. I shouldn't have said anything."

"No, please. Tell me." He didn't want to put her in an uncomfortable position, but the fact that there were important things he didn't know about Chavi ate at him. He needed to know. The need was a physical sensation, the same way he needed to breathe.

"It's not—"

"I've got to know. I mean, I just—I need to know."

Rivka took a deep breath, as though steeling herself. "You know Chavi was expelled from the Academy, yes?"

"Yeah."

"They got into a fight. A boy who had been bullying Jasmine."

That seemed in character for both Yale *and* Chavi. "They are...very protective," Harvard conceded.

"That they are," Rivka laughed fondly with a sad smile, which soon faded. "But they went too far. Put the boy in the hospital."

"Is he alright?" Harvard asked.

"He is," she nodded. "But he can't...he can't speak properly anymore. Chavi accidentally broke his skull and it...affected him neurologically. Chavi knew they could get in serious trouble, and that no one was going to hire me after, so..." To Harvard's surprise, Rivka Chakrabarti began to cry. He froze, watching wide-eyed as she wept, feeling completely useless. What was he supposed to do? "They're a good kid, you have to believe me," she wept. "They try so hard to be good."

Harvard found himself at a loss. He didn't know where all this was coming from. He tentatively reached out for her hand.

"I know that," he reassured her.

"And you," Rivka sniffled, "you make them better. Really, you do. They are happier than I've ever seen them when they're with you."

Hearing that gave Harvard that warm ache in his chest. "I'm glad."

She grasped Harvard's hand tightly and looked in his eyes.

"Please don't leave them," she pleaded.

Suddenly Harvard understood. She was afraid she'd just ruined her child's relationship, which, from her perspective, was one of the few good things happening in Chavi's life.

"I won't," Harvard whispered.

"I love Chavi more than anything,"

"I know. I do too."

She pulled him closer. "Do you really?" she asked with a hopeful smile.

"Yes."

Rivka let go of Harvard's hand, leaning back in her chair, wiping her tears with the back of her hand and laughing at herself.

"I'm so sorry," she said. "It seems every time the two of us talk, one of us ends up crying."

Harvard laughed. "It's really okay," he said. "It actually makes me feel a lot better, to be honest."

Rivka didn't seem to have heard him. "And to think, you came here looking for a gift idea and I've given you nothing."

"Actually?" Harvard said. "This has given me an idea. And I think it's a pretty good one."

That evening, walking back home, Harvard thought about what Rivka had divulged to him about Chavi and the boy from the Academy. It was...disconcerting, but Harvard could live with it. After all, it wasn't like they'd killed anyone. Well, there was Lyle, but that was an accident. Chavi was impulsive. Harvard knew this. He could make peace with their mistakes. He was hiding his own past from them, too. Didn't they deserve to have secrets too? Well, this was...it was a big secret. But Harvard could manage. They would bring it up when they were ready. He would just have to wait.

* * *

"Surprise!" Harvard said, uncovering Chavi's eyes to reveal the only tattoo parlor in Lower Bastion that had been willing to make a deal with him.

"A tattoo?" Chavi asked, and Harvard could tell they were surprised, but he wasn't sure if they were surprised in a good way or a bad way. He panicked. How could he be so presumptuous to assume that Chavi would want something permanent on their body?

"I'm sorry," he blurted out. "This idea was stupid. You don't have to if you—"

"No, Harvard, it's great!" Chavi laughed. "I've always wanted one! But—how are we gonna pay for it?"

"She said she'd do it for free if I did some designs for her," Harvard said. He guessed this was probably a pretty poor trade on the part of the parlor, given that the owners of every other tattoo parlor he asked had more or less laughed in his face. The proprietor of this one, though—a little old lady with ink up and down all her limbs—had flipped through Harvard's sketchbook and said, "Oh, sweetheart. Of course, honey."

"What will it be of?" Chavi asked. "Or do you want me to choose?"

Harvard pulled a folded piece of paper from his pocket. "You don't have to do this one, but...I did make a design for you." Harvard was pretty proud of his design, though he did feel a little nervous about it when the old lady had peered down at it through her thick glasses and said, "I don't understand it, sugar, but it's up to you."

Chavi folded Harvard's hands over the paper and pressed it back into his chest.

"Actually, don't show me," they said. "I'll see it when it's done."

"Are—are you sure?" Harvard asked.

"It's your design, right?" Chavi smiled. "So I know I'll like it."

Harvard didn't know much about the tattoo process. He knew it involved needles, but he didn't know his present for Chavi basically amounted to having them get stabbed repeatedly. He had to cover his eyes for most of it, though Chavi, oddly, seemed to enjoy it.

"It actually feels kinda good after a while," they reassured him, though Harvard couldn't imagine that was actually true. They were probably just trying to spare his feelings. They had selected their right wrist for the tattoo placement, and while the inked woman bent over their arm, they watched Harvard, smiling the whole time.

"All done, kids," the woman announced, cleaning Chavi's wrist with a wet towel before wrapping it. Chavi started to unpeel the wrap, but the woman caught their hand. "Wait a few hours," she instructed, and Chavi looked crestfallen.

They couldn't have been walking home for more than twenty minutes when impatience got the better of Chavi. They paused on a street corner and ripped off the wrap, looking over the lines that had been inked into their skin: a simple outline of two hands, one bandaging the other.

Harvard watched Chavi expectantly, waiting for some kind of response. They just stared at it. Maybe they didn't get it.

"It's the day we were reunited in the dusts," Harvard explained, "and I bandaged you—"

"I know what it is," they said absently. Harvard shifted nervously.

"I picked it because it was the first time you ever let me care for you," he explained. "You always want to protect me, but...I want you to carry around a reminder that I'm here to protect you too."

Chavi pulled Harvard into a sudden embrace. "It's perfect," they whispered.

There was always a voice in Harvard's mind trying to convince him that Chavi didn't mean what they said, that this was all temporary, that Chavi was only pretending to love him.

In that moment, that voice was quiet.

CHAPTER NINETEEN

The Sand Crystal

Chavi checked the Ivies' funds at a points kiosk again in the vain hope that maybe something had changed, and they wouldn't have to do the job tonight after all. But no, August hadn't even started working on the townhouse again, so they hadn't received a single payment since the one from the Delian Group. Well, maybe tonight would go well. Maybe they'd be the new breadwinner in the household.

"Money troubles?" asked a voice so close it made Chavi jump. They saw Devrin standing just beside the kiosk, leaning with performative casualness.

Surprise morphed into irritation in an instant. "Are you following me?" Chavi demanded.

"Following you?" Devrin laughed. "Of course not. I'm a very busy man. Not everything is about you, you know, Chaverim. I'm merely out for a stroll. So. Financial difficulties? I gave you so much money and you spent it already?"

"None of your business."

"You could always take another job for me, you know."

"And you're not gonna threaten my boyfriend this time?" Chavi spat.

"Pft." Devrin rolled his eyes. "That was just to get your attention. I was never *really* going to hurt him."

Chavi blinked. "You broke his fingers."

"That was nothing. I mean I could have *really* hurt him. You know..." He gestured vaguely with one hand. "Put him through agony that he would feel the echoes of for the rest of his life. You get the idea. But I only broke his fingers, because I'm just so charitable like that."

"What is wrong with you?" Chavi asked, which Devrin completely ignored.

"So. Job?"

"Are you serious?" Chavi asked. "I will *never* work for you again."

Devrin shrugged. "Well, we'll see."

"We won't. I hope I never see you again."

"Careful, Chaverim," Devrin said, holding a hand to his chest in feigned offense. "I'm the one looking after *your* safety, remember?"

"Since when?"

"Since before you were born. The Delian group has lasted for hundreds of years, and the Delian Group is mine."

"The Delian Group has never done shit for me," they asserted, and as far as they were aware, it was true. The Galvin Conference was the first interaction they'd ever had with a Delian guard, and they did *not* feel very protected that day.

"If you don't notice our work, that means we're doing our job well. Listen." He gave them a pitying kind of look. "I'm only asking for your own sake. You seem so worried about providing for your dear little Harvard."

"We're doing fine," Chavi lied, but Devrin ignored them, leaning on the kiosk dreamily.

"Ah, young lovers. Clawing at each other in such a desperate attempt to get closer that they end up tearing each other apart."

"And what would you know about it?" Chavi snapped.

"Everything." He sighed, suddenly looking wistful. Or pretending to be wistful, maybe. Chavi didn't believe this man was capable of feeling human emotions, let alone being full of wist.

"I understand that when you love someone that much, you want to give them everything. You'll go to any length to show them how much you care. It must be difficult for you to know you can never provide for him the way his family used to. A little heart breaking, isn't it?"

Chavi stared blankly at him. "What are you talking about?"

And in that moment Chavi saw an emotion cross Devrin's face that they had never seen there before: genuine shock.

"Founders, do you really not know?" he asked. "I must say, this is a bit of a rarity for me. I'm in the habit of *knowing* things, you see, and I had no idea that he *didn't tell you*. I'm a little thrown off, if I'm honest."

"What are you talking about?" Chavi repeated.

Devrin leaned forward. "I have the pleasure of being the first to tell you," he grinned, "that you are in a relationship with the progeny of Bastion's Founders."

"Are you trying to say that Harvard is part of the big six families?" Chavi asked.

"Do you even know his real name?"

Chavi bristled. "Ronan," they said.

Devrin smile grew wider. "Ronan *Bell.*"

Chavi was silent for a moment, eyes searching Devrin's face.

"You're trying to fuck with me," they finally decided.

"I'm not!" Devrin sounded almost offended at the notion, was which comedic considering how often he was, in fact, trying to fuck with them. "I assure you that had I known you weren't aware, I would have tried to find some way to use it to my advantage, but honestly I'm a bit perplexed. Why would he keep that from you? I thought he trusted you."

"He does trust me!" Chavi shot back. "You're just trying to make me suspicious of him, cos you're a...a..." Suddenly no insult felt cruel enough. "A bad person." Dusts, that was weak.

Devrin shrugged.

"Look into it, if you don't believe me. It wasn't too hard to piece together."

"Oh yeah? And how did you 'piece it together?'"

He looked delighted that they'd asked. "When we first brought him in, he mentioned something to Pierce about his family. That was what first clued me in the fact that perhaps I didn't know the whole story about dear Harvard. I had Pierce ask him for his real name while seeing to his injuries. And you were so kind as to volunteer his approximate age. Bastion is a big city, sure, but not big enough that it was too much trouble to shift through all the Ronans that were born within a rough time period."

"Well, you're thinking of the wrong Ronan!" Chavi snapped. "Harvard's parents wouldn't let him leave the house cos they thought he had a blood disease. He ran away when he was—"

"Fourteen?" Devrin guessed.

Chavi inhaled sharply. "How did you know that?"

Devrin looked altogether too pleased with himself. "By some strange coincidence, that's the exact age that the Bells claim their Ronan had to be institutionalized after a 'nervous breakdown.' Isn't that strange? That both Ronans—whose descriptions match up almost exactly, mind you— disappeared at exactly the same time?"

Chavi gritted their teeth.

"That doesn't make sense," they said. "Why would he become a scavenger if he were one of the Bells?"

"Well I'm sure I don't know," Devrin laced his fingers together. "Makes you wonder what he's hiding, doesn't it?"

"No, it—look, he has a right not to tell me things if he wants to. It—even if it is true, I'm sure he has a good reason for not telling me. I trust him."

Devrin nodded. "That's good," he said. "It's very important that you trust him. Even though, it seems, he doesn't trust you."

Chavi rolled their eyes. "Shut up with your stupid...mind games! You're not going to manipulate me!"

Devrin looks genuinely wounded. "First of all, my mind games are never stupid. They're very smart. But I'm not playing with you, Chavi! I'm completely serious!"

"Harvard and I love each other, and if you think you can possibly get in the way of that, you're a fucking idiot."

Devrin feigned offense, placing a hand over his heart.

"Me? Step in the way of young love? I would never. Founders know I wouldn't dream of ruining it for you. I just wanted to make sure you know who you're dealing with."

"I'm not 'dealing with' him." Chavi shoved the slip of paper in their pocket, turning toward the door. "And you probably made that shit up anyway."

"Easy enough to verify," he said with a shrug. "All you have to do is look at Saoirse."

"Who?"

"The chief executive officer of Bell Enterprises. Also, a good personal friend of mine. Also, Ronan Bell's mother. Would you like to see a picture of her?"

The answer, of course, was yes. Even if Chavi didn't believe him—which they were pretty sure they didn't—seeing a picture of Harvard's supposed "mother" would confirm what they already believed. And they desperately wanted that confirmation. But they also wanted to trust Harvard, and more than that they wanted to prove to Devrin that they trusted Harvard. They didn't know why they cared what Devrin thought of them, what he thought of their relationship, but suddenly they did, and they wouldn't let him win.

"Leave me alone," they said, shoving their hands in their pockets. "Leave all of us alone. I don't want a job, and I don't want your help."

As they turned to walk away, they could hear him say, "But what if I want *your* help?" They didn't think he expected them to answer.

Chavi didn't want to let the interaction bother them, but it still did, like a wound they tried to ignore and that only meant it got infected. *Clawing at each other in such a desperate attempt to get closer that they end up tearing each other apart.* They didn't like that imagery. Besides, that was stupid. He didn't know what he was talking about. And Harvard wouldn't lie to them. *But you're lying to Harvard,* they thought with a pang of guilt. *You refused to tell anyone about crab disease, and now look what happened. Someone's dead because of it.* Then again, that would have happened regardless of whether or not they'd told.

It's not lying, Chavi decided, if the other person doesn't need to know. And Harvard simply didn't need to know. Not about Harmony, and not about the creature that lived in their blood.

* * *

Chavi revived their suit jacket from the Galvin conference, but decided it looked a little more interesting with a shimmery shirt underneath. They swiped one of Harvard's new bow ties—black. And for a final touch, they wore fishnets with shorts, something they hadn't sported since they were sixteen. They decided it was a subtle nod to the Fisher's Union. They let their hair down so it reached their shoulder, keeping it pushed to one side, then examined themself in the mirror.

Not bad, they thought. Sufficiently hot. They briefly considered ditching the glasses, but they didn't love the prospect of stumbling around the club blindly all night, plus they always thought they managed to wear glasses in a cool and sexy way that others weren't able to pull off. Many of their classmates at the Academy certainly thought so. In fact, preparing to go out reminded them a bit of getting ready for a party in high school. They missed those times, a bit. Everything had been simpler then. All that mattered was having a good time. Now they had so many responsibilities. Why couldn't things just be like that again? Perhaps tonight would be a nice escape.

When they were reasonably certain Harvard had fallen asleep beside them, they slipped out of bed, put on their carefully chosen outfit, and crept out of the house without waking anyone. They could hear the thrumming of the music once they were within a few blocks from the club. Once they neared, they thought they could feel the street vibrate with the pulses of the beat. No sign adorned the entrance, but the flashing lights that spilled out into the street beyond made it obvious. That and the two bouncers posted by the door, though Chavi guessed they were more for show than actually turning people away. The bouncers didn't even turn to face them as they entered—and why would they? Chavi looked like they belonged here.

Chavi was surprised to find how comfortably they slipped into the heaving mass of people. They hadn't been to any kind of party since the Academy.

"Chavi!" they heard Ariel call as they pressed through the crowd, looking for some kind of bar. Ariel, Mellie, and some of the other Harmonizers were standing together in an iridescent column, glittering in the lowlights of the party. In fact, Chavi now realized that the whole room was full of glittering columns in different colors—all different hues that could be found in a handful of sand.

"Hey!" they said, nearly shouting to be heard over the din of voices and music. Ariel approached them, drink in hand. Their hair cascaded down their front in a delicate twist, with sparkling gemstones weaved in. They wore a sheer black dress that clung loosely on their body.

"I'm glad you could make it," they said.

"Wouldn't miss it," Chavi smiled. *Plus, I kind of have to be there. You did imply that.* "So, uh, what are we doing here?"

"Having a good time!" Ariel raised their drink hand to indicate the rest of their cohort, who were chatting and laughing and dancing. Mellie winked.

"Okay." Chavi drew out the word. "But what about the job?"

"Don't worry about that for now." Ariel gave Chavi's shoulder a friendly squeeze. "What's important right now is that you enjoy yourself. That people *see* you enjoying yourself. Go on, get a drink. And once you've caught up with the rest of us..." Ariel smiled that warm, disarming smile of theirs. "Let's *dance.*"

* * *

Harvard found himself pretending to be asleep a lot these days. He made his breathing deep and even as he watched Chavi quietly dress and slip out the door.

He trusted Chavi.

He did.

But also what could they possibly be doing in the middle of the night? And why hadn't they told him? He know that a good, trusting boyfriend would have faith in his partner and go back to sleep, but his need to *know* was so visceral it twisted his stomach.

So he climbed out of bed the moment Chavi left, and started dressing to go follow them.

Harvard.

Harvard jumped. He turned to see Speedy perched on the windowsill. It had been a long time since Speedy had spoken directly into his mind like that. He'd almost forgotten what it felt like. "Speedy! Where have you been? Where are you?"

I was visiting my father. We had much to discuss.

"What did you discuss?"

Speedy was silent for a long moment. Then he simply said, *Do not follow Chavi tonight.*

"So you know where they went?"

I know that nothing good will come of you following.

Harvard frowned. "Listen, Speedy. I know you just want to help me. And when I was actually in danger, yes, I needed that help. But now we're back in the city. I know the city. I'm used to it. I can take care of myself." And it felt good to say, because it was true. After years of feeling so out of control, Harvard was back where he belonged, in the city he'd come to know so intimately.

Am I not your friend, Harvard? Crab though he may be, Speedy was easy to read. Harvard saw the hesitancy in the shuffling of his legs and the hurt in his voice.

"Of course you are," Harvard assured him.

Please, heed my warning as you would that of a friend.

"Just because someone's a friend doesn't mean you always listen to them."

With that, he slipped out of the room and hurried down the stairs, hoping he wasn't too late to trail behind Chavi. He kept a sizable distance between them, keeping to the shadows, and Chavi led them both into the Cusp.

Harvard didn't know the Cusp very well. Even during his days at the Shack, he'd avoided this area. It had frightened him. Not because he believed everything his mother said about Lower Bastion—he knew by then that most of that was made up. The Cusp was full of things he didn't understand, and it made him feel like a child, and he hated that feeling.

Hearing the din of voices and the pounding of bass, he felt that familiar sensation—dwarfed by a world that was not his own. He wanted to fit in, but he had no idea how. He unbuttoned the first two buttons of his shirt, thinking it might make him look cooler, then decided that was stupid and buttoned them up again. He attempted a saunter, with his hands in his pockets, but then he decided that "saunter" was not really in his physical vocabulary, and just walked normally.

A bouncer put a thick hand in front of his chest as he neared the entrance.

"Hold up a minute," she said. "How old are you, kid?"

Harvard looked up at her where she was perched on her high stool.

"I—I'm twenty," he stammered.

She raised an eyebrow.

"Really?"

"I am! I'm twenty!" he said, flushing with indignation. He'd just seen Chavi walk in with no issue, and the two of them were the same age.

"You got any identification?"

"Identification?" Harvard repeated. What did that mean?

"A citizenship card?"

"Um, no?" Harvard said, flustered. He'd never heard of that. Was he supposed to have one? Did his parents have one for him when was little? Did Chavi have one?

"Oh, just let 'im in!" said a voice behind Harvard, and he jumped. Another bouncer was leaning against the wall on the opposite side of the door. "He looks honest enough. Right?"

"Um. Yes."

The first bouncer fixed him with a skeptical glare.

"You're not gonna get into any trouble tonight, are you?"

Harvard shook his head rigorously. The bouncer shared a glance with her compatriot and sighed.

"Alright. Go ahead in."

Harvard hurried inside, berating himself. He'd only just arrived and already he was having problems. He glanced around, taking in the place. He'd entered into a hallway, where patrons were coming and going from a shrouded doorway that seemed to lead to the dance floor. Some patrons headed to the right, which looked like it led to the bathrooms. Others, often in pairs or groups of three, headed to the left, where there was a series of cushioned booths fashioned with curtains that could be pulled closed. Harvard panicked at the sight of them, and at the sight of the giggling patrons who had just claimed a booth for themselves, and hurried toward the doorway to the dance floor.

He steeled himself and pulled aside the curtain. He was blinded by flashing lights, and the music was so much louder in here that he had the instinct to cover his ears. He knew he'd look like an idiot, though, with his ears covered and eyes squeezed shut, bumbling around the place, so he forced himself to act as normal as possible as he made his way into the crowd. It smelled like sweat and alcohol, and also a lot of other smells that Harvard didn't recognize. Everyone was jumping and screaming and dancing—though he wasn't entirely sure if he qualified a lot of what he saw as "dancing." Definitely there was movement involved, and often in pairs, but was it a dance?

A hand grabbed him by the waist and pulled him in.

"You look like a lost little puppy," said the woman holding him. She had stars painted on her face, and paper stars woven into her hair. Her comment made his face burn. What was it about him that made him look so scared? Why was it so hard for him to just look normal?

"Maybe you could use some company tonight?" the woman continued.

That actually sounded great to Harvard. If this woman could help him find Chavi, things would be a lot easier.

"Yes, actually!" he answered.

"How about I take you back to my place, little puppy?"

Harvard's stomach dropped. He realized he had misread the situation.

"Oh, that's not—No, I'm fine—"

Another hand grabbed him by the shoulder and turned him around.

"Is that old creep bothering you?" said a person with glitter on their face, wearing what looked more or less like shiny underwear to Harvard. And nothing else. Was that allowed?

"Um, a little, yes." A wave of relief washed over him, thankful someone had come to his rescue.

"Some people." The glittery person rolled their eyes. "Maybe I can help you."

"Yes please! I'm looking for someone—"

"Looking for someone, you say?"

"Aren't we all," laughed the star woman behind Harvard.

"Maybe it's me you're looking for," said Glitter.

"No, it's someone specific—" Harvard clarified. He thought he'd been pretty clear about that.

"I think it's me." Glitter pulled him closer. "Why don't you come with me to one of the booths out there?"

"No, I—I don't want to—" Harvard stammered.

"No fair!" Stars interrupted. "I saw him first!"

"Fine. We can share him."

"I don't want to—" he tried to pull away, but with one hand on his waist and another on his shoulder, he couldn't gracefully extricate himself.

"You don't *think* you want to. But trust me, you *do*."

With a burst of determination, Harvard ran, breaking free of them and diving into the crowd. He could hear them laughing behind him, and he wondered if they had been joking the whole time. They didn't actually want anything from him. They just wanted to play with him. Was this what normal people were like? Or worse, was this what *Chavi* was like? Was Chavi full of secret desires that they kept concealed, that Harvard could never fulfill? Was that why they ran off tonight? To find someone—or someones—willing to sequester themselves in one of those booths with them and do salacious things that Harvard didn't want to do? Or *couldn't* do? Was it his personality that was deficient, or his very body? He was powerless to change either. The thought made Harvard nauseous. Not the thought of Chavi with someone else—the thought that he just wasn't enough.

* * *

Chavi didn't need to be drunk to be confident. That was a bit of a secret of theirs in high school. So long as everyone *thought* they were drunk, they could get away with all kinds of things with alcohol as an excuse. That was why only a few drinks in, Chavi was more than happy to allow Ariel and Mellie to pull them up onto the bar, dancing on a makeshift stage.

They were surprised at how natural it felt, slipping back into this part of themself that they'd given up as lost. When Chavi became Yale, they thought they'd completely given up on having any fun in their life. Now the past four years of their life seemed to fade into the background, like they'd never happened.

More patrons of the club climbed up onto the bar, and Chavi found themself passed from dance partner to dance partner. They didn't really mind so much. They were happy to move with whoever pulled on them.

"You better save some time for me," Ariel said as they pulled Chavi into an embrace, smiling sweetly.

"Of course," they said.

Ariel leaned over to grab a bottle of champagne from behind the bar. They popped the cork, and it shot out into the crowd. They held the bottle up and poured it over the two of them, the liquid dribbling down like sweet, sticky rain. Chavi laughed, and when some of the champagne got into their mouth they found it tasted chemically and strange, nothing like the wine on Haven. Still, being on this bar felt like being on a stage, and the people in the crowd were cheering, so they opened their mouth to drink more, and pulled Ariel closer.

* * *

Harvard stood frozen to his spot. He watched Chavi dancing, smiling and laughing, and he wondered when was the last time he saw them this happy. Had he ever made them this happy? Had he ever really known them, or what they really wanted?

Harvard realized with a sinking sensation that maybe Chavi was not the person he thought they were at all. He had fallen in love with Yale, captain of the Ivies. What if Chaverim Chakrabarti was someone altogether different? Someone who didn't love him. Someone who *couldn't* love him.

Harvard felt like an idiot. His throat tightened, and though he fought to hold back tears, one rolled down his cheek regardless, making him feel like more of an idiot. Here he was, in the middle of a party, crying. He wanted to wipe the tears away, but he froze, eyes fixed on Chavi, so he just let the tears fall. The whole crowd was moving around him, shifting and pulsing like ocean waves, and here he was in the middle of it, still.

Suddenly, everything was too much. The music was deafening, the room was too hot, and everyone was too close, crushing him. There were too many smells and sounds and sensations and he needed them all to stop. He should never have come here. He needed to get out. He needed to leave.

Chavi locked eyes with him.

They froze, and Harvard couldn't tell if the expression on their face was confusion, embarrassment, terror, or some kind of combination.

It was too loud to hear them speak, but he could read their lips as they said: *"Harvard?"*

Harvard's face burned, his whole body burned, and he needed desperately to be anywhere but here.

He whirled around and shoved through the crowd, making for the door. He'd started crying in earnest now, but he didn't care.

* * *

Chavi leapt off the bar, eliciting some cries of surprise and confusion from the people standing nearby.

"Harvard!" they shouted, even though they knew they couldn't be heard. Was that really him? It had to be. But what was he doing here? How did he get here? And—the next question made Chavi feel dizzy to think about—what was he thinking, watching them dance with everyone like that? Did Harvard see this as a kind of infidelity? It hadn't occurred to Chavi that dancing could be cheating, and now they felt stupid for never considering it.

Chavi shoved people aside, spilling drinks and stepping on toes. A few people cursed at them, but they didn't care.

"Harvard!" they shouted again. They had to get to him. They had to explain everything. The room suddenly tipped dangerously, and Chavi wondered if they'd had more to drink than they thought. "Harvard!"

They caught sight of him pushing his way toward the door off the dance floor, into the hallway beyond. Chavi managed to close in on him in the hall, just before he made it to the front door.

"Harvard, wait!"

He paused. Out here the roar of the crowd was not so loud, and he could hear them better. Chavi could see he was trembling, and his fists were clenched. So he was mad at them, then. Well, Chavi supposed that made sense. In retrospect, they were mad at them too.

"Harvard." They reached for his arm, fully expecting him to pull away. He didn't. Chavi turned him around to face them. His face was streaked with tears. It made Chavi's chest ache.

"Do you not want to be with me?" Harvard demanded.

"What?" Chavi asked. It was the last thing they'd expected him to say.

"You sneak out in the middle of the night to go drink and dance and hang out with your friends and—am I not enough for you? Do you not want to be with me?"

"No, of course I want to be with you!" Chavi gripped both of his shoulders, still baffled.

"Then why—" Harvard sniffled, "why are you—"

"Look, Harvard, I can explain everything, alright?" Chavi sighed, their mind racing to try and figure out a way that they could, in fact, explain everything. "After the last party we went to—I mean, that didn't go so well, right? I thought maybe that kind of life just wasn't for you. And I missed it, but I didn't want you to feel left out, so...I left when I thought you were sleeping."

"You snuck out...because you didn't want to hurt me?" Harvard sniffled, seeming mollified.

"Yes!" Chavi said, trying to convince themself that this was technically true. That justification turned them into a hero, kind of. Bravely sacrificing to protect Harvard's feelings.

Some of the hurt seemed to fade from Harvard's expression. "That's...really nice of you."

"See?" Chavi pet Harvard's curls. "Of course I want to be with you. I just didn't want you to feel pressured to do something you wouldn't enjoy."

"Well..." Harvard wrung his hands. "I might enjoy it."

"Really?" Chavi asked, trying to mask their skepticism.

"I don't know," Harvard shrugged. "I've never been to a club before. And now that I'm with you...I mean, maybe I will have fun." He sounded unsure, but optimistic.

Chavi considered this. It wouldn't be a *problem* having Harvard around, especially since they weren't even working yet. Maybe it would even be *fun*. "Okay, how about this: we'll go back in there, have some drinks, dance together, and then we'll see how you feel?"

"Yeah," Harvard smiled, and seeing that smile was like seeing the sun peek over the horizon after a long and painful night. "That sounds nice."

Chavi breathed a sigh of relief. "Good. And—I'm sorry I hurt you. I didn't mean for that to happen."

"It's okay. I just want you to know that you can be honest with me."

Chavi tried not to wince. "Right. I know that."

"Okay. Good. Let's go."

Chavi guided Harvard back onto the dance floor, this time with an arm around him to assure him that they weren't going anywhere. They watched his face carefully, looking for any signs of residual hurt. Luckily, he seemed satisfied after their conversation out in the hall. Maybe this would be okay. Maybe they'd even have a fun night together. Maybe Harvard could even be part of the job, and then they'd make twice the points.

When Chavi got back to the iridescent column, the Harmonizers were there again, taking a break from dancing.

"Hey guys," Chavi said, hoping that Harvard's addition wouldn't be too unwelcome. "This is my boyfriend, Harvard. Harvard, you remember Ariel, right?"

"Yeah. I do," Harvard gave a tentative wave, and Ariel nodded with a smile.

"This is Mellie," Chavi gestured for her to come forward, and she shook Harvard's hand fervently.

"I've heard *so* much about you," she said.

"Really?" Harvard asked, glancing at Chavi. He looked so pleased at the idea that anyone would deign talk about him.

"Oh yes," Mellie continued, "Chavi just won't shut up about you."

Harvard flushed.

"Can I speak to you for a moment, Chavi?" Ariel sidled up next to them.

"Sure."

They pulled Chavi aside, toward the dark edges of the room that were a little less packed. Ariel pushed them up against the wall with surprising force, still gripping their arm.

"What is he doing here?" they hissed, and their sudden urgency left Chavi stunned.

"I don't know!" they said. "He must have followed me—"

"Get rid of him." Ariel's easygoing air and light smile were gone. Their face was hard, harder than Chavi had ever seen it.

"Why?" they asked.

"He can't be here when we begin. It could be dangerous."

"Dangerous?" Chavi repeated. "Is the job we're doing going to be dangerous?"

"Hopefully not," Ariel said, "but it's been planned very carefully. Any unanticipated complications"—Ariel nodded to Harvard, who was currently laughing at something Mellie had said—"could make a mess. And you don't want him to get hurt, do you?"

"No!" Chavi said reflexively.

Ariel's grip loosened slightly. "Right," they said. "We begin at one. You need to have him gone by then." Chavi didn't have a way to tell the time, but Ariel showed a slender watch on their wrist, beaded with little glass flowers. It was already almost midnight. They had an hour.

"Okay. I will. He'll be gone by one. I promise," Chavi said.

Ariel's smile returned, and despite unease beginning to settle in Chavi's stomach, they still couldn't help but trust them.

"Perfect," they said, releasing Chavi and melting back into the crowd as though nothing had happened. Now they *had* to figure out what was going on, so they could back out while they still had the chance. Chavi pulled Mellie aside the first opportunity they got.

"Do you know what we're doing tonight?"

Mellie smiled, biting her bottom lip, and nodded, her pigtails bobbing.

"Is it dangerous?" Chavi asked.

"Not really." She crinkled her nose. "Just a normal job like always."

"What is it?"

"Oh, I can't tell you that!" She punched their shoulder playfully, as thought they'd just told a joke. "We don't talk about it until we're Harmonized. That's the rule. We'll meet in the far back booth at one, and Ariel will explain everything."

Chavi glanced at Harvard. He was swaying a little with the music, watching the other Harmonizers dance, but not dancing himself. Mellie followed their gaze.

"I'm guessing you know he's gotta go?" she asked.

"Yeah," Chavi said. Mellie grabbed their hand and slipped something into their palm. It felt like a flimsy sheet of paper, or thin plastic.

"Here," she said, folding Chavi's fingers over it with a coy smile.

"What is this?" they asked.

"Something to help you get the little guy out of the way."

"What do you mean?"

"Put it in his drink. He'll be out like a light."

Chavi tried to give it back to her. "Are you serious? I can't drug my own boyfriend."

"What's the alternative?" She pushed their hands back.

"I mean—"

"Look at it like this," she said, draping an arm over their shoulders. "Harvard takes a little surprise nap. We do what we gotta do. He wakes up none the wiser. Sounds good, right?"

No. In fact, it sounded awful. "It just...feels wrong."

Mellie shrugged. "Yeah, it feels wrong. Everything we do feels wrong. But deep down, you know it's right."

Chavi thought back to Harvard's betrayed expression just moments ago. That was already more guilt than they could bear. "I already hurt him once tonight," they decided. "I can't risk doing it again."

"Don't you want to keep him safe?" Mellie asked, her eyes wide with feigned innocence.

"Of course. Always."

"Well right now, he is in danger. Either you fix that, or you don't."

Chavi opened their hand to examine the tab. It was no more than a square inch in size, pale and translucent. "Will it hurt him?"

"Hurt him?" Mellie laughed. "He'll be asleep!"

"This is a bad idea," Chavi groaned.

"Actually"—Mellie flipped her hair with a sense of pride—"I think it's a pretty good idea. You'll thank me later."

Chavi told themself they hadn't decided what to do, but as they slipped the tab into one of the pockets of their jacket, they felt as though the choice had been made for them. They approached Harvard, who looked happy to have their attention again.

"Where have you been?" he asked as Chavi placed a hand on his back.

"Just talking to friends," Chavi shrugged. "Are you having fun?"

Harvard's smile faltered. "Sure," he said, "but I was hoping to spend more time with you."

"Why don't we dance?" Chavi asked. Maybe if they tired him out, he'd go home on his own. His smile disappeared completely.

"I don't think I can dance," he said. "I don't know how. I'd embarrass myself."

"Didn't you dance on Haven?" Chavi asked.

Harvard looked away. "That was different."

"How?"

"I don't know. The people were different."

"C'mon," Chavi said, pulling Harvard toward the bar. "Let's get you a drink. You'll feel better."

They went up to the bar and ordered two cocktails so full of synth juice and sweeteners that it would be overpowering. When the drinks arrived, dyed red to imitate the fruits they were supposed to taste like, Chavi turned around to see Harvard wasn't watching them. He was looking at the people in the crowd, almost longingly. They pinched the flimsy tab between two fingers, willing themself to believe that they were doing the right thing. Logically, yes, it made sense.

But they remembered what Harvard had said to them back before Haven, when he'd almost drowned before August grabbed him. *You're not responsible for me. You know that, right?* Besides, Harvard had been the one to save all of them at the Ceremony. If Chavi had forbidden him from taking any risks on their behalf, all four of them would have died. They couldn't make this choice for him. They could, however, confess everything, and let him make a choice for himself.

They laid the tab on the bar.

"Look, if you can't do it yourself, just ask," Mellie said from behind them, reaching for one of the cups. She took the tab back with one finger, fluidly dropping it into the cocktail so quickly Chavi almost didn't see it happen. Mellie tapped Harvard on the shoulder.

"This one's yours," she said, handing him the drink.

"Wait—no—" Chavi stepped between, them, but Harvard had already accepted the drink. "That one's not—Don't drink that!"

Harvard frowned. "Why not?" He glanced at the bar, where Chavi's identical drink still sat. "You're drinking it."

"Well, I mean, yeah, but...you don't even like alcohol, remember?"

"Yeah, Chavi's right," Mellie said with a fiendish grin. "It's probably too strong for you." As if to illustrate her point, she threw back her own drink easily. "Here, give that one back to me. I'll get you juice or something."

Harvard's grip on the cup tightened. "You think I can't do it?" he asked.

"What? No!" Chavi said, but Harvard's eyes were fixed on Mellie.

"I mean, don't get me wrong," Mellie said, her voice dripping with condescension, "it's just, I hadn't considered that you must have a low tolerance. I mean, you're just so *small*."

Harvard tensed, and Mellie smiled victoriously. She held out an expectant hand. "Cup. Please," she requested with an innocent bat of her eyelashes.

"Harvard, don't listen to her," Chavi said. "I mean, *do* listen to her, but—hold on—"

Harvard downed the cocktail, dribbling some sticky red liquid onto his chin. Chavi watched helplessly as he finished the last off, wiping his mouth with the back of his hand and grinning defiantly.

"You didn't have to do that," Chavi murmured.

"Well I *wanted* to," Harvard insisted. "I can be fun. I can do the stuff that you like. You don't have to do it in secret." Before Chavi could respond, he took their hand. "We're going to dance now, just like you wanted," he declared.

At first, Chavi wasn't sure they saw any change in Harvard—at least, no more than they'd seen when they'd shared the ceremonial wine in Haven. He smiled and laughed more freely, touched them more openly, but this was nothing like the time when they'd first returned to Bastion and he'd been dazzed out at a party. Part of Chavi hoped Mellie's tab hadn't worked at all. They could enjoy an hour of fun with Harvard, then send him home before their work started. It reminded them of the way he'd been on Haven when he proposed they steal the ceremony wine— gleeful, liberated, and (probably for one of the few times in Harvard's life) confident. They wondered how different he would be if he were always free of his inhibitions. They longed to see him free himself like this again, without the aid of any substance. Was it possible?

Then Harvard started to dance with a reckless abandon that Chavi had never seen in him before. He began pulling at the lapel of their jacket.

"C'mon...c'mon..." he slurred. Chavi wasn't sure if this was the drug taking effect, or if Harvard was just more drunk than they'd realized.

"What?"

"Follow me..."

Chavi allowed themself to be guided into the hallway, until they saw he was headed for the row of curtained-off booths. They tensed, resisting his pull.

"Um...Harvard?" they asked. "I don't think you're really...in the best state of mind for...I mean, maybe let's wait..."

Harvard found an open booth and tried to push them in, but he wasn't quite strong enough, so Chavi allowed themself to fall onto the amply cushioned plush bench. Harvard went back to the entrance and yanked the curtain closed.

"Listen, Harvard, I don't know what you have in mind—"

"Sh sh sh shhhhh" Harvard put a finger to their lips, pushing them against the velvet-lined wall.

"I am going...to dance for you," he slurred.

Chavi's brow creased. "Um...you are?"

Harvard nodded. His eyes were half closed. He started running his hands through his hair along his body. He kept losing his balance and catching himself. This was not the same, liberated dance that he'd done less than an hour ago. This was a performance, and Harvard had told Chavi he'd never liked performing. It wasn't like his performances on Haven, either, when he'd been free to make mistakes and have fun. He was trying to dance like the people he'd seen in The Sand Crystal. Like the person he thought Chavi wanted him to be. Like *Ariel*.

"Why are you doing this?" Chavi whispered.

"To make you happy."

"You don't have to—"

"Sh sh shhhhh" he placed a finger to their lips again, or at least tried to, but missed and ended up just kind of rubbing his fingers across their whole face.

He continued the dance—if it could be called a dance—and Chavi found it painful to watch. This wasn't *him*. And they hated the fact that they had made him think he had to try this hard for them to find him attractive. *I did this to you*, they thought, shaking their head. *I wanted to help you get better, but I made you worse.*

"Stop," they whispered, but he couldn't seem to hear them.

Harvard stumbled over his own feet, and hardly seemed to notice as he flopped forward. Chavi leapt up to catch him, barely managing to scoop him up in their arms before he hit the ground.

"Harvard?" they asked, lowering him to the bench. He didn't respond. His breathing was already deep and even. Chavi shook him, just to ensure that Mellie's gift had worked. Harvard remained unconscious. Chavi stood, then peered behind the curtain to ensure the hallway was empty. No one else in sight. They went back to the bench and wrapped one of Harvard's arms around their neck, lifting him.

They located a custodial closet and managed to open it with their foot. They knelt, gently propped Harvard up in the corner, nestled between some mops.

"I'm sorry about this," they said as they stroked his hair, then planted a kiss on his cheek before standing, closing the door behind them and leaving the sleeping Harvard in darkness.

After depositing Harvard in the relative safety of the closet, Chavi sought out the Harmonizers' booth. They pulled back the curtain only a moment past one. The rest of them were all already seated on the floor in a circle, Ariel at the back of the booth, sitting cross-legged. They nodded their approval of Chavi's arrival, and Chavi nodded back as if to say, *"I did it. He's gone."*

Mellie moved over to make room for Chavi next to her.

Ariel placed a metallic cylinder in the center of the circle. At first Chavi thought it was a candle, but when a plume of amber mist shot into the air, they realized it was a vaporizer, not unlike the canisters they'd used to ward off the scuttlers in the desert. As the mist dissipated, the Harmonizers closed their eyes and breathed deeply. Chavi took their cue and did the same. The mist didn't burn the back of their throat the way that dazzle smoke had when they'd first tried it. It was smoother, warm but not hot, and instead of that burnt floral taste, it was sweet, like fruit juice. Chavi could hear the vaporizer giving rhythmic puffs, filling the room with warm, sweet-smelling fumes.

Chavi didn't feel anything happening. Smoking dazzle would have kicked in by now. They cracked open an eye to survey the other Harmonizers. They all wore satisfied smiles, their chests rising and falling. Hm. Maybe it just didn't work on them. They'd heard that was possible. Some people just didn't have the brain chemistry for certain drugs. They'd know a guy in high school who could never get dazzed, no matter how much he smoked. Maybe Harmony was just like that for some people. They shrugged and continued to breathe in the vapor. At the very least it *smelled* nice. And it tasted good, too. It reminded them of the orange cakes their mother used to make when they were little. Synthetic oranges were not cheap, so it was always a special occasion to have an orange cake in the Chakrabarti household.

The vaporizer halted abruptly. There were no hallucinations, heightened senses, no rapid-fire neurons firing. Chavi felt...well, they just felt normal.

And then they opened their eyes.

Ariel was the first person they locked eyes with. Consciously they knew that nothing about Ariel had changed, that they were the same person they'd been a few minutes ago—but looking into their eyes now, Chavi had the sensation they were looking directly into Ariel's soul. They turned to Mellie. She met their gaze, and Chavi felt as though the irises of her eyes had opened up to swallow them, and for that moment they knew exactly what she was feeling, exactly what it was like to *be* her, to live in her body, to exist in her skin. *Founders*, they thought, *I'm reading her mind!*

They shifted their attention to one of the other Harmonizers in the circle. As soon as they locked eyes, Chavi felt it. They weren't discreet thoughts as much as feelings, sensations, like they were experiencing everything he was experiencing, and including what they themself were feeling, and they were caught in an ongoing feedback loop of feeling and knowing and feeling and knowing and understanding. *I can read people's minds*, Chavi thought again, *holy shit, I can read people's minds*. And the euphoria that came with it, the joy of knowing and being known, was something Chavi could never have imagined. They formed a link with every Harmonizer, a transcendent understanding, as they watched each member of the circle in turn, for one fleeting moment, there was no pain. Their body was not their own. Their body belonged to all the Harmonizers, which meant the pain was shared, which meant the pain was gone. Everything was beautiful and nothing hurt.

Ariel started handing out masks—party masks for Founder's Festival. Plenty of stores were already selling them in preparation for the festivities. Chavi recognized these particular masks as animals from the Creatures of Ruin tale. These masks were common amongst children, who enjoy dressing up as ancient animals. A small part of Chavi wondered what Ariel was handing them out for, but most of Chavi trusted Ariel, and knew they had a reason for everything they did.

Mellie selected her own mask, and one for Chavi as well. She put the Brown Dog mask over her own face, and pressed the Black Cat into Chavi's hand. They slid the mask underneath their glasses. Ariel now wore their own mask, the Crow, and looked at the faces of the animals staring back at them—Rabbit, Pig, Horse, Cow, and Squirrel.

"Bristull Paccen is the man who owns this club," Ariel said. "He is also the patron of the Harmonization circle that serves as our supplier—they call themselves the Concertos. The Concertos' circle has had control of us for too long. They've charged us extra, skimming money off the top for themselves. They revel in controlling us, mock us for it. They've even threatened our friends and family. The tyrannical reign of Concertos is over. We'll confront Bristull ourselves, and we'll no longer be beholden to those who would see us exploited."

This all made perfect sense to Chavi. Why would they keep paying the rival circle when they could get the Harmony directly? Ariel stood, and the rest of the circle stood with them. The group moved with fluid ease to the maintenance staircase at the back of the hall.

"From here, we can access the residential part of the building," Ariel explained. "He lives on the top floor."

Everyone nodded. Nothing more needed to be said. Everything was simple and easy and straightforward. They passed two floors dense with apartments, and then arrived at the top floor, which only had one. The hallway, which was really more of an entryway, was decorated with red wallpaper and lamps that gave off a warm yellow glow.

Ariel didn't knock. They kicked the door, and the wood splintered. They gave it another kick, and the door swung open, wood chips spraying the deep blue carpet. This was a very efficient way to enter a room. A very wise choice.

"What the f—hello?" said a voice from within. The Harmonizers followed Ariel into the interior of the apartment, which Chavi saw was decorated with the same iridescent columns as the club below. There were paintings on the walls, and sculptures on pedestals. Living in the cramped townhouse with the other Ivies, Chavi couldn't imagine having enough room in their living space to display a sculpture, let alone multiple.

They found Bristull, a spindly man whose lounge clothes contrasted with this lavish home, seated at a marble table, eating some kind of seafood. Real seafood, Chavi noted, not synth. Did this man eat fish every day?

"Thank you for agreeing to meet with us," Ariel said in the same warm, congenial tone they used to greet everyone.

The man's eyes swiveled around at the animal faces that loomed over him.

"I didn't," he said, his surprise melting into frustration at being interrupted.

"You will," Ariel said, nodding to Pig, who withdrew a knife. It wasn't like the hunting knives that the Commission lent to scavengers—this was a kitchen knife with a smooth blade fit for chopping coarse synth vegetables and meat.

Bristull regarded the knife with performative indifference, as if to say, *"what, you think you're the first kids to try and stab me? Grow up."* He wiped his mouth with a napkin, tossed it aside, and sighed.

"What do you want?" he asked, crossing his arms and leaning back in his chair. Chavi wouldn't have picked up on the subtle creases of the man's face without the assistance of Harmony. With their heightened awareness, they guessed that this was not the first time Bristull had spoken to Ariel. Perhaps they'd even had this same conversation before.

Ariel gestured for the Harmonizers to move forward, and without exchanging a word, they encircled Bristull in a ring of animals. Ariel sat on the table, facing him directly, with Rabbit and Squirrel on either side. Chavi stood right by the chair with Mellie hovering just behind them, Pig on the other side, and they could smell that despite being alone in his apartment at night, the man wore cologne.

"We have a proposal for you," Ariel said.

Bristol scanned the animal faces that stared down at him. Pig held his knife close enough to be threatening, but not so close that Bristull was truly afraid. Still, Chavi could tell as he scoffed that he was truly trying to cover up the deep unease settling in his stomach.

"A proposal? From a bunch of low-lifes like you?"

"You get your Harmony directly from your contacts in the Zuri Institution, correct?" Ariel ignored him.

"Yes," Bristull said, as though he wasn't sure what Ariel was driving at.

"And the other Harmonization circle you supply for, they pay you in tokens so that the payments cannot be tracked, correct?"

"Yes?" He was growing impatient, Chavi could tell.

"Perfect. Then we want your contacts, your tokens, and any Harmony that you might have around."

Bristull laughed. "And why would I do that?"

Ariel nodded to the knife. "I thought we made that clear."

"You're not gonna hurt me."

"Do you want to test that hypothesis? Besides, a few tokens are everything to a few low-lifes like us." Ariel threw his words back at him. "To a businessman like you, surely, they're nothing."

"Fine," he shrugged with forced casualness. "I keep the tokens under the bathroom sink."

"And the contacts?"

He eyed the Harmonizers. His gaze landed on Chavi. They surprised themself by being completely unfazed. Bristull looked at them for a long moment, and some of his facade melted. He could pretend he wasn't scared of Ariel. But for some reason, he couldn't pretend that he wasn't scared by the black cat that hovered over him. It was as though Chavi was an omen of portents to come.

"Under the bed," Bristull said, like a man trying to weasel out of fate.

"And any excess Harmony?"

"The front closet." he sighed, sinking back in his chair.

Ariel nodded. "Excellent. I appreciate your cooperation. One more key question."

"Founders, haven't you kids done enough? I'm trying to finish my dinner." A weak display of bravado. He was terrified. Chavi knew now that they wouldn't have known it if it weren't for the Harmony. He kept his voice hard and confident, his movements relaxed. But in the moment that Chavi had looked into his eyes, they had seen into his soul. They knew he was afraid for his life.

"No, we haven't done enough. Because only a finite amount of Harmony was ever produced, and we need to secure as much of it as possible. So we need to know: will you continue to sell to the Concertos?"

Bristull's face darkened. "You know I have to."

"I don't know that," Ariel said curtly. "No."

"I have a business to run."

"I do too." Ariel gestured to their Harmonizers. "I have to take care of them."

"Listen," Bristull hissed, "I already gave you want you wanted, alright? You don't get to decide who gets Harmony and who doesn't. That's not your choice to make."

"Well that's why I'm here, making it my choice. Promise me you won't sell to them anymore."

Bristull shook his head. "I can't do that."

"Well, I guess we'll have to get rid of you then."

Bristull leaned back, studying the Creatures, judging whether or not this was a bluff. "You won't kill me," he said.

"We will, I think," Ariel countered, and Pig slashed the knife across Bristull's throat. The movement was so fast and brutal that Chavi and Mellie were sprayed with blood.

The sudden gore jerked Chavi out of Harmony's spell for just a moment. Was this man really dying? He looked up at Chavi pleadingly, grasping at their jacket with a slick wet hand, blood pooling as his lips and dribbling down his chin. Chavi only stared into his dying eyes and couldn't help but make a tenuous connection with him, a thread compared to the ropes that bound them to the other Harmonizers. Chavi didn't realize they were holding Bristull, keeping him from flopping on the floor, until he died in their arms.

Ariel hardly seemed to notice. They'd already started giving orders.

"We split now, in case we're pursued. Elco and Isobel, you take the contact list. Mellie, Alibek, and Jonas, tokens. Kaita and I, Harmony. Chavi, deal with the body."

You want me to what? asked the small rational part of Chavi's brain that was out of Harmony's reach. The part of their brain that was attuned to the others, though, nodded, knowing that they were lucky to be a part of the whole, and everyone had a role to play. The Harmonizers moved swiftly and efficiently around them, and Chavi tore down one of the curtains to wrap the body in. It was messy work, but they managed it. If they could just get it out of the building, they could carry it to the city wall and leave it out in the dusts, where scuttlers would pick it apart. They didn't know how they were going to get it out of the building, but they trusted their Harmonized brain to figure it out.

Then they looked up, and everyone was gone.

Chavi was suddenly alone. They did not want to be alone, not when their mind needed another person to latch onto.

They stared down at the body, Harmony still twisting their mind. Why didn't those eyes look back at them? Why couldn't they form a connection? It felt wrong, so wrong that they lost themself, and they didn't snap back into reality until they heard the stomping of booted feet in the corridor. Delian Group officers, they realized. Here already. Someone must have heard the confrontation and put in a call.

Chavi couldn't run, not now. They didn't know where the officers were coming from – maybe everywhere? All they could think to do was hide in the closet, and as they closed the doors behind them, they berated themself for being so stupid. All they'd succeeded in doing was trapping themselves here with the police. Some light shone through the wooden slats of the closet door—not so much that Chavi would be visible, but enough that they could make out the movements of the officers as they poured into the room, weapons raised.

"Poor bastard," one of them said, lowering her weapon as she nudged the corpse with her foot. She bent down to touch the body. "Still warm. They might still be around. You, search the perimeter. You, search for anything they might have left behind. There are too many people in this city with a motive to narrow it down."

Chavi covered their mouth for fear that one of the officers might hear their breathing. The one who the leader had commanded to search the room started poking around, under the table, on the bookshelf. He neared the closet. Chavi held their breath. The officer stared at the wooden door. Chavi was almost certain he could see them through the slats.

Chavi stopped breathing.

They stared into the man's eyes.

He wasn't Harmonized like they were, but still they felt they could see into his soul, that they could see what he was seeing, and know what he knew.

He could see them. They knew it.

Before the officer had a chance to say anything, Chavi kicked the closet door, so hard it came off its hinges, sending the Delian officer in front of them stumbling backward. Before any of the others had a chance to respond, Chavi darted for the front door of the apartment. As they slammed into the wall of the hallway, they could hear shouts behind them, though the words were an indistinct blur. They aimed for the service stairwell. Gunshots peeled off behind them. They didn't think. They just ran.

The heavy door to the stairwell slammed behind them as they started down the cement stairs. The door slammed for a second time when they were only one floor down, and they could hear shouts and the pounding of booted feet. At this rate, they'd never make it out. They glanced over the stairs railing. They were still two floors up. Without thinking, they slung themself over the railing and plummeted the rest of the way down.

Somehow, they managed to land on their feet, but the impact of the landing shook their whole body. It vibrated their bones. They made for the door the moment they hit the ground, pushing into a hallway that was much more crowded than the one they'd left from.

With a sinking sensation, Chavi realized they'd gone for the wrong stairwell. This wasn't the one they'd ascended on. They were at the back of the building, and if they wanted to get out, they'd have to push through the entire crowd. They gritted their teeth and started shoving bodies aside.

"Hey! Watch it!" a girl screamed, her glass shattering on the ground. A few other people protested, but their voices were more and more drowned out the closer Chavi got to the dance floor. By the time they made it back to the main room, they could hear nothing but the thrumming of the bass and the beating of their heart.

That is, until gunshots cracked in the air.

After a split second of quiet, the crowd shifted from a party to a mob in an instant. If the Delian officers were yelling something at the crowd, Chavi couldn't hear it. Someone screamed, and then soon the people were trampling each other, clawing their way toward the exit, asking each other who fired the shots and why. If the Delian Group didn't catch them, Chavi realized, then they'd probably end up being trampled in the crush of people pouring out of the building. At this point, they couldn't tell if they were pushing through the crowd, or if the crowd was pushing them.

Somehow they made it onto the street, and at this point their lungs were burning, but they couldn't stop running. They bolted across the street into one of the alleys beyond, weaving through the maze of mismatched buildings that morphed from the Cusp into Lower Bastion.

When the only sound they could hear was the sound of their feet on asphalt and their own ragged breathing, they paused, leaning against a cool brick wall to catch their breath. They started to glance around the corner to check and see if they'd been pursued, but the sound of shouts echoing through the alley made them press themself back against the wall, as if they could melt into it and disappear. The officers were still after them.

Chavi continued down the back alley they'd found themself in, but without the lights of the street beyond, they had no idea where they were going. They didn't know how to navigate the city like Harvard did. He seemed to have the entire city map memorized. They wished he was here—except they didn't wish that, because they would never want him to be in danger.

Chavi stopped short just before they barreled into a brick wall. They backed up a few steps to see they'd stumbled into a dead end—nothing but the back end of an apartment building that stretched at least four stories up, and a pile of trash bags haphazardly discarded from the windows above. Chavi turned, only to find that the sound of boots and shouts was growing louder.

The officers were closing in on them, and they were cornered. If they backtracked now, they might end up stumbling right into their pursuers. There was nowhere to run. They glanced at the pile of trash bags, then behind them to the mouth of the alley. All they could do was hide.

* * *

Chavi had the strange sense that they were watching events unfold from outside their body. They watched the Delian officers pile into the alley, flashlights up, weapons raised, so certain that they'd managed to catch their prey. They watched as the police glanced at each other in confusion. One of the officers nudged another, indicating a pile of trash. They nodded to each other. Chavi watched as the Delian guards fired shot after shot into the heap. Only after they'd showered the heap in bullets did they start tearing it apart. Chavi found themself surprised that they didn't see the guards uncovering their corpse.

Because that would have made sense, after all. That they'd hidden in the garbage. Surely, they couldn't have really sprouted crab legs and scaled a four-story building. But they watched from the rooftop as the officers uncovered nothing, their quarry having vanished, giving each other perplexed looks before retreating.

Chavi straightened up, stepping back from the edge of the roof.

This wasn't real. This wasn't happening.

Slowly, Chavi turned their head to the side and saw four crab legs on either side flanking them like a protective exoskeleton. They held out a shaking hand and experimentally curved their fingers inward. The legs curved with them. Chavi gave an involuntary whimper.

They reached out a hand and touched the chitin. They flinched away. The surface was warm, and slick with blood. Their own blood.

"This isn't real," they said aloud, and as they said it the legs retracted with such force that it made Chavi's back arch. They sucked in a breath, suddenly dizzy.

Touching a hand to their back, they found not one but eight bloody chitin patches peeking out through holes in their suit jacket.

Chavi bent over and retched.

As the sun rose over Bastion, Chavi curled up on a rooftop and cried.

* * *

"Ariel!"

Once they were certain the coast was clear, Chavi had snuck their way back to the ground and went straight to Ariel's building. The Harmony still stirred their brain, but not enough that they felt any more loyalty to Ariel and their Harmonization circle. They'd almost been killed, and it was Ariel's fault, and they would have to answer for that.

"Ariel!" they pounded their fist on the door. No answer. They wondered if Ariel even lived here, or if this was just their base of operations. It had never even occurred to them that Ariel might live elsewhere. Now it seemed so obvious. They wouldn't run their organization from their own *home*. Of course this wasn't where they actually slept.

They tried the knob. It was unlocked.

"Ariel!" they called again, stomping into the living room.

"Founders, you trying to wake the whole building?" said a voice from the corner. Chavi turned to see Mellie sitting in the corner on one of Ariel's cushions. She was still wearing her dog mask, and she still had blood staining her crop top and skirt. She was eating a bag of rice puffs.

"What are you doing here?" Chavi asked.

Mellie shrugged. "Snackin'." She stood, brushing crumbs off her skirt, and approached Chavi. "What are you so worked up about?"

Looking into her eyes, Chavi still felt their connection with her was Harmony-enhanced. *Stop stop stop stop stop* they told themself, but the Harmony still clung to their mind with a vice-grip. *Mellie is a friend*, it whispered. *She loves you. She wants to help you.*

They shook their head as if they could dislodge the thought.

"We killed someone!" they said. How could she not understand this? They were supposed to understand each other perfectly.

She only grinned. "First time?" she asked. Chavi gaped.

"You've done it *before*?" Chavi asked. "Ariel used us! They played us! Open your eyes!"

"No, you open your eyes," Mellie scowled, suddenly on the offense, pressing a hand on their chest and backing them into the wall. "We're a Harmonization Circle. Don't you know what that means? We take care of each other. And we work together."

We put the community over the individual.

We care for each other.

We accept these words as holy.

The words echoed in Chavi's head. The Haven Principles. And they'd *scoffed* at those. Mellie was right, though, and Chavi couldn't tell if she was really right or if the residual Harmony only made them think she was. This time, the bond formed with Harmony was not something euphoric. It was a chain, tethering them to Mellie with unbreakable force.

She drew a finger across their chest to pick up some of the still-wet blood. She worked her finger between their lips and into their mouth. They didn't resist. They couldn't. Harmony wouldn't let them.

The blood of Haven now runs through you.

"Taste it," Mellie said. "This is ours. You're one of us. You can't back out."

"And what if I do?" Chavi whispered.

She leaned in, and Chavi wasn't sure if the sharp iron scent was the blood on her face, or the blood on their own. "Then I tell your little boyfriend what you've done."

"No." The word came out quiet, somewhere between a plea and a command. "Please."

Harvard. Kind, perfect Harvard. What would he do if he discovered what Chavi was becoming? What they had already become. *He already knows*, they thought. *He saw what you did to Lyle.* But that was different. Chavi had no excuse for the blood that now painted their chest.

"Harvard!" Chavi gasped. "He's still there! At the club!"

"Then go get him," Mellie said with a shrug.

"I can't! The Delian Group they're—they're looking for me. They chased me—"

Mellie removed their glasses, and slid the cat mask off their face, showing it to them. "What do you think this was for, genius?" She pressed their glasses back into their hand. "No one will recognize you."

"But—My clothes—the blood—"

Mellie stepped back, gesturing toward the rooms further in the apartment. "Check the bedroom," she said. "Ariel always keeps spares."

Chavi remembered what Mellie had said earlier: *First time?* Of course Ariel had spare clothes for the Harmonizers here. They probably had everything they could possibly need here. This wasn't their apartment. It was the center of operations. They'd done jobs like this before. They'd killed before, and they would expect Chavi to do it again.

"Why me?" Chavi asked as Mellie headed for the door. "Why was I the one that got left with the body?"

"Because you're the newbie," she said over her shoulder, and before closing the door added, "Think of it as a rite of passage. Just imagine how much fun you'll have next time!"

CHAPTER TWENTY

Empty

Harvard woke up and soon regretted it. He felt like someone had taken a sledgehammer to his skull. He groaned, rolling over to see Chavi seated beside the bed, mug of coffee in hand, their leg bouncing.

"Good morning!" they said, and though Harvard knew they were speaking normally, it sounded like they were shouting. Why was the world so loud today? He groaned again and covered his ears. "How are you feeling?"

"Bad," Harvard said, rubbing his eyes. He sat up, and his stomach lurched. "Oh no," he moaned, and flopped out of bed toward the bathroom, his legs getting caught up in the sheets. He extricated himself, stumbled into the bathroom, and emptied the contents of his stomach into the toilet. A nagging voice in the back of his mind told him he should be embarrassed, but he felt too miserable. Chavi rubbed his back as he heaved. When he was finished, Chavi helped him up and handed him a little cup of mouthwash.

"Better than brushing your teeth," they explained, "because you don't wanna rub all that stomach acid in. That's what they told me in high school, anyway."

Harvard swished and spit, then made his way back to the bed. He overwhelmingly felt like he never wanted to leave the bed again. Chavi stood in the bathroom doorway, watching him with barely disguised concern. Why? Was something wrong? What—

Harvard's stomach dropped as a wave of terror washed over him, and he feared he'd vomit again. "I don't remember what happened last night," he said. His heart hammered, and he started trembling. He knew he'd followed Chavi to the club, and he'd cried and Chavi had comforted him, and then...when he reached for the memory, there was nothing. "I don't remember! I don't remember anything!"

"Relax," Chavi said, sitting on the bed next to him and rubbing his back again. "That's normal."

"It is?" Harvard asked. Chavi nodded.

"Alcohol does that. You blacked out."

"Has this ever happened to you before?" Harvard asked. Chavi laughed.

"Oh yeah. All the time."

Harvard took a shaky breath, his trembling subsiding. He still didn't like having a gaping hole in his memory, but at least it didn't mean there was anything wrong with him.

"So...what happened, then? Last night?" he asked.

Chavi shrugged. "Not much. You had some drinks. We danced. You had a few more drinks. We danced more. You wanted to stay out, but I could tell that you'd had a little too much, so I took you home."

"And that's it?" Harvard asked.

"Yup. That's it," they said with a reassuring smile.

Harvard exhaled slowly, leaning back.

"I feel terrible," he said.

"That would be a hangover. Also normal. You stay right here. I'm gonna get you some water, and maybe some food your stomach can handle."

Given that Harvard's stomach lurched just at the word food, he doubted it could handle anything at all. He didn't protest, though, because he worried if he even opened his mouth he might vomit again. He only nodded his assent, and Chavi slipped out of the room.

How was your night?

Harvard jumped. He turned to see Speedy perched on the windowsill—and though he was still learning the nuances of desertwalker expressiveness, he was confident that the way Speedy had crossed his claws in front of him like folded arms was the crab equivalent of a contemptuous gaze.

Harvard groaned. "Please stop."

Do you now wish you'd heeded the warning of a friend? Speedy asked innocently.

"If you're only going to make me feel bad about it, then you're not much of a friend," Harvard grumbled, rubbing his temples.

I'm only trying to protect you.

"I'm tired of having people try to protect me," Harvard complained.

Yes, I imagine you are.

Harvard clenched his jaw. He felt nauseous again, and this time he worried it had nothing to do with the hangover. He willed Speedy to stop, but he pressed on, *Isn't it ironic, then, that Chavi claims to want protect you, something you've expressed you do not want, and then—*

"Speedy! Enough!" Harvard snapped. He wasn't sure he'd ever heard such ferocity in his own voice. "Just leave me alone, okay?"

I wish I could, but I fear you will stumble into danger. You always do, Speedy said, and the note of condescension in his voice was painfully familiar.

"You sound like Skrack," Harvard observed.

I do not, Speedy protested too quickly. Harvard could sense he'd struck a nerve, and on any other day that would have been enough to dissuade him from pressing the matter further. Today, though, he was sick and tired and most of all *angry.*

"You do," he insisted. "You sound just like him."

I am entirely unlike my father, Speedy asserted, stubbornly supercilious, just like his father.

"You're both patronizing," Harvard pointed out. "And sometimes mean."

I'm mean? Speedy sounded genuinely wounded, and Harvard knew that meant he'd done enough damage, but couldn't resist one final barb.

"Sometimes, yes!" he doubled down.

I am sorry, Speedy said. He sounded earnest. *This was not my intention.*

Harvard didn't care if he was earnest, though. In that moment, he didn't care about Speedy at all. "Just leave me alone, okay?"

Of course. I would not want my disobedience to be construed as "mean."

Harvard couldn't tell if he heard acid behind that comment, or sincere remorse. The little crab was even more like his father than Harvard had initially realized. Skrack, too, seemed to never decide if his disdain for Harvard outweighed his genuine care.

Harvard wished he'd handled the conversation more gently. No, that wasn't true. He wished that he *wished* he'd handled the conversation more gently. In truth, he was left with a wicked sense of satisfaction, as though he'd just released something he'd been holding in for a long time. But Speedy hadn't deserved that, not really. He'd just been a convenient target, and Harvard wanted to bring himself to regret it, but he *couldn't.*

He threw up again.

* * *

Avi had said it would take a few days. She'd taken Chavi's blood, explained some science things Chavi didn't really understand (What's an antibody? Why would things in your body be *anti* body?) and said that the process would take time.

"What if you hurry?" Chavi asked. Avi suppressed a smile. Chavi knew that look: the look she wore when they said something hilariously stupid, but Avi was trying not to make them feel bad.

"*I* don't actually do anything," she explained. "It just takes time for the precipitate lines to form."

So they'd waited, hoping that maybe the longer it took, the less they would think about it. Instead, the thought remained like a festering wound. When Avi appeared at their doorstep a few days later with a file in hand, the relief that washed over them almost overpowered the terror that settled in their stomach.

"What does it say?" they asked, hunched over the lab results splayed out on the kitchen counter.

"I don't know," Avi said.

"What do you mean you don't know?" Chavi demanded. "You're looking at it."

Avi cringed. "I mean...I don't understand."

Well, that couldn't be right. Avi understood *everything*. "What?"

She inhaled sharply, eyes fixed on the indecipherable documents. "Your blood is not human blood."

Chavi stared at her for a long moment.

"What?" they repeated.

"Your blood," Avi said, meeting their eyes. "It's not human blood."

"But...I am human," Chavi said, but they didn't sound as confident in the assertion as they'd intended to.

"I know. I know that," Avi said, and maybe Chavi was just reading into things at this point, but she didn't actually sound convinced. She used that tone you might use with a child when assuring them, *"Yes, of course I believe you'll be a corp head one day!"*

Panic flashed hot and cold all over their body. Their *human* body. "Am I not?" Chavi demanded. What did that even mean?

"No, you are," Avi said hurriedly. Too hurriedly.

"Then if the blood came from me and I'm a human, how is that not human blood?"

"I don't know!"

Chavi shuffled through the papers, looking at them as though they would be able to comprehend any of the data, which they obviously wouldn't. "Can you explain what it says to me?"

Avi contemplated, biting the inside of her cheek—a habit she'd no doubt picked up from Jasmine. "Think of it like...okay, so you know how when you're born, you're registered with the city?"

"Yeah, sure."

"And everyone has a name, and that's their official name, and everyone's name is different. I mean, not everyone, but like it's pretty rare to meet someone in Bastion with the same exact name as you. Do you see what I mean?"

"Um, sure?"

"You have the name of someone who does not exist. Which means we don't know who you are."

Chavi's eyes darted helplessly across the pages, looking for some kind of answer that wasn't there. "I...I'm me."

"I know," Avi said, reaching for their hand. They withdrew it instinctively.

Tears blurred their vision, which made them furious, because being upset about this meant there was actually something to be upset about. "I'm *me*," they repeated, and their throat tightened around the word.

"And this doesn't change that."

"Yes, it does!"

"It shouldn't matter—"

"How can you say that? How can you say it when you're not the one sprouting new limbs? How can you say that when you're not the one with another skin growing under your skin?"

"I'm just saying that—I mean, your mind is the same—"

"And how does that help me?" they demanded. "I'm stupid, Avi! I've always been stupid! My mind is *worthless*. The only thing I've ever had going for me is my body, and for a little while there, out there in the dusts, I could actually make some use of it. But if I don't have control over my own body, then what do I have? Nothing! I have nothing!"

Avi winced as though this wounded her, which was even more infuriating. What did she have to be upset about? She had everything, including human blood.

"You have us," she murmured.

"Do I? Because if I'm not me anymore, I don't think you all are going to be keen on sticking around." Okay, they could see how that was probably hurtful, but they couldn't help it. Like the tears that had already started to roll down their cheeks, the words were spilling out.

"That's not true," Avi said.

"You'd still be here for me? Even if I was a monster?"

"Of course."

Chavi stared at Avi until she started to fidget under their gaze. They wanted desperately for that to be true, but they couldn't dismiss the image of Bristull Paccem bleeding at their feet, the sound of their own footsteps on pavement, and the sensation of desperation so animalistic that it forced alien limbs to burst from their body. It didn't matter what was in their blood. Their actions alone made them a monster already, and inevitably, Avi would find out.

So they told her honestly: "I don't believe you."

* * *

Chavi had weighed the pros and cons of the Harmony Circle. On the one hand, they were complicit in a murder and Mellie was liable to make everyone aware of that fact. On the other, there was a non-zero chance that whatever creature Skrack had unwittingly planted in their blood would eventually outgrow them, eventually sloughing off their human shell entirely.

Harmony would not prevent that from happening.

It would, however, temporarily allow them to forget that it was a possibility. Not a long-term solution (they weren't certain that a long-term solution existed) but something to keep them from falling into complete and utter despondence.

Just once more, they promised themself as they stood at the points kiosk, transferring what remained of the Ivies' funds. *Just long enough to figure out what's happening to me.*

They sat cross-legged in the circle, sullen, refusing the other Harmonizers' attempts at conversation. A timid knock turned everyone's gaze to the door on high alert, but Ariel waved a hand to indicate calm.

"That should be our new addition to the group," they said, standing to open the door. In stepped a timid looking girl with curly dark hair and cautious, calculating eyes. Chavi tensed. They knew that face. They'd only seen it twice in their life, but they'd never forget it.

"I'm Maya," the girl said. Chavi had known her as Twix. "It's nice to meet all of you."

Ariel placed a gentle hand on her shoulder, introducing each of the Harmonizers in turn. Chavi's instincts told them to flee before she spotted them. The first time they'd met this girl, her crew had taken the Ivies captive. The second time they'd seen this girl, they threatened to have Skrack annihilate all her friends. They should leave, *now*. But where would they go? She was standing at the only door. Maybe for once in their life, luck would smile down on them, and she wouldn't recognize them.

"And this is our newest member, Chavi," Ariel gestured to them, and their eyes locked with Maya's. She gasped quietly, eyes wide. Yeah, she definitely recognized them. Chavi's self-preservation instincts took over, and they stood.

"I think I should go, actually," they said. They didn't understand what they were feeling right now, but they didn't like it. They didn't like being around this girl. They didn't like the thing they remembered when they were near her. It made their fingertips sting with the memory of clawing at the walls of their prison.

Chavi stepped across the Harmonization circle and reached for the door.

"No, I—" Maya fidgeted, "I didn't mean to make things—I'm sorry. Should I leave?"

"Of course not," Ariel said to her, then grabbed Chavi by the arm. They drew up close so no one else could hear them. "Chavi?" they asked sweetly. "What's wrong, love?" Suddenly Mellie was next to them too, holding their other arm.

"I need to go," they whispered.

"But we're a circle," Mellie said, "and you can't break the circle."

"I don't want to be with her." They tried to pull away from Mellie, but her grip was surprisingly strong.

"It's important that our circle grow," Ariel murmured, and they sounded almost like a cat purring. "So we can't be rude to the newest addition to our group."

"You promised me you would stay," Mellie whispered, and Chavi tasted phantom tang of blood on their tongue, and smelled iron. "You *promised.*"

They thought of their conversation with Avi earlier that day. The chitin patches burning holes in their back. The creature that lived inside them yearning to be free. For just a few hours, they could escape all of that. What Maya had done to them seemed to pale in comparison to the treachery of their own body.

"Fine," they whispered. "I'll stay."

Six hours of Harmony slid by like liquid. Chavi tried to avoid Maya's eyes, but they inevitably caught sight of them, and when they did the Harmony took over, and Chavi felt their souls link against their will. They hated that they understood her. They hated that they couldn't hate her the way they wanted to.

When the session was over and the sun was starting to rise, Chavi made for the door immediately, throwing their hood over their head and running down to the street in hopes that Maya wouldn't try and stop them.

"Chavi! Wait!" they heard her call behind them as they turned on to a narrow side street.

Dusts, how did she manage to get her so fast? She must have run after them.

Chavi whirled on her. "What do you want?" they demanded. Maya recoiled, her hands flying up to cover her face, as though she feared they would strike her.

"I just want to explain," she said, lowering her arms.

"What is there to explain?" They forced themself to look in her eyes, even though looking in her eyes triggered the Harmony, and the Harmony made them want to care for her.

"I know you must hate me," Maya said. "I would too. But there's a lot you don't understand. You want to know, don't you? It bothers you, why that happened to you? I know it would bother me."

She was right, of course. Ever since The Chocolates had sold them, Chavi had wondered what made them do it, but they'd chalked it up to the thing they'd been told ever since they'd become a scavenger: the dusts make people crazy. But Jas had always insisted that "crazy" was an unscientific term, used by people who didn't want to take a deeper look at the motivations of others. And here Twix—Maya—was, offering that deeper look. They couldn't resist.

"Okay. Fine," they said. "But be quick, okay?"

"I'm sorry," Maya said, clasping her hands together, and the Harmony told them that she meant it. "I'm so sorry. I know sorry doesn't fix anything but—"

"You're sorry?" Chavi gave a hollow laugh. They couldn't help it, the visceral part of them that *wanted* to hurt her. "Do you know what it's like to choke on dust?" The memory was so vivid. Of course it was. They dreamt of it nearly every night. And knowing she was the reason for that, the reason they were haunted by depths and darkness and the sensation of suffocation, it was so satisfying to watch her squirm.

"No," she murmured. "I—I didn't know what they were going to do to you."

"But if you did, you would have done it anyway, would you?" they guessed.

"Yes," Maya admitted, wringing her hands, "But—"

"But?"

"I *have* been buried alive," Maya said. "I had a building collapse on me. Out there in the dusts. Steelmites. I was trapped under rubble for days before my crew found me. I know it's not the same, but…What I'm saying is…I was a scavenger for six years. And I was desperate to get out."

"So you sold me and my crew for supplies?" That didn't really seem like a way out to Chavi.

"No," Maya said, stepping forward. "*They* promised us a way out. If we sold five scavenging crews, they said they'd set us up for life."

"Who?" Chavi demanded.

"The Delian Group."

Chavi stared at her. "The Delian Group?" they repeated, grappling with the implications. That didn't make any sense. Devrin didn't care about scavengers. "Why would he—why would they want scavengers killed?"

"I don't know," Maya said. "They're doing a lot of stuff I don't understand. We weren't alone out there, either. There were others they sent. Researchers."

"Researchers?" Chavi repeated, remembering O'Neill.

"I think so? I don't understand what they're doing. But they tamed that pinchdragon and gave it to us, so they must understand something about desertwalkers that we don't."

"And they gave you a gun," Chavi said. Maya looked away again.

"Yes," she admitted, scuffing her shoes on the concrete. "They gave us a gun. When they first approached us, I didn't want to agree to the deal. But Snickers was the captain and—"

"You don't disobey your captain if you want to survive," Chavi repeated the same rule they'd been lectured about when their disobedience got Minty killed, and the same rule they'd lectured Harvard about when they'd grabbed his wrist in training. It was the first time they'd failed him. The first in a long, long string that Chavi couldn't seem to put a stop to.

"Exactly," Maya said, looking relieved that they seemed to understand. "So I didn't have a choice. It was my crew against everyone else. You've been a scavenger. You know what it's like. You know how badly you need to protect your crew. Wouldn't you have done the same?"

"No," Chavi said automatically. They'd made mistakes in the past, sure, but they would *never* do that.

Maya tensed, her eyes glittering with tears. "Then I guess you're a better person than I am."

"No," Chavi said. They could be honest enough with themself to admit they were not a good person. "I just think I have a better crew. My crew would rather die than have five scavenging crews sacrificed for them."

"How are they?" Maya's voice softened, as though she was afraid of the answer. "Are they...I mean..."

"They're all alive, if that's what you're asking," Chavi said.

Maya sagged with relief. "And how—"

"We're surviving," Chavi cut her off. "What about yours?"

"I don't know," Maya admitted, rubbing her arms. "I left after—after you took everything away from us. Snickers did too. Oh, uh, Trevor. That's his real name. He started his own Harmonization circle. He kept trying to get me to join, but I didn't want to see him anymore. The relief he promised, though...it was hard to say no to. Mars and Milky stayed at the Commission, I think. Maybe they're on a new crew now. I don't know. I...miss them. Not Trevor, obviously," she added with a grimace. "But the girls. I worry about them. They were too young to be doing that job."

"I'm sorry," Chavi said, though they didn't know why. What reason did they have to be apologizing to her?

"You found your fourth member though?" she asked.

Chavi reared back. "Yeah. How did you know?"

"I saw him. When—you know." Right. When they'd 'taken everything' from the Chocolates. "The ginger one."

"Yeah. We found him." It was such a warm memory, reuniting with Harvard. Hugging him. Strangely, they yearned to return to that time. Everything was simpler, then, when their only responsibility was keeping everyone alive. At least that, they could manage.

"Good," Maya smiled. "I was worried he was dead."

Chavi's brow knit. "You didn't even know him."

"I know. But it still makes me sad to come across a team of three scavengers. I have to wonder. Is he alright?"

"Yeah," they said, though they weren't fully sure that was true. "He's fine."

"Good."

It was sickening, somehow, to have her be happy for them. Maybe it was because they didn't want her to be happy. Or maybe they felt like the happiness they presented was a sham. Either way, they were eager to be done with her. "Is that it?"

"Yeah. I guess that's it. Unless—" Maya looked away again.

"What?" they prodded.

"Do you want me to leave these Harmonizers?" she asked. "I will. I just couldn't go back to Trevor. He's...not stable."

Chavi sighed, thinking over her offer. Tempting, but unfair, especially now that she'd linked with the group. As much as they still loathed her, it was hard not to pity her, too. "No. You don't have to leave."

"Thank you," Maya breathed, burying her face in her hands as though she may cry.

Chavi shrugged, watching her warily. Would they become this dependent on Harmony? Were they already? "Yeah. Well. No problem."

"Maybe..." Maya lifted her head, meeting their gaze, "I mean, what with Harmony and all, maybe we'll even become friends?"

"No. I don't think so," Chavi turned their back on her before the chemicals in their brain could implore them to do otherwise, leaving her in the alley alone as they headed for home.

A part of Chavi, admittedly, pitied Maya. She had, after all, only tried to look after herself and her crew. And while Chavi had been adamant their crew would not have asked them to do the same...how far would they go, to save Havard? They'd already killed for him once.

That's different, they told themself. Of course it was different. Because this wasn't one killing that made everything go away. The Chocolates had sold scavengers to the sandheads again and again and again. Chavi wouldn't have done that.

Right?

No, Chavi couldn't stay mad at Maya for long, but they could stay mad at the Delian Group for putting her in that position in the first place. Some people lived a life where they never had to make hard choices at all.

Ronan Bell, Chavi suddenly heard Devrin's voice in their mind. They shook their head, as if to dislodge the thought. It was stupid.

What if it wasn't?

Chavi had spent their whole life making hard choices. Did Harvard ever have to make a hard choice? It was so easy to imagine that his life had been like theirs. What if it wasn't? What if he'd come from another world entirely? *This doesn't change anything*, they promised themself. *Even if it's true, it still doesn't change anything*. But it did, actually, because if it was true, then it was be so much easier to be angry at Harvard than to live with the guilt of hurting him.

Chavi stopped in their tracks. They wondered if this was a bad idea. They decided it was, but that they would do it anyway. They whirled around, seeking out a place Jasmine had taken them dozens of times. Chavi did something they had never done in their entire life: they *willingly* went to a library to do research.

If they could just find an image of this Saoirse lady—and if she was as important as Devrin said she was, a picture shouldn't be too hard to find—then they could prove to themself she wasn't related to Harvard, and put the whole thing out of their mind. They went to one of the libraries in Midtown since it was more likely to be better stocked with old newspapers. They strode past students in Rubira school uniforms and librarians stocking the shelves, into the back room where old public records were kept. They sifted through file folders full of newspapers, checking the business section of each one. That's where she would be, if they were going to find her. Her name came up a few times, which at least confirmed that she was the head of the company, but no images.

Chavi opened a new file folder to see Harvard's face on the first page.

They lifted the paper into the light to see it better. No, it wasn't Harvard. The face was older, much older, and the frown lines attested to that. Harvard could never muster an expression as withering as the one that the woman on the page wore. But that was his red hair, though much longer than he kept his, those were his greenish-grey eyes, and his freckles.

"Shit," they breathed. The paper fell from Chavi's fingers and drifted to the floor. They didn't know why their heart was racing. "This doesn't change anything," they whispered to themself.

But it did. They knew it did.

* * *

Jasmine sat at the kitchen counter doing some of the administrative work she'd taken on for the University, hoping August didn't realize she was waiting for the postal delivery. She'd sent in her applications, and she should be hearing back...well, today. August, luckily, didn't seem to be paying her much attention. Today was the day he had elected to paint the living room—which was pretty much the only downstairs room in the whole place—and he was too focused on the task to pay her any heed. She was actually quite impressed with him as she watched him work. He'd learned all these skills in the past few months.

After they'd worked in silence together for an hour, Jasmine heard a clink as he dropped the paintbrush in the metal paint tin.

"Jasmine?" he said, still facing the half-painted wall. He'd painted the white wall a cream color that didn't look that much different from the original shade. He'd wanted to pick a bright color, but Avi told him that it was her parents' property, and they wouldn't like that very much.

"Yes?" she asked.

"Do you feel sad?"

The question was so unexpected that her head snapped up. She placed her pen down, unsure how to answer. "I...don't know," she said slowly. "I haven't really thought about it. I've been trying to keep busy."

"That's what I mean," August said, still looking at the fruits of his labor, the bland paint that hardly made a difference. "It feels like all we're doing here is keeping ourselves busy. Now that I know what's out there..." He nodded in the direction of the ocean. "Bastion just feels...so small. Dry. I mean, do you remember those trees? The gardens? The food?"

"Yes. I remember." She wished she didn't. It hurt to remember. Somehow, abandoning Haven felt like a personal failure. That could have been their lives forever, but they'd turned away.

"Compared to those vegetables...I mean, our synthetic shit just tastes like sand. I can hardly taste anything anymore."

"Yeah. Me too."

August turned to face her, and she saw he was almost on the verge of tears.

"I never knew a city could be beautiful," he said. She remembered he'd said the same thing when they'd walked together in Haven. "I never thought that could be the point of a city. A city is a thing you use, and live in. But everything about Haven was beautiful. The people were beautiful. And I don't just mean they looked beautiful, I mean...the way they lived. Every single person has someone else to take care of them. Can you imagine that? Having a companion, like they do? And they community, the community takes care of them too. Jas, I had to join the scavengers to pay for my dad's medical bills. Do you think something like that would ever happen in Haven?"

"Do you think they have proper doctors in Haven?" Jasmine retorted. She understood what he meant, but...surely his father had received better care in Bastion than he could have in Haven, right?

"Yeah, I do," August said resolutely. "Whatever they have is better than no doctor at all, which is what my dad got, in the end."

"August..." Jasmine said, turning his words over in her mind, "do you want to go back? To Haven?"

It somehow felt like a dangerous question, so Jasmine was relieved when August said. "What? No. I just...I just want more than this." He wore that same pensive expression she'd seen on him in Haven.

"Yeah. Me too," Jasmine said quietly. *I'm trying to get that, August,* she thought. *I'm trying to get that for all of us.* "This place is a start," she added, gesturing to the house. "We've got a home now. This can be...our little Haven. Haven Mark 2. Alright?"

August studied her for a long moment, then gave a sad smile. "Alright," he nodded. "As long as I get to name the dog."

"Fine," Jasmine shrugged, smiling despite herself. "You can name the dog."

The mail hatch clinked, and Jasmine's stomach leapt.

August hardly noticed. He went back to work. Trying her best to appear calm, Jasmine crept over to the door and picked up the single delivery. But the package that waited for her was not the thick admission package she was expecting. Instead, it was a single flimsy letter. She tore it open and inspected it. She didn't process the sentences fully, only individual words.

Revoked. Denied. Fraud.

The hand holding the letter began to tremble. Her payment to the university had been found fraudulent.

Her account was empty.

CHAPTER TWENTY-ONE

Concertos

Chavi wished they could continue to convince themself the tunnel was a dream. When they fell asleep and found themself in a subterranean burrow, desertwalkers of all shapes, sizes, textures, and breeds all marching toward some distant destination, they wished they could pretend it was just a bizarre nightmare.

But now they knew better.

They didn't look at themself. They didn't want to know what they looked like here.

You're back.

That same voice as before. They heard it without hearing, and turned to find the hulking crab towering over them. Skrack wasn't the largest of the creatures that scuttled and slithered and wriggled down the tunnel, but he still dwarfed Chavi by comparison.

Where am I? they asked, and somehow they managed to ask it without speaking aloud.

You mean you don't know? Oddly, there was no derision in the crab's voice. Only genuine surprise, and a bit of reverence. Not for Chavi. For this place.

No, Chavi said, though they wondered if maybe they did know, and they just didn't realize it yet.

Skrack gestured with a claw to the winding tunnel. *This is the path to the Serenity.*

What is the Serenity?

There are no words in your human tongue to describe it. It is known only to desertwalkers.

And me, Chavi added.

Skrack was silent. Chavi didn't want to dwell on what that silence meant.

I've been here before, they realized abruptly.

Yes. I took you here when I preserved your life.

I've seen it? The Serenity? They could just feel it on the periphery of their memory...they thought they were already dead, and Skrack had spoken to them, and there was a sensation that their very being was dissolving...

You remember?

I think I do, Chavi said. *It was...warm.*

Skrack nodded with the whole of his shell. *Yes.*

Chavi remembered feeling as though they could disappear into that sweet light forever and be happy to do it. They felt like their entire past, present, and future all melted away, and nothing existed, had ever existed except for the warmth, with them basking in its glow.

Will we get there? Chavi asked. *To the Serenity?*

That, Skrack said, lumbering down the tunnel, *has yet to be seen.*

"Get up."

Chavi awoke abruptly to the sensation of something cold and smooth pressed against the bottom of their jaw. A figure stood above them, silhouetted by the glow of streetlights from the window. They wouldn't have been surprised to find Devrin in their room again, recruiting them for another mission. But they knew his voice by now. This was someone different. Someone younger.

They squinted. They *did* recognize that face, but they hadn't seen it for a long time. They reached for their glasses and clumsily put them on to get a better look.

"Snickers?" they asked blearily.

"That's not my fucking name. Now move."

The gravity of the situation slowly settled on Chavi. Snickers, the scavenger that they'd nearly had Skrack crush to death, was *here*. And he wanted something.

Wait. Harvard.

They flipped over to find Harvard still sleeping peacefully beside them. Hovering inches above him was the point of a knife, and gripping that knife was Maya.

Chavi locked eyes with her for a fleeting moment, and she looked away.

"Just do what he says, okay?" She pleaded. Chavi turned back to Snickers—Trevor—and now that he stood a pace away from the bed they could see what he held. A gun. *Their* gun. It felt like centuries ago that the Ivies had taken it from the Chocolates, and now here it was, back in Snickers' hands.

"Move," he hissed.

Chavi willed themself to stay calm and did as commanded, careful not to wake Harvard. They worried what the Chocolates would do to him if he awoke and started to panic. Besides, the gun terrified them. They'd been shot before, and they'd like to avoid a repeat experience if at all possible.

They stood, hands held slightly aloft to demonstrate they were compliant. Snickers nudged them to the door, and only then were they aware of the other figures in the room. One stood guard by the doorway, and the other was quietly picking through the room and pocketing things.

"Who's this?" Chavi asked.

"My Harmonizers," Trevor said, and Chavi picked up on a note of pride in his voice. "The Concertos."

He pressed the muzzle of the gun into the small of Chavi's back.

"Let's go."

* * *

Harvard waited until the footsteps receded before he opened his eyes. His heart hammered so hard he felt blood pounding in his fingertips.

When he'd awoken to the sound of voices, he'd nearly sat up and asked Chavi what was the matter. His instincts, however, told him to listen, so he kept his breathing even, feigning sleep until he was alone.

He leapt out of bed silently. Was Chavi really involved in something dangerous they hadn't told him about? What had Chavi called—Snickers. That name was from somewhere, wasn't it? That was a pre-Quake brand. Scavengers? Was this a team of scavengers?

Harvard peered around the bedroom door. He saw the four intruders just at the foot of the stairs, Chavi in tow. He waited until he heard the front door shut before he followed. If he was careful, he could follow just a few paces behind without anyone noticing him. After all, people hardly ever noticed him.

* * *

The streets were empty. Lower Bastion was always quiet through the night. No one wanted to get hurt. That meant no one was there to see the

Concertos herd Chavi down the street. Their pulse thundered in their ears. They took slow, deliberate breaths in hopes of calming themself down.

It did not work.

"What is this about?" Chavi asked, forcing themself to sound casual.

"Your Harmonization Circle hit our patron," Trevor said from behind them. "We want our quake-scourged money back."

"Wait. He was *your* patron?" Chavi asked, but as they said it they realized they already knew. Ariel had told them about the rival group that was marking up the Harmony costs. "I'm sorry to disappoint, but I don't know where the money is, either. Ariel took it, and—"

"It's right here," said one of the Concertos. She held up a backpack that clinked with tokens.

"How did you—"

"Maya gave us an in with your Harmonizers," Trevor said. "We visited their session today to let them know what we thought of their last move."

Dread settled in the pit of their stomach. "What did you do to them?"

Trevor laughed. "What do you *think*? I was disappointed to see you weren't there. You're really making us go out of our way here."

"How did you know where to find me?" And more importantly, *why*? If they already had what they wanted, why go through the trouble of seeking them out?

"Ariel. I told them we'd let them live if they told us where you were." The latent part of Chavi's mind still warped by Harmony felt the sting of betrayal. Ariel had understood them on a transcendent level. They wouldn't sell them out. It wasn't possible.

It was, though, and they had.

"And did you? Let them live?"

"No."

So Ariel was dead. It didn't feel real. Chavi was surprised to find themself utterly numb. What about Mellie? Guiltily, Chavi had to admit they didn't care much about the others. Strange, how when Harmonized, Chavi had been convinced the other Harmonizers were their best friends. Now they couldn't remember their names. And then there was Maya. Maya had joined the sacred trust of the circle, and shattered it.

They turned to face her, though she kept her gaze fixed on the ground. "You know, I actually believed you. When you said you were sorry." It stung to say. How had they been so stupid? "You really got me. I thought you meant it."

"I did mean it," Maya murmured.

"So what's this about then?"

"You know what this is about."

"Harmony, yeah. Well, if what you said is true, then my whole circle is dead." Still didn't feel like it could be true. But Chavi remembered the graves of all those scavengers at the Congregationalist camp, and they knew this boy was more than capable of it. "So if my circle is gone, why come after me?"

"Because you came after us in the dusts," Trevor said. "And I haven't forgotten that."

"So you're doing this because you're petty?"

"I'm doing this because last time I thought you were dead, you came crawling back just to fuck me over," Trevor said, his voice closer now. "And my Harmonization circle got robbed, lo and behold, there you were. I'm doing this because you won't leave me alone, and this time I know that if I want to be free of you, I'm just going to have to kill you myself."

Dusts. He was really gonna do it, wasn't he? Up until this point, they'd clung to a sliver of hope that they could somehow talk Trevor—or at least, Maya—out of this. But that wasn't going to happen, was it?

They were about to die.

"You don't have to do this," they said, weaker than they intended.

"No, I do."

They grasped for another desperate tactic. "What about my crew?"

"I couldn't give a shit about them."

"That's not what I meant. You think they're not gonna trace this back to you? That they're not gonna come after you for this?" To be honest, it was a bit of a bluff. Would the rest of the Ivies allow themselves to get dragged into a series of blood debts they may never escape from? Harvard would want to, they had no doubt. Chavi might have been the only person in the world who could see this, but deep down, Harvard was bloodthirsty. But Jasmine would probably be too smart for that. And with good reason. It would be better, actually, if she kept Harvard from seeking out the Concertos.

"As far as your crew knows, you abandoned them."

It was a nauseating thought. The prospect of the Ivies believing Chavi had willingly chosen to leave them was worse than the looming spectre of death.

"Someone will find my body," they said.

"I don't think so," Trevor said.

They had reached the city gates, and Chavi stood on the precipice of the dusts. A hand shoved them forward.

"Move. Pick a grave."

Interlude Ten: Oman

Oman wasn't sure why he did it. He told himself he was only doing it out of a sense of charity, but he knew that wasn't it. He simply never managed to escape the pull of his curiosity. No one stopped him as he walked through Delian Towers. They knew who he was. Well, that wasn't entirely true. Most of the people there didn't know who he was, but they knew he was allowed to do what he wanted, so they didn't give him any trouble.

He went to the table with coffee machines and bowls of fruit and bagels. He poured hot water into a teacup on a saucer, and dropped an herbal tea bag inside. He carefully carried the saucer over to the elevator, and ascended to the top floor.

He watched the swirls of tea slowly diffuse in the water as the elevator took him skyward. He started to smile at a memory, then stopped himself. *He's not the same boy you met all those years ago,* he reminded himself. *He's changed. He's corrupted.* Oman dunked the tea bag a few times and the clouded water turned a uniform burnt orange. But if he really believed all that was true, then what was he even doing here?

Pierce wordlessly allowed him into the office, though a momentary look of surprise appeared on his face, before it was replaced with his usual professional stoicism.

Devrin was, as usual, working at his desk. He was scribbling things down, occasionally murmuring to himself.

Oman placed the saucer on the table with a clink. Devrin glanced at the tea, and a slow smile spread across his face. When his gaze lifted to Oman his eyes lit up, and Oman had to admit it was at least a little bit endearing. Devrin clapped his hands in delight.

"You're here!" he said. "How wonderful!"

"I'm here," Oman nodded. Devrin patted the desk to indicate that he should sit down. Oman scoffed, opting for the chair opposite him. "I'm fine with the chair, thank you."

Devrin pouted. "It's just so formal to have you sitting across the desk from me. You should be by my side!"

"No, I shouldn't be by your side. I shouldn't be here at all." He hesitated, drumming his fingers on his cane. "But I admit I want to see how all this plays out. So I'm here as an impartial observer."

"Well, you say that now," Devrin smiled, producing a battered black notebook, "but just wait until you see what I have to show you."

"Allura still being a nuisance?" Oman guessed. Devrin winced. "She's been running her operation much longer than you, you know," Oman reminded him. "Much longer. She was gunning to be the first to expand the city even back when you and I worked for her."

Devrin waved a dismissive hand, placing the notebook on the table. "Never mind her," he said. "Look." He flipped through pages of notes and sketches until he landed on a schematic. He laid the book out in front of Oman, who studied the diagrams with reluctant interest. They depicted a machine, one that must have dated back to the pre-Quake days. Oman inspected them carefully.

"Are you aware of what this machine does?" Oman asked.

"I am," Devrin nodded, hands clasped.

"The world has not seen anything like this in centuries."

"The world has had no need of it. Until now."

Oman looked up. "Until now?"

Devrin slipped a single sheet of paper across the desk. Oman lifted it. His breath caught.

"Is this real?" he asked. Devrin nodded, grinning. "How did you find this? Not by stealing her methods, I hope. I always told her it wasn't right to force the hand of evolution."

"Luck, really," he leaned back, spinning a pen in his fingers. "And, if I'm being completely honest, some ingenious maneuvers on my part. But really mostly luck."

"And does she know?"

He shook his head. "She doesn't know a quaking thing. And I have gone to *great* lengths to keep it that way. It was all a bit of a production, honestly but—"

Oman held up a hand. "I don't really care." It was a bit cruel, but he only said it because he knew Rin would get that crestfallen look he always got when he didn't get to explain the thing he was so proud of himself for.

"It was a lot of work," he added pettishly. "But my point is..." He leaned forward conspiratorially, and it reminded Oman of the days that the two of them would spend together in secret, planning all their big dreams that they knew would never see the light of day. "We can actually do it, you know," he whispered. "Build our own city from the ground up.

Build a *human race* from the ground up, even. Everything we ever talked about is at our fingertips, and *she doesn't even know*."

He's not the same person he was, said a voice in the back of Oman's brain. *You don't know what he did to make this happen. You don't know how many people died for this.* But those voices were quiet now that the thing he'd always dreamed of was sitting right there in front of him. He didn't want to admit it, but he didn't have a choice.

"I'll do it," he whispered. He couldn't say no. Not to this. Not to him.

"Oh, Oman," Devrin said. "You've missed so much." He placed a gentle hand on Oman's. "I can't *wait* to fill you in."

CHAPTER TWENTY-TWO

Monsters

Harvard had ducked in and out of alleys, watching the grim procession from afar. They were speaking, but Harvard could only hear snatches of conversation. He heard the name "Ariel." He recognized that.

His stomach dropped when they reached the city gates. How could he follow them into the dusts without being spotted? If they got too far away from him, he'd have to give himself away. He peered around a corner as Chavi led the pack into the desert.

Once they were a good few paces away from the threshold of the city, Harvard dashed forward and hid himself behind one of the columns of the gate. Where were they going?

The group stopped. Two of them grabbed Chavi's arms to keep them from fleeing, and one stepped in front of them. He held something that glinted in the moonlight.

Harvard gasped.

That was *their* gun. The Ivies' gun. Sure, they'd never used it, but it still belonged to them, and it was *theirs* to never use.

He ran.

* * *

Snickers glanced back toward the city.

"This is far enough," he said. "We leave you here for the scuttlers, and there'll be nothing left by morning."

Now would be a great time to summon their crab powers that might also be a hallucination, Chavi thought as two Concertos gripped their arms. But it wasn't like a muscle that they could flex. They willed themself to *change* and it just didn't happen. They wondered if they should try and break free so they could make a run for it. Just to get shot in the back, though?

"Harvard will come for you." It was one last, viscous swipe before it was all over. "You think he won't but you're wrong. He knows I wouldn't leave him. He'll figure you out and he will hunt you down."

Maya's brow knit. She seemed to believe them. Chavi didn't realize it until they spoke it aloud, but they believed it, too. They believed every word. Harvard could be viscous when he had to be.

Maya placed a light hand on Snickers' shoulder.

"We have the money," she said. "We can go. We're already in enough trouble as it is."

"We had it made, Maya!" Trevor shouted. "If it weren't for their stupid crew, we would be living like the Upper Bastioners! Milky and Mars—they would be with us!" Dusts, he was near tears. Maya had been right. He was unstable. "They'd never have to go out in the dusts again in their life. We were *so close.*"

His grip tightened on the gun. Chavi jerked away reflexively. The other Harmonizers held them in place.

"This isn't going to change anything!" Maya pleaded.

"It'll at least give me some peace of mind."

Chavi could hear their blood pounding in their ears.

Do something, they told themself, *anything*. But there was nothing they could do except watch, helpless, as Maya and Trevor debated their fate.

"Let's go back to the city, okay?" Maya said. "We can—"

"Shut up!" Snickers screamed, shoving her away. She fell on her back. "Shut up! Shut up! We started this, and if you don't want to finish it, then fine. But I'm going to. And I'm going to do it before you try to change my mind."

He raised the gun.

"You don't want to do this," Chavi warned.

Trevor took one long stride forward, the muzzle of the gun almost touching Chavi's face.

"Actually," he said, "I really, really do."

* * *

"Stop!" Harvard screamed. "Sto—"

He froze.

The words died in his throat.

* * *

Chavi didn't mean to do it.

They didn't even know how they did it.

They hadn't felt it happen. Not at first, anyway.

First there was a gun pointed at them. Next thing they knew, Snickers was hoisted in the air by a crab claw, gun discharging into the sand. For a fleeting moment, Chavi thought maybe a desertwalker had arrived to rescue them, but with a wave of nausea they discovered the truth.

That claw was theirs.

It extended from the back of their right shoulder, a chitin appendage that ended in a pincer that had closed around Trevor's chest.

Chavi didn't mean to do it. But they were scared and angry and confused and they felt the claw close and they could feel Snickers' ribs snap and he started to scream but he was choked off as blood pooled in his throat and dripped down his chin. And Chavi wanted to drop him but they didn't know how, and they became aware that their feet were no longer touching the ground, and a full set of carcine legs now extended from their back and held them aloft, and one of the people who had held them was pinned to the ground with a crab leg through the stomach. The other one was grasping at his throat and Chavi realized they must have stabbed him in the neck with another leg.

Maya wobbled, looking pale, then her knees buckled and she flopped onto the sand, unconscious. Chavi wished they could do the same.

They willed the claw to open, and it felt like willing an arm to move when they were waking up, still half in dreams. The claw obeyed, and dropped Trevor's corpse to the ground with a sickening splat.

They hadn't meant to do it. But suddenly they were surrounded by four bodies in the sand.

The legs and the claw retracted, and their feet touched ground and they were human again. They took a shaky breath and wondered if any of this was really happening or if this was just another in a long series of nightmares that never seemed to end even when they woke up.

They turned back toward the city.

And there was Harvard.

He was standing only a few paces away from the carnage. He watched Chavi with wide eyes and an open mouth.

He wasn't shaking.

He was standing perfectly still.

"Harvard?" Chavi asked tentatively. He didn't respond.

They took a step toward him. He bolted.

"Harvard! Wait!" they cried, chasing after him. Chavi chased him back into the city, down the empty central street, back toward home. They had to explain. They could explain this. They had to catch him and let him know that everything was okay, that it was still them. They had to catch him. If they didn't catch him then he could get away.

* * *

This isn't real this isn't real this isn't real, was all Harvard could think. Chavi had been in danger and he wanted to save them—but then there was something *else*. Something he didn't understand, but whatever it was there was death and blood and then there was just Chavi, except it *wasn't* Chavi, it *couldn't* be, and he had to go, he had to run, because the thing was after him and it was calling his name and *none of this was real it wasn't real it couldn't be real.* He didn't know why he clung to this conviction, but whatever he saw wasn't human and it wasn't desertwalker either. But it was wearing Chavi's body.

But he could hear the sound of his bare feet on concrete, and his lungs were burning, and his breaths were ragged, and nothing had ever felt as real as this moment, and nothing was more real than Harvard's animalistic need to outrun an imposter.

* * *

"Harvard! Stop!"

He kept running. He was faster than them. They knew that. But now Harvard moved faster than Chavi had ever seen. They pumped their legs in a futile effort to keep up with them, but their lungs burned.

They slowed to a stop. And let him go.

Chavi took a moment to catch their breath. They felt like an idiot. They should never have gone after him. If they were scared, they could only imagine what he must be feeling, having watched that whole thing. At least being in the middle of it they had been spared most of the gore. Harvard had witnessed it all—what was he doing there?—and to make things worse, Chavi had tried to keep him from running away.

It had all just felt so fragile, in that moment. Like Chavi was barely human, and Harvard was the only lifeline they had, the little silver thread tying them back to the rest of humanity. And if they lost Harvard, they lost everything.

But you haven't lost Harvard, they reminded themself, panting. *You just scared him. You can still fix this.*

They took stock of their body. Nothing hurt, not even so much as a bruise, There was only a splatter of blood on their worn t-shirt. They didn't know whose it was. They took off the shirt and turned it inside out to hide the little evidence of the evening that still clung to them. *You can fix this.*

Not now, though. They couldn't very well follow him home after this. So they had nowhere to go. Well, almost nowhere. There was one place they could think of.

* * *

Rivka Chakrabarti awoke to the sound of someone pounding at her door. She threw on a robe and ran through the kitchen, to the living room, and peeked through the peephole.

She unlatched the door. Her child stood before her, looking harried, face contorted as though they were about to burst into tears.

"Chavi?" she asked.

"Hi mom," they said. "Can I stay with you tonight, please?"

* * *

Harvard did not sleep that night. He didn't even bother trying. He paced the room, wringing his hands, pulling his hair, trying to puzzle together exactly what had happened, what exactly it was that he had seen.

It really was Chavi who killed the boy on Haven that night.

Whatever Skrack had done to save their life, it had changed them. It made them...carcine.

Harvard sat down heavily on the bed.

Chavi was becoming a desertwalker.

That didn't bother him.

He sat with that for a moment.

Should it bother him?

It should bother him, shouldn't it?

It had scared him, that was for sure. The first time it had happened on Haven, he wasn't even sure he had seen it. Now he knew what he had seen, but it was all so...so visceral, he had struggled to make sense of it. And there had been so much blood and death that he didn't even know what he was looking at, so he had run. He felt so guilty about it now. He'd abandoned Chavi in the middle of all that just because he'd been scared.

But now he understood. It was okay. And it didn't scare him anymore.

Well, that wasn't true. It scared him a little. But most things scared Harvard, so that wasn't anything new.

I was hoping you wouldn't witness something like that.

Harvard jumped. He'd been so shaken he forgot his carcine companion was perched on the dresser. Speedy watched him with impassive eyes, but somehow they looked sorrowful nonetheless. "Did you know this was going to happen to Chavi?" Harvard asked.

Speedy was silent.

"Speedy!" Harvard pleaded.

Chavi was warned, Speedy said simply.

"What do you mean?" Harvard asked.

They had a choice. They could die, or they could change. They chose to change. It was their own decision.

"I don't understand," Harvard shook his head. "Where does the change end?"

I do not know, said Speedy. *This is...unprecedented. None of us know.*

"You're not really here to look after me, are you?" Harvard asked. "Skrack *did* send you here. Skrack wanted to keep an eye on Chavi."

I may have...misled you, Speedy admitted. *But I also told you the truth. I am here to protect you, Harvard. And have I not done well? Did I not save you in Haven when your plight was dire?*

"You lied to me!" Harvard gripped the edge of the bed. "You knew this would happen! If you really wanted to protect you would have told me, so I wouldn't have had to—so Chavi wouldn't have—"

Harvard cut himself off, burying his face in the heels of his hands. No wonder Chavi had been acting erratic lately—they were going through something unimaginably terrifying. No, not unimaginable. Harvard knew what it was like to feel alien in your own body.

I did not know what would happen. None of us knew. But even if I did, Speedy continued, *would it really have changed a thing? If I'd warned you, would your situation be any different?*

"Yes!" Harvard cried. "Because then I would have known!"

That's not a meaningful difference.

"It is to me."

Harvard—

"Leave me alone!" Harvard snapped. "I thought I could trust you. Now I know the only person I can really trust is Chavi."

Speedy said nothing.

"You don't think I can trust Chavi, do you?"

Speedy shifted his claws awkwardly.

"Get out," Harvard said. "I don't care where you go. Go back to the dusts for all I care. Just...get out."

Speedy leapt off the dresser and crawled forlornly toward the window. He clawed his way up the curtains and landed gracefully on the windowsill.

I will see you again, Harvard, he said.

Harvard shook his head. "I don't care." He did care, of course. Harvard cared about everything. Right now, though, he wanted to wound.

When he turned around, Speedy was gone.

* * *

Chavi awoke in their childhood bed. They wished they could put the events of the previous night out of their mind, but they were plagued by a desperate need to understand. What exactly had happened to them? Could they make it happen again? And if they really were...transforming into something else, then where would the transformation stop?

They rolled over and examined the gun they'd scooped up off the desert floor. They weren't sure why they'd bothered to retrieve it. They'd never used it. But it still felt like it belonged to them—at least, to the Ivies—and there was a strange security in having it. In being armed with anything.

Maybe I don't need it anymore, they thought. *Maybe I am a weapon now.*

There was a knock on their door. Chavi hurriedly covered the gun with the blanket.

"Come in," they said.

Their mother tentatively pushed the door open.

"Hey, honey," she said. "Do you wanna talk?"

Chavi sat up in bed. "Not really."

Rivka sat at the foot of the bed.

"What's going on?" she pressed. "You have a fight with your boyfriend?"

Chavi blinked at her, amazed she could deduce that so quickly. Moms were just like that. They doubted she'd be able to deduce the crab part, though. "Uh. Yeah."

"And you're sure you don't wanna talk about it?"

Chavi sighed. "I fucked up. I know that. He has every right to be mad at me."

Rivka rubbed their leg on top of the covers. "Well, you know you're welcome here any time."

Chavi snorted. "What, you think he's gonna kick me out for good?"

"I'm not saying that," Rivka said. "I'm just saying that fights happen. I want you to know that you have someplace to go."

"Thanks, Mom," Chavi said, and they meant it, even though her reassurances barely scratched the surface of their fears. What if he did kick them out for good? What if after last night, he didn't want anything to do with them? Chavi's throat tightened, and tears welled up in their eyes.

"Mom," they rasped, "I think I'm a monster."

"Oh, love," she laid a gentle hand on their shoulder.

Tell me I'm not a monster, they willed her. *Please tell me I'm not a monster.* She pulled them into a hug, and they wrapped the sheet over their shoulders so she couldn't feel the places where their skin gave way to chitin carapace.

"If you're a monster," she said, "then you're the most lovable monster in the world."

Chavi sobbed into their mother's shoulder.

* * *

"Where were you so early in the morning?" Jasmine asked as Chavi entered the townhouse.

They mumbled something so incoherent that even they had no idea what they were saying.

Jasmine rolled her eyes, which Chavi noted was a distinctly un-Jasmine thing to do. But they could worry about that later. Harvard was priority number one right now. After this was sorted out, then they could figure out what was going on with the best friend that wasn't also their boyfriend.

"Harvard around?" they asked.

"Still asleep, I think," Jasmine shrugged.

"He's in the room?"

"Haven't seen him."

Chavi took a deep breath, steeling themself, and ascended the stairs. They knocked tentatively on their door.

"Harvard? It's me. You...you don't have to open the door if you don't want to. I just wanna talk to you. I wanted to say—"

The door swung open abruptly. Harvard stood there, looking up at them, his face unreadable. He grabbed them by the hand and pulled them inside, furtively glancing down the hallway to see if anyone had seen, then slamming the door behind them.

Chavi stood by the dresser, befuddled, as Harvard sat down on the bed, hands pressed between his thighs. They waited for him to speak, but the silence became unbearable.

"I'm sorry I ran after you," they said. "It was a stupid idea. I just—I didn't know you were there. And when I saw you—I freaked out a little. I didn't want you to see that. And then when you ran away, I thought—" *I thought you were scared of me.* The thought made them feel sick. Harvard *had* been scared of them. They knew that for a fact.

"I saw you kill three people," he responded numbly, staring at the floor.

"Yes."

"They tried to kill you."

"Yes."

"Why?"

"I...don't know," Chavi lied. It was a weak lie, and they could tell as they said it, but they hoped Harvard was too shaken by the whole event to notice.

"Did you know you could do that?" Harvard asked, and they didn't need to ask what he meant.

"No. Well, yes. I don't know. I knew something was happening to me, but I...I didn't want to believe it. I'm sorry. I should have told you. I was trying to forget."

"I've been trying to forget about Haven too."

Right. He touched the scar on his cheek reflexively. Chavi wondered if it would fade, or if he'd bear that memory of Haven on his face forever.

"Ariel," Harvard said. "They mentioned Ariel. Wasn't that your friend from the party?"

Chavi shrugged. How nonchalant was too nonchalant? How would they be acting if they really didn't know why they'd been taken out in the desert to be shot?

"They weren't really my friend," Chavi said. "Only kinda knew them."

"Do you think...do you think they were involved in something bad?" Harvard brow creased. "Something illegal?"

"Seems likely. We need more information," Chavi ran a hand through their hair, hoping Harvard couldn't see their mounting panic. "There could be more of them. They could come back for me—or you, maybe. Or the rest of the Ivies. We have to do something. But—Founders, Harvard, I don't know who to go to. I don't know who I can trust. And even if I did, I wouldn't even know where to find them. I—"

"The Founder's Festival," Harvard interrupted, looking distant.

"What?" Chavi froze, staring at him.

"We go to the Founders' Festival."

"How would that help?"

"Well," he reasoned, "the Chocolates were after you and Ariel. What about the rest of your friends from the Sand Crystal? Did they get hurt too? If any of them are still alive, maybe they know what's going on. The Festival is only time that pretty much the entire city comes together. Don't you think it's likely that they'll be there?"

"But—but the Festival is massive!" Chavi stammered. "I'll never be able to find anyone in that crowd."

Harvard shrunk visibly.

"It was just an idea," he mumbled.

"No! No! It's a good idea!" Chavi corrected, raising a hand to their mouth, "and it may be all we can do. Why not give it a shot, right?"

Harvard brightened.

"I mean, I have always wanted to go."

Chavi laughed despite themself. "You've never been?"

Harvard shook his head, and despite everything, Chavi found themself grinning. *Of course he's never been,* they realized. *He's a Bell. He wouldn't have been allowed to do anything fun.* Their smile faltered.

"Alright. Let's make a day of it," they said, shaking their head as if to dispel the thought. "The Founders' Festival, you and me. Jasmine and August too, actually. I don't want them to suspect anything is off."

Harvard nodded, and for the first time in the conversation, his mouth quirked up into a cautious smile.

Interlude Eleven: Kathy

Kathy Bell did not often broach a topic of conversation with her mother. While Saoirse Bell seemed to recognize her daughter's acumen, and therefore her usefulness, that didn't mean she relished being pulled into a conversation with her daughter, though, especially not during her work hours, or worse, during the few leisure hours she afforded herself.

Still, Kathy found herself at a dead end with all of her half-baked research, and she wanted to know if her mother knew anything about it. She started by asking her mother if she could help her with anything, and she'd only waved her away, hunched over her desk doing some ledgers, by the looks of it.

"Do you know anything about the theft at the Galvin Conference last year?" she tested. Her mother didn't even look up.

"No, though I expect it was something to do with the corp rift."

"What corp rift?"

This time her mother did look up, and she looked oddly surprised, as though Kathy was supposed to know this already. As though she weren't the very reason that Kathy didn't know all the ins and outs of the family's business.

"The Delian Group and the Satsuki Group have stopped working with each other," she said, as though this was obvious.

"What?" Kathy asked. "But the Delian Group relies on the Satsukis. I mean, how else would they get their guns?"

"Well, that's just the thing..." Saoirse leaned back, spinning her pen in her hand. She seemed uncharacteristically excited. "Rumor is, the Delian Group has decided to start producing their own arms."

"What, making their own guns?"

"Possibly. The Head Enforcer is notoriously tight-lipped about this kind of thing, even to his closest allies."

"You mean you meet with him?" She hated that despite the fact she would inherit the family business one day, so much was kept from her.

"Yes. Regularly. He's a delightful man. But he has secrets to keep, of course, so I only press when I feel I must. People talk, though."

"And what are they saying?"

"The Delian Group is developing bioweapons."

"Bioweapons? What do you mean?"

"Well, keep in mind the Zuri Institution and the Delian Group have always been closely partnered. Think of what they could build together—biological weapons aimed at maintaining the city's safety."

"How...how does that maintain the city's safety?"

"Well if the Satsuki Group does not have our best interests at heart...weapons might be necessary."

"You think there will be a war?"

"War? In Bastion?" her mother laughed. "Never! The common people have no idea any of this even happening, and I'm sure they never will. But just in between the corps..."

"There's going to be violence?"

"No. At least, Not involving anyone important. Bastion is too civilized, my dear," she said with a note of condescension. "We've advanced past that."

"And you trust the Head Enforcer?"

"Completely. He's the most trustworthy person I know. After all, he holds the safety of the entire human race in his hands. You don't get a job like that without proving your reliability. And he has proven to me, personally, that he is very reliable." *Trustworthiness and reliability are not the same thing*, Kathy thought, but she stayed silent. "After all," her mother continued, "I trusted him with the most important thing I had, and he did not let me down."

"What was that?" Kathy asked.

"My legacy." Kathy's silence must have given away her confusion, because her mother looked up and smirked. "What, you think I had time to raise children when I first inherited the company? *Someone* had to take care of you when you were a mewling, puking little thing, and it certainly wasn't going to be me. I hired an assistant."

Kathy hadn't known any of this. She only had the vaguest memories of the various caretakers and tutors who had tended to her in her childhood, but certainly no recollection of her infancy.

"Your assistant became the Head Enforcer?" she asked.

"Well certainly not by chance," her mother scoffed. "I played no small part in the appointment. Now if you don't *mind*," she said pointedly, indicating her ledgers.

Kathy gave a deferential nod before retreating to her room. She didn't have a full picture of what was going on, she knew one thing for sure:

Ronan was somehow involved in this, and it was up to her to get him out. But how could she find him if—

"And Katherine?" her mother called after her. "You'll stay in tonight. They're doing that dreadful festival again."

She paused mid-step, and gasped. Ronan always said he'd wanted to go to the Founders' Festival. Their mother had always forbade it, of course, saying it was a celebration for the masses and the Bells were not a *part* of the masses and she would be dead before she saw a member of her flesh and blood cavorting with the rabble.

But Ronan was free, now, and he could do whatever he wanted.

Kathy went searching for Camilla to ask her if she could find a way to subtly secure her a mask.

CHAPTER TWENTY-THREE

The Founders' Festival

It was the thickest crowd Harvard had ever been a part of, thicker than the Galvin Conference by far. And everyone wore costumes—some looked intricately hand made, and others only store-bought gestures at a disguise. Jasmine handed Chavi a mask. They hadn't bothered to buy one early. It was the black cat. They frowned.

"Do you want to switch?" Harvard offered.

"No. It's fine," they said abruptly. Harvard donned his mask. In the distance, he could hear drummers beating out a rhythm, and musicians tuning their instruments. Lots of different musicians, actually. There was no schedule, no rules. Everyone could play their own music if they wanted. Harvard thought that was exciting. That was how music should be, right? Everyone can play whatever they want.

The procession began to ascend the stairs to Upper Bastion, and Harvard's excitement gave way to panic.

"What's going on?" he asked.

"Right!" August put the heel of his hand to his head. "You've never done a Founder's Festival before! Which probably means you've never been to Upper Bastion before, either."

"Nope. Never," Harvard said.

"Well this is the one time a year that they actually open the gates for us. Anyone can enter Upper Bastion on festival night!"

"Maybe we can stay down here?" he asked. What if his mother was there? He knew she'd never stoop so low as to participate in the revels, but if she somehow managed to catch sight of him—

"And miss our one chance a year to see that place? No way! It's insanely pretty. You'll love it."

"Okay," Harvard nodded meekly. He was wearing a mask, he reminded himself. Even if his mother did spot him, would she even know it was him?

The Ivies ascended the stairs in a current of other revelers. The crowd flowed into the central Upper Bastion Square, around the stone fountain.

The drummers sat on the lip, and now their beat was so loud Harvard could feel the vibrations in his throat.

"What now?" he asked.

"We dance!" August grabbed his hand and pulled him out further onto the cobblestones. Well, that wouldn't be so bad. Harvard liked the idea of dancing. Especially dancing with Chavi. Especially after the other night. It would be nice to go back to having fun together. They hadn't spent any time with each other just doing something nice since they stole the wine on Haven.

He glanced over his shoulder to summon them, but someone else pulled on Chavi's hand leading them into the rabble. A girl with pink pigtails. Harvard had seen her at the Sand Crystal. Her name was Mellie. He felt a stab of jealousy, so visceral it made his stomach hurt.

"Would you like to dance with me, Harvard?" Jasmine asked. It was a kind offer, but he wondered if he could take her up on it. Could he really manage to look her in the eyes for a whole song, still haunted by what he'd seen the previous night, and keep his composure? He nodded meekly, and took her hands.

* * *

Mellie wordlessly pulled Chavi into a dance, and they didn't protest. Their curiosity propelled them. She pulled them in tight, which they knew Harvard wouldn't have liked, but it was the best way to speak to each other without being overheard. They were pressed so close together they couldn't see each other's faces, just speak in the other's ear.

"You're alive," they said.

"So are you," she responded.

"How did you survive?"

"I have someone taking care of me," she evaded. "How did you survive?"

Chavi didn't answer. They didn't want to say it out loud. That made it more true.

"You killed them," Mellie said. It was a statement, not a question. "I thought so. How many?"

"Three." Maya had escaped. That had been mostly an accident, but despite her betrayal, they were still oddly glad of that. They still somehow pitied her, even though she set them up to—Chavi felt a sudden flash of fury. How had Mellie *known* to hide? To seek protection in the first place?

"You knew this was coming," they said. Mellie hadn't been there. She'd known just like Maya had.

"I did."

"You didn't warn anyone."

"I couldn't."

"Ariel is dead."

"I'm aware. There's nothing I could have done about it and you're just going to have to trust me on that. I only just got back."

"Back? Back from where?"

The song ended, and Mellie released them. She gave an over-exaggerated bow.

"It's nice to see you're still breathing," she said before disappearing into the crowd. They reached for her, more questions on their lips, but she was gone.

* * *

Harvard focused all his energy into seeming normal, but the weird thing about seeming normal was that once he stopped and thought about it, he had no idea what normal was. Jasmine didn't seem herself, either, but Harvard couldn't quite pinpoint what it was about her that was different.

"Something is wrong," she finally said, and Harvard's heart fluttered. She knew. She knew about the Chocolates, the people Chavi had killed, everything. He didn't know how, but that didn't matter. Jasmine was the kind of person who just *knew* things.

"I don't like keeping things secret, Jasmine," he whispered. She looked surprised.

"*You* know about what's been going on?" she asked.

"Yeah," Harvard said. "Do you?"

Jasmine pursed her lips. "Not the whole story. It's driving me crazy," she said. "Tell me everything, Harvard. Please."

He didn't know where to begin. "Jasmine...Chavi did something bad."

He hated how juvenile it sounded, but the words didn't form right in his mouth. He desperately needed to say it, but he didn't know how.

"What do you mean, Ha—"

Before she could finish, a hand shot out and grabbed her by the arms, just as the song reached its conclusion. A girl with long pink pigtails spun her around and bowed deeply. Harvard scowled. Mellie, *again*. Was she determined to take everything away from him?

"May I have this dance?" she asked with excessive formality. Harvard couldn't help the feeling that they were being made fun of, until the girl lifted her head and he saw the intensity in the way she stared at Jasmine—and pointedly ignored him. He could feel his frustration begin to boil. He slunk away, and decided he would poke around to see if he could find Chavi again, and ask if they'd discovered anything new.

* * *

The pink-haired girl pulled Jasmine into a surprisingly intimate dance. Despite herself, Jasmine blushed.

"I need to talk to you," she whispered in her ear.

"I don't know you," Jasmine said.

"But you would like to," the girl smiled. Jasmine was tired of this. She was tired of being left out, tired of feeling like she was playing a game that everyone knew the rules to but her.

"What do you want?" she demanded.

"Do you want to know what Chavi's been up to?" the girl asked.

"What are you talking about?" Jasmine asked. As far as she knew, Chavi wasn't "up to" anything.

"I'll tell you everything."

"Why?" Jasmine asked. "Do you want something from me? I have nothing to give."

The girl shook her head, and her pigtails danced.

"I've already been paid."

* * *

Harvard meandered through the crowd feeling sorry for himself. He'd always wanted to go to the Founder's Festival. Now here he was, in a crowd and yet completely alone, harboring this secret weighing down his chest. It didn't feel like a party. It wasn't fun. He wanted to go home. He wanted the past few weeks, with Snickers and Adri and The Sand Crystal and everything, never to have happened. He wanted to be back on Haven, where everything was simpler. Their parties weren't like this.

A hand caught his wrist, and Harvard's head jerked up to see who'd grabbed him. Behind a simple, elegant white mask, he saw his own face, grinning triumphantly.

Harvard's stomach twisted. He knew that smile. He'd seen it on his very last night in Bell Manor. It was the smile Kathy Bell wore when she knew she'd beaten him.

"Ronan? It's really you, isn't it?" She had the audacity to sound relieved, as though she weren't the reason he left in the first place. And of course between her grip on him and the crush of the crowd, he could hardly run away. It was so devious, so like *her*, to catch him when he couldn't escape.

"Let me go," he demanded, and she ignored it.

"It's okay," she said, as though she were calming down a scared kitten. "You can come back home now."

"I have a new home," he insisted, but it sounded like a lie even though he knew it wasn't.

She flinched as though he'd slapped her. "Don't say that. You belong here." How could she say that, after what she'd done to him?

"No, I don't. Let go!" He tried to pull away again, but her grip was firm.

"Stay with me. Things will be different," she promised.

He shook his head. "Things are *already* different."

* * *

That fateful day when Chavi had gotten themself kicked out of the Academy, Jasmine could not find it in herself to be angry with them. She was angry with Carter, with Principal Santos, with the school, but most of all with *herself*. If she hadn't been such a tempting target, Chavi would never have felt the need to protect her. So clearly it couldn't be *their* fault.

For the first time, Jasmine wondered if she was wrong.

Because now? She had a lot to blame them for.

She found Chavi near the edge of the upper level, on the ledge right above the fountain. She would get the truth, and she would get it from Chavi directly. They must have read her frustration in her face, because theirs fell when they saw her approaching. They grabbed her hands as if to dance, but Jasmine didn't feel much like dancing, especially not with them.

"Jasmine? What's going on?" they asked, taking her through the movements of a simple dance.

"I'm giving you a chance to tell me the truth on your own," she said, fighting to keep her voice level. She watched their face for any sign of recognition. She thought she saw a flash of fear but, it disappeared instantly.

"What are you talking about?" they asked.

"You know what I'm talking about."

"I really don't," they gave a nervous laugh.

"The University rejected my application because the account was empty."

"You applied for University?" Chavi gaped.

"Why was it empty?" Jasmine asked. Her voice was tight, but she would *not* cry.

"Jasmine, why didn't you tell me?" Chavi looked wounded, and a small part of her wanted to pity them, but that part of her was rapidly shrinking.

"What did you do with the money?" she asked.

"Jas, I didn't know—"

"Tell me."

Chavi's brow creased behind their mask, and they bit their lip. They looked pained, and Jasmine knew she'd cornered them. "I can't," they whispered. Jasmine realized with a sinking sensation that this was as much of a confession as they were ever going to give her. She thought then of Simon Foster, and something he'd said to her years ago as the two sat together in an empty courtyard. *"Chavi needs everyone to like them so much that they can't just own up to their mistakes. And I'm just never going to believe the truth until I hear it from them, so I think we'll be stuck in this loop forever. Chavi won't tell me, and I'll pretend like I don't know."*

Her eyes rimmed with tears, she whispered, "You never could help yourself, could you?"

She shoved them.

For a fraction of a second, Chavi's eyes widened with alarm and surprise, and Jasmine knew her face must have matched. She'd never, ever done anything to hurt them. In fact, other than punching Snickers, she was fairly certain she'd never done anything to hurt anyone. Beyond that, she didn't know her own strength.

She hadn't intended to hurt them. She didn't think she had intended anything. It just happened. But it didn't matter what she'd intended, because when Chavi stumbled away from her, they backed into the ledge and toppled over the side.

* * *

Jasmine knew. She knew everything. This was Chavi's last thought before suddenly they were falling, and their stomach lurched as the world shifted unsteadily around them. Then everything flashed white when their head crashed into something hard, and before they could cry out they were already coughing up water.

* * *

Kathy pulled him into an embrace—not a hug, no. She had never hugged him, and he doubted she was about to start now. She intended to dance with him. He tried to pull away, but her hand was already on his back.

"Why?" she whispered. "Why are you back?"

Her smile grew wider as she saw the panic on his face. He tried again to pull away but her grip on his hand was tight.

"No," she said firmly. "You're not leaving again." She was enjoying his fear, a cat toying with her prey.

But Harvard was not prey anymore.

The moment Kathy turned her attention to the fiasco near the center of the circle. As she turned, Harvard used the opportunity to rip away. He followed her gaze and saw a crowd forming around the fountain where someone had—

"Chavi!" Harvard cried, bounding toward the growing crowd.

"Ronan!" Kathy called after him, her trap thwarted.

"Why?" she demanded, and she sounded like she was near tears. "*Why?*"

But her voice was soon drowned out by the voices of the crowd.

* * *

Chavi hadn't been knocked unconscious by the blow they took, but the whole thing was disorienting. The first thing they became aware of was a blossoming warmth where they'd been struck, and touching a hand to their temple they discovered their head was bleeding. The second they became aware of the faces staring down at them, then the cold of the water that they thrashed in, then a hand gripping theirs, and another on their shoulder, then a familiar shock of red hair.

"Chavi? What happened?"

* * *

Jasmine stood frozen for a moment as she watched the scene unfold below her, most onlookers a combination of surprised, confused, and entertained by the drama that transpired before them. Should she feel guilty? She didn't. Should she go down and help? She didn't want to. The anger still boiled in her chest, and in that moment, she couldn't care less if she had hurt Chavi. She didn't care what happened to them next. What was wrong with her?

She balled her fists and darted away, back to the townhouse. Her townhouse. The one in her name. The one she'd worked hard for. The one she'd once shared with the person she'd allowed herself to believe was her best friend.

* * *

By the time Chavi got to their feet, most of the musicians had gone back to playing, and most of the crowd had ceased staring at them and gone back to dancing.

Harvard fussed over Chavi, checking the wound on their head where they'd crashed into the stone of the fountain.

"Are you okay?" he asked, not waiting for an answer. "Did you get hurt? How did you fall? Do you want a change of clothes? I know you hate water. We could—"

"I'm fine, I'm fine," they waved Harvard away, looking up at the ledge. Jasmine was already gone. Harvard followed their gaze.

"What happened?" he asked again.

"She pushed me," Chavi said, dazed.

"Who?"

"Jasmine."

"What?" Harvard gaped. "But she would never—why would she—"

"I don't know," Chavi lied, "but we've got to find her."

"Hey!" August puffed, jogging up to the two of them. "What's going on?"

"Jasmine disappeared," they said.

"So you...jumped in a fountain?" August narrowed his eyes. Chavi had neither the presence of mind nor desire to explain.

"Where did she go?" they asked. August scanned the crowd, sucking his teeth.

"Lotta people here, bud," he said. "She could be anywhere."

"Let's go home," Harvard pleaded, rubbing a hand on Chavi's back. They hated the sensation of the wet cloth being pushed onto their skin, but feeling his arm around them was still a small comfort in the face of everything.

She knew. Jasmine knew.

"Yeah. Let's go home."

CHAPTER TWENTY-FOUR

Drowning

"I don't get it," August said as the three of them walked back toward the townhouse. "Why would she do something like that? It seems so...un-Jasmine."

"I don't know," Chavi repeated, though they weren't sure why. Wasn't it only a matter of time before they found out the truth? They scanned the empty streets. It was strange, seeing the city so desolate. Even after so many years of attending the Founders' Festival, they'd never seen how deserted the rest of Bastion looked when nearly all its occupants were crowded on one end. The silence was eerie.

This was somehow worse than the Chocolates marching them to their death. Because at least that would have been the end. What Jasmine was about to do to them, they would survive, which meant afterward they had to keep living.

Can someone just shoot me again, actually? Chavi thought as they unlocked the front door. *I won't get back up this time, I promise.*

When the door swung open, Jasmine was waiting, her arms crossed, her eyes were alight with fury. Chavi had never seen her this angry.

"Jasmine, what's going on?" August demanded.

"Are you okay?" Harvard asked.

"Chavi has been lying to us," Jasmine said. Her face was impassive, her voice cold.

"What?" August asked. "About what?"

"They used our money to pay a fee for a...a drug cult."

"What?" August laughed. "Jas, that's ridiculous."

"That's what I thought," she said. "When I got the notification the account was empty, I felt like I was losing my mind. But then the girl at the Festival who keeps the records showed me the receipts. Chavi had paid her. To be part of this...this group."

"Chavi." Harvard turned to face them slowly. "That's not true, is it?"

Chavi suddenly felt dizzy, and it wasn't from the head wound. "I can explain," they held up a hand.

"Wait, so it is true?" August gaped.

"It's not a 'drug cult!'" Chavi said.

"But you stole *our* money?" August asked.

"I didn't steal it!"

"But you took it without telling me and Jasmine. That is stealing!" August took a step toward them.

"I was doing it for *us*!"

"How was that for us?" Jasmine demanded, stepping toward them too, and suddenly the room felt suffocatingly crowded.

Chavi knew their justification made sense to them, but how could they possibly explain it in a way that would make sense to anyone else? "Because if I don't...if I don't find something to help me control whatever's happening to me, then I'm afraid of what it'll do to me. And what *I* might do to all of *you*."

"If you thought that...Harmonization...was so important," Jasmine asked, "then why didn't you just tell us?"

"Because I didn't think you would understand. And obviously you don't! You don't understand!" They didn't mean to start shouting, but they did. They started to feel that same sensation they had when Harvard had locked them out—drowning, and these three were the only ones who could save them, but instead they were just watching them sink. The last one on the boat, abandoned to drown, and they didn't even have a right to complain about it because it was their own choices that landed them here.

"Is this why those people were after you?" Harvard murmured. Chavi whipped around to look at him. They had agreed not to talk about the Concertos incident.

"People were *after* you?" August repeated.

"I thought we weren't going to talk about that," Chavi hissed.

August crossed his arms. "So Harvard knew, and you told him not to tell?"

"And this is where you've been disappearing to at night?" Harvard asked.

"Whoa!" said August. "Why is this the first time we're hearing about this?"

"You told me you wouldn't hide anything," Harvard said. "You told me you wouldn't lie *to me*."

Chavi felt like a cornered animal, running out of escape routes. Even Harvard had turned on them, which they hadn't believed possible. They lashed out before they knew what they were doing.

"You can't believe *I'd* lie?" They laughed, and it was humorless and hollow and cruel. "You can't believe that I'd lie, *Ronan*?"

Harvard reared back. "Why did you call me that?"

"Oh, sorry." Chavi whirled on him. "Would you prefer I called you by your title, *Master Bell*?"

Harvard recoiled as though struck. So it *had* been true. Unbelievable. Jasmine gasped quietly, but August was still baffled.

"What the hell are you talking about?" he asked.

Harvard didn't answer. He reddened, his fist clenched.

"Why—how—" he stammered.

"Like, the famous Bells?" August asked. "The rich ones? You're saying Harvard is related to them? That's not true, is it Harvard?" Harvard said nothing, just smoldered. He glared at Chavi, and they realized this was the first time they'd ever seen him angry with them. It was terrifying.

August shook his head. "What about the blood disease?"

"There was no blood disease!" Chavi said. "He made it up!"

August looked between the two of them before his eyes settled on Harvard. "Holy shit. It really is true." Now it was his turn to be furious. "Dude, you were rich this whole time and you didn't tell us? You could have helped us! You could have saved us!"

"It's not like that," Harvard said.

August took a step toward Harvard and backed away, eyes wide. In a flash, August was Princeton again, berating Harvard for his latest mistake. "It *is* like that! We've been working our asses off, starving, and you could have asked your parents—"

But Harvard wasn't the same person he'd been all those months ago.

"You don't know what you're talking about!" Harvard snapped with such ferocity that August flinched back. "Do you know what would happen if I went to my family asking for money? They would laugh in my face. They hate me!" He was trembling again, but this time with fury. So much anger in one small body. "Why do you think I became a scavenger? Because I would rather *die* than spend another day in that house. So congratulations." He turned back to Chavi, and his face contorted with a combination of rage and betrayal. "You did it, Chavi. You found the thing I hate most about myself, and you dragged it out in front of everyone. My family doesn't want me. Do you want a prize? Do you want a medal or something? Because I've worked really hard to make *this* my family, but apparently that's not enough for you. You call me Harvard all you want, but at the end of the day you can't see past the name I was born with."

Chavi stared at him, stunned. "I wasn't trying—"

"No, I know what you were trying to do," Harvard spat back. "You wanted to catch me in a lie so you could feel a little tiny bit better about the lies you told. Well guess what: my lie didn't hurt anyone. I didn't steal from anyone. I didn't make anyone think they were going crazy," he added with a gesture to Jas. "So if you think this makes things any better, well, now you're just lying to yourself."

With that, he stormed off up the stairs. Chavi could hear the bedroom door slam closed behind him. They turned to the other two.

Jasmine, who had watched the whole exchange in silence, stood still. August looked after Harvard in wonder.

"Ronan Bell," he wondered aloud, then shook his head. "That little shit."

"I'm sorry," Chavi said, mostly for Jasmine's benefit.

She just shook her head.

I'll deal with them later, they thought, and took off up the stairs after Harvard.

* * *

Harvard stared out the window, his jaw clenched, trying to tame the tempest of emotions that churned his stomach. Behind him, he heard the door open and close. He'd left it unlocked. He didn't want to continue this conversation, but he knew it was going to eat him from the inside out if they didn't.

"How long have you known?" he whispered. He didn't turn around. He couldn't bear to look at them.

"A few weeks," Chavi said behind him. "Devrin told me."

"And you believed him?" Harvard turned, surprised to see Chavi looked strangely small, their arms drawn around themself protectively. *Don't fall for it*, he thought to himself. *Don't feel bad for them.*

"Was he wrong?" they asked.

No, he wasn't. Harvard's shame weighed heavy on his chest. He feared ever since they'd returned to Bastion that he'd be caught in this lie, still, it stung to know that Chavi had trusted Devrin's word over his.

"Don't you trust me?" Harvard murmured.

"I did," Chavi said. "Which made finding out so much worse."

"And this makes everything *you've* done better, I guess?" Harvard snapped. It was an evasion and he knew it, but he couldn't help feeling like his personal background was his own business, whereas Chavi's stealing was everyone's.

Chavi bowed their head. "No. Of course it doesn't. I'm sorry."

"That doesn't fix any of this," Harvard said.

"I know."

"What else?" Harvard said, and the moment he said it he started to feel dizzy, like the room was pitching around him.

Chavi's head snapped up. "What?"

"What else do I not know?" Harvard asked. He hated that he had to ask, but he knew there was something. He stumbled, placing a hand on the wall for support. His reality was shifting, the whole world was shifting, and he could barely stay upright.

Chavi shook their head. "I don't know."

"You don't *know*?"

"No, I just mean—"

"What really happened the night I blacked out?"

Chavi looked away from Harvard. "I did a job with the Harmonizers."

Harvard remembered how violently ill he was the next morning. Speedy's warning, and his reprimands after.

"What did you do to me?" he whispered.

Chavi winced. They still wouldn't look at him. "I tried to stop you from drinking it. I did. I didn't want to give it to you, but Mellie…"

"Chavi, no." He didn't know what he meant by it. Maybe he was begging them to say it wasn't true, or denying that it had happened at all. That they wouldn't let that happen. But they did.

Looking at them now, Harvard felt that same double-sight he had when he'd seen them dancing at The Sand Crystal. Chavi was a different person than they were in the dusts. Chavi was a different person than Yale. Yale had shown Harvard a modicum of kindness, and he'd fallen for them so easily, because he'd never had anyone care for him before, and he yearned for it. Who was Chavi compared the captain that Harvard loved? He gripped the key around his neck, and suddenly it didn't feel like such a sweet gift anymore.

"Were you Harmonized when you gave me this?" he asked.

They squeezed their eyes shut. "Does it matter?"

"You were!"

"No!" Chavi insisted. "But what I'm saying is—I mean, if I found a way to be better version of me, then shouldn't I—"

"So did I fall in love with a 'better version' of you?" Harvard asked. "Or did I fall in love with *you*?"

"I—um—" Chavi stammered.

"You don't know. How can you not know?"

"I was just...I was trying to be better for you."

"I don't know you at all," Harvard whispered, shaking his head. He took a step back, remembering the conversation he'd had with Rivka. Chavi had permanently injured someone when they were sixteen, and never told Harvard about it.

"You do!" Chavi insisted, stepping toward him.

"Stay back," he said without meaning to, and he could see the hurt on Chavi's face.

"I'm not gonna hurt you, Harvard," they said.

"You already have."

Harvard yanked on the key, and the cord broke.

* * *

Before Chavi could assure him they'd only ever cared about him, that it was all for *him*, Harvard lobbed the key at them. They ducked just before it pelted them in the face. The metal projectile crashed into the mirror, leaving spider-web cracks on the glass. Chavi looked at the broken mirror, and their own jagged reflection in it, in a combination of shock and horror. *He doesn't mean this*, they thought, *he can't possibly mean this.*

But when they turned back to Harvard, his eyes bore into them, his fists clenched, and they knew they were losing him. Drowning again. Harvard was the only person who could pull them to safety. The desperation hit them like a building caving in, and they fell to their knees.

"Harvard, listen to me," they begged. "I can explain it all. I promise—"

"Founders, I'm so stupid!" Harvard buried his face in his hands. "I saw you hit Adri just 'cause you were a little jealous! I saw you kill three people! I saw you *burn down Haven*! And I forgave you for all of it! Because I was the idiot that actually thought I knew you."

"You do know me!" Chavi insisted again.

"Really? Because all I know is you promised me you would tell me if there was something I should know and you broke your promise again and again. All I know is you keep dragging me into things I don't want to be a part of and you don't have the decency to even tell me about it. And now I know you're more than happy to tell everyone about the thing I've spent my whole life trying to run away from. I thought...I thought you were good, Chavi! I thought you were good!"

"I—"

They couldn't protest. Because they weren't good, were they? They never were. The teachers at school knew it. The principal knew it when he expelled them for putting Carter in the hospital. Marcel knew it the moment he met them. And Devrin? He had known all along, hadn't he? That's why he wanted to recruit them. He knew what they were. They could blame it all they wanted on the beast living inside them, but that was only an excuse. If anything, their body was only just starting to reflect the person they'd been all along.

Destructive. Uncontrollable. *Violent.*

"I can change," they finally said, their voice tightening with tears.

"Then why haven't you?" Harvard asked.

At that, every last shred of pride Chavi had vanished, and their desperation only deepened. *I can't lose him, I can't.*

They grabbed at the hem of Harvard's shirt.

"Please," they begged. "Please believe me. I love you. I love you. I love you." Not so long ago, Chavi had struggled to say those words. Now that they were a desperate lifeline, they came so easily. "Please, please Harvard. Please listen to me. I love you. Please."

Harvard's face hardened in a way Chavi had never seen before.

"Don't touch me," he said, placing both hands on their shoulders and shoving them away from him. They fell back, astonished, staring up at him and, to their surprise, shaking. *It's over. I've lost him.*

"I think," Harvard said coolly, "you should leave."

Chavi took a shaky breath and picked themself up. There was nothing to do but nod. It pained them moving toward the door when all they wanted was to wrap their arms around him, to hold him close and assure him they'd never, ever hurt him again, to cry into his shoulder while he pet their head. But he wanted them gone, and that knowledge hurt like a gut wound.

They placed a hand on the door frame, wondering if they should ask the question that tormented them. They turned back slightly, and could see Harvard watching them go.

"Do you...still love me?" they asked.

Harvard winced.

"I...I don't know," he admitted.

Chavi nodded slowly, still holding back tears. And they left Harvard alone, just like he wanted.

* * *

It shouldn't have felt good. Hurting someone should never feel good. But Harvard was just so angry, it had given him a kind of satisfaction to see Chavi so wounded, to know that he had that kind of power over them. He'd never felt that powerful before. But it was wrong, and he knew that, and the moment they were out the door he regretted all of it.

Of course, he still loved them. Love didn't just dissipate that easily, especially not his. Still, it would take the two of them a long time to get past this. There would be more difficult discussions and more tears. But he knew he wasn't just going to let them go that easily, and he felt like an idiot for letting his anger get the better of him. He shouldn't have made them leave.

He thought back to his dismissal of Speedy, and August's response to finding out the truth of his upbringing. If the Ivies didn't want him anymore, and Speedy was gone, then who did Harvard even have?

Harvard ran for the door, starting to go after them, but he stopped himself as he closed his fingers around the doorknob. Chavi would come back eventually. He knew that. And when they did, he would tell them everything. They'd make up and they'd snuggle on the bed and things would be just like they used to be.

Harvard let go of the doorknob, threw himself onto the bed and buried his face in the pillow, willing Chavi to come back and willing himself not to cry.

* * *

Chavi let the door slam behind them as they walked out into the hot summer night. They walked a few paces before they slammed their fist against the wall.

"Fuck!" they cried. They'd ruined everything, hadn't they? Part of them wanted to curl up right here and sob, but they wouldn't let themself do that. Walking at night always made them feel better. So, they made themself walk.

They wound through side streets, hoping they could lose themself. Part of them wanted to disappear into the night and never return. Just to stop existing altogether. It was a delicious thought. *Just pull yourself together,* they told themself, *then you can go back.* They remembered August's words when he had pushed them in the bathtub. *Is your shit together? Say it. Say you have your shit together.* The thought would have made them feel better if it wasn't a reminder of how August probably hated them now, too.

A silhouette appeared at the end of the street.

Chavi froze. It was probably nothing, just someone out to smoke late at night, but still, Chavi had lived in Lower Bastion long enough to know that you want to avoid encountering strangers in the dark. They turned around, only to see another figure appear at the other end of the street. Too many of the streetlamps out here were broken for Chavi to make out any features, but they recognized the voice behind them.

"Fancy meeting you here, Chaverim! Out for an evening stroll? I suppose it is a nice night for it."

"What are you doing here?" Chavi demanded, turning to see Devrin. They had no doubt it was Pierce approaching from the other end. They even wondered if there were other Delian Guards hiding in the shadows.

Devrin shrugged. "Enjoying the night air, of course. It's a good thing I ran into you, though. I've been wanting to pass along my apologies."

"You're apologizing?" Chavi asked.

"Yes, I'm very sorry to hear about that falling out with your friends. Poor Harvard especially must be devastated. You really messed this one up, didn't you? No coming back from that one." He tsked, shaking his head. "Yes, I fear you've burned those bridges completely."

"What are you talking about?" Chavi said, though the real question was *"How do you know what you're talking about?"*

"You *know* what I'm talking about. The little spat that got you kicked out of the Ivies. Don't worry about them. Jasmine will make an excellent captain in your stead."

"She's not—what are you—"

"Oh my dear," his brow creased in a caricature of sympathy. "I really *did* think it was going to be obvious by now. You honestly think I would let Harmony circles exist in the city without keeping an eye on them? You thought the Zuris hadn't been meticulously tracking its circulation? And Jasmine glimpsed your transaction record by sheer chance?"

Chavi inhaled sharply. "Mellie..."

"Is my employee, yes," Devrin nodded. "So long as my agents report back to me, I let their little crews get away with misbehaving every now and again. As a treat. Thanks to Mellie's help, the rift between you and your friends looks totally organic to the outside observer. And believe me, there *is* an outside observer. This has got me thinking. You just lost your crew—"

"I didn't lose my crew!" Chavi said, though admittedly they were beginning to feel like this wasn't true.

He gave them a pitying look. "I wouldn't be so sure about that. You stole from them, lied to them, and you even researched Harvard's little secret behind his back—"

"*You* were the one who told me—"

"I know I did," he covered his mouth as he giggled, as if to say, *"Oops!"* "Silly me. Point is, I can't expect they'll be forgiving you any time this century."

Chavi shook their head. "You don't know them."

"I'm afraid I know all of you a bit better than you think. Which is why I came up with this silly little idea. You need a crew. I could use some assistance. Why don't you join my team?"

"I'd rather die," Chavi spat.

Devrin cocked his head, considering this. "Well, I can make that happen, but I was rather hoping it wouldn't come to that."

That searing sensation burned in their veins, one that was all too familiar by now. Devrin didn't know about what they could do, about the desertwalker that lived in their blood. They could kill him so easily, and he had no idea. For this first time tonight—for the first time in a long time, actually—Chavi had the upper hand.

"You think you're so smart," they said. "You think you have me all figured out."

"Chaverim, I do," Devrin said.

"You don't know what I can do. You don't know what I'm capable of. If you think you can manipulate me anymore, you're an idiot."

"What, your new party trick?" he raised an eyebrow. "Yes, I'm well aware of that. That's precisely why I think you'd be such an excellent addition to the team."

"Wha—" Chavi started. Everything snapped into perspective.

"I told you. I know all of you better than you think. All I needed was a sample of your blood, and you very kindly bled for me that night you fought the scorpioncrab. I sent you on a vacation to keep you out of the way while I did my research, and it turns out I was right. You're *exactly* what I need. You can try to run away now, if you want, but I assure you it's too late."

"I have killed people," they hissed, tensing. "And if anyone gets too close to me, I'll kill them too."

"Oh, no one will be getting close to you," Devrin waved a hand. "No need. Remember that venom you got for me?" He produced something thin and sharp from his suit pocket. A dart. "It's not lethal, but it does make an awfully convenient tranquilizer. You know"—his eyes looked Chavi about and down appraisingly—"like you might use on a wild animal."

Chavi found themself caught between fight and flight instincts. They wanted so badly to let loose the creature inside, to tear Devrin apart—but if what he said was true about the tranquilizer, they wouldn't last very long.

Devrin took one step toward them, spinning the dart in his hand. "Go ahead," he said. "Run."

Chavi ran.

They bolted down an alley toward home, their feet pounding on the asphalt.

"Harvard!" they shouted. "Harvard!" He could probably hear them from here. He wasn't so angry with them that he'd completely abandon them when they called, right?

A dart bit into their calf. They pulled it free before it could pour much of the venom out.

"Harvard!" they shouted again. He had to hear them. They were getting so close. They could make it back home if they just—

Another dart pierced their shoulder. They moved to pull it out, but already their limbs grew heavier. They suddenly became aware of the sound of their own heartbeat in their ears, and it was thunderous, and it was slowing down. Every footfall took momentous effort.

They pulled the dart free.

"Harvard?" they asked, but suddenly it was too much effort to yell. Another dart hit their neck, and by now it was too difficult to lift their arms and remove it. They weren't sure when they stopped running, but the ground came up to meet them and they realized they were on their hands and knees, taking labored breaths.

"Harvard," they whispered, and now they knew it wasn't a call. It was only a wish.

"He's not coming, I'm afraid," Devrin said, and Chavi could hear his casual footfalls on the asphalt. He knelt in front of them, and gently lifted their chin so they were looking at him. "No one is coming, actually. You see, no one loves you anymore. You belong to me now, Chaverim. But don't you worry. I'll take such good care of you, dear, and we'll do such wonderful things."

He let go of Chavi's face, and their head fell. They were unconscious before their face hit the asphalt.

* * *

Harvard fell asleep waiting for Chavi's return. In his dreams, he could have sworn he heard them shouting his name.

Interlude Twelve: Kathy

Kathy couldn't remember the last time she cried, but now, she sobbed. She sat at the foot of her bed, buried her face in a pillow and screamed. All the years of her life she'd been chained to her guilt over that idiot boy. She'd been weighed down by the secret knowledge that she'd been to blame for his death.

And now?

He wasn't even dead. And he didn't even want to come back.

Which meant she'd been torturing herself over nothing.

She wanted to hate him. She wanted so badly to blame him for all of it, for ruining her life, for making her the monster that she was.

Somehow, though, she still couldn't do it. There was still a seed of remorse inside her that refused to die.

Well, no matter. Maybe she couldn't get herself to hate him. But a torrent of rage still churned inside her, and she hoped she'd never, ever see his face again.

Somehow, she expected she wouldn't be so lucky.

CHAPTER TWENTY-FIVE

A Choice

Chavi once again dreamt they were being buried alive in that familiar metal box. Their head pounded, and they groaned weakly as they shifted their weight—

No.

This wasn't a dream.

They reached their hand out as their awareness slowly returned. Cold metal inches from their face. Slim shafts of light streaming in from a grate just in front of their face. Instinctively they reached up to press against the ceiling, but they found their hands manacled, chained so they couldn't raise their wrists any higher than their waist.

They slammed their fists against the wall in front of them. It reverberated with a metallic clang.

"Hey!" they shouted. They tried again to raise their hands to claw at the grate, but again the chains yanked their wrists down.

"Hey!" they cried again, this time throwing their weight against the front of the box. Nothing moved.

"Let me out!" they screamed to no one. They looked out the grate. They could see a cinderblock wall in front of them, but even straining to look from either side, they couldn't see anything else. If anyone was there, they were out of view, and they made no effort to help.

"Let me go!" Chavi begged, repeatedly ramming their open palms against the metal walls. They struggled in their restraints until their wrists were bloodied, and they screamed until their voice was ragged, but nothing changed.

Defeated, they slumped against the wall of their claustrophobic cell. There wasn't even enough room to bend their legs and sit.

Only then did Devrin appear in front of the grate. He gave a cheerful wiggle of his fingers.

"This isn't happening," Chavi groaned.

"It is, I'm afraid," Devrin pouted.

"Let me go," Chavi begged again, already exhausted from their initial pleas. How long had Devrin stood there while they pleaded? An hour? Two?

"Or you'll do what? You're not very threatening, Chaverim. At least, not right now. Not to me."

Chavi felt a surge of panic.

"Harvard!" they exclaimed. They imagined him in a metal crate of his own, terrified and alone. "Jasmine, August—Are they—"

"They're fine," Devrin waved a hand. "I don't care about them anymore. The only thing that matters now"—he placed a hand gently on the grate that separated their faces—"is you."

Chavi deflated a little, leaning back against the metal behind them.

"I don't want to matter," they said.

"Too late," Devrin shrugged. "You mattered the moment you and your compatriots became the second human beings to make a contract with a desertwalker."

Chavi stood up straighter, eyes wide. "How do you know—wait, second?"

"How do I know?" Devrin laughed. "Why else would a group of scavengers, fresh from the dusts, have any interest in rescuing a baby crab? I mean, we knew the scuttlers were going to try something at that conference, but we didn't actually think they'd rope humans in again, not after last time."

Chavi reeled, struggling to grasp everything. "What does *that* mean?"

"It means things are changing, for humans and desertwalkers alike. I want you to join my team."

"I told you, I'd rather die."

"And that's a choice you have a right to make," he nodded. "But like I said, I rather hope it doesn't come to that. Allow me to explain: there is a war going on in Bastion. The city must expand, and whoever controls that expansion controls the future of humanity. The war is invisible to the citizens, but it has been waged for years where no one could see."

"The Underground City?" Chavi guessed, remembering what Avi had overheard.

He nodded. "You must understand, if we allow Allura to control the shape of the future, she will drive all of us to extinction. If she founds her new city before we found ours, then we've already lost. I'm working toward a future where humanity survives by any means necessary. And *you* are the poster child of survival. You sustained a fatal wound and *adapted*. There's a lot we can learn from that. Allura has always tried to brute force nature to bend to her will. I often told her I thought it was pointless, even dangerous. And then I stumbled upon you. Now, I don't believe in fate, but sometimes I'm tempted to. It's like I was meant to find you, you beautiful freak of nature. And I want you on my side."

"I'm not on anyone's side!" Chavi protested. They didn't care if Bastion expanded, and they certainly didn't care who was doing the expanding. They didn't want to be a beautiful freak of nature. They wanted to go home.

Devrin frowned pityingly. "I'm afraid that's not how this works. You're always on a side. And if it's not mine, it's the enemy's. You see, you are a powerful weapon, Chaverim. And I cannot risk a powerful weapon falling into enemy hands."

A weapon. So that's what the desertwalker in their blood had reduced them to. An oddity. A monster.

Devrin must have read the despondency on their face, because he hurriedly added, "No no! You misunderstand. I'm doing you a *favor*. I'm protecting you. You're much better off with me than with Allura, I promise you that, and I can guarantee you that if you weren't with me— if I hadn't taken great pains to keep her from finding out about you—you would be much worse off. I know you don't like me. But Allura? She's *evil*."

"*She's* evil?" Chavi repeated incredulously. "You put me in a box!"

"Well, that's as much your fault as it is mine," Devrin asserted defensively. "If it weren't for the box, wouldn't you have killed me already?"

Chavi didn't answer, but their manacled hands curled into fists so tight their fingernails bit into their palms. He was right, of course, and that was infuriating because he knew it and he was all smiley about it.

"So." He tapped on the metal demonstratively. "Box! But if you would, try not focus on the box so much as the benefits. This is a trade offer, really. I provide you safety, and in return you'll give me some help."

"So what do you want from me?" they asked.

"Your service. Your loyalty. Be a soldier in my army."

Chavi paused, considering this. If it meant that their friends were safe..."Would I have to kill?" they asked.

Devrin looked at them incredulously. "What exactly do you think a soldier *does*, Chaverim? The thing is, I think you'll enjoy it. You've killed before. You said so yourself."

"But I didn't want—I didn't mean to—"

"A good soldier never wants to kill. But they still enjoy it."

Chavi pressed their back against the cold metal. Carter, Minty, Lyle, Bristull, Trevor. It had to end. They *needed* it to end. "I can't do it. I can't."

"Such a decision should not be made rashly. I'll give you some time to think it over. An hour, as a matter of fact," he said, glancing at his watch. "And once I've returned, you tell me your decision."

Maybe the only way to end the string of bodies left in their wake was to make *themself* their final victim.

So Chavi did use their hour to think. And by the end of that hour, it didn't seem like much of a decision at all.

Interlude Thirteen: Speedy

When Speedy returned to the familiar sands of the dusts, no comfort awaited him. It was not that his brethren did not welcome him. As he weaved his way through the dim corridors of the den, his siblings extended their claws to stroke his carapace in welcome, some chittering their congratulations. Speedy did not feel congratulations were in order. His first independent assignment has been an unmitigated disaster, and he feared his siblings already knew this, which made their pitying platitudes all the more humiliating.

Speedy found his father in the central hollow of the den, in conference with the Empress Myrk. When Skrack caught sight of his son, he requested the Empress's pardon, which she readily gave.

Welcome back, Guardian-to-Be Bryk, the Empress said with a cordial tilt of her carapace. For a fleeting moment, Speedy forgot that Bryk was *him*. He'd become so accustomed to the name that Harvard had gifted him so long ago that he had nearly forgotten his true name. And it *was* his true name. It was past time that he doffed the silly diminutive Harvard had presumptuously placed on him. He was Bryk, and one day he would be a Guardian of the Southwest Plains.

Today, though, he was nothing but a disappointment.

I have failed you, father, Speedy said once he and his father were alone. His father already knew what had transpired—Speedy had kept him apprised via his tether to Essence—but he still felt it his duty to announce his shame.

Failed? Skrack repeated, extended a claw to Speedy. He dutifully climbed upon his father's pincer. *No, my child. It is the humans that have failed you. It is I who has failed you, infected by the goodwill of the Empress. In a moment of weakness, I succumbed to the will of the humans. I gifted my blood to one of their kind, and in doing so, unknowingly gifted my Essence. The humans have something holy in their possession, and yet they exile you? For no crime other than serving as their Guardian?*

Guardian, Speedy reflected. Not Guardian-To-Be. Speedy's father saw him as a proper Guardian.

Do not hate them, father, Speedy pleaded. *At least, do not hate Harvard.* Despite the unfortunate circumstances under which they parted, Speedy could not find it in himself to be angry with Harvard. Only sad for him.

No. No, I do not hate Harvard, Skrack admitted.

I am glad.

But I must correct my error.

His tone was dangerous in a manner Speedy did not understand. He tilted his little body up toward Skrack inquisitively, meeting his father's inky eyes. *What do you mean, Father?*

The abomination must die.

CHAPTER TWENTY-SIX

The New Captain of the Ivies

Jasmine stared into her coffee, hands cupped around the mug for warmth. She wasn't cold. Still, the heat felt nice on her skin. Right now, she just needed something in her life that felt nice.

"Good morning," she heard August say as he clomped down the stairs.

"It doesn't feel like one," she grumbled. "It's a pretty awful morning, if I'm being honest with myself."

"Yeah," August dropped down in the seat across from her. "It really is, huh?"

"I feel bad about last night," Jasmine said. "Not guilty-bad, though. Just generally bad. Is that terrible of me?" She looked up at August for affirmation. He shook his head.

"You didn't do anything wrong," he said.

"I do think maybe we were too hard on Chavi."

"Nah." He waved his hand. "They totally deserved it. If everything you said is true."

"It is, unfortunately."

"Then this was all long overdue. And I'll be expecting some big apologies today."

"No," Jasmine looked down at the bubbles in her coffee. "I'm tired of apologies."

She heard Harvard's gentle footfalls on the stairs.

"C'mere, little dude," August waved for him to come over. Harvard slunk over to the chair next to August, who draped an arm around him as he sat. He propped his head up in his hands, as if he was struggling to hold it up. He looked exhausted. Jasmine wondered if he had slept at all.

"How was the rest of your night?" August asked, overcompensating with cheeriness. Jasmine thought back to the day of the Conference, which now felt like decades ago, when August had distracted Harvard with games. He was surprisingly sensitive when he wanted to be, wasn't he?

"Bad," Harvard said into the heel of his hand. August glanced over his shoulder, toward the stairs.

"Is, uh, is Chavi still upstairs?" he asked. Harvard shook his head.

"Chavi didn't come to bed last night. They went out. I figured when they got back, they'd sleep on the couch..." he trailed off as he leaned back to look past August, at the vacant sofa.

"I've been up since five," Jasmine said. "They haven't been in."

"Wait a second," August said, and she could hear a fresh wave of anger under his words. "After everything that happened last night, they just...left? Just like that?"

"No, it's..." Harvard wrung his hands. "I told them to. After you all went to bed, we kept fighting, and...I sort of told them to get out." He looked to Jasmine as if for approval. She didn't know what had passed between them, but if Harvard had wanted Chavi out, then he was within his right to say so. She nodded knowingly.

"Okay, so...where the quaking fuck are they?" August asked.

"Where they always go when they're upset, I expect," Jasmine sighed. "Their mother's house."

"Can we go get them?" Harvard asked. August snorted. "I feel guilty. About last night," Harvard explained. "I need to talk to them."

"Why do you two feel so quaking guilty all the time?" August asked. "We were in the right! We don't owe them anything! We have nothing to feel guilty about!"

Harvard bowed his head.

"Last night, when we were alone...I said some things I shouldn't have said. Bad things. Things I didn't mean. I need to...I just need to see them. Now."

August gave an exaggerated eye roll.

"Sure," Jasmine said, "we can go get them."

She hoped she was right about Chavi being at their mother's.

"So you guys—" Harvard started, then cut himself off.

"What?" August asked. Harvard seemed to shrink in on himself.

"You guys aren't mad at me, too? For lying."

"Your past," Jasmine said, "is none of our business. Our money is. There's a big difference between what you did and what Chavi did, Harvard."

He let out a shaky breath that Jasmine guessed he had been holding.

"I do wish you'd been honest with us," she continued, "but I don't hold it against you."

"What she said," August agreed, standing. "Now if we're gonna go, let's go."

When they arrived at Rivka's, she seemed delighted and confused to see the three of them appear at her door.

"Oh! I didn't expect you all would be coming today. Come in, do you—"

"It's alright," Jasmine cut her off. She didn't really feel like being here longer than she had to. "We won't be long. We're just looking for Chavi."

The crease in Rivka's brow deepened. "Oh. Well, they're not here. I would have assumed they were with you?"

"Are you sure?" August asked, and Jasmine surprised herself when she felt an urge to snap at him. Yes, of course she was sure. Wouldn't you think she would know if her own child was in her own house?

"I mean, they were here two nights ago," Rivka offered, then with a tentative glance to Harvard as though she were asking for permission. "They were upset."

"We got into a fight two nights ago," Harvard clarified for the benefit of the other two, scratching the back of his head. August looked down at him.

"About what?" he asked.

"August!" Jasmine scolded.

"I'm just asking!"

"It was...it was nothing," Harvard said. "It wasn't even a fight, really. Just a...misunderstanding."

Rivka nodded slowly. "Well, that's good to hear. They were...very worried about you." She reached out and gave his shoulder a squeeze. "They care about you so, so much. You know that, don't you Harvard? All of you." She looked at the other two, and though Jasmine did her best to school her face, Rivka must have noticed something off.

"Is everything alright?" she asked.

"Yes!" Jasmine said too quickly. "Everything is fine."

Rivka didn't look convinced. She frowned, crossing her arms. "I know it's none of my business," she said, "but whatever they did...I hope you won't be *too* hard on them. They mean well."

"We know," Harvard said quietly.

Their farewells with Rivka were awkward and uneasy, and Jasmine felt guilty for worrying her, she was starting to worry herself.

"So what was the fight about?" August asked Harvard again. This time Jasmine didn't protest. She did want to know.

Harvard wrung his hands. "So...I didn't know about the Harmony situation at the time, so I didn't really know what was going on, but...another group of Harmony people tried to kill them."

"What?" August gasped. "How could you not tell us this?"

"Chavi made me promise not to tell."

"Of course they did," Jasmine grumbled. She felt there was more to the story Harvard wasn't telling them, but right now, she'd heard enough. Besides, she was hungry, and as soon as she got home all she wanted was to make herself something to eat with the meager food they still had lying around.

She couldn't afford herself that luxury, though, because almost as soon as they got home, someone was pounding on their door. Jasmine answered it to see Avi standing there, her eyes uncharacteristically wild.

"Where is Chavi?" she demanded, pushing past Jasmine.

"We don't know!" August said, throwing himself onto the couch. "We had a sorta fight last night when we found out about all the shit they did, and instead of apologizing like a normal person, they ran away."

"They did apologize," Harvard said quietly, but Avi didn't seem to hear him. She sank into a chair, holding her head in her hands.

"No no no," she was saying to herself, "shit shit shit."

"What's going on?" Jasmine asked.

"Chavi is not coming back," Avi said into her palms. "And it's my fault. I didn't realize it soon enough, and—"

"Whoa." August lifted his head. "What are you talking about? They're just off somewhere having a little pity party. They'll be back."

"They won't," Avi insisted, "because the Delian Group already has them."

"If the Delian Group wanted them detained, why didn't they do it before?" Jasmine asked.

"Listen, I—" Avi made a claw-like gesture with her hands, as though she were grasping for the right words but couldn't. "I made all the wrong assumptions. About this city about how it works. I thought they could do whatever they wanted. But they can't. Because they're racing the Satsuki Group to something."

"But the corps work together," August said. "That's what we were always taught."

"How much of what we were taught about this city is actually true?" Jasmine asked.

"They've formed alliances," Avi explained. "And the Delian Group needed a weapon of their own. And since they're already allied with the Zuri Institution—"

"A bioweapon," Jasmine whispered.

Avi nodded gravely. "Once he was able to confirm his suspicions, all he had to do was keep an eye on you. And ensure that you had a reason to kick Chavi out of the house when the time was right, so no one would think it amiss when they disappeared."

"Are you trying to say that Devrin made us fight? You actually think he did that on purpose?"

"Where do you think Harmony comes from?" Avi asked. "The Zuri Institution makes, sells it, and keeps track of its sales."

"The girl at the Festival," Jasmine cut in. "The one with pink hair. She didn't have to tell me, or show me the account slips. But she did. She said..." Jasmine pulled at her hair. "She said she'd already been paid."

Harvard stood up abruptly. Jasmine realized he'd hardly spoken this whole time. He'd listened to Avi intently as she gave her explanation, his face unreadable. Now he stumbled over to the kitchen sink and vomited. Jasmine didn't move to help him. She didn't feel like she could move at all. She couldn't believe she'd been stupid enough to allow herself to be manipulated, to be turned against her best friend. She'd been coaxed into expelling Chavi the same way they'd been coaxed into the Harmony Circle in the first place. She looked at Avi, who stared forward, blankly. Only August seemed unaffected.

"So, what are you saying?" he sat up. "That Chavi is just like, gone? Just like that?"

"I don't know what the Delian Group wants with them." Avi shook her head. "But if what they want is a bioweapon—"

"We'll never see them again," Jasmine whispered, but the words didn't feel real. Harvard retched again.

"This is all my fault," he groaned. Jasmine knew he was wrong, but she couldn't find it in herself to contradict him. She discovered she was trembling. Steadying himself on the kitchen counter, Harvard turned, wiping his mouth with the back of his hand. "There's gotta be something we can do," he said, and his voice sounded frantic. "Some way we can get them back."

"Right, like when we traded to get Harvard back!" August said, running his hands through his hair. "Maybe he wants us to do another job."

Avi shook her head. "I don't think any of this was ever about getting you to do a job."

"There has to be a way we can get them back," Harvard insisted. Avi bit her lip.

"The aquarium," Jasmine said. "If anyone intends to meet with us, that's where they'd be. If we're supposed to make some kind of trade, that's where we'd be expected to go."

Avi and Jasmine exchanged a look. They had nothing to trade. What good could come of it? Still, she couldn't fathom doing nothing. She'd been furious with Chavi, sure, but she didn't want them *gone*. She wanted them to be *better*, not *dead*.

"Okay," Avi finally said.

When they stood outside the aquarium, Jasmine had the dizzying sensation of having come full circle. It didn't feel like too long ago that they'd stood outside this same building in the hopes of saving Harvard. She never thought she'd be gripping a gun in the desperate hope of saving Chavi.

"Guys," August said, "before we go in there, I think—"

Harvard ran ahead of the group and shoved the boarded up doors aside.

"Harvard, wait!" Avi cried.

"Chavi!" Harvard called, his voice echoing in the cavernous building. "Chavi!"

The other three followed suit, charging into the decrepit wreck that now felt oddly familiar to them, Harvard's cries growing more and more desperate. Once they reached the same room where they'd first traded for Harvard, all four of them stopped.

Pierce leaned against one of the tanks. He regarded the Ivies with the same tired indifference that an old dog watches a kitten trying to attack. In fact, his face did bear a striking resemblance to an old dog—tired and scruffy with big sad eyes.

"Where is Chavi?" Jasmine demanded. She pointed the gun at him for extra effect, but he didn't seem to notice.

"Gone."

"Then why are you here?"

"To tell you they're gone."

"That's it?" August asked. "We don't have to go to another island or fight a crab or—"

Pierce sighed. "No, because that's what *he* does. But he doesn't even know I'm here. He'd probably have forbidden it if he did. But I..." Pierce looked on the Ivies pityingly. "I was a scavenger. I knew what crews are like. I know how attached you get to each other, even after you return to the city and start living your own lives. You just can't be the person you used to be. You're just not the same person without the other three there. You start to see yourself as a piece of the group. I mean, look at you all. How long has it been since you've been scavengers? And you still call yourselves the Ivies. You see the four of you as a whole, and you always will."

"Just answer the question," Avi snapped.

"What I'm trying to tell you," he said, "is that I'm here because I know that when a member of your crew disappears, your instinct is to find them. And I'm risking a lot right now to be here and tell you: *do not do that.*"

"We're going to get Chavi back," Harvard said.

"No, you're not," Pierce rubbed his face. "And you can't. You just can't. And you're only going to get hurt trying. You're just going to have to accept—"

"I'm not going to accept anything!" Harvard shouted, charging Pierce. August lunged forward, wrapping an arm around his waist to restrain him. "I want Chavi back! Give them back!" Harvard struggled against August's grip, but he couldn't break free. Pierce only looked sad. He sighed.

"I didn't wanna have to do this."

They immediately tensed. Jasmine cocked the gun.

"I'm not gonna hurt you!" he said, sounding more annoyed than frightened. "I just hate being the bearer of bad news. But if you really won't listen to me, well...you've left me no choice."

He produced a leather band from his pocket. Jasmine sucked in a breath.

A captain's band.

Pierce strode forward and gently removed one of Jasmine's hands from the gun. She was too stunned to pull away. He placed the band gently in her palm and closed her fingers around it.

"I think they'd want you to have this."

"What does this mean?" Jasmine demanded, but she already knew the answer. Pierce regarded her with sympathetic eyes.

"I thought," he said, "it would be easier on all of you if you didn't know the truth. You could live the rest of your lives believing that your friend was still out there somewhere. But they had a choice, and—" he cut himself off. He turned to Harvard, who was looking at the band in Jasmine's hand with wide eyes.

"I'm sorry, Harvard," Pierce said. "I've been there before. I know it's not easy."

"No," Harvard said absently, shaking his head, "you're lying to us."

"I'm not," Pierce said. "I did my best to get you all to trust me, and I have no control over whether or not you do. But right now, I need you to believe me." He inhaled slowly, locking eyes with Jasmine. "Chavi is dead."

Jasmine's breath caught. She believed him.

"No," Harvard said again, his voice breaking. August laid a hand on his shoulder.

"If Chavi is dead," Avi challenged, "then where's the body?"

Pierce looked at her ruefully. "You really don't want an answer to that question."

Avi crossed her arms. "I do."

Pierce sighed. "Given that Chavi is a bit of a medical anomaly," he said, "the Zuri Institution has requested...research privileges."

August made a hissing sound. Harvard groaned quietly. Pierce only shook his head.

"I'm sorry," he repeated. "I wish there was more I could do. But I'm afraid..." He looked directly at Jasmine. "I'm afraid you're on your own now." He reached for her, and Jasmine tensed, even though she knew he would not hurt her. He only patted her on the shoulder, and whispered quietly enough that none of the others could hear, "Take care of them, alright? You're the captain now. That means something."

Then he strode toward the door, leaving the Ivies alone.

Jasmine examined the band in her hand, then looked at the other three. Harvard was hugging himself, staring at the ground, his face unreadable. August had a hand on Harvard's back, but he was watching Jasmine. Avi, too, kept her eyes on Jasmine, her face schooled to show none of the emotions that Jasmine knew were there. She had so many questions she wanted to ask them all. Did they believe it was true? What should they do next? What would happen now?

She couldn't bring herself to say anything at all.

August nodded to the captain's band in her hand. "Put it on," he whispered. Jasmine swallowed. Putting on the captain's band felt wrong. Felt like cementing the fact that Chavi would not be coming back.

"I can't," she rasped.

"He was right," August said. "It's what they would have wanted."

Jasmine turned over the worn leather in her hands. Slowly, she wrapped it around her wrist, and fastened the buckle in place.

Only then did Avi start to sob.

* * *

Harvard didn't really know what happened after they left the aquarium.

He was vaguely aware of the walk home, of people speaking to him but he couldn't hear what they were saying, of time passing, of day turning into night turning into day turning into night. He could only think one thing: *Chavi is dead and I killed them. Chavi is dead and I killed them.* If he hadn't forced them out of the house—if he'd only told them that he still loved them—none of this would have happened.

In his mind, he played back every moment they'd made him smile. The piano. Their dinner together, and the ride in the pedi-cab that followed. The night they'd shared wine on Haven, drunk on their own mischievousness. The tattoo Harvard had drawn for them, a permanent reminder of the way they took care of each other.

When he got home, we went to his bedroom and found the key he'd thrown at the mirror, and he saw for the first time cracks in the glass. He turned it over in his hands. The only gift that anyone had ever given him, and now the person who had given it to him was dead. The only person who had ever loved him, and they were dead. He remembered the way he sat at their bedside after the Conference, willing their eyes to open. All he'd had to do was say their name. Now there was nothing he could do. He felt like he could hear the sound of their voice and the touch of their hand on his back, just out of reach. As though if he imagined hard enough, they would appear. He willed them to appear in the doorway, laughing, saying this was all some horrible practical joke and everything was fine, actually, and they'd never do it again.

He wanted to go back to last night, to grab their wrist and say, "Don't go. I love you. Please stay. I love you." Maybe it wouldn't have mattered. Maybe Devrin would have come for them anyway. But at least he could have been there, put his body in front of theirs, and said "if you want them, you'll have to kill me." Chavi would have done the same for him. He knew that.

Jasmine and August and Avi all checked on him to see if he was okay, but they knew that he wasn't, so there was nothing to be done. He'd sometimes become aware of them watching him, encouraging him to eat or drink or speak to them, please, just say something, but it all felt like a dream, and he couldn't seem to bring himself to do anything. All he could do was sleep, because in his dreams Chavi was there, and it was the only time he got to see them again.

Every morning, Harvard woke up expecting to find Chavi next to him. Every day he walked downstairs into the kitchen and expected them to walk through the doors. He expected them to take him in their arms and say, "I told you I would always come back for you."

And they had told him that, hadn't they?

They promised.

That was their final lie, and it hurt the most, because when they'd said it they hadn't even realized that they were lying.

But days passed, and Chavi did not come back for him.

Weeks passed, and Chavi did not come back for him.

The weight of their absence, and the knowledge that he only had himself to blame, pulled him down like a stone in water. Eventually, it was too much of a struggle for him to even get out of bed. He lay there, knowing that Chavi would never come back for him again. And then one day he decided it was too much. He grabbed the satchel that had been with him now for so long and slung it over his shoulder.

He packed the gun.

He could not be Harvard anymore. He had tried being Harvard, but he'd failed.

He could only be Ronan Bell.

For the last time in his life, Ronan Bell ran away.

This time, he had the courtesy to leave a note.

It simply read: *I can't do this anymore.*

Epilogue

At first, Ariel didn't feel the pain. Just the impact, as though they'd been punched, and the air forced out of their lungs. The hands holding them allowed them to drop, and they fell forward onto their hands and knees, one hand clutching at the hilt of the knife still buried in their gut.

"Thanks for everything, Ariel," Trevor said, and they wanted to say something, anything to him, but already blood worked its way up their throat and onto their lips. The arm supporting them buckled, and they fell onto their side. From the ground, they could only see the movement of the Concertos' shoes as they left the room, and closed the door behind them.

Ariel was left to bleed out alone.

As they drew ragged breaths, they wondered if they deserved this.

They were only trying to do a good thing. And Harmony *was* a good thing. They still believed that, after everything. They believed in the power of their circle, even though most of them were dead. They couldn't bring themself to think that they'd actually done anything wrong—even selling out Chavi, since clearly Trevor was after them regardless. Chavi would understand, surely. They were part of the circle. And the circle understood each other.

At least they could die without regrets.

The door opened.

Ariel saw a pair of work boots enter the room, easily sidestepping the bodies as though they weren't there. The boots paused in front of Ariel's face. With great effort, they turned their head to face up, and they saw white wings, and the glittering of many eyes. For a moment, they were put in mind of the pre-Quake legends of angels, winged helpers of gods with wings and infinite eyes. Had an angel come to visit them at the moment of their death?

"Hm," said the angel, who Ariel now saw was not equipped with wings at all, but instead wore a billowing lab coat. "This is a very unfortunate scene indeed."

The angel sat down beside Ariel, blood seeping into the hem of the lab coat. With a better view, Ariel could now see she was a woman with greying brown hair tied in a messy bun, pencils and pens stuck through it. Her many eyes, as it turned out, were actually just glasses with all sorts of additional lenses that could be flicked into position.

"My name is Allura," she said conversationally. Ariel responded by coughing up blood. Some of it got on the woman's work boots. She didn't seem to mind. "I'd like to offer you a job," Allura continued.

"I'm dying," Ariel rasped.

"I noticed," Allura adjusted her many-faceted glasses. "It's not an ideal trait for an employee, but I can overlook it. In fact, when I save your life, you can consider your payment. What follows, after all, will not be pleasant."

Ariel groaned. They tried to inhale, but blood coated their throat.

"You see, I have this associate," Allura continued. "His name is Devrin. We used to work together, but he betrayed me. And believe it or not, he's betrayed *you* too. It's his job to keep Bastion safe, and yet he knew that one boy's little club was going to come over here and kill your little club, and he didn't do a thing about it. In fact, he saved your friend Mellie, but he didn't bother saving you. I think that's a bit rude, wouldn't you say?" She looked down at Ariel as though waiting for a response, but Ariel only managed to gurgle up blood.

"So I was thinking," Allura mused, "how about we team up and kill him together?"

She looked down at Ariel with a hopeful grin.

Ariel answered by passing out.

END OF BOOK 2 OF THE BASTION CYCLE

ACKNOWLEDGEMENTS

You would think that releasing a first novel would be scarier than releasing a second one, but it turns out releasing a sequel is a whole lot scarier. I am beyond thrilled that so many people enjoyed the first book, but that also meant I had to reckon with exciting and terrifying concepts like "expectations" and "being perceived" and other nightmare fodder. I am so thankful I had so many people to make this journey fun and enjoyable, and who made this book everything it could be.

To start off with, I would be nowhere without the support of my (as of this year) spouse, Noa. His confidence in me is what keeps me going.

An enormous thank you to William C. Tracy for guiding me through this process, seeing right to the heart of the story I wanted to tell and helping me achieve it. I appreciate your patience, your care, and your faith in me. I sing your praises every chance I get.

Thank you, Courtney Brooks, for taking on the herculean task of copy editing something I have written (not once, but TWICE!) I think I finally figured out how to use an em dash, so at least we don't have to worry about that anymore.

My fantastic writers group, The Silent Notetakers Writers Collective, were the first people to read a draft of this novel, even before the first Empress was picked up. I am so grateful to be a part of such a caring and insightful community, who contributed so much to the development of both books. So much gratitude for those who gave me feedback: Shaoni C. White, Yarrow Syskine, J.R. Steele, Delphi Foster, Grace Griego, and H.R. Owen.

I could not have asked for a better cheerleader than Riley Lamarre. They were a beta reader of the second draft, someone to bounce ideas off of, and a kind voice any time I felt down. (Also their original character Eeee for Creature of Ruin cracks me up every time I think about it)

Thank you to everyone who had kind words to say about the first book, especially those who contributed their quotes: Sue Burke, Rob Greene, Alasdair Stuart, Aimee Ogden, and Dawn Vogel.

And if we trace it all back to the beginning, I have my parents to thank for encouraging me to pursue a creative lifestyle and be unapologetically weird.

ABOUT THE AUTHOR

Alex Kingsley (they/them) is a writer, comedian, game designer, and amateur mycologist. They are a co-founder of the new media company Strong Branch Productions, where they write and direct the sci-fi comedy podcast *The Stench of Adventure* and other shows.

Their short fiction has appeared in *Translunar Travelers Lounge, Radon Journal, The Storage Papers*, and more. In 2023 they published their short story collection, *The Strange Garden and Other Weird Tales*. Alex's sci-fi play *The Bearer of Bad News* premiered in LA in 2022 produced by the Annenberg Foundation, and their sci-fi play *Unplanned Obsolescence* premiered in Philadelphia in 2023 as part of Cannonball Festival.

Alex's SFF-related non-fiction has appeared in *Interstellar Flight Magazine* and *Ancillary Review of Books*. Their games can be downloaded pay-what-you-will at alexyquest.itch.io. They live in Chicago, Illinois, with their partner Noa and their cat, Ford F150. You can find them at alexjkingsley.wordpress.com, on BlueSky at alexyquest.bsky.social, Instagram at hitchhikersguidetothealexy, Mastodon at alexyquest@podvibes.co, and on TikTok at alexyquest.

Please take a moment to review this book at your favorite retailer's website, Goodreads, or simply tell your friends!